THE
MALL WALKER

Jack Krause's Private War

A NOVEL BY
Desmond Drue

Cover Design: Hannah Linder
hannahlinderbooks@gmail.com

ISBN: 1543115551
ISBN 13: 9781543115550

DEDICATIONS

This book is dedicated to my father Bernie, one of the Greatest Generation, who saved the world from tyranny.

A special thanks to Dr. Andrew Kwait for his support and counsel in the writing of this book.

Most importantly, this book is dedicated to the estimated nearly 60,000 men and women who were killed in the Vietnam War along with the 150,000 gravely wounded. To all of the nearly 3 million who served in one of history's most "questioned" U.S. military involvements. To each and everyone one of you, please know we salute you. You are all true American Heroes.

AND THEY SAY I'M NOT ALONE

I find him difficult at times
To be with
He carries so much of the old stuff with him
The reruns of another day
When he felt more significant than he now feels
Or thought he'd be
Or so he says
I don't believe him

His youth fluttered by on butterfly wings
And then one wing clipped at a time
He found himself in free flight
Falling through an unrecognizable haze
And there he was without a clue
Not a damn one

Vietnam was a cesspool and nothing more
It's relentless sun ate through my skin
The stink of the fortunate dead
Free from this repulsion
Stung my nostrils
I didn't taste a fresh breath for over two years

Where the hell was the glory my young man asked
It was there on the TV screen, John Wayne, Aldo Ray
Never let their country down, they were heroes, dug in
But for moral reasons survived to fight again
Not so it seemed with me

I see none of this around me
Just frightened, naive dog soldiers scared beyond their years
Droppings in their pants, wondering if they will ever fit in again

There is so much distance between them and the others
And more before it ends and it will
And the price that always is with war, immeasurable

I take cat naps, there is no restful sleep for me,
I still sleep with one eye open,
With the whirly gigs resonating through my head,
I have collateral damage all around me, it comes in the form of
family and friends,
AND THEY SAY I'M NOT ALONE

I'm Jack Krause

Table of Contents

1

Bad Hair Day

"Your father's losing it!"

I can't believe my wife told my daughter her dad is going off the cliff. It must have been the ponytail. Ever since I told Gerti I was growing one, she looked at me like I lost my marbles.

"Christ Jackson, you're sixty-nine years old and you're going to grow a damn ponytail - why?"

"Cause I always wanted one and since I've retired and don't have to answer to anyone - so why do I - to you - I'm slowly flipping the pages of the last chapter of my life - like I'm in the single digits now - like what the hell?"

"Damn it Jack, that's where you're wrong. You still have to answer to me, I'm your wife - you damn well have an obligation to me, your partner of forty plus years, not to make me look like a fool."

When I heard these words, something snapped inside me - I was wound so tight I was beginning to scare myself. *Make her look like a fool.* I have never made my wife look like a fool, in fact, broke my butt for thirty three years loading damn UPS trucks, eight hours a day, to the point my back ached so much, I can't recall having a restful nights sleep for the last decade.

Making her look like a fool, my ass. I never made my wife, kids, grandkids look like fools - anything but - yes, anything but ...

"Jack, I'd really like you to reconsider the ponytail. You should cut it off right now before anyone takes notice."

"Gerti, like I said, I ain't cutting it off. I'm damn well doing what I please from now on."

"Well, grow your damn ponytail then and make a fool of yourself, the next thing you'll be coming home with tattoos all up and down your arms."

"You never know Gerti, you just might never know."

I heard enough of this crap. At sixty-nine years, I've earned the right to do what I please. In fact I earned it a hell of a lot of years before - I fought for it - I FOUGHT FOR IT. I walked past Gerti. She had contempt in her eyes. She really hated when I didn't listen to her. I told her not to take it personal - I listen to no one.

"Where you going?" she asked.

"Where I go every morning since I retired, I'm going to the mall to meet Dirt and Rhino."

"Dirt and Rhino, what stupid names, like kids - I wish you guys would just grow up". She had to interject.

I ignored her and I walked to the closet and grabbed my worn Reebok bag. It held my heavy sweatshirt, my Boston Red Sox hat, two pair of Asics and a pair of soiled sweat socks. I threw it over my shoulder. Gerti looked at me with disdain. She turned her back. I walked toward the kitchen door.

She shouted out, "You spend more time with those guys than you do with me."

"They shoot straighter Gerti - straight and true".

I got to the mall just when the doors opened. It was nine o'clock. I was usually the first in the pavilion but today I was running a few minutes late. There were ten or so mall walkers ahead of me. I recognized several.

Getting to the mall early allowed me to spend a few minutes warming up. The older I get, the more limbering I need. I was beginning to feel the change in my body, especially over the last few years. Getting old sucks. My grandfather used to say, "growing old son ain't for wussies". I loved my grandfather. He grew old but unlike me, he did it gracefully. Me? I'm fighting every step.

I always arrived earlier than Dirt and Rhino. Dirt, got his nickname when we were kids. Wherever he was, he left a pile behind him. He was just an unclean kid. It was like he never wanted to get near water and a bar of soap. His real name was Danny Kearney but after we started calling him Dirt, the nickname held. He never refuted it or provided any pushback. He just went with it. If he knew what a deterrent it would be in his later life (especially when trying to pick up women) my gut tells me he would have butted against it. Dirt never had a steady girlfriend or got married. Appallingly, he never had the good hygiene to get physically, nonetheless emotionally close to anyone, except Rhino and me. We loved him as friend, a Vietnam Vet and couldn't give a damn how he looked or smelled.

Rhino got his nickname because nobody could ever pronounce his real one, Steven Anthony Radaskiewicz Junior. There was no way he was going to burden his kid pals with that. He became Rhino, and eventually at six feet two inches tall and two hundred and thirty pounds, the name naturally held.

I stood at the mall's entrance waiting for Dirt and Rhino for nearly twenty minutes. As prompt as I was, they always seemed to run late. But they were my army buddies, two of my "Band Of Brothers". The others if they weren't dead, I never kept contact with. I wish I did but Nam was a long time ago and there's been a lot of water under the bridge but none of it washed away the scars that were left. Forty some years later, they're still there. I've been lucky because for the most part, I've been able to manage through them, which is not to say that I was ever the same after returning from my tour. Nobody is. The people who think a man or woman can return unscathed from the human depravity of war, are just plain stupid, dumb as a box of rocks. I hate people like that, stupid ignorant butt holes, who look at us vets, either volunteered or drafted, as the unclean who do the dirty work of war. Most of them don't look at us as the true American heroes we are and were. What really grates me is their lack of respect. Screw them!

I remember transitioning home in 1967, one mixed up twenty-four year old. After my tour, I wanted nothing more than to return, to embrace what I left behind, the support of my family (of which I never quite thought I had) the love of a girl, the familiarity of my friends, the security of being in an environment that was non-confrontational. *What the hell must I've been thinking?* I heard about the turmoil going on back home, all kinds of crazy stuff and here I was with my platoon, stuck in a cesspool jungle arboretum full of wild birds, panthers, snakes, pigs, sweat, jack ass goons who wanted to kill us and thousands of lonely frightened, disenfranchised G.I.s, who wanted nothing other than getting their dysentery butts state side.

Finally, Dirt walked in. Crazy Dirt. He was brain dead before he went to Nam and worst when he returned. He lived no normal life. He was homeless and lived at Lifebridge. He scrambled everyday to earn, beg or steal enough money to eat and stay alive. I gave him five dollars everyday. Dirt was my own private charity. I never asked him what he did with it. He could eat, drink or throw it away for all I care. He was one of us and no matter where he was in life, it made no difference, he was a brother until death and beyond. He was wearing the same old military sweatshirt that read **"KILL THEM ALL…. LET GOD SORT THEM OUT"**. He carried the usual backpack and worn tattered Boston Red Sox baseball cap stained across the brim. He had a scraggly beard and dark circles under his eyes. His skin had a yellowish tone. He spoke to me.

"Jackson, my boy, how da hell are ya?"

"The same as I was yesterday and the day before, not much different. Dirt, you ask the same questions everyday, nothing really changes from one to the next."

"Screwed up ha?"

"Ya, like you, to a fare thee well."

"Ya, me too."

"Shit, you've been screwed up since I've known you. Where's Rhino?"

"Ain't com'n today."

"Ex-wife trouble again?"

"Ya."

"That shit never goes away."

"It's like Nam Jack. Look at me, I'm now living in a box."

"What, shit for brains? You now say you're living in a box?"

"Ya, in a wooden crate behind Marshalls"

"Marshalls?"

"Ya, Marshall's, the clothing store and such."

"I didn't know!"

"Know what?"

"I thought you were living at Lifebridge?"

"Ya, well, ain't now - I did until last night, when they threw me out."

"The same old shit?" I asked.

"Ya, the same old - damn it Jack, like …… I just can't help myself. It just comes over me."

" Dirt, you got to get this anger thing under control, it's gonna get you killed or you're damn well gonna kill someone else. Let's walk."

Dirt and I set out on our forty minute walk, six times the periphery of the inner wall, the last one on full burner, taking us around as fast as our legs could carry us.

For a sixty-nine year old guy, I was in pretty good shape. I always prided myself on that. Even before Nam, I could do a hundred pushups and sit-ups and more if I had to but I set the bar because I didn't see any reason to do a hundred and one. The main thing that challenged me now was my belly fat. Where did it come from? I had a roll around me like a flat tire. It drove me crazy cause I worked out with obsession to get rid of it. It just never went away. My daughter Riley said if it really bothers me, then get it sucked out. She must be crazy, *well she is kinda crazy*. Look, I'm a sixty-nine year old Vietnam veteran. Guys like me don't get the fat sucked out.

I looked at Dirt. He was sweating profusely.

"Shit you're sweating like a pig Dirt."

"And you're not?"

"Not like you."

"So why do you give a damn?"

"Don't be such a hard ass - you're my bud - I'm just looking out for you."

"Ya, I know how to look out for myself."

"You're living in a wooden box - behind Marshalls Department Store - by nobody's standards you're doing alright for yourself."

"Dirt turned toward me, sweat pouring into his eye sockets, "Screw you Jack, just screw you to a fare thee well."

2

The Same Shit – All the Time

When I got back home it was 10:45. I should have gone to the diner but didn't. I went every day. Retirement is all about eating. Where do you go for breakfast, lunch, and where can one get the best *early bird special?* Everyday it's the same stuff. Today I broke the breakfast and lunch cycle. I wasn't hungry. I didn't want to eat. I just decided to go home but what for? Gerti would be there and I would have to drag her to leave the house. Home to her was like a ball strapped to a convict's ankle. It just held her back from doing anything that wasn't house centric. The only time I could get her out was to eat. Gerti loved staying in (she became more isolated as she grew older) but she hated to cook. She would do anything to avoid it. She won't be happy to see me back so early. My presence would mean she would have to scurry up something for lunch. She was lucky. I didn't feel like eating. If I did, I would have provided for myself.

I unlocked the back door. I walked to the kitchen. Gerti was sitting reading the Boston Globe. She was surprised to see me. I startled her. I heard my last few steps. She snapped the paper to her lap.

"Christ, Jack, you scared me."

"Sorry!"

"You should be - you almost gave your wife a heart attack."

"Like I said, I'm sorry!"

"What are you home for? I thought you would be at the diner with the boys."

I turned and walked to the Kenmore, opened the refrigerator door and grabbed a carton of milk.

"No, not today, Rhino is sick again with his intestinal thing." I lied because because I didn't want to alert Gerti to his marital troubles.

"Well, what about Dirt?"

"Dirt - Ya, Dirt, got really pissed off at me - because I jumped all over his sorry butt cause he's living in a wooden box in the back of Marshall's, plus I can't take him to the diner anymore, cause he scares people and smells.

"Marshall's?"

"Ya, Marshall's, the discount department store."

"So that's what it has come down to in his life, divorced, bankrupt, his kids hate him, now living in a wooden box in back of Marshall's - and late October, he's gonna freeze to death when winter comes."

"Wrong guy Gerti. You're talking about Rhino."

"I guess I got them confused."

"Ya, Dirt's never been married."

"A pity."

"Ya he's had a tough time of it."

Gerti looked at me with dismay.

"You better get yourself some new friends, Jack."

Every time Gerti said this to me it made my blood boil. She hadn't a clue who Dirt and Rhino are - not an inkling. I grew up with them, they were the closest to the brother I wish I had, *my own was a distant remembrance.* We all went to Nam and returned, not physically broken but fractured inside. We remain that way today - not that anyone cares - they all should but no one really gives a damn. Our war experiences made us different than most, especially the rage exploding in our veins made our bond even stronger. We were wedded together in heart and spirit. Gerri didn't get it and to my chagrin she never will.

"I don't want any new friends. My old ones are just fine."

"You're wasting every hour you spend with those guys".

"It's my life. It's my time to waste .... and Dirt, he'll be alright."

"Sure, he's made his own bed. He's got to sleep in it."

I filled my glass and put the milk back in the frig. I turned to Gerri.

"That's really funny Gerti."

"What?"

"He's made his bed and he has to sleep in it, him living in a box and all."

"There's nothing funny about it, it's the damn truth."

"Ya, I see like always your lack of compassion ."

Gerti threw the newspaper on the kitchen table and stood. She always stood arrow straight when she wanted a fight.

"Compassion for your friends, why should I have compassion for them?"

Gerti walked towards me.

"Talking about compassion. Riley came over today."

"Oh yeah?"

"Yeah!"

I walked over to the kitchen table and sat down. The Boston Globe was lying there. The cover story read "Six Firemen Perish In Chelsea."

"Don't you care that our daughter Riley came over today?"

It always comes down to that question whenever we discussed our daughter.

"Christ, Gerti, do we have to go over this again?"

Gerti takes two steps forward and points her finger at me.

"You're damn right we have to go over this again, it's about your daughter, you thick headed fool, our daughter, our one and only and our granddaughter Bellows and her kids, your family - you know the one you never want to see."

"Bellows, what a stupid name." I said, I really didn't know what else to say because it was indeed a dumb ass name and it was a disservice the day my daughter burdened her kid with it and it will be after I'm dead and for the rest of eternity.

Gerti raised her voice, "Gees, is that all you got to say, Bellows is a stupid name. You're really an ignorant man Jack. I haven't a clue what I ever saw in you, in fact, whatever possessed me to marry you?"

Gerti just has a way of pissing me off. So I hadn't seen or spoken to my daughter for several months. I told her if she continued allowing that loser Humphrey to keep living under her roof they'll not see me no more. And if there is anything I am, I am a man of my word. Gerti hated I cut my daughter and her family out of my life but I saw no other choice than surrounding myself with a bunch of do-nothings. Gerti damn well better get over it, she damn well had better.

I couldn't take this crap any longer. I had to get away …. It's the same old shit all the time and it just wears me down - grinds my gears - makes me want to scream my bloody head off. I rose from the chair and grabbed the Globe. I figured I'd ride to Lynn Shore Drive and sit by the ocean. I needed a little piece and quiet, a little read time to catch up on the local events, the sports page, the business section, whatever's in the Globe to take me out of this moment.

I walked pass Gerti. "Now where the hell are you going? You just came back here and you're already out the door - can't stand to be with me but for a minute can you?"

I turned to Gerti, placating. "It ain't that way hon, you didn't expect me anyhow. In fact, I probably interrupted your day and all. I'll be back around 5:00 and we'll catch the early bird somewhere, maybe at the diner, or Deleo's, you know that Tuesday night special, salad, ribs, all you can eat - the $9.99 special, *you know the one*.

3

Band of Brothers

I walked out the front door of my cape. The hinge holding it squeaked like it has for over a year. I told Gerti I would repair it but like the other hundred chores I should get done in the house, I didn't have the ambition. There really wasn't anything urgent. It wasn't like it was falling apart. It was more it needed a little TLC. The truth was my whole life needed some but it was one more thing I neglected.

I stopped and looked around the neighborhood. My house even with the little attention I gave it compared to the others was a stately mansion, not in stature but damn well in upkeep. The hood was going to hell in a handbag. Thirty-two years ago I moved here and it was a decent neighborhood. Guys like me coming from Nam worked our asses off to get together a down payment to purchase a small house for our families. My house cost me $23,700 and I was so damn proud when I signed the papers - Jackson Krause home owner. I had a piece of the American dream and beamed with joy as Gerti returned the smile, delighted and proud she could put a roof over the head of our two young children.

The neighborhood started to go into disrepair about twenty years ago. As my neighbors died or pulled up roots, the new occupants just didn't seem to care as much about their homes as the previous. I watched with disbelief as the houses one by one, turned over to a new set who kept very much to themselves. In twenty years, I bet I haven't said ten words to any of them. Honestly, I don't go out of my way to reach out to people who don't to me. It's just not the Jack Krause way. It never has been and that's just the way it is. Gerti doesn't reach out either. She's very much a "leave me alone" kind of woman. In fact, the both of us in this particular manner are very much the same, although we are quite different in just about every other.

I can't say that I don't have contempt for my new neighbors. I do. I have for anyone who negatively effects who I am. My neighborhood now, I see as a cesspool. A place, where way too many people other than the owners, go in and out of the houses all day and night. It's like revolving doors. There's cars everywhere, motorcycles and noise every damn minute. It never ceases. I remember when people had respect. When you could open your windows in a pleasant evening and hear nothing but maybe a few kids crying, or the faint play by play of a Boston Red Sox game coming from a neighbors TV or just folks getting together for a chew and chat. These were sounds of a solid suburban neighborhood where people were conscious and courteous towards their neighbors, where they really gave a care. It's not that way anymore. What's going on in my neighborhood just mirrors that to what is going on in the world. It ain't pretty, no, it ain't pretty at all.

Lynn Shore Drive was just twenty minutes from my house. It is on the ocean. I liked to park my 1998 Mercury and people watch. I am always amazed at the various types who come together on a perfect autumn day to partake in the beauty of New England before it gives way to winter. I've spent way too many winters here. Sometimes I think I've spent way too many, PERIOD.

I was surprised I found a parking spot on my first pass. On a beautiful day like this, it usually took several. It seems people just come out of the woodwork when the sun beats down on the ocean blue. It's some kind of renewal. Its coming together is like magic. It draws all types. I can people watch for hours, just me and my Dunkins. I don't have to take any crap from anyone when I'm sitting here. I turn off the radio. I crack the car window. If my damn cell phone rings I don't have to answer and I don't. I damn well can do and think anything I please - just me, my Dunkins and my Merc.

I took a snooze. It was only for a couple of minutes - five at most - I went out like a light. It was like I was in Nam again. The only thing I liked there was the early morning sun - I'd see it break through the thick vegetation and reflect colors that somehow took me to another place. Everything else about Nam sucked. I will hate it until I die, it will probably be the constant nagging away at my soul that finally kills me.

I took off my cheap drug store sunglasses and rubbed my eyes. I felt like I had been sleeping for hours. I put them back on and looked up and down the concrete walkway. There were people everywhere. They flowed like a wave, constantly in motion until I noticed a group of guys making their way down from Nahant beach walking towards the Hawthorne Restaurant. It seemed they were shoving people out of their way. Just pushing them like they were bowling pins. Young kids, old people, they didn't seem to care. It was like they were on a mission. It was a mission of "get the hell out of the way, I'm better than you and if I ain't, there's more of us and that makes us considerably so."

What's with the disrespect? I've asked myself this a million times. I remember the comedian Rodney Dangerfield saying, I guess it was his trade line, "I just don't get no respect". I would like to pull Rodney from the grave and say to him, "Like really, Rodney, you get no respect! Today, nobody does!" It's just the way things are now. There just ain't enough to go around. In fact, the truth is I can't remember the last time I saw anybody go out of their way for someone or a person holding the door for another, or a young man (or anybody) giving up their seat for an elder or for that matter, just somebody saying "Thank you". It is now so uncommon, I don't think kids today have any clue what it means or when and how to use it.

Yeah I have no question Rodney would damn well be down on his luck and probably unemployed today being that "no respect" is common and his not getting any isn't a big deal anymore.

I couldn't stop watching these kids making their way down the concrete walk. I lost them for just a moment in the glare of the sun coming off the water but before I knew it my eyes were honed in on them again. There they were bulldozing their way past the crowds pushing people aside. Just then, I spotted a Met Cop on horseback followed by another not ten yards behind. The first cop was at medium gallop, which easily caught him up with the punks on the walk, pushing and ram-rodding through the others sharing the path. The cop galloped alongside them and then in front, signaling them to stop and step aside. As the young men looked behind them, they saw there was another metro policeman, on horseback not ten yards following quickly closing quarters, allowing no pathway for the young men to escape.

One thing I immediately noticed is how the patrolman mounted on his horse dwarfed the boys he spoke to. The horse was ten feet tall from hoof to the tip of his ears. I could see the kids were edgy, it was damn well apparent they had a disdain for authority. They were tatted all over their arms and wearing the same attire as if in uniform, black oversize jeans that fell below their butt crack and white T- shirts cut to their shoulders with very thin straps, baseball hats and layers of chains around their necks.

The police had a very quick discussion with one of them, who obviously was, the alpha male because he stepped right up to one of the cops and the others followed in sequence. Within minutes the conversation ended and the kids were on their way again sauntering down the concrete walkway towards the restaurant Hawthorne By The Sea.

These youth reminded me of myself, Dirt and Rhino, when we were their age. We along with several other guys, Johnnie Franco and Kats Jenkins (where they are today, I haven't a clue) spent hours on the walkway doing exactly what these kids were. We too, saw the park stretching from Swampscott to Nahant as our personal turf and walked it with arrogance, aligned with youth. This stretch of landscape was our world. We lived within its confines, very seldom journeying outside, other than a day trip to New Hampshire or the Cape. Our views of the world were so restricted. We just "didn't know, what we didn't know" and we didn't know a lot and if there was anything I was damn well assured of is even with the experiences we now had as older men there is so much that constantly goes over our heads (worldly stuff) and we still remain, in many ways, the same kids we were with our then restricted thought.

If there is one thing that really upsets me as I look back, it is I always saw myself, Rhino and Dirt, as followers instead of leaders. It was in our DNA, we were always falling behind someone, who we thought could lead us to the Holy Grail. We finally learned but too late, that indeed, one did not exist and those we followed, as pigs to their slaughter, didn't know as much as we thought. In fact, in many cases, a lot less. But we followed them anyway, because that's who we were, followers, and basically what we still are today and it's unfortunately what has created the somewhat unfilled, damaged lives we live.

If we were still young, we would probably fall in amongst those five guys on the walkway, boldly parading our facade, right behind the leader talking to the cop. We would probably take his lead, without great thought, doing what we were assigned, very much like we did in Nam, just filed in, stood in line, sucked up as best we could, killing, maiming, destroying the enemy and ourselves, and really never thinking through why, not that it would have made any difference but I would like to think that perhaps, just maybe, *it might have*.

4

Home Sweet Home

I really didn't want to visit. By every measure I was a lousy father. I knew it. My wife knew. My kids knew. The world knew. There was no way coming back from Nam I should have had kids. In fact marriage was the furthest thing from my mind and probably the worst thing I could have done. In a lot of ways it is like jumping off a diving board. It all comes down to the initial approach. If it starts off bad there is no recovery. The diver in midair can play it back a gazillion times in his mind but there is nothing he could do about it now. He was launched and the outcome was a shitty ass splash entry into the pool, and a bad start to a marriage is the same but to a substantially greater degree - splash, splashy - splash - tread water- tread water - gurgle - eventually drown.

Gerti and I had a crappy marriage but unlike most couples who do, we didn't try to hide it. We had a general disdain for each other. I think the majority of times she looked at me, she wanted to scream. I can't imagine how she tolerated me all these years. Ninety percent of the dysfunction I caused. I can lie to myself about a lot of things but I can't about this.

"I don't want to go."

"Damn it Jack, you haven't seen your daughter's family in nearly six months. She thinks you died and she wasn't invited to the funeral."

" Well if I did I would be surprised if any of them would show."

"Don't be an asshole Jack, you damn well know what I mean."

"It might be best if I did die. She doesn't need me in her life anymore, none of them do."

"I think it best to allow her to decide that", snapped Gerti.

There she goes again - damn it, she's always right – yeah Gerti's always right (go ahead and ask her), I don't think she ever did a wrong thing in her entire life, except for marrying me - the biggest and worst mistake she could have ever made - in fact THE MOTHER OF ALL MISTAKES, that made up for a million others she wished she had made instead.

"Okay Gerti, damn it okay. I'll go, but will that crumbum be there?"

Gerti looked at me with utter contempt, "You mean Miley's boyfriend?"

I really riled her when I said, "Yeah, that sorry crumbum."

"Damn it Jack, don't do me any favors and come if you are going to be an asshole. These visits are hard enough so if you are going to make them harder you can stay home with the cat."

"It definitely would be more fun."

Gerti threw me the finger. "Then just stay home, you moron." She walked toward the kitchen, turned and looked at me one more time, opened the back door, walked through and slammed it shut.

I damn well knew there's going to be hell to pay when she gets back - bitch'n and moan'n how my daughter and granddaughter wanted to see me and again I have disappointed them - as I have always - I am just one universe of disappointment.

I grabbed Mustard, my tabby cat, who was licking the hell out of himself off his pillow bed in the kitchen and put him under one arm and walked to the frig where I pulled a cool PBR, *Pabst Blue Ribbon* the best beer ever made for blue collar scumbags like me. I took a long draw and nothing could have tasted better - in the quiet, with my tabby - with a six pack of PBR.

I looked at this as a reprieve, knowing damn well I would soon be in the penalty box. I turned on the set. The Sox were playing the Rays at home. They were losing 12-2. They stink. I sucked down another three quick beers and fell asleep in my tattered chair. I didn't have a clue where Mustard went and actually, I couldn't care less.

5

A Punk Ass Kid

It was with mixed emotions I read for the fifth time the invitation to attend my 50th high school reunion. I attended Lynn Tech and fooled everyone, my parents, teachers and fellow students alike when I graduated with my class in four years. The odds were similar to drawing an *outside flush*, no, worse than that, a thousand to one odds, the proverbial snowball chance in hell this would ever happen. I didn't lie to myself. I was really a poor student, and to tell the truth couldn't understand how I ever found myself walking up to the stage of the Lynn Tech auditorium to receive my diploma. At the time I thought I was really getting the best of everyone and remember thinking, those ignorant drones, (referring to my fellow students) they busted their butts to get this sheet of paper and here I am receiving mine and I did the bare minimum, that is if I did anything at all. I looked back and I thought I bested the system and made fools of the student body, my teachers, especially my parents, who constantly told me I wouldn't amount to anything and hadn't a chance of ever getting out of high school. I remember thinking, I was one pretty smart street wise guy and would use this model to make the rest of my life play out - yes, I would use "trying to get somewhere with the least possible effort" my mantra - Jack Krause cunning as a fox -street punk intelligentsia - system "upside downer".

Unfortunately, for me, it didn't take long before I realized I didn't know, even the most basic fundamentals of getting through life and was prepared for absolutely nothing after leaving high school. I never thought about going to college because it was never in the picture. Neither of my parents attended and I believe they never had any faint aspiration from the moment of my birth that I would. I recall them mentioning it twice, once referring to a son of one of my mother's best friends. "Guy got accepted to Community, he's a smart kid, Ellie should be so proud". My father grunted out a response. "Yaw, good for him", and that was it, like the whole thing passed like a light fart streaming off to find a draft ventilating to the outdoors. The second and last time was when the Vietnam War was being protested in various colleges throughout the country and my father was referring to headlines of the deaths in the Kent State demonstration leading to an escalation of stronger outbursts throughout the states. I remember him responding to the headlines, "ignorant jerks" and then he folded the paper and threw it against the wall where it fell on the floor finding a home near our shabby cat's feeding bowl. I never really knew what my father thought of the Kent State demonstration because I didn't know who he was referring to as "jerks", the students or the cops. I guess I could have asked but I didn't. Truthfully, at that time, I couldn't give a care. Vietnam was the furthest thing from my mind and didn't mean anything to me. It was just something happening I paid no attention to, although the military was drafting every available able-bodied man because the war was expanding and they needed a lot of young, naive male flesh to throw against it. I never worried about the draft because I was Jack Krause, yes that Jack Krause, the smartest son of a bitch of them all who got through high school by barely opening a book and turning a page. Why would I have to worry? I bullshitted my way this far, and damn well knew I would the rest of my life.

My draft notice arrived in the mail on April 25th, 1970. When my father handed it to me, all he said was, "congratulations my boy, you have been drafted". I couldn't help but notice there was a little smirk on his face, that said as I perceived it, *"Gotcha, my punk ass son... so you think you're such a wise guy ... the Army's got you by the short hairs. Well halleluiah ... my punk ass son ... VIETNAM, HERE YOU COME!!!!."*

I remember my mother turning around from the stove when my father handed it to me. It was a really quick glance to see what kind of response I would have to my father's words. She didn't know I was looking at her as well and waiting for some kind of emotion to fix her face, something really transparent, like a motherly concern for her eldest son who was now sitting in the kitchen with a draft notice in his hand, waiting to open it. *There was none.* I finally realized at that moment, whatever emotion my mother had was stripped away by her twenty eight year marriage. Whatever feeling she had for me was also part and parcel of the dysfunctional relationship she was in. This was the whole deal, for all intents and purposes our home was a dead place, with near hardly a heartbeat - the coldest of blood running through its veins, with but maybe one gorilla tear ready to manifest, if indeed one was left or then again, a reason to shed the last remaining.

I believe it was the day my draft notice arrived that my ties to my family became shredded, leaving just a marginal emotional tie and that was to my kid brother Bobby, a sibling so very much different than me in just about every way but the only reason I could conceive ever coming back home again - if indeed I was truly being drafted after reading the notice, which after opening I found I really was.

I never really thought about what to expect or how I would react. The reality was I thought I would never receive one. For the same reasons I survived to graduate from high school I was impervious to being drafted by the US government.

Not me, "no way in hell" did I ever venture a thought that I, Jack Krause would someday be drafted. The military didn't take kids like me, I was too damn smart, or either too lucky. I was the "Teflon Kid", and shit just rolled off me and there would be no reason it wouldn't again.

In disbelief I read the notice. I was being asked to report for my physical in three weeks at the City Hall in Lynn. My face turned flush as I read it. This was the real deal, and I hadn't a plan to get out of it, because as I indicated, I had no reason to ever think I would get in. I kept staring at the paper, what scared me is it looked so official. There was an importance to it, one I didn't see in my high school diploma, one that rendered a significance, extremely more important than my driver's license.

I stared at the paper for another moment or so and then put it down on the kitchen table. My father was hidden behind the Time Ledger ingesting the evening news. He dropped the paper several inches so I could see his eyes and he said to me "I guess your luck has run out hot-shot." My mother turned from the stove where she was preparing the everyday Wednesday evening meal, spaghetti and meat sauce and said, "Geez, Gunther, is that what it says, that Jack is going to war. HE'S GOING TO WAR?"

"WAR", what the hell was she talking about? I'm not going to 'WAR", just to City Hall to get my physical that's all. It's no big deal, because as *Teflon* and as *lucky* as I am, there was no way I was going to pass. It's the Jack Krause way, "cheated death - again."

My father broke his silence, "Did you hear me Jack?"

"Ya, I heard you Dad."

My father spoke again.

"Well, maybe Vietnam will make a man out of you?"

"What's with you Dad, what do you mean?"

My father replied, a man, yeah, ya can't screw around with the military. They'll damn well shape you up and make a grownup out of you. God knows, as much as we don't want to admit it, your mother and I have failed."

There is no other way to put it but I hated my father. What's not to hate. I never knew him as a person, just as an authoritarian who lived under the same roof as my mother, my kid brother and me. He spoke in word farts, little tiny sound missiles that were propelled with malice, as if he held a gas bubble within and as it grew disproportionately to his ability to contain it, let it blow through his butt hole with no regards for those around him. My father didn't speak in sound bites, he didn't speak to engage, to cure an interest, to gather an opinion, to solicit a understanding. He spoke only to injure, maim, abuse, defame, with the greatest malice of forethought. There wasn't a nice bone in his body and each day as I returned from school, I carried a heavy heart because I just didn't want to share the house with him.

Why my mother didn't leave him, I could never understand. As miserable as my life was, hers was even more. She was with him all the time, she was dealt a husband dose of bullshit every day, little carvings of disrespect that whittled away at who she was as a person in the most injurious of ways. He called her fat, ugly, her meals despicable, her house unclean, terrible word assaults a man would use to demean a woman, causing her to feel she had no worth and there was probably no other man who would want her and therefore she had no recourse to be anywhere, with anyone else other than where she was.

I lost respect for my mother years ago. She just wasn't strong enough to fight back, to hold the barbarian that my father was at bay. When she spoke to him you could hear the reflection in her voice. It quivered as if it lost strength and velocity and fell upon his ears with such weakness and surrender he barely responded back, as if nothing she said had any importance.

It was 51 years back that my home became a living hell. It was the day my father got his full disability and didn't have to work no more. He said he slipped in the pressroom at the

Eastman Printing Company where he was employed for thirty-two years. My father hated his job but never made or saved enough money to ever think about retiring. Each morning he left for work, he seethed with resentment that at the age of 56 he could never retire on Social Security alone and was stuck in a dead end job, earning a minimum wage barely allowing him to cover his monthly bills. When he returned home, routinely at 7:00 p.m after consuming a couple of Boiler Makers (a shot of whiskey followed by a beer chaser) with a few of his buddies. He would be so full of rage, my mother would serve up his dinner as quickly as possible which he would consume like a ravaged dog, retire to his favorite chair in front of the TV set, barely speaking a word for the rest of the evening. Then when he did, spitting out enough vile driving my mother to the bedroom until he retired at 11:00 p.m., when she would exchange places, her going to sleep in his chair and him retiring to his bed.

My brother and I learned very early, to try to avoid him. We really had no other recourse. Our father was a large burly man who was not to be deterred in his thinking and opinions. My brother learned early how to deal with him. As lucky as I thought I was, I was just stupid enough to lock horns, making my mother and brothers life so much less tolerable. Then without notice, all our lives went from bad to worse.

It was obvious my father had something up his sleeve. It was for about three weeks in the fall of 1967 that he seemed to be out of character. He spoke a bit more although as with all his conversations, there was really nothing worth listening to. It was cheap "fill in the empty cracks of my lousy life" banter. It was noise disallowing the time to pass unencumbered. My father just ran his mouth about stuff he had to do around the house, some things needing attention - which was totally out of character with who he was - being we never saw him pick up a hammer or paint brush or do anything to repair or maintain our small two bedroom home. The truth was it was becoming a rundown cottage in total disrepair with the roof badly leaking and the furnace occasionally not working (our family froze five months out of the year living there). It was like he never really cared and when we complained he would refer to some blankets stacked in the basement closets. One, two, three, four blankets just weren't enough to keep all of us warm. My brother and I would opt to go to bed right after supper, hoping we would survive the night. Obviously we did, but waking and greeting my father every morning in our small kitchen, made me despise him more. He couldn't even keep his family warm and his lack of shame cut into me like a sharp razor.

It was within a couple of weeks, my father morphed from a healthy 56 year old man to one who was hunched over and now had a limp. It was a Tuesday in October that he returned from work mid-morning and told my mother he had applied for disability at the Eastman because several weeks before he had slipped and badly injured his back and he had been, during that time, claiming his disability as career ending - that is if you consider stacking magazines seven feet high on a skid a career, which obviously he did.

He told my mother he's done with work, been working since he was fifteen and had it up to HERE - as he reached over his head - meaning he was drowning in it, the work thing.

Sixty days later my father was home permanently. He was now on the dole, meaning he did nothing all day but just hang around, until 3:00 p.m. when he would disappear to his favorite watering hole the Fairlawn Tavern, then return at 5:00 p.m. just before dinner. It was also a miraculous recovery from his back pain and cane, because it seemed whatever routine he now found himself was incredibly beneficial to his health. He walked straight up again and I saw him lift items that six months before he wouldn't attempt. After a few drinks my father was smug as hell. He not a few times, told my mother, brother and I what a "smart-ass" street merchant he was, reaming it up the

Eastman's butt, faking a false disability and getting away with it. I remember him saying to me.

"You see Jack, that's the difference between you and me, I can figure shit out. It might take me a while, but your old man is fox smart and damn well can survive.

My father now points at me, "You, I just don't know whether you can make it in this world. You buck up against everything and everyone. You just don't get it at all."

I couldn't believe what my father was saying, like he was a genius or something. A flaming genius my ass, working a crap job for thirty some freaking years until like the "fox-smart bastard" he thought he was screwed the system with false pretense and a stupid lie. So, this was the example I was supposed to follow - a shit ass job, a shit ass house, in a shit house neighborhood, a shit ass dysfunctional family - well if that is what my future held - the hell with it - it damn well just wasn't worth the effort.

As I sat at the table pondering my draft notice the kitchen door opened, my brother Bobby walked in. From the moment he was born, I was the odd man out. It seemed everything he was, I was not. He was tall and good looking, smart, ambitious, cunning - although I knew he was a mistake because I damn well knew after me, my parents wanted no more kids. I was enough for them, the energy and attention to me was minimal - but then came Bobby and my parents now had a "WONDERCHILD". It seemed they were doting on him at my expense and doing a pretty good job at it. It was apparent that all the brains, talent and ambition my parents held was wrapped up in my little brother. He just set out at his own pace, and if he were one of God's favorites. He had innate abilities at the youngest age to distance himself from the family disease and fend for himself. It was as if God bestowed him a free pass to travel the toll roads of his formative years arriving at his destination as an adult at thirteen.

I had mixed emotions concerning Bobby. Sometimes, I loved him being who he was, an ingrate armed with "special powers". He was an A student with minimal effort. I barely made a C- average in high school. He knew exactly how to handle and what to say to my parents in almost every situation, as if to lull them with complacency that he was above everything they were concerned with and that he was in total control of his life.

"Where are you going at 7:00 p.m. on a school night?"

"I've put in three hours of study for my math test tomorrow but I think I need to study a bit more. I'll be off to the library till 9:00" my brother answered.

"You're one smart kid", my father would reply, with my mother cheering Bobby in the background.

When asked a similar question, I was compelled to answer, "I don't know, I'm just going out."

My father would snarl back, "Going out on a school night and not knowing what for - you're damn well bullshitting me. Until you know where you're going and why you're staying home where you belong."

I often found myself in the soup, especially when my brother would reinforce his position with excellent grades and me nearly passing.

As I sat there at the table with draft notice in hand, "Wonderboy" was home. My father put down his paper. My mother turned from the stove.

My father addressed him, "Bobby, how was your day?"

"It was good, Daddy", Bobby spit back.

"We'll then, a hell of a lot better than your brother's."

I looked up at Bobby from the unstable chair I was sitting.

Bobby responding, now looking at me. *"Jack, is there something wrong?"*

6

Daddy Dearest

It was 1972, Rhino and I just got back from Nam. We hit stateside within thirteen days of each other. We had been back about three weeks and as strange as it seems - in some ways, it felt we hadn't left - and even stranger - in a lot of ways - we no longer belonged.

It was weird coming back to my house, it was always a house to me, never the home my father's behavior disallowed or at least never allowed me, and finding my room still waiting for me just the way I left it - except everything was in order - contrary to how I reconfigured it when I left.

My final evening at home before leaving for boot camp was Tuesday, May 19th, 1970. I remember it well - the detail is etched in my memory and is shelved in the very same footlocker in my mind, where I stored all my old service memories - all good and bad - my last night at home, was one of the latter.

Abandonment is one of the worse of the cardinal sins. It is unforgivable in its natural form. I will never forgive my parents for doing it to me. They may not believe they had - but in my mind's eye, there was no doubt.

I remember being in my room packing my bags with the little personal things I thought were allowed an inductee, which I learned when I signed in were nothing but the clothes on my back. I should have read the correspondence. I didn't. They

35

replaced what I was wearing with official US Military garb right down to my boxer shorts and sent my civilian clothes boxed back to my home address.

I was in my room selecting my clothes for the big day; a pair of blue jeans, a plaid red and gray flannel shirt and brown work boots and hearing my parents and brother reacting to a repeat of the Phil Silvers Comedy hour where he portrays Master Sergeant Ernie G. Bilko, an arrogant, rebellious con-man, who runs the motor pool, prone to mischief and mayhem and with always women, alcohol and gambling, his chief distractors.

For the last several weeks, there was barely mention of my leaving and tonight at dinner, there was hardly three sentences spoke. I couldn't believe my family was so removed from the experience I was about to go through, and how incongruous it was they were watching "make believe" when there was a lifetime drama being played out in a room, one floor above. The oldest son in the family was being drafted and spending his last night home and there was nothing, NADA - not a blessed thing. More attention would have been given a kid leaving for summer camp not that I would ever know - being I never went because my parents didn't have the financial where-with-all, or the inclination to send either my brother or I.

I remember just sitting on my bed looking at the small pile of items I readied for the coming morning, the insignificance of them- blue jeans, shirt, underwear, work boots and toiletries which did nothing to overcome the seriousness of I AM BEING DRAFTED AND PROBABLY WILL BE SENT TO VIETNAM WHERE MY DEAD BODY WILL COME BACK IN A PLASTIC BAG AND MY UNCARING FAMILY DOESN'T GIVE A CRAP.

I could really feel the rage building. It was a tidal storm of emotion cresting as it moved through my body attacking every neuron traveling at warp speed eventually arriving at its destination igniting a fire-storm.

Within seconds I found myself on my bed, bouncing from mattress to ceiling, smashing through the plaster with my fist. I jumped from it and locked my bedroom door and then pushed my bureau against it to reinforce it from opening. I then grabbed one of the two small lamps in the room and smashed it against the wall. Shortly after following with the second. *SCREW THEM BELOW… THEY'LL DAMN WELL PAY ATTENTION TO ME NOW.*

"What the hell are you doing up there?" I heard my father yell.

"None of your damn business" I screamed back.

"I could hear him now, walking toward the stairs. Weighing two-hundred and twenty some pounds, he had a heavy gait. As a young kid just hearing him move around the house unsettled me because his behavior was unpredictable. It took from me all feelings of wellbeing, but for some reason at this time, he didn't frighten me at all damn it. I was being drafted and probably going to be sent to Vietnam - AND KILLED - how the hell could the mortal presence of my father scare me now?

I looked at all the trappings of my room - now as collateral - being I had an inclination to throw, break, damage, separate that which was part and parcel of the civilian me. I started sweeping the items from my bureau top and as they went tumbling to the floor, I kicked through the wall. My father was now pounding on my bedroom door.

"What the hell is going on in there?"

He was now pulling on the door - the only thing that kept the beast from me - but could not get it unlatched.

"Screw you, go away" I said, "leave me the hell alone."

"Goddamn it Jack, let me in."

There was no way I was going to let my father interfere with my rage. I emptied out all my bureau drawers and threw the contents on the floor. Whatever I could break I broke. Whatever clothing I could rip I ripped. Whatever I could deface I defaced. I grabbed a Magic Marker and scribbled on the walls (the writing made no sense but I scribbled anyway) I was out of control and relished the fact everything I did and the mayhem my father heard on the other side of the bedroom door was just me separating from the shit in my life, the accumulation over the last eighteen years. If I could had parlayed everything I owned, every experience, every emotion - everything - all of it, I would have put it in a pile and fired it up - leaving just the residue of who and what - the civilian part- Jack Krause was - into a little pile of ash.

It was just minutes later, my father could not be deterred. He was motivated to break through the door and there was nothing that would now prevent him. I could hear my mother and brother, who had now joined him in the stairwell.

"Gunther what is the hell is going on up there?" My mother asked in a terrified voice.

"Your demented son is in a meltdown." He responded angrily.

"A meltdown... what do you mean?"

"I mean he's destroying the place - his being drafted and going to Nam, has got the best of him."

"He can't do that," I heard my brother Bobby say, "That's my room too."

"FUCK IF IT IS NOW", I heard myself say. And *going to Vietnam*, was that what this is about? No way in hell. It was about getting my family's attention. It was about showing them something significant is happening here and it is being overlooked. It's about being downgraded to nothing, to where a rerun of a TV show plays more significance in the lives of my family than I did. THAT WAS WHAT THIS WAS ABOUT - PAY SOME DAMN ATTENTION -WOULD YOU NOW PLEASE - PAY A LITTLE RESPECT - DISPLAY A LITTLE SEPARATION ANXIETY - WILL YA PLEASE - LIKE JUST A LITTLE - CAUSE I'M IMPORTANT TOO - AIN"T I - DAMN IT – AIN'T I?

"What are we going to do?" I heard my mother ask.

"I'm going to break through this door and kick the living shit out of him."

I could hear and feel my father putting his shoulder to the door and it finally becoming separated from its hinges. It took three or four assaults on it before it finally gave way pushing into the bureau creating now a space where he could squeeze through.

I retreated to the far left corner of my shared 10 X 12ft bedroom. It gave me a good perspective of my father's face as he pushed through the door. It was chili-pepper red, his eyes were bulging from their sockets, the veins in his forehead were breaking through his skin. They looked like they were about to burst and part of me hoped they would.

I knew from the beginning what I was getting myself into. For whatever reason I just didn't care. I needed to express myself. I needed to purge and let my dammed up emotional waters run free. I needed to close out my civilian me and present tomorrow a clean canvas from which the army could paint the soldier they wanted me to be, that I needed to be to survive.

Seeing my father's bulldog face I thought for a fleeing moment I might have made a big mistake. Perhaps even greater than that. Perhaps, probably - **THE BIGGEST MISTAKE, THE BIGGEST MISCALCULATION OF MY LIFE.**

It became frighteningly clear to me I was not going to die in Vietnam, I was going to right here in my small shared bedroom of my house. This damn well will be my demise, if I indeed was reading my father's face right - there was little doubt I could be wrong - there was no margin of error here - I was indeed screwed.

What to do next? I had but just seconds to think this through. If my father got his hands on me, I was toast. I made the quickest most calculating decision I could.

There was absolutely no time to waste. In two steps I was at my bedroom window.

In one quick motion I broke the latch and opened it and kicked through the screen. My father missed grabbing me by one inch as I exited through the window making my way to the roof of our small bungalow. I jumped to the only tree in our yard that was hanging on to a pittance of life. No one ever took care of anything in or around our house, the walls were decaying and crumbling around us. It was seldom cleaned, there were cockroaches, spiders and mites everywhere, paint was peeling off the walls and in regards to our yard it was an afterthought. Nobody gave a darn, nobody ever cared. I grabbed onto the only sturdy branch on the tree, that under my weigh couldn't hold. I heard it crack and I fell the eighteen feet or so to the ground with a thump. I hit so hard, I felt my internal organs rearranging themselves. The fall knocked me for a loop. I was in a semi-conscious state but realized as I cleared my head, my father was still screaming at me from the window.

"You stupid shit - I can't believe what you have done to your room - you sick asshole. You think this is funny, well I hope you get your drafted ass shot off in Vietnam."

My father quickly disappeared from the window. He was replaced with my mother and brother Bobby staring out in amazement. My mother screamed.

"Jackson - you're just an insane child" and then in such a caring and motherly voice, "now listen to what they tell you to do and make sure THAT YOU DON'T GET KILLED OVER THERE."

GET KILLED OVER THERE - the only thing I was worried about was getting killed over here.

My brother yelled out, "Don't forget to kill some gooks for me - man, you really messed up our room."

I was half way down the block by then. I stopped to look back and saw my father about twenty yards away, panting heavily in his feeble attempt to catch me. He threw me the finger and screamed out "YOU SHIT - YOU DAMN WELL ARE NEVER WELCOMED BACK HERE AGAIN."

That was the last frame in my mind. The only thing I wanted was to get as far away from my dysfunctional family as possible.

I made my way to Rhino's house. His parents took me in for the night. They felt sorry for me and knowing their son was inducted a few months prior thought it was indeed the Christian and patriotic thing to do. God bless America, God bless the Radaskiewiczs!

That was the last time I ever saw or communicated with my father. I was well into my tour when I received a notice he had died. I was just involved in the Battle of Ban Houe Sane, and trying to deal with the experience the best I could. I admittedly was un-nerved, frazzled to the bone. I was reconciling, knowing I was part of a unit who had experienced the same and that if I alone could not endure, then me, being a part of the team definitely would.

I was approached by my buddy Joey Ratel. He looked as out of sorts and confused as me.

"Major wants to see you."

"Where?"

"In his tent."

"You know why?"

"Didn't say - mine is not to question why - mine is just to do and die."

"Funny!"

"Tough out there, ha?"

"Sucked to a "fare thee well""

"Major says he wants to see you now."

"Ya, ya - I'm going."

I made my way to the Major's tent. I hadn't a clue why he wanted to see me. I had no rank, just another draftee - another dog soldier. I approached the door, knocked and asked permission to step in.

"Granted", I heard from within.

I entered. There was a figure standing with his back to me. He turned around. It was Sergeant Major.

"Krause?"

"Yes sir."

"Tough out there today?"

"Yes Sir - tough out there."

"Yes, this war is a bitch - unfortunately we soldiers are cursed in that we have to fight our country's wars and our own personal ones as well."

I hadn't a clue what the Sergeant Major was talking about.

"Yes, sir."

"We'll Krause - I regret I have to inform you - that I just received notification your father died."

I stood there, void of emotion.

"Did you hear me Krause - your father has died?"

Again, the words rolled off me like beads of water off the down of a young duck.

"Krause, you alright - say something?"

I didn't know what to say.

The Sergeant Major approached me.

"Krause - you o.k. - hey, you need someone to talk to?"

'Ha?"

"Ya, like you need a chaplain or someone?"

I snapped out of it.

"Do I need a chaplain or someone? No...no sir." What I really wanted to say was, *"No sir, what I needed was a father"*.

Sergeant Major walked right up to me and stared me in the eyes.

"Well, O.K., then Krause, I delivered the message, you're dismissed."

"Yes, Sir."

I saluted the Sergeant Major and took my leave. I retired from the tent. I learned a few weeks later my father died of a massive stroke. Since I left home he had gained almost thirty pounds and was weighing in at a stout two hundred eighty. He was scary enough at his previous weight. He must have been frightening at his new. It wasn't his mass that warranted being guarded if you were around him. It was his moroseness, his demons that occasionally played out. My father had the darkest of sides and his demeanor could change at a moment's notice, like a cold icy breeze breaking through an August night.

I never saw a good side of him. His personality's baseline was tolerable. We could live in the same house with him but it was best to avoid him at all costs. In our house familiarity bred contempt. From tolerable, his only direction was spiraling down when his inner hell broke from him, like rancid air, it sucked the life from everyone in the room. There was no one who was safe, except sometimes, my younger brother Bobby who he occasionally let leave the room before his tirades began. Bobby, who my father thought was the anti-me, me, who I knew deep in my heart of hearts he despised.

My father met his demise at the trough. He was at the local watering hole, The Fairlawn Tavern, where he routinely spent the hours from 3:00 to 5:00 p.m. He was somewhat tolerable with a drink in him, almost beyond human, with several or more.

I was told the Boston Red Sox were playing the New York Yankees and my father got into a pissing contest with a couple of transplanted New Yorkers whose allegiance was still to Appleville. They were tested and true and looked upon the Yankees as the second coming of Christ. My father had no such regard. He hated the Red Sox and the Yankees too. To him they all sucked. He was green with envy they were all as he said "fucking millionaires playing a kid's game". He berated them often and made it known their status and salaries were a insult to the average hardworking men and women of America who slave away every day in the factories and production lines (that is if they were damn well lucky to have a job) laboring until they grew ill or tired supporting the lying crooked scumbags who ran big business. "None of this shit is fair" he would say. "It's an American injustice. I'd like to put a hot poker up all their butts and spin them around on it."

The Red Sox (so I was told) were winning 5 to 3, in the eighth inning. My father's consumption was about one Boilermaker every inning and a half. He was working on his fifth, just hanging at the bar, listening to the two outliers who were sitting adjacent to him. They were nursing their bottles of Sam Adams (after they were told by Butchy, the bartender the Fairlawn Tavern was a blue collar bar and didn't serve no designer beer) and bitching about Boston as compared to New York and the Sox versus the Yankees.

It was late in the eighth that the Sox scored another 3 runs. My father really didn't care but being antagonistic to the bone, wasn't about to let a prime opportunity pass - not to bust these guys "balls".

"The Yankee's suck!"

Telling a New Yorker that his prized Yankees sucked was paramount to stabbing him in the eye with an ice pick.

"Fuck. I didn't hear what I think I heard?" responded one in a thick Brooklyn accent.

"Ya damn well did that is unless you have shit in your ears." My father responded in his thickest Boston brogue.

"Why so damn unfriendly? Is it all the assholes in the world live within the confines of Rt.128?"

"Don't have a clue what you're talking about?" responded my father.

"You Bostonites, all shit for brains every damn one. Your Red Sox suck, your Patriots suck, your Bruins suck."

"It's Bostonians - you stupid asshole."

Then I was told one of the New Yorkers gets up from his barstool, a six-footer, two hundred pounder himself and grabs himself by the balls and says. "Here asshole, you damn well can suck this."

Butchy the bartender (I'm again told) senses there is elevation in the room and tries to calm things down. "Yow, guys, let's calm it down in here - we don't want no trouble."

Then as the story goes, my father, pissed and red faced, slams down his shot of Bourbon, gets off his barstool, gags and falls to the ground, dead."

The two New Yorkers, astonished, walk over to him. "I think the bastard's dead." They throw two twenties on the bar and leave..

Butchy calls the ambulance and they take my father away and that was it. His life ends like a petrified dobber in a snot rag.

My father's only joy in life was to threaten and antagonize. When I heard the circumstance of his passing I wasn't surprised. It was a tolerable ending for not too tolerable a guy. It was alright by me, he damn well wouldn't be missed. I was now fatherless but I was fatherless all my life. Now it just became official. I felt more like a robot than a person. I tried to think through my relationship with him - hoping to capture some good times we shared. Unfortunately there were none.

I had not one tear to shed upon hearing of his demise. I had not one regret with him involved. I had not one parting thing I wanted to say to him - if indeed I had the chance. It was as if he were although a part of my life, the bit part he played, if not inconsequential - ***was the darkest of theatre***.

7

Peter Strong

He was staring at me, staring at him. I knew he thought I was focusing on his prosthetic. I was. It wasn't that I never saw one before. I saw a lot, probably a few hundred or so during my service years. In and out of Walter Reed, the prosthetic and the wounded warrior wearing it was not an uncommon sight. It just reinforced how ugly war is, how painful its cost.

For some reason I couldn't take my eyes off him, this twenty something year old, who was in turn staring me down as he sat not twenty feet away at the Danvers Northshore Mall. It was 9:00 a.m. and I was waiting for Rhino. I was always waiting for Rhino. His being on time would be a first. Not that his presence could have distracted me. I found myself locked in a stare with this kid and found I was unable to break away. Like two elk locking horns, neither he or I were backing down. What began as an innocent glance was now becoming more than uncomfortable. For whatever reason, I wanted to walk the twenty feet to him and knock him right off the bench as he sat. Something raged inside me, something I had not felt for a number of years. It was like this kid, with his thin goatee and combed back greasy hair, dressed in a purple Adidas sweat suit, wearing in your face bright orange sneakers was egging me on - like he was questioning me *"Who the hell are you to stare - you old crusty bastard - who the hell are you to lay eyes onto me?"* and I wanted to tell him who exactly the hell I was - I was Jack Krause - the proud veteran Jack Krause from Lynn Massachusetts. The Jack Krause who served his country admirably in Vietnam - who raised his two semi-dysfunctional kids but by today's standards kids a cut above (who was I kidding myself, they were dysfunctional) the Jack Krause who worked his stupid butt off for thirty plus something years for UPS to put a roof over his family's head and food on the damn table. That's who the hell I am and I'm damn proud of it. So okay sonny boy, who the hell are you? *Yeah, just who the hell are ya?*

"Hey guy, I'm Peter Strong."

I must have been in a trance. I must admit, I didn't see the kid get up from his bench and walk the twenty feet towards me and now standing right in front of me. I didn't see him at all. This scared the shit out of me, frightened me to a fare thee well.

I just wanted to ask Scotty to "beam me up- get me the hell out of here." I quickly gathered myself and looked at him.

The kid was rolling a cigarette around in his fingers.

"Hey old man, you got a light?"

The arrogant little prick I thought to myself. This young punks got some kind of an attitude. Old man, my ass!

"No I don't smoke - only assholes smoke."

The kid moved a step closer to me. He indeed was encroaching on my personal space, getting into my private circle pushing into that invisible moat surrounding me, which was really beginning to piss me off.

"Well like they say old man, opinions are like butt holes, everybody's got one."

"That may be true sonny boy, but some opinions are just dead right and others are just dead wrong and people who smoke cigarettes are dead wrong assholes and that's my educated opinion and I'll hold to it." And then just like that I asked, " Where did you lose your leg?"

"What's it to you?" he asks.

"Just curious." I responded.

"Iraq 2008."

"That's a bitch."

"It is what it is." The kid responds.

I don't know what it was but this arrogant butt hole was bringing out the worst in me. I feel like I drank five cups of Starbucks and was teetering on the edge. I should just back off and shut my big mouth but that indeed would be new to me, me, Jack Krause never knew when to shut my yap and hold my opinion. So why begin now?

"Come on now sunshine, you for real?"

"What are you asking?" the kids responds.

"I mean your retarded answer, it is what it is."

"It ain't retarded at all, I'm trying to move past all the crap in my life, and honestly don't need some old fart like you getting in my face, questioning who and what I am - like I have to answer to you."

"Iraq 2008 huh?"

"Yeah Iraq 2008, IED. You serve?"

"Ya damn right I served, Vietnam, 1970-73."

Rhino arrived none too soon. The conversation with the kid was going nowhere. It seemed both of us were getting tied up in our jockey shorts. I didn't know what the kid felt but I welcomed the reprieve. Rhino in spite of himself, timed his arrival well.

I turned to him and greeted him with "Rhino, late as usual."

"What's new, my internal clock runs on Rhino time."

The kid looked at us both with contempt. There was no way he could hide it. I sized him up that he lost a leg and probably held it for the world. He turned three hundred sixty degrees and started to walk away from us as he threw his right arm high into the air and threw us the "bird". I could barely hear his last utterance, " Old Ignorant Assholes."

"What the hell was that all about?" questioned Rhino.

"The kid and me got into a staring joust. We just started looking at each other and it got away from us. I think I got caught up staring at his prosthetic, lost a leg in Iraq."

"Leg or no leg the kid seems like a punk to me."

"Screw it Rhino, give him a break, he's really pissed at the world. You know he probably saw some really bad shit there and it's tough to forget every morning when he puts on his pants and looks at the stump."

"Screw him", retorts Rhino "I'd still categorize him as one flaming arrogant punk".

"Shit Rhino, remember when we returned from Nam. There were no bigger shitheads on the face of the earth then you, me and Dirt. You talk about attitude - remember what we brought home?"

Rhino walks the few feet to the bench I was sitting, puts down his torn baby shit green gym bag, then bends over to tie his sneakers.

"Ya, I remember, but we had every right to - we returned to a bunch of scumbag "commies" calling us "baby killers" and throwing garbage and spitting at us, long haired hippie assholes, having no idea we were saving their yellow delicate cowardly asses as they were running over the border to Canada."

"Shit Rhino, as hard as you want to be on those idiots you got to remember they for the most part were right. It was a screwed up war."

"And this Iraq, Afghanistan shit isn't?"

"Damn it, let me finish Rhino, like I was saying, it was a fucked up war and of course what war isn't. They're fought on the backs of ignorants like you and me who thought there was a morality about it and we were fighting to save the world from communist "Domino Theory" shit. We didn't know crap and I guess if those asshole "hippie" types didn't do all the stuff they did the Vietnam War would have gone on forever."

"Yeah Jack, ignorants like you and me - and let's not forget all the other poor bastards, who had less options than us - you know the left behinds - the ones who didn't have a chance in civilian life but who damn well were good enough for the military - the disenfranchised, the leave behinds - they didn't know anything other than being drafted - unlike you and me who "didn't know what we didn't know" but knew enough to figure our way out - but we didn't, we just let the pols serve the war up to us - and like the fools we were, swallowed it hook, line and sinker."

"Rhino - can we ever get over this?"

"Jackson, can we ever get over a failed marriage, a death of a child, an abusive parent, a heroin addiction, our dog getting run over by a car, our siblings stealing money from us? The answer is NO, there is just some crap that chips away at us, compromises our sense of wellbeing, makes us feel at any moment everything we have and are will be taken out by some killer meteorite, some kind of Darth Vader drone and puff just like that we are vaporized."

"You have one really absurd imagination Rhino."

"No imagination at all Jack - you, me and Dirt, us three — yes, are three of the sorriest bastards I know - you know why Jackson my boy?"

"No Rhino, prey tell - you damn well are cutting into our walking time."

"Well then I'll just tell and enlighten you, or rather us to the state we're in. We are indeed sorry ass souls because we now live in the world of "We and Them". "We" who had the honor and privilege of living and fighting in the jungle swamps of Vietnam and have to live with what we saw and did every damn minute of every damn day and no matter what we do, drink, drug, psycho blab - can't even, maybe only if we're lucky, break but for a brief few seconds escape from it's horrors - and then there are "them". "Them" are everybody else in our lives who didn't serve - and even if they have some kind of inkling or rendering of what war is about, haven't a clue except for what they see in the movies, on TV or on their computer. War isn't X-BOX Commando 3 it's "WAR", with real blood and carnage."

"Whoa, Rhino, you're on a roll."

"Ain't finished yet Jackson, the pity and shame of it all is that our interactions with those who didn't serve are bullshit, because what we experienced is always in our heads and those innocents that we share our lives with are so far removed from us and our demons it is a miracle we have anything in common and can communicate and co-exist with each other at all."

Rhino's words somehow hit home - that shroud he was talking about now lay upon my chest sucking the air from my lungs, depleting the great energy I had not minutes before I met the kid and then Rhino dropped a "Rhino" bomb on me - a big black Rhinoceros turd that set my heart spiraling into an abyss of despair.

"Christ, Rhino we're here to walk - not to psychoanalyze the world and our role in it - walking is what I need to do and now I don't even feel like doing that - screw it! SCREW IT! **SCREW IT!** - no walking today."

I reached down and garbed my bag. I stuffed my sweatshirt into it and searched for my keys and sunglasses. I looked up at Rhino and he had this confused look on his face.

"Where the hell you going?" he asked.

"I'm going to go visit Dirt."

"I just came from there. Peaked in his box. He was still sleeping, by the looks of the empty bottles he had a big night."

"Great. Well, I'm going to go see him anyway, maybe he sobered up and I can buy him some bacon and eggs."

Rhino chimed in, "We'll then I'll join ya."

"Ya, sure Rhino, it's always been the three of us. But no more talk about this war shit - *that's just what made Dirt the drunk he is.*"

8

Living in a Box

I followed Rhino out of the mall to his beat 2002 Ford F150. The truck was dying of cancer. The wheel panels were rusting out and there were enough holes to see the New England Winter ate out the undercarriage as well. Every time I rode in his truck, I expected it to be my last. There was no doubt in my mind the brake linings were also rusted through and would give at any moment, sending the truck, as a rogue missile rolling over anything in its path.

"You got to get rid of this rusted truck Rhino. Damn it, I can put my foot through the floorboards."

"Ya, sure Jackson - ya gonna lend me the twenty grand to get a new one?"

"A new one, who's talking about a new one - you can get a used one for like maybe five or six."

"Like I said Jackson - you got the five or six grand to lend me?"

"Damn it, Rhino, if I had, you damn well know I would give it to you, but I don't. I got just enough to pay for Gerti's and my retirement. You damn well know that."

"Okay, so stop bitch'n about my truck."

Rhino drove me to the back entrance of the mall where I picked up my 98' Mercury. Unlike Rhino's truck, my Merc was in great shape and looked showroom new. I babied the hell out of it. I bought it new and cleaned, polished and maintained it to ad nauseum. For a seventeen-year old car, my Merc was a showpiece.

Gerti said "You spend more time messing with that car, than you do with your family." She was right. Gerti used to say "You love that car more than you love me." Again she was right. Several years back, she never mentioned my car again. It wasn't really worth her time cause I never listened to her anyway.

I followed Rhino to Marshall's at Vinnin Square in Swampscott. Tracking him reinforced my opinion, he was going to kill himself in that truck - or worse yet, a passenger (probably me) or anyone in his path. I committed to myself I would avoid riding in it anytime I could. I clearly saw the writing on the wall as Rhino swerved like a wild man over the dividing lines from lane to lane, barely missing the vehicles surrounding him.

We pulled off Paradise Road into Marshall's parking lot. It was just

10:20 a.m., and there were at least fifty vehicles parked there. *Who the hell are these people who shop at Marshall's at 10:20 on a Tuesday morning? Different folks than me* I thought. Then again I asked myself, *Who are these guys who are visiting a friend, who lives in a crate at the back of Marshall's building? Different folks, then they,* I answered.

We pulled our cars to the back of the building. The crate was one of those large bulk sea freight containers, measuring 8 feet by 6 high. It had been left there for several months and now seemed to be abandoned - that is, until Dirt found it and now had squatter's rights - or at least thinks he does.

Dirt was homeless. He has been that way ever since he returned from Vietnam in 1972. He was one of the "totally left behinds" who couldn't after his return, measure up to any societal expectations. He returned home a broken man and acquiesced into a life on the streets and seemed to have never aspired for anything more. A few months before he was living at the shelter in Salem until he came in drunk one night and disobeyed the shelter's rules. They were cut and dry, "NO DRINKING, NO DRUGGING, NO VIOLENCE, NO GUNS, NO SEX. Dirt lived up to them all except the "NO DRINKING". He was a bonafide alcoholic - one of those who could not stop at one drink, but needed another, and then one following, then too many to keep count as he drank himself into oblivion not having a clue to where he was or what he had done. He had been this way for the last forty something years. It amazed Rhino and I he hadn't died years before or that someone hadn't beat him within an inch of his life, because Dirt wasn't just a drunk - he was a nasty, belligerent one - who could piss off everyone he came into contact - beyond the tolerance of their last patient neuron.

Rhino and I parked our cars and walked over to Dirt's freight container. We pulled open the door and there he lay surrounded by empty whiskey bottles and a bunch of other crap but it was too dark to see. The stench from the carton was almost intolerable. It pinched my nostrils and sucked back my ears as my face contracted to the rancidness of the odor. It was as if there was not one rodent but a number had died in there and then the biggest one of all, who yet had hopefully not, Dirt. Rhino and I pulled back the large container's door further and the light from the sparkling October day hit Dirt right in his eyes and he pushed back against the container's back wall to try to avoid it..

"Who the hell's there?" questioned Dirt.

"Who the hell do you think is here?" I responded.

"Fuck if I know."

"It's me Jackson and Rhino, the only friends you have, you asshole."

"Just go away", he retorted.

"No, we're not leaving until we see how you're doing and get you some breakfast."

"How am I doing (in a voice carrying the weakness of a deflating balloon) how do you think I'm doing - *I LIVE IN A FUCKING BOX.*"

9

The Salem Diner

I returned home after Rhino, Dirt and I had a late breakfast at the Salem Diner. Dirt looked like death warmed over and smelled the same. This was really the first time in a while being close to him offended me. I had reservations walking into the diner, thinking that perhaps this was a really stupid thing to do. Not only did Dirt stink but there was no doubt alcohol was oozing from his skin. I now fail to see how bringing him there was the sane thing to do but I was hungry and I knew Rhino was as well. In regards to Dirt, there was no doubt he hadn't a decent meal for some time now. I guess I justified Dirt's assault on the diner as something motivated by my sense of duty to my wayward brother. It certainly caused me to pause when Alycine, the waitress motioned we sit in a little alcove, the farthest from the rest of the occupants. She beckoned us as if it were urgent we follow her lead, as she hurried us past several empty tables anchoring us to the booth closest to the "john". My take was Al (as we called her) probably hoped the smell emanating from the bathroom would overcome any association with the three of us. It didn't, it compounded it.

"You ready to order?" She questioned. Alycine was a stressed, tattooed woman in her fifties, who reminded me of Phyllis Diller, but her voice was more manly than the comedian's.

"Just got here." I answered. "Haven't even had time to look at the menu."

"What? You order the same damn thing every time.", Al pressed us.

"Okay, okay, eggs over easy, rye toast, hold the butter, a glass of orange, coffee black. Thanks Al."

"How bout you Rhino?"

" Ah, western omelette, home fries, english muffin, orange as well, butter and jam, if you got it, coffee with milk" ,volunteered Rhino.

"Dirt, whatcha havin?"

"Ah, give me a four egg omelet, a stack of blueberry pancakes, a side of ham and bacon, bowl of fruit, a plateful of home fries, keep the orange juice coming and every few minutes refill my coffee", Dirt spit out.

Alycine looked at Dirt wild eyed. Rhino and I looked at him with amazement.

"You gotta be kidding, right?" she questioned.

"Kidding my ass - bring it all as soon as its ready."

She gave a frown, turned and hurried to the kitchen. I could see her through the crack in the door talking to the cook. He was shaking his head in amazement..

"You must really be hungry?" questioned Rhino.

"A guy who lives in a crate usually is."

"Why don't you go back to the shelter?" I asked, "at least you get three squares there."

"Screw the shelter. I don't need no charity, I can fend for myself. I did in Nam for them two years and anyway, everybody in that place don't have a clue. They're drunk and drugged up and have to leave it all behind to enter the place - but mark my word, as soon as they leave the shelter they're back at it. It's all bullshit. I know who and what I am - it ain't pretty but it is what it is and I'll be damn if I have to bullshit anybody - ya know, cause I'm a US Vietnam Veteran, a drunk and a druggy - but a US Vietnam Vet and I'm damn proud of it."

"Ya, we get it Dirt - you forget, we're Vets too - we get you don't have to make excuses for being one. "

"You're damn right I don't", Dirt spits out, ' Yeah, you're DAMN RIGHT I DON'T."

Several minutes later Al returned with our order. The cook Jamie must be the fastest ever. I got a feeling both he and Alycine wanted us out of the place - why - I hadn't a clue (other than the smell we emanated) I just sensed it, that's all.

There was so much food delivered, Al had to put some of it on a neighboring table.

Rhino and I start to eat. Dirt looks at all the breakfast laid out before him, takes one bite of the eggs and then lays his fork down and pushes back on his chair.

"I can't do it!"

"Can't do what?"

"Eat. I thought I could but I just can't do it."

"After you ordered all this food, you're telling me now you're not hungry?"

"Ya, that's what I'm telling you. Like it all sounded good - I mean as I read the menu. It all sounded good but once I laid my eyes on it - it kinda makes me sick just staring at it."

"Damn it, Dirt" I injected "This here's a forty dollar breakfast. I mean Rhino and I are going to split it - but it's still a forty dollar breakfast - I don't take my wife out for a forty dollar meal."

Dirt throws up his arms. "What the hell do you want me to do? I said I'm damn well sorry. I guess like they say, my eyes must be bigger than my stomach."

Alycine sees neither of us are eating, and comes over to our table.

"Anything wrong here?" she asks.

Just when I was ready to respond the diner's door opens and in walks five guys. They were dressed in gang apparel. Orange and gold bandanas, denim jackets cut to their shoulders. Three were of medium build, one slight and the other solidly configured with a wide neck that showcased his beard. All of them had pumped up pecks and arms. They all were tatted, two just their forearms, three with tats covering their wrists to their shoulders.

"Hey, waitress ... table now", one screeched.

Alycine shrugged her shoulders walked toward them and beckoned them to follow.

We watched as they approached us with Al sitting them not two tables away. All five of them glanced an eye at us with us returning the gesture. They sat down. We continued our conversation.

"Like I said Dirt, if you didn't want to eat that much food - damn it you should have started with something small, like a couple of poached eggs or something - not the whole damn menu." I can't say I wasn't pissed since I was now living now on a fixed income and all.

"Christ", Dirt responded, "What the hell do you want from me? My stomach's shrunk - so what's the big freaking deal?"

All of a sudden, our conversation was broken by one of the new occupants of the diner.

"What the hell, what do I smell, it smells like crap?"

Damn it, I said to myself, if there ever was a time to take leave it was now. It was so vividly clear to me taking Dirt to the diner was worse than a bad idea. Here I sat, my breakfast turning cold and hardy eaten. Rhino eagerly shoveling the food off his plate, his mouth so full, he could barely speak. Dirt smelling up the place and starting (I was absolutely sure) an alcohol and drug induced melt down. I was also damn sure I would be the one paying out the forty bucks because it was always me who paid for Dirt's missteps, not Rhino.

The truth was Rhino didn't like Dirt. He did once when they were young, in fact they were best friends, but after Nam, there was a real cooling off. Dirt was too much for himself and Rhino didn't have that one extra "giving" gene, a mega-one needed by anyone who had to deal with Dirt. Dirt just torpedoed his life and Rhino couldn't stand for it. The fact was Rhino saw a lot more action in Nam than Dirt and I. He was a member of Bravo Company, Ist Battalion, 26th Marine Regiment. He was involved in the battle of Khe Sanh, one of the bloodiest of the Vietnam War, one lasting eleven weeks, with a Marine Battalion of 5,000 men battling 3 NVA battalions of 20,000. It was a battle of legend, at the cost of thousands who died and debilitating lives for those who survived. Rhino spoke of it once to me. I never heard him mention it again.

"What the hell Dirt?" I heard Rhino cutting through my thoughts.

"Ya, what the hell, I'm ready to blow, this place".

Rhino looked at me.

"Your buying, because you damn well know I'm not."

What's new? I said to myself.

I looked at the guys two tables removed. They were still kavetching.

"Son of a bitch, what the fuck's up with that smell. It smells like someone shit in their drawers."

Dirt, Rhino and I got up from our chairs. I put my baseball cap on and pulled my ponytail through the back end. It felt balanced on my head. I wore the cap constantly. It was another bone of contention between Gerti and me.

"Will you take that damn hat off?" she would yell. "That ponytail is stupid enough but with that foolish hat you look ridiculous."

"RIDICULOUS" my ass. I was very much proud of it. It was a Vietnam Veterans blue cap embroidered in gold with a series of service bars going across. I got in the habit of wearing it, like many of my brethren who understood the value of their duty and after years of denial and guilt embraced their service and now wear it as a deserved badge of honor.

I took two twenties and a ten-dollar bill from my front pant pocket. I had a habit of keeping my money there. With just a touch of a finger, I knew whether my stash was with me or not. It might seem weird but I felt I had control over my life when I had control over my money, not that a hundred dollars in my front pant pocket really makes any difference but for the weirdest reason, it seemed to me it might.

As I laid down the fifty on the table, I kept thinking Gerti would kill me if she knew I blew $50.00 with tip on breakfast with Dirt and Rhino. I never spent $50 on anything for her. She would think it a stupid waste. The two of us had money issues all the time. It wasn't we were broke, we weren't. One thing about UPS, they have a damn good pension plan for their workers, not to say those who received it didn't work our sorry butts to the bone to deserve it. We did, every one of my UPS brethren, knew how to hustle, that was the mantra of the job.

Yes, Gerti and I had money issues all the time because although as cheap as she was, hording every dollar she could from her series of part time jobs over the years, spent my money as quickly as it came in on my daughter, granddaughter and her kid with no husband for my daughter and my granddaughter's do-nothing boyfriend. We supported the lot.

"It's our responsibility", Gerti would constantly say,

"No way our responsibility", I would retort, "They're the responsibility of the lame brained, lazy bastards who knocked them up."

"No, it's our responsibility and our duty under God's eyes, to take care of our family and like it or not, your daughter, granddaughter, great granddaughter and yes, Bellow's fiance Humphrey, fall into that box."

"Christ Gerti, fiance? Are you kidding me? He's nothing but a leach."

"Jack, he's committed to Bellows and Miley."

"Committed my ass. If he were committed he would get a job to support them."

"He's looking Jack".

"Looking bullshit. Didn't you ever hear that God helps those who help themselves?"

"Helping them may be the one thing you've ever done in your life that will get you a pass when you die - I sure as hell can't think of another."

When Gerti said that, all she ever did was really piss me off because I WAS IN NAM, and she forever looked at my service as inconsequential, like it was nothing more than a group of guys going to Boy Scout camp, just hanging out enjoying ourselves, ONE BIG CIRCLE JERK. It was anything but - and that was a big divide between her and me, once a small abyss, now becoming a Grand Canyon of division and misunderstanding, getting broader and deeper every day. My frustration is that the meaning of my service would be forever lost on her. She didn't care then and didn't now. Her life was tied up in her daughter, granddaughter and great granddaughter Miley and nothing else mattered. I didn't matter.

I've been living with that for years and now at sixty-nine, I've come to terms with it, that is as well as I can. Living with a woman who deep down in her heart of hearts, hasn't loved or taken me serious for years and for that matter, probably never did and never will.

I figured I would leave a ten dollar tip for all the mess Alycine had to clean up.

"Leaving a ten spot - big man - big tipper," Rhino spurted out.

"Let's just get the hell out of this place," I responded.

Rhino and I waited for Dirt to slide out of his seat. He looked terrible. I wish he ate something, with all the good food, sitting untouched on the table, it was just a terrible shame he ate nothing - a waste of food - a waste of life.

As Dirt passed me, his stink attacked my senses. I was a fool to bring him here, just a stupid fool - what must I've been thinking? We started to walk out of the diner and passed the table the five gang members sat.

As we passed, one of them yelled out 'Hey, stink pots, ya want a dollar for a bar of soap - you guys fucking stink." Dirt and I just kept on walking. It was the smartest thing to do because the truth was we did, or rather Dirt stunk enough for us three. Rhino however had a different nature, as big as he was, giving him license to never back off. He took five steps backwards and turned and just looked at the five guys staring up at him. Rhino's girth overshadowed them all. He just stared at them and to my surprise, not a word was passed, and then he just turned and walked away, the occupants of the booth not uttering a sound, Rhino not looking back.

I was pleased the incident ended as it did. This was unusual for Rhino, he had a very short fuse and it didn't take much to set him off. I surmised he had the comfort of a full stomach and whatever was spurted out by one of the five guys, was right on the mark ..... a shower and a bar Dirt sorely needed - there was no denying - so that gave them a little license - and a reason for Rhino to walk away.

We left the diner and I drove Dirt back to his crate. During the short journey I recalled I saw those five guys before. It was while I was parked on Lynn Shore Drive, and they were involved with the incident with the pedestrians, bumping them out of the way until the mounted police intervened. Yes, I concluded they were the same - just looking for something or someone to ignite them - to fire them up - any reason, then again, for none at all.

"I know those five guys". I volunteered.

"From where?" questioned Rhino.

"Assholes!" interjected Dirt.

"Walking the wall near the Breakers on Lynn Shore Drive."

"I might have seen them around too", added Rhino.

"Assholes", again added Dirt.

"No dickhead, we were the assholes, or let me say this, I was, thinking no one would take issue with the way you smell - you got to get yourself cleaned up Dirt and out of that crate."

"It's my home."

"Ya, if you were a dog."

"I should have kicked the shit out of those guys," injected Rhino.

"And why didn't you - I asked?"

"Too much eggs and bacon - ***oops I gotta fart.***"

10

We All Live in Crates

It was 1:50 p.m. and Marshall's parking lot was full. Winter had ended, Spring was in the air. It looked like everyone wanted to spruce up their wardrobe, everybody but Dirt.

Dirt got out of the car and walked towards his crate. It was surreal. I never thought anyone I knew would ever live in a crate, now my social circle included one. I didn't know whether it spoke well of me or not. Without a doubt life has its intriguing twists and turns and they culminated as one of my "Band of Brothers", once one of "America's Best and Brightest" made his way to his makeshift home.

"Doesn't that beat the crap out of you?" questioned Rhino.

"Beat the crap out of me, meaning what?" I responded a bit indignant.

"Dirt living in a crate?"

"We all live in crates." I responded.

"We don't all live in crates - you know what I mean."

"Ya, I know what you mean but we all live within the confines we either have inherited, accepted or designed into our lives."

"Shit, I don't see it like that."

"See it anyway you like Rhino - that's my limited perspective."

"You're telling me, Dirt designed this life for himself?"

"I'm telling you - well look at him - this might seem a bit weird - but he seems pretty comfortable with what he's doing."

"You've lost me on that - he's no dog."

"No Rhino, I'm not saying he is - but Dirt wouldn't be living in a crate if he didn't want to - he seems to have accepted his sorry ass life and isn't doing a damn thing to better his situation."

"Honestly Jackson, I think the man's an imbecile."

"No, not an imbecile - just a guy caught up in the abyss of self-pity. He sees himself as the ultimate victim and wants to make sure the world sees him as such as well."

"He could have gotten help after Nam."

"It wasn't readily offered and he didn't seek it out - he chose one shelter after another and now this crate - he'll be back to another shelter as soon as it gets cold. That's what he does."

I started my Merc and drove Rhino back to his car. We agreed to meet at the mall tomorrow at 8:00 a.m. our usual time. I wondered if I should go back to Dirt and schedule meeting with him as well. He kinda lost his motivation to walk with us over the last few months. What he had for moving his life forward seemed to disappear with his decision to leave the shelter or rather get drunk and get thrown out.

Being in Nam was like rust on a car. It slowly destroyed us from within. Initially, we came home and were a basket case, especially arriving to a bunch of catcalls of "Baby Killer", "Rapist" and "War Monger." Then months or years later we tried to muscle though it with a pharmacy of drugs, a distillery of booze, and with as much denial as humanly possible. We thought we were doing all right but we weren't. We were just sweeping the shit under the carpet, putting on a pretty face when it covered the scars and torment of a fractured soul. No matter how we tried to hide or disguise it, it seemed to always break through. A pig with lipstick is still a pig. A car rusting from the inside is still a pile of rust, and its presence will eventually rise through the facade, showing the world there has always been a cancer within, and consistent with this dreadful disease, there has or will be a terrible price to pay.

The tragedy of wars is young people fight them, BECAUSE THEY DON"T KNOW SHIT! I knew nothing at eighteen, but if you listened to me then, I would tell you I knew a whole lot. Like the rest of my generation at that age, I didn't know what I didn't know. Youth is primed for war. They are the stupid ones who go over the hill, because they are told to, the innocents who during their youth saw Cruise, Deisel, Stallone, Schwarzenegger, Van Dam, Smith, Walberg and the like (John Wayne, Gary Cooper, and Aldo Ray, if they were my generation) take the insanity of war dead on and return to honor and glory as they live another day.

The glory of War is the big deceit. No matter for what reason we became soldiers, there was a part of us, whether the most miniscule or grandiose that we felt (all of us, I think, cause my fellow soldiers and I spoke of it often) that what we were engaged in would bring some sort of good. It didn't make sense to us we would be put in harm's way and be asked to kill and destroy, if indeed there was nothing honorable to come from it. Nam wasn't like World War II where the Nazis were trying to take over the world, where if it wasn't for America's intervention, we all would be speaking German today, that is all the Arians, cause there would be no others left but them, once Hitler scrubbed everyone else from the face of the earth.

In Nam, we were all told it was much the same thing. In retrospect it wasn't. It was a different war, fought for different reasons, having a different result and here I am, forty-five years later wondering what the hell it was about, my body and mind screwed up to an extreme, and now today it seems the whole world is waging it. I guess those I killed in Nam were killed for no reason. I guess the American heroes draped in the RED, WHITE and BLUE were the US price of admission. I still don't get it. I probably never will. I'm too old now to give a damn but still am no less affected. I appease myself by saying I was involved because it was my duty to serve the good old United States of Amercia. I wish it was as clear then as I see it now. When I was drafted, I just didn't see it this way. Maybe because I was drafted and dragged, screaming and yelling. Well, far from that…but I went reluctantly - I really didn't have a clue, regrettably - ***not a damn one.***

11

The Prodigal Son

Gerti and I are at it again.

"Christ Jack, it seems you're never home."

"Things to do Gerti."

"You're retired Jack!"

"Just from the UPS, Gerti, not from life."

"Jack the way it seems - from the UPS - me and your kids."

"Bullshit Gerti."

"Well you haven't seen your daughter, granddaughter, great granddaughter and your son Hendrix - he's wandering the face of the earth somewhere - and we haven't heard from him for decades. He might be dead for all we know."

"Like I told you when he gets tired, hungry and broke, he'll find his way home. When he's finally big enough to man up."

"Jack, twenty some years letting him leave like he did, might be the sorriest day in our lives. We've lost our son, I damn well know we have. In fact, I know he is dead - a mother knows such things."

"Gerti, it wasn't like it was a casual leave. Hendrix ran away from his bond. Remember his bond, remember the two thousand we put up to get him out of jail - the two grand we scrapped together to get his sorry butt out...?"

"How the hell can I forget - you remind me all the time?"

"That's horseshit - I'm now trying to forget."

"You'll never forget ...!"

"And how do you expect me to do that? The fact is our kid, yes, YOURS and MINE was a drug addict and a dope pusher who ran away from his bail because he couldn't face the consequences - and screwed you and me royally, flushing our two grand down the toilet."

We haven't seen our son for twenty-seven years. He just left one morning and never returned. It was after he was arrested for selling Heroin by the Lynn Police. When I heard he was dealing again and arrested, I went ballistic. I mean, what parent wants his kid to be a pusher, selling poison, rolling towards a dead end future.

I had to put up two grand of bail money after the hearing. Two grand to me was a lot of money and putting it up to support my drug addicted, drug pushing son was way too much for me. Gerti was right. I did go ballistic. I just wanted Hendrix to know where I stood. No addicts, no drug pushers would be in my family. I just would not tolerate it.

I wasn't born yesterday. I knew what drugs were about and what they did to people. I was no innocent, I smoked pot and took some uppers and downers and did a little acid and cocaine but it stopped there, *well not really, Gerti and I were on our "Magical Mystery Tour" for a good three some years before the kids arrived*, but I did stop. Especially after I saw what it did to a lot of guys in Nam. Some of them were doped up all the time and I knew there was a major penalty to pay. Many a good US soldier met their deaths because they were so blown away they neglected their duty, not even seeing the enemy coming, and when they confronted it, so toked up and non-functional they were less than non-effective.

My kid taking drugs and peddling them - I guess I just couldn't deal with it. I should have known the kid was cursed the day Gerti and I named him. She wanted to name him Bartholomew after her father Bart. I hated that name, Bart Krause didn't do it for me. I wanted to name him Reynolds, after one of my good friends and fallen brethren in Nam, Reynolds Dileo killed in "The Battle Of Route 62". Gerti wasn't high on that name either, so after a couple of glasses of wine, *that is for me but none for her because of her pregnancy - but she damn well wanted some,* we decided to name our son Hendrix if a boy and Henrietta if a girl after Jimmy Hendrix who the Rock & Roll Hall of Fame named the greatest instrumentalist in the history of Rock & Roll.

Gerti and I loved Jimmy Hendix's songs. "The Wind Cries Mary", "Red House", 'Purple Haze", "Hey Joe"and Foxy Lady". I remember us getting all wired up and screwing all night, sucking down Tango Screwdrivers and pulling on weed, dropping acid and everything in between. "Along the Watch Tower" (lyrics by the great Bob Dylan) was one of our favorites. The lyrics still resonate after all these years and every time I hear it, takes me back to what were probably the best years of my life. I often wonder If I wrote the song what it would say?

It would go something like this…

ALL ALONG THE LYNNWAY

All along the Lynnway and no fresh air to breath,
There has to be a way out of here, we try so hard now, to believe,
There's just too much confusion as we greet the day
Policemen try to arrest us
The drugs, they try to test us,
As we scratch to find our way

What a foolish man my wife, she said to me
To work and still have nothing renders a man a fool,
We don't have much but a gentle touch

That brought us where we are
Now the two of us and soon to be three
How stupid, how bizarre

The crazy man above us who lives in the one room
flat
Drinks all night and runs his mouth and doesn't stop at
that,
Cause he sees himself when he was young and it isn't a
pretty sight,
So he sleeps all day
To run away and drinks all through the night

My wife she strangely looks at me and her eyes are a distant
gray
But there's no chance to pull back with a child soon to
come our way,
I'm going to be a daddy and there's no chance in hell
That Gerti would abort the kid but there's no way to tell
That the kid is truly mine
And hers was meant to be
That once was one, and now is two
And soon now, to be three

All along the Lynnway and no fresh air to
breath,
There has to be a way out of here, we so hard try to believe
There's just too much confusion as we greet the day
We never had much use for God

But now begin to pray

"Damn it Gerti, how many times do we have to talk about
this - I didn't have an inkling he was leaving. If I knew he felt

as scared and hurt as he did - we could have talked, like adults-through it."

"Talk like adults - you kidding me - the older you and I get, the less adult conversation we have - and the truth is Jack - and you will have to live and die with this - is that you never spoke to your kids civilly - you talked at them, never with them and that's why you had and have such a estranged relationship with Hendrix and Riley, none at all. And with me, shit, I hardly know what to call what we have today and have had for the last forty some years."

God, I hated this crap but in truth backing off would have been the smartest thing to do, but I just didn't feel like it today - screw it, I was all in.

"A MARRIAGE - they call what we have a M-A-R-R-I-A-G-E."

"You could've fooled me, I call it anything but - maybe an arrangement, maybe a contract, maybe roommates, maybe a prison sentence, maybe an understanding, but never a damn marriage."

"And you have no one to blame but me?"

"Jack, we've gone over this a thousand times - there's enough blame to go around - but you should take the brunt of it because you were never the same after coming back from Vietnam. You tell me all the time you were a whole different person. I should have ended it there knowing Nam took such a big part of you before we met. I should have known there would never be a place for a woman and children in your life. I was just foolish thinking there would. I was just damn foolish. I should have left you a long time ago."

I was getting pissed. "It was there all along Jack, but it wasn't all about Vietnam - it was in the Krause bloodline - I should have known you would be abusive - all I had to do is look at your father - you've told me he was a terribly abusive man - look at how he treated your mother - you followed right in his footsteps!!"

Gerti was stepping way over the line. I despised my father. He was abusive to me as he was to anyone - he never gave me a break - just stomped me into the ground, just me being around pissed him off. I was a burr in his saddle and he rode the shit out of me. A comparison to him? I would no way accept.

"DAMN IT, NO, NO, NO, - NEVER, NEVER, NEVER, make a comparison of my father and me - NEVER, NEVER, NEVER!!!! - or I'll walk away and never come back."

"Maybe that would be the best thing of all!"

"Maybe it would" I responded, "Yes, maybe it would for everybody."

I had had enough. There was a regular pattern of abusiveness in our relationship that had a consistent rhythm. Our arguments would go on for twenty or thirty minutes - no longer - the words would get more profane and our voices more amplified. This was kind of where we were right now. Then when we arrived at that plateau, both of us would back off. It was like we delivered enough damage to each other and this was indeed another difference between me and my father - my father would never back off, he would keep going until he was drunk and eventually pass out. Sometimes, more that I could count, the three of us, me, my brother and mother hoped he would never wake up.

It was 6:30 p.m. and Gerti and I were worn out.

"You want to catch dinner at Joey's?" I asked.

"After the conversation we just had you want to eat now?"

"Gerti, you'll never have enough energy to scream and abuse me like you do if you don't."

"You're just one badly screwed up person Jackson Krause."

"No shit Gerti, but rather, one screwed up hungry one."

"So, okay, okay, I'll put a little face on and then, well you're right, I guess we have to eat."

I watched Gerti turn her back on me and make her way into the bathroom. In many ways she was right. Maybe I was too hard on her and the kids? Maybe Nam messed me up way more than I realized? Maybe like so many other Vietnam Vets, I am functional but no way really together? Maybe the price I made my family pay was way too dear and that it would have been far better off if they had another husband and father who never went to war or then again never returned. Another father who was very much unlike me - a gentler, kinder spirit without the constant turmoil and paranoia eating away inside.

It was really hard for me to face the problem we had with Hendrix. Gerti always blamed his misbehaviors on me and she was probably right. I was just really hard on both my kids, especially him. There was something uncontrollable in Hendrix that scared the hell out of me - as it sometimes came to the surface, exposing itself in both words and actions. I wanted like a hammer to a nail, drive it back into its host. The truth was my son and I were estranged from the earliest years of his life.

"Dad, do you really love me?"

I couldn't believe my kid was asking me that. I couldn't believe I didn't readily have an answer.

It was a very long "telling" pregnant pause. I didn't know what to say. My first compulsion was *Yes, I kind of love you.* A red light went off in my head warning me to not let those words leave my mouth. How the hell can any parent ever tell his or her kid- *Yes, I kind of love you?!* But in my heart of hearts that was the way I felt, because that was the way I felt about myself, *Yes I kind of love myself too* and the way I felt about my daughter, my wife, my job, my life - of just about everything and everyone.

What scared me and was the crux of the matter was this, where did it kind of begin and end? Was it 49-51 percent, 60-40 percent, 70-30, 80 -20? What percent was the LOVE and then again what percentage as the OTHER?

I walked into our bedroom and opened up the lower drawer of my three drawer bureau. I lifted up several sweaters and retrieved a worn leather jewelry box I had for years but could never remember the origin. I opened it and there it was **THE LETTER.** It was addressed: DAD. I've read it a hundred times. I never shared it, not even with Gerti. I still have never accepted or come to terms with its content. It was indeed the point of the spear … and I felt like Christ on the cross, with each reading just like a lance plunging into my ribs ….. it was destroying me one word, one caustic pierce at a time.

Dear Dad.

You failed me. If I indeed had the power to choose any father in the world …. It would not have been you.

I don't know what a kid should expect from his Dad so I never had any great expectations … but even the smallest I never realized. I can't remember you ever playing baseball with me. I can't remember you ever watching a Red Sox or Patriots game and inviting me to sit by your side. I never ever recall you asking me about my schoolwork or what I wanted to accomplish in my life. It seemed my presence always interfered with something you were too busy with. It seemed you were always living in another world. I don't know what kind it was, or is, but I do know it wasn't kid friendly.

I know what I am, I am an addict and drug pusher and understand I can't blame everything I am on you but I have come to realize there is a whole lot to go around and you better ACCEPT YOUR SHARE.

I'm leaving. When you find this letter, I will be gone. I haven't a clue where I am going but it's time. Yes, I do know I am breaking bail and there will be a warrant out for me. I also know you will lose the $2,000.00 you put up for my bond. In a way, I feel bad about that, but the loss of the money is a small consequence for you to pay for the void you have created in my life.

I wish the two grand could buy enough shit to fill the hole in my heart but I've come to realize there isn't enough money in the world to do that.

Writing this letter as a nineteen-year old greatly pains me. I would have thought by now I would have elevated myself beyond the victimization stage but I have not.

I hope in your heart that you can see fit to wish me the best but honestly I cannot extend to you the same.

Hendrix

P.S. I hate my fucking name.

I knew I should destroy this letter because I knew in my heart of hearts its bullshit. I was a damn good father, well okay, maybe that is a bit of an exaggeration, but I did the best I could. I never took a belt to my kids like my old man. I never degraded them or used any demeaning language at all. I was just a busy guy. If there is a penalty for being such, as I clearly knew from my son's letter there was, then yes, I am now paying for it.

I couldn't now bullshit myself. Was I one hundred percent involved in my kid's lives? No, what father is? My family wanted stuff and it was my duty to provide. Not to say that the United Parcel Service didn't pay me well, it did, but the more I made the easier it was to grow into spending it. That's what we did, a renovated house, a newer car, a swimming pool (above ground) in our back yard, an SUV for Gerti, a camper and all the other stuff the average American family covets and yes, the kids education.

If there was anything that was a waste of money, it was that. Both kids dropped out their sophomore year. My daughter because she got knocked up by a "shit for brains" lying bastard she is no longer married to – look I could expand on all the reasons she left him but it would take days- and my son because as he said so succinctly told Gerti and me "School is too lame for me. Anyway, I don't need it. It's so boring. I haven't learned a damn thing. I'm out'a there."

My kids couldn't give a damn I spent nearly five grand on their college education. No, they could have gone to a local college, Salem or North Shore Community but both weren't good enough. No, they had to go to UMass, Amherst. No way they could as Gerti and I hoped made it easy and board at home but out they went so they could learn to mature through independence. What hogwash. My daughter became a sperm receptor for a bunch of lame brains and eventually one of their seeds took, and my son got lost in the world of experimental drugs finally addicting him to a spiraling abyss of insanity.

I worked my ass off for my wife and kids and now it seems they couldn't give a damn. I fought in Nam to keep the "commies" at bay, so my family could live a free and privileged life and not have to do the service I did. And what do I get for it?... *figlio di puttana*. My service meant nothing to them, an American Vietnam vet and they couldn't seem to care. They damn well owe me one, they damn well do.

I looked at the letter and read it one more time. It would be the last. There was no way now I was going to continue punishing myself with this "left behind" from my imbecilic kid. I squeezed it into a little ball and put it in my front pant pocket. I burned it once I left the house.

I was at the mall early the next morning. It was 7:00 o'clock as I looked at my watch. I should have stayed in bed. It was a really cold February morning. One that makes you think Florida, complete with humidity, snakes, bugs, gaters and a universe of old dying people might in a few years be the wisest choice. Florida wasn't calling me yet but a few more winters like the last and I will hear it loud and clear.

I called Rhino last night and for some reason he didn't pick up his cell. This was very much unlike him. I left a note for Dirt as well informing him I would be at the mall really early today because I had some errands to do mid-morning. He had now moved out of his crate in back of Marshalls and was again living at the Lifebridge facility on Derby St. in Salem. Somehow he must have gotten lucky and they let him back in. It was way too cold to live in a box but Dirt pushed it as far as he could, almost to New Years. The truth was he was freezing his ass but couldn't let himself admit it. There was something heroic for Dirt to live in his crate. I just didn't get it. The guy had nothing, absolutely nothing, just some left over pride which nobody gave a damn about.

I put my sneakers on and took off my winter coat. I removed my sweater. I slipped my New England Patriots 38th Super Bowl Champions sweatshirt over my head. I love the Pats, what's not to love? I replaced my Vietnam Veteran's baseball cap back on my head and was now in full combat gear. I was ready to take on the mall. I felt good. This might be a new goal for me, six times around the perimeter, maybe a good six miles plus.

I figured I would give Rhino and Dirt another fifteen minutes. It was getting near 8:00 o'clock and that's all the time I would allow. They probably got caught up in the bullshit in their lives. It's not like it hasn't happened to them before. It's not like I can't walk alone. I've walked by myself many times and to be honest, sometimes I preferred it that way. It gives me some time to think without the constant chatter and bantering back and forth. Rhino and Dirt weren't quiet walkers. Walking with them was like with a bunch of girls. They just never stopped talking. It was incessant. Between my wife Gerti, beating on me every day and my friends never allowing me any quiet, I welcomed the down time. The hell with them, I looked at my Timex. It was 8:03am, time for me to walk.

I threw my knapsack on my back and gave the lower tier of the mall one more look. No Rhino, no Dirt, just three middle-aged women dressed in Florida pastels, green and pink, way out of season, barreling around the profile of the building with water bottles in hand, balls to the wall walking at warp speed as if they were in the walkathon of their lives.

Following right behind but at a much slower pace were six old farts like me. They were walking in two bunches of three. I've seen these guys before. They must belong to a walking club that is probably preceded or followed by a coffee clutch. I can see these old farts jammed up at some Dunkin' Doughnuts or Starbucks for hours, absorbed in their "chew and chat", discussing all the shit going on in the world, and unfortunately, like the lot of us, not having one bloody thing they could do to affect it. Wound up to an extreme, I see them returning home full of angst, driving their wives (if they still have them) up the proverbial wall.

The "Mommy Dearest" group, as I affectionately call them, was now beginning to come in. These were the young mothers with kids and strollers. It was really a support group allowing the moms to get their kids out of the house for a few hours. The infants and toddlers held captive by the Boston winter, I imagined welcomed a change of scenery, but probably not as much as the mothers who were held captive by their every need. With less then two hours before it opened, the mall was starting to have some major activity. The managers and shop clerks were now opening to clean, spruce and polish up their stores.

I hoped to get my walk in before the mall got any more traffic. It's a bitch trying to zig and zag through it trying to get my walk in. Many times, getting to it too late, I wanted to scream at the top of my lungs to all the walkers encumbering me *GET THE HELL OUT OF MY WAY ... CAN'T YOU SEE I'M A WORLD CLASS MALL WALKER AND YOU'RE BLOCKING ME?"* Yes, well I wanted to say it but I never did, and even if I had, like every other time in my life – nobody would listen.

I started my walk and there he was, right next to me, the "no leg" kid.

"How many times around?"

" Too many for you." I replied.

" You're one sorry ass bastard."

" Screw you."

"What makes you so damn angry?"

"None of your nosey business."

"Nam really messed you up, ha?"

I started to pick up my pace. I didn't want to talk to the kid. In fact I couldn't give a darn whether he could keep up with me and if it looked like I was trying to get away from him because frankly I was, but he held close to me like a dog to a bone. I picked up my pace.

I turned to him, "Leave me alone - I'm trying to get my walk in."

"We'll that suits me fine, I've been known to walk and talk at the same time."

Shit! I thought. *Dealing with this kid is the last thing I want to do this morning.*

"So what's with you old man?" What's with the attitude?"

"Buzz off, will you kid?"

"No man, I'm stuck on you like glue."

I turned to him again, "don't you have anything better to do with your time than to harass a tired old man?"

"Shit the one thing I have is time. Can't you see I'm a Wounded Warrier? I'm missing a leg here if you haven't noticed, but I see you have two."

"Ya. Like sorry for your loss."

"Wow, that sounded like you really meant it."

We were not halfway around the first lap of the mall and this kid was driving me freaking nuts.

"Hey man, cut an old Vet a break and give me some damn peace. Just leave me alone will you now?" I pushed back.

"No old man and about my leg - you don't give a shit do you?"

This punk kid was really starting to piss me off, leg or none, I wanted to get him off my back. I just stopped in my tracks. Before he knew it he was five steps in front of me. I guess his prosthesis didn't have really good brakes. He turned and aggressively walked toward me.

"What's with you man?" He asked with a little bit of anger in his voice.

The elevation triggered me, "No, not what's with me but WHAT THE HELL'S WITH YOU?"

"I don't get your attitude."

"I don't get you being in my face and wanting to make me feel sorry for you."

"Feel sorry for me, what the hell are you talking about? I'm not looking for any sympathy from you, and what for?"

"You guys, think Desert Storm was the only war ever fought."

"Old man, you must have a screw loose. I have no idea where you are coming from?"

I tried to bring my temperature down but this kid really grated me, so screw it. I went right after him.

"You don't get it, do you?"

"Don't get what?" he spit back.

Several of the mall occupants started staring at us. We didn't care and continued.

" You blasted guys come back freaking heroes - like you know."

"Like no, I don't know."

"Let me finish, like you know I'm sorry about your leg but ...."

I hesitated too long, he jumped in.

"My leg is my leg, I lost it and have to deal with it."

"We'll ya, I guess you do but you have no choice."

"I don't get you."

Smugly I said, "I agree...like there's nothing you can do about it."

"Old man, that's where you are wrong, there's a lot I can do about it. Desert Storm buried my leg, it didn't bury me."

I had to cut to the chase, I had errands to do and told Gerti I would be home in a hour. It's already been one and a half and she'll really be pissed, so what the hell is new?

"So kid, where you going with this?"

"And cut with the cute condescending "kid" shit. My name is Peter ... yes Peter Strong. In fact Sergeant Peter Strong who proudly fought in three campaigns, two Iraq and one Afghanistan."

"It ain't no Nam kid. That was my generation's war."

"Well "Shock and Awe" was my generations, and screw you up your butt!"

With those words, the kid turned around and threw up his middle finger. "See you around asshole". He moved through the mall's crowded building. ***He was gone**.*

12

Riley's

When I arrived home Gerti was there. I knew I was more than an hour late. There would be hell to pay. Gerti didn't waste any time.

"Always thinking about me again, I see."

"What are you talking about?"

"You know damn well what I'm talking about. After Dirt and Rhino, I fall in line, unless there are others you spend your time with I'm unaware?"

"See, you're wrong again. I spent no time with them."

"Then who were you with? If you weren't with anybody then you damn sure should have been home with me."

"I know Gerti, I know. I just kind of lost track of time that's all."

"Ya, sure Jack, like you lost track of your marriage."

"Shit Gerti!"

"You deserve it and a hell of a lot more Jack."

"Okay, okay… so what's up?"

"Well, you said you would spend the rest of the day with me so I'm going to hold you to it."

"Okay like I said, you got me for the rest of the day. Where we going?"

"Riley's."

"Damn it Gerti, I ain't going to Riley's!"

"She's your daughter and you're damn well going to see her."

"No damn way."

"The hell you aren't."

"You know I hate to go over there and see Riley, our granddaughter Bellows and her uncontrollable kid and listen to her *asshole whatever he pretends to be today roommate*, and the dump they're living in - it's depressing."

"He's not her roommate. He's Bellow's soon to be husband."

"Right, and that makes everything even worse."

"And as for the apartment it's the only place Riley can afford."

"And who's to blame for that?"

"These are tough times Jack."

"Like you're telling me that "Bozo" can't get a job?"

"Shit Jack, you know jobs are hard to come by. Remember the meltdown… 2008, it ain't the times when you were looking for work."

I can't believe Gerti wants to drag me over to our daughter's place. In one small apartment lives our daughter Riley, our granddaughter Bellows, her lazy dysfunctional boyfriend Humphrey and their untamed kid Miley. After Riley's divorce she took pity on her daughter and took Bellows and her family off the streets. She said it was the "motherly" thing to do, and there would be no excuse for her not going to Hell if she avoided her moral responsibility.

"Moral Responsibility", my ass. The truth was our daughter, didn't have two pennies to rub together or a pot to piss in. She survived on welfare and food stamps. After getting knocked up, dropping out of UMass and eventually getting married to and divorced from the "Prince of all Losers" - her life became a total train wreck. Now she has taken three more dysfunctionals under her roof, with neither our granddaughter or her boyfriend making any attempt to support themselves and my wife defending their irresponsibility and dysfunction at every turn. If it wasn't for the money Gerti and I give them every week, they would starve.

"It ain't the times when you were looking for work". Like those were easy times .... my wife must be crazy."

I could pull out the little hair I have left. My wife must be delusional, I dug freaking holes, shoveled cement, shingled and roofed houses, anything I could do to put food on the table and provide clothing and shelter before I was lucky to land with the UPS. I can't believe she doesn't remember. We spent half our lives without the slightest luxury. USP was a Godsend. Although not as religious as I used to be before Nam, I still take a minute every night and thank God for the Parcel. Gerti, I can't believe she could have forgotten the bad times, yeah like these are the good ones. I can't believe it.

"Where were you those early years of our marriage?"

"What are you asking?"

"What I am asking is where the heck were you when we were struggling in every way, with hardly enough money for nothing .....NADA, NADA ...... THE BIG "ZERO" NOTHING?."

"Emotionally supporting your sorry ass and raising your two kids."

"Oh, now they're my two kids. I think there's enough guilt to be shared by the two of us."

Gerti and I were now standing toe to toe. She had that crazed PMS stare. I could have sworn her irises were turning various colors, like there was a tidal wave splashing around in her head, getting stronger and more violent by the moment as it crashed against her inner cranium.

My decision was now to back off or be totally in. I chose the former. It's already been a hell of a week, I felt discretion here was the better part of valor. I walked away from her, to the kitchen, opened the back door and gestured Gerti to follow.

"Well, you coming or not?"

"The only place I'm going with you is to see our kids.."

"Yeah, sure, okay, whatever - the kids it is." *The kids my ass.*

Gerti walked by me and brushed her shoulder against mine. I knew damn well there would be more aggravation coming today because if there was anyone that could grate the hell out of me, it was my granddaughter's loser Humphrey. That lazy, unworthy son of a bitch. We were like fire and water.

It took eleven minutes to drive to Riley's. She lived in a four decker in the west side of town. The neighborhood was anything but inviting, in fact it resonated as a place not to be after hours, and probably during the day as well. This was not lost on me and as brave and stoic as Gerti often was, I couldn't help notice her uneasiness.

"What a dump!" I said.

"Christ Jack, we're not even at her door and you're starting."

"What do you want me to do Gerti, shout out how pleased I am how well our family is doing?"

"Jack, all I'm asking is for you to be civil, you haven't seen your family in over four months - a little civility will go a long way here."

"I turned to Gerti to look her in the eyes. The bright August sunshine profiled her face and reflected off the windshield catching the texture of her skin just right. At sixty- five years, it looked loose as it cascaded from her eye sockets down to her chin finally resting at her neck. Her face was falling. Gerti and I were getting old.

In her younger years Gerti was a decent looking woman, no beauty but more than passable. She was never one to really take care of herself. She never did the "girlie" stuff like massages, mineral baths, obsessing about her weight, or pampered herself in anyway. She just wasn't into it. She kind of let her body have a life of its own. She had gained over twenty pounds since we got married, ironically I lost almost the same during that time. She never exercised or used little if any makeup. It was as if the kids were the center of her life to the exclusion of everything and everyone else, including herself. Then they were gone and she still didn't do anything for herself. She just caved into getting old, lamenting her screwed up kids and waiting for Hendrix to knock on our door which I resolved would never happen. He was lost to us forever.

I remember trying to buy her some new clothes for her birthday in 2015. I really wanted to buy her something nice, because well, she damn well deserved it. Dealing with the kids was not an easy task. She thought I overlooked how really hard it was but the truth is I didn't. Dealing with me was a whole other subject. She dealt with it well, kinda. I didn't overlook that either. I just didn't bring it up.

Our kids were challenging but the reality is I was even more. So I woke up a few weeks before Gerti's birthday and decided I would surprise her by informing her I wanted to go shopping to buy her a birthday present. She looked at me like I was crazed. Shopping, I never went shopping. It was something I never did. I never found any pleasure in it so me announcing I was volunteering to do it knocked her off balance, like I threw a weight at her almost dropping her to her knees.

Also as far as birthdays, they were very seldom celebrated. When the kids were young sure, we made a little fuss, a cake, a token gift, maybe inviting some of the kid's friends for a piece of cake and a few games. I figured rightly or wrongly and Gerti concurred, whatever they didn't have, the kids wouldn't miss. I was convinced neither of them would ever be invited to a highfalutin kids birthday party, catered with clowns and ponies, and enough Toy's R Us presents to inflate the company's bottom line. We were a family from Lynn trying to make ends meet. That's just the way it is. My kids went to public school, not the private St. John's Prep in Danvers, where them Lynnfield, Marblehead, Swampscott, Manchester By The Sea kids go. That's just the way it is and my kids would just have to live with it.

I didn't know whether I was happy or sad she responded in such a way. I mean it was *shopping*, no big freaking deal but I guess she just wasn't prepared for my announcement.

"Jack, what's with you? You don't like shopping, you hate it."

"Hate may be just too strong a word?"

"No, you hate it. You've told me a hundred times you'd rather pass a kidney stone than spend an hour at the mall."

"No, I said, I would rather be staked to the ground and burned alive."

"Same thing!"

"Not really."

"….. Same thing!"

"Shit Gerti, I go to the mall all the time."

"You sure as hell do, hanging with those creeps Dirtsy and Rhiny."

"A little sarcasm there?"

"No, a lot."

"Well I walk with those guys."

"Yeah, three or four times a week and when in our entire marriage have you ever spent an hour with me there? Well, I'll tell you, NEVER, NEVER, NEVER. You hear me Jackson Krause? Never ever- so I don't get today."

"Gerti, I can understand you beating on me when I go wrong, but Christ can't you see I'm trying to do a little right here. I mean, why beat up on me for that?"

"Because there's something going on here with you that is not upfront, some conniving thing I can't get a handle on."

"Like what?"

"Well, like I used to know who you are Jack. Don't change now."

Honestly, if I knew offering to go to the mall would create so much angst I wouldn't have mentioned it. I would have just gone by myself for my usual exercise. Inside the mall was the popular place to be. It was just too damn hot to walk outside.

That's the trouble with Boston, either it is too hot or too damn cold, plus the Sox suck, at least this season. I damn well should have gone myself and might have found Dirt or Rhino to accompany me. Maybe soldier boy Peter Strong was waiting there to continue his lecturing on good soldiering, good victimization and all the other crap. Maybe he'll get another medal because of his great positive outlook. If there ever was a ultimate victim, he was the perfect one.

"Well, Jack, an invite from you is a bit out of character but at least you didn't forget my birthday, that in itself is a big surprise but - I ain't going. What the hell can you buy me, another pair of slacks, a sweater to sit in my closet, I have enough of this stuff and where the heck do we ever go Jackson.? When was the last time you ever took me somewhere nice?"

I turned my back, I was just not that kind of guy. We stepped out of the Merc and onto the cracked cement pavement in front of Rileys.

Gerti asked in a quivering voice, "Jackson, you sure nothing is going on here? Is there something you want to tell me?" Gerri looked at me, "What are you staring at?"

"Nothing, nothing at all. I'm just trying to get my sea legs under me before we go in." I replied.

"Well, you better be on your best behavior because God only knows the last time you were here - it was a disaster. I damn well don't want to go through that again."

"Cross my heart, I'll be at my Jack Krause best." I crossed my heart.

"Jack, I just hope that's good enough…yes, I do, I just darn hope".

Gerti and I get made our way to the front steps of the four story tenement. The wooden stairs cracked under our weight as we both stepped on them at the same time.

"Careful Gerti, these steps should be condemned."

"Jack, you heard me, good behavior, okay?"

"Okay, PROMISE."

Gerti banged on the door.

Our granddaughter Bellows opened it. I stared at her belly. I just couldn't believe she was pregnant again. I was livid Gerti didn't tell me but allowed it to be dropped on me like a lead fart.

Bellows then opened the screen door and we walked in. The place was dirty and unkempt. There were clothes and toys all over the floor. The dishes were stacked up in the sink. I could hear our great grandkid screaming from the bathroom.

I walked over to an old wooden captain's chair and removed three layers of clothes, revealing enough room to sit.

Gerti and Bellows cleaned up the tattered couch allowing them to sit as well. I felt awkward as hell - I really didn't want to be there - I hope it wasn't as apparent as I thought. There was a large pregnant pause in the room. Finally Bellows broke the silence.

"Well, grandpa, nice to see you, your pony tail has grown at least three inches since I last saw you."

"Ya", and I wanted to retort, *"Ya, like I see your stomach is three times as large as it was the last time I viewed you. Is that all you and your do nothing boyfriend do is make babies you can't afford?"* I bit my tongue on this one. I really wanted to spit it out but damn well knew there would be nothing but hell to pay.

"I see you're pregnant."

"Yes, obviously I am, has it really been that long since we've seen each other."

"Well, yes, unfortunately it has, sometimes things get in the way of what's really important, especially today when everything seems to be so damn complex."

"Yeah, complex and scary as well."

My daughter Riley comes out of the bathroom with her granddaughter in hand.

"Hey mom and dad, how are you doing?"

"Fine darling" answers Gerti, "we are doing well thank you."

Doing well my ass, I said to myself.

"Well, that's great, as you can see we are doing okay also." Our great granddaughter Miley runs several feet from the center of the room and jumps on the couch now where Riley just sat and Gerti and Bellows were sitting. She nearly misses kicking her mother's pregnant belly.

"Christ, Miley" Bellows said agitated, "watch what you're doing, you're going to hurt the baby inside of me."

Miley jumps from the couch and runs to the small kitchen. Seconds later she comes running back. She is ADD to the nines, bouncing from one piece of furniture to the next, from Gerti's lap to mine, me sitting in the old worn captain's chair, that could barely hold my weight, then running back from where she came. The girl, aged three was out of control. It was obvious she took after her father Humphrey Kerrs. He was beyond control himself, couldn't keep one meaningful thought in his head and act on it. Some people would call him ADD but I just called him fucking lazy.

Out of nowhere, I turned my head and there he was ascending from the basement. Out of all the men in the whole wide world, my granddaughter (like my daughter Riley) had to hook up with a no good guy, this one a Humphrey, the only person, I ever knew with the name outside of some long dead president Hubert. He was standing there in his oversized jockey shorts, Guinea T, white athletic socks and work boots.

Bellows was indignant, "Damn it Humphrey put on some pants, you're half naked standing in front of my grandparents".

It looked like he was half pregnant too with his large stomach pushing through his stained T-shirt. He had this totally disinterested look on his face, shrugged his shoulders, turned and walked toward his bedroom.

It was obvious things weren't getting better here. Riley looked agitated and hadn't spoken but a few words and they weren't forthcoming but seemed had to be pried from her. Bellows looked beat and with another baby coming there was no way she would find any long-term relief. Without a doubt things would be going from bad to progressively worse with a new infant to feed and baby essentials being as expensive as they are. Also, Humphrey hanging around the house at 1:45 p.m. was the worst of signs. Obviously, he wasn't working again, unless he participated in a second or third shift job. The smart money bet was he wasn't, probably something else Gerti inadvertently forgot to tell me - like Bellow's pregnancy that quite literally escaped her mind.

"Whoa, what's going on with Humphrey?" I asked Bellows.

"Hey", she answered back, it's the economy, believe me, he's been looking for work, believe me he really has. He did have a job, for the last six weeks."

"Ya, like doing what?" I asked.

"Like detailing cars in Danvers."

"And what happened?"

"Humphrey said he made more money staying home and collecting welfare and food stamps than he did working. He said only a fool would work if there was no reason."

"So how are you feeling Riley?" Gerti broke in to break the tension.

"Okay, I mean nothing out of the ordinary. It isn't like I haven't traveled this road before. It's just..." She hesitates.

"What?" Gerti questions.

"Well, you know, nothing's easy. Especially now with Bellows and her family living with me and another baby on the way. But we'll manage and I damn well would rather have them here with me than living somewhere on the street."

Bellows starts breaking out in tears. "Damn it Ma, I know we are a burden for you, but I promise the first thing we'll do when Humphrey gets a job is find a place of our own. It just hasn't been easy. I'm okay, but it's just that I feel I'm drowning some days. I feel the weight of the world is falling on my shoulders and for the love of God, I don't see any way to dig out. You've really been a Godsend Ma ...you really have."

Riley turns on the couch and grabs Bellows hand "It's okay baby, I'm your mother."

Gerti turned and gave me a stern look, like all this crap going down here was all my fault. She blames me for everything, every damn thing, I resent the hell out of that.

Humphrey walked back into the room, now wearing a pair of soiled pants that seemed like they were two sizes too big, if that was possible, seeing that he had to be fifty pounds overweight.

"So what's going on here?"

"Your wife is crying, that's what's going on." I firmly stated.

Humphrey screams over to Bellows, "Whatever it is baby, suck it up. We don't have any room for crybabies around here."

Gerti became outraged, "Don't you ever speak to my granddaughter that way."

"She's my fiance and she'll do as I tell her and I'll do as I please and speak to her as I wish and that's just the way it is ..... if you don't like it then get the hell out ..."

Promise or no promise, I wasn't about to sit there and take this shit from this piece of do nothing scum, do nothing. There's a lot of crap I can tolerate but Humphrey was the culmination of everything I disdained: lazy, a user, disrespectful, vulgar, and worse of all, a degenerate bully. He was no more transparent then he was now, huffing and puffing spitting a lot of hot air into the room. The tension was heating up and as the beads of sweat broke from my brow, I had enough.

"You stupid asshole, if I ever hear you raising your voice or your hand to my wife or granddaughter, or any of my family again it will be a sorry ass day in hell for you. Mark my words. Bellows and I have had our differences but we're family here and don't you ever be foolish enough to think I would ever abandon protecting her."

My great granddaughter came running into the room again, she grabbed my leg. I tried to release her grip. She held onto me like a vice.

Humphrey suddenly disappeared. Within minutes he returned, wearing a Boston

Red Sox jersey and carrying a baseball bat and spaced himself between Gerti and me.

"Now', he said, "Get the hell out of this house- both of you."

"I couldn't believe what I was hearing from this "shit for brains." This lazy cowardly punk stood in front of me with a bat in his hands, as if he had the balls to swing it. If there was one thing I knew about Humphrey he was a cowardly shit. No man in his right mind or for that manner, having one ounce of courage would ever resort to this idiotic behavior. As far as I was concerned, Humphrey was ball-less. There wasn't a courageous bone in his body. Courage, as I saw it, was getting his lazy fat ass off the couch and off the dole, and do what men are supposed to, go out into the world and make a damn living to support their family. Yes, that is what courage is about, at least a path to find it. Yes, that is what brave men would do, but Humphrey, the lousy cowardly prick he was, couldn't pass muster and my stupid granddaughter Bellows, of all the men in the world, opened her legs for him.

I looked over at Gerti. She was terrified. My granddaughter just sat there with Miley now on her lap, tears pouring from her. I looked at my wife again, she was now caulk white, moving around the room consumed by nervous energy. I got up from my chair. Humphrey took two steps back.

"I can't believe you're threatening me, shit for brains!"

"Jack, you and your wife aren't welcome here anymore - do you understand what I'm saying?"

"Lets just say Humphrey I'll let your little threat pass, because if I truly believe what you're saying, was what I think you might be thinking - then it's all over for you."

"Meaning what?"

"Meaning the two hundred a week that miraculously shows up in your mail each Monday will mysteriously disappear, starting today."

I pulled the envelop from my pocket and pulled the twenty ten dollar bills from it. "Like this money here, like there will be no more charity for you."

Humphrey didn't know what to say. He turned to Bellows. "What's he talking about?"

"It's true what he's saying." Bellows replied sheepishly, "My grandparents send us a two hundred a week and have been doing it for several years now."

"Damn it Bellows and you never told me."

"It's money I use for food and clothes for our kid, soon to be kids. Humphrey, we would never been able to get by if it weren't for that money. With welfare and food stamps we'd never be able to exist. The money is a Godsend." Humphrey throws the bat against the wall shattering the one lamp that lay in it's path. It is obvious he is deranged. ENOUGH IS ENOUGH. It was time to leave.

I got up from my chair and walked over to Gerti. For every step I took forward, Humphrey back-peddled several. I knew he didn't have the balls to confront me. I saw him as a lazy cowardly bastard and he did nothing to prove otherwise, in fact everything he did today confirmed it.

As I extended my hand, Gerti grabbed hold of it, lifting herself from her chair. She was paper white. Although always being confrontational, she now said nothing. I brushed our great granddaughter from grabbing my leg, we made our way to the door. Humphrey just stood in place wearing his faded blue Boston Red Sox jersey, the super-sized "wannabe" that he was.

Bellows escorted us the few feet to the door. There were tears in her eyes as she moved closer to Gerti - she bent over and kissed her on the cheek. She then tried the same on me but I gently brushed her away.

"I'm really sorry, grandpa", she said.

"I'm sorry too", I answered, "sorrier than you would ever imagine ….. someday, maybe you'll listen to your grandfather."

Gerti gives me a jab with her elbow, "Jack, not now, Christ, this is not the time."

I opened the apartment door and Gerti and I walked out.

"It sure as hell been real - a really great few hours spent."

"I'm really sorry Grandma and Grandpa, we're really better than what you have seen … we really are."

"Sure, we damn well know you are", I said in my most sarcastic tone.

"Save it for later Jack, will you please save it for later?"

"Sure Gerti, maybe until we get into the car."

We just sat there basking in the summer sun. Being it was ninety-four degrees outside, it seemed strange that Gerti nor I complained. We were just too messed up to pay attention as the sweat started to pour from us like a broken radiator. Finally, Gerti noticed.

"Open the damn window Jack."

I opened them. It was just as hot on the outside as it was in the car.

"Damn it Jack, close the damn windows and put on the air-conditioner."

"Christ Gerti, now which is it, open the windows or the air-conditioner?"

"The damn air-conditioner,"Gerti spit out.

"Like I said, Gerti - THAT'S THE LAST OF IT … I told you before and I'll tell you for the last damn time … I NEVER, NEVER, NEVER … ever want to go over to Riley's again… LIKE NEVER AGAIN!"

Gerti put her hands over her ears, "Alright, okay, alright again. I hear you but mark my words, you're being an ass about this. Hey, I'm not saying that Humphrey isn't a jerk and Bellows couldn't have done a whole lot better but it is what it is and it's the price we have to pay to see our great grandkid - soon to be great grandkids."

"The great grand kids. I don't even know who my great granddaughter is. She's like so outrageously out of control. I mean, does she ever stop? I mean have you ever had even one conversation with her? Now be truthful Gerti, do you even know whether she's able to speak? And as far as Riley and Bellows are concerned they made their beds and now have to lie in them. They just never listened. I don't think either one ever listened to one word you or I ever spoke … and as far as thinking things through, I don't think either gave their futures one minute of serious thought. Well perhaps now that their worlds are spinning out of freaking control."

"You're really sympathetic Jack. You damn well have a big heart. Obviously it shows in everything you do and say." Gerti stated sarcastically.

"Let's get out of here Gerti. I'll be damn if I'm going to sit in front of Riley's house for the rest of the afternoon. Let's go home."

The ride back was the longest eleven minutes of my life.

"Do you think there's something wrong with us Jackson?" Gerti suddenly questioned.

"Us meaning …and wrong meaning?"

"Yes US, like YOU and ME. Do you think there's something wrong with us, like our life together , in how we raised our kids - I mean like all of it , all of it combined. I mean really, is there something wrong with us?"

I wanted to rephrase the question. I wanted to say, *Is there anything right with us?* This would have been a lot easier to answer because there really wasn't anything right with us. There hadn't been for years, in fact probably from the day we married.

I answered like I usually did, delivering to Gerti, what I thought she wanted to hear, another BIG FAT LIE because I damn well knew she didn't want to hear the truth. No matter how she sliced it, if there was indeed something wrong then she would have to take half the blame because there was just the two of us, married "for better or worse" and there was no plausible way in the world she could deny responsibility for her half. Was there anything wrong with us? You damn well bet there was, *in every single way*.

13

She Knows

"She knows!!!"

"How do you know she knows?"

"How do I know she knows? I've lived with the woman for forty-six years, there's just no way she doesn't."

"Well, then that's just the way it is, you're just going to have to deal with it Jack."

"Like she turned to me Julie, when I was walking away and asked me. "Is there something you want to tell me?""

"And …..?"

"I didn't say a word, not a damn one and went in the bathroom and took a shower."

"You didn't say "No", just walked into the bathroom and took a shower?"

"Yes, that's right."

"I don't know whether that was the best move Jack. I mean you should have said something. I mean you should have said anything. I mean saying nothing … I mean she's gonna wonder."

"She caught me flat-footed Julie. I was like paralyzed, like a deer in the headlights."

"Well, then like you said she probably knows. It ain't easy what we are doing."

"'Ya, that's for damn sure. Living a lie is hard work."

"Living a lie? Now Jack, so what part of this relationship is a lie?"

"Sorry Julie, a bad choice of words …we're getting a bit testy here aren't we?"

I met Julie seven years ago at the Lynn V.F.W. I was at the bar waiting for Dirt and Rhino when she walked in. She was long-legged and went out of her way to show several of her best assets. Her tight dress was cut at the thigh. It revealed her long smooth back and was just a tad below Sunday church acceptable leaving little to stir the imagination of the twenty or so Vets sitting at the bar, oozing over her like it was their last "WILL AND TESTAMENT".

Julie had long curly dyed blonde hair that spiraled from her head falling to her shoulders. Under the bar lights her dark roots were visible. She wore three inch pumps that put her about five feet eleven inches tall fully platformed. She didn't have a beautiful face but rather one that reflected hard times with deep furrows running down her cheeks, only to be broken at her lips, which seemed to be botoxed to their limit. She had a look suggesting great vulnerability but even greater strength (paradoxical as it seems) but when the whole package was viewed from about six feet away, she was alluring in a very strange manner. Weird but intoxicating, there was a mysteriousness and extreme sexiness about her.

Julie seemed to be a fish out of water at the VFW. The majority of us were dress- downs, she on the other hand, was a dress up, a peculiar attire to be worn behind a bar. We were used to seeing Ray, the regular bartender who dressed one grade below throw-away. The guys at the VFW were all vets, who judged each other on their service to their country and didn't give a damn about how they looked now, because most knew the best of them was left in uniform somewhere, only to be remembered in dusty pictures, framed, sitting on a mantel in some quasi-respectable place.

Julie was magical behind the bar. She worked it with a surgeon's precision. She had a rhythm that easily supported her as she mixed one drink after another without interruption. The bar was packed this early December night. It was the NFL playoffs and our beloved Patriots were pairing up with the Denver Broncos, which had the earmarks of being one of the best, if not the best rivalry of the season. Brady versus Manning, it just couldn't get better than this but it did, because Julie was there and her presence added to the excitement in the room. She was like the frosting on the cake and not one of us seated at that bar, now packed like sardine, did not fail to notice.

"Wow Jack, who's the new bartender? questioned Rhino who finally arrived, late as always but astonishingly lucky to find an empty barstool right next to me. Rhino with a shit-eating grin on his face turned to me "This is a good sign Jackson, this empty stool right beside you. It's a sign from Heaven everything is lining up with the stars. The damn Pats are going to win tonight, not only win, but large, really large, like running Manning and the Bronc's right off the field right out of the stadium. There's no doubt, they are going to kick some Bronco tail. Yep, and here we are with ringside seats and a new saucy bartendress to boot. We must be the luckiest guys in the world."

"Where's Dirt?"

"He's sick again."

"Again?"

"What'd you expect from the life he leads? So Jack again, who's the new cocktologist?"

"Her name's Julie. She's taking Ray's place tonight. He came down sick too and regards to the "luckiest" guys in the world, wasn't but a few months back we had to suffer through that really shitty Red Sox season. The Red Sox suck."

The night seemed to fly. The game was a drilling. The Patriots left their A game in the lockers at Gillette Stadium.

It wasn't pretty and the only thing making it tolerable was the new bartender.

For whatever reason, maybe it was my imagination but as the bar continued to thin out, she seemed to be giving me a lot of attention, significantly more than she was the other ten or so guys still sitting there.

"So what's with you Vets and your hats?" she asked me.

"So what are you asking?"

"You old vets, well, I mean like you know what I mean. Like I mean you guys who fought in the old wars, like Vietnam, Korea and such, it seems I see a lot more of you wearing campaign hats, than say ….. well World War II vets and those returning from Irag and Afghanistan?"

"Well you're damn well an inquisitive one aren't you?"

"Yeah, like inquisitive minds want to know."

"Well, I guess I see it like this, turning to Rhino to get his agreement, we, like you don't see too many second World War vet's strutting their stuff because the majority of them have died off and the remaining are either spending their last days in a convalescent or veteran's home. As far as the Iraq and Afghan vets, I dare say I see a few sporting their caps, but for the most part I think they have a lot more on their minds than wearing their colors, like maybe assimilating back into society, getting used to their family again, and vice a versa, getting a job and in this economy in the last few years is a big daunting thing. Plus these guys came back heroes, in many cases really screwed up, but heroes nonetheless. Maybe they don't want to wear their glitz because they want to forget where they've been and what they've done. Maybe they just don't want to talk about it and give people a reason to."

"Well, they damn well are heroes in my eyes."

"Yep, why the hell not, they served their country well."

"Okay now, then what about you and the Nam guys, why so many?"

"I guess, if I can be blunt..."

"Blunt away!"

"Well, we are proud of our service too …really damn proud but when we came back from Nam we weren't perceived as heroes ….. hell no, we were insulted, spit upon, called names like "RAPISTS" and "BABY KILLERS." The majority of us returned to a really shitty circumstance that really screwed us up. We were in the jungles of Nam one day and when our tour was done we were in the States forty-eight hours later. It was just one huge cluster SNAFU …."

"SNAFU?"

"Yeah, military lingo … SITUATION NORMAL, ALL FUCKED UP."

"Oh, let me get another round of drinks out and I'll be back."

I looked at Rhino sitting next to me and he nodded his head, confirming what I was saying. Julie was back.

"And the hat thing?" she questioned.

"Well, as I was saying - very few of us after returning from Nam found the States to be a friendly and welcoming place. So that being said, only the most foolish among us, and there were not a few, wore anything that brought attention to us because as I stated before we were the rapists and baby killers and all of us hated that, hated what we were pulled into, being way too young to know what the hell it was, way too vulnerable and innocent to see we were just literally pawns in a big political game. Like every soldier in every damn war ever fought. The whole war thing really sucks, it sucks to a fare thee well."

"So then again, for the umpteenth time, I'm asking, why do you guys seem to be the ones wearing the caps, the campaign jackets, all that stuff?"

"Okay, okay, we're old now and most of us don't give a crap what anybody thinks. We are way beyond that now. In fact light years, and to cut to the chase - as Vietnam Vets we are really proud we served, and you might just say we are "Flying our Flag", showing our colors, parading the fact that we are the damn proudest of the proud. Before it's too late, before everyone forgets, before we're all dead and gone."

Rhino shook his head in affirmation.

"And you and that ponytail?"

"Whoa, you're getting really personal and we haven't even traded the first kiss.'

"Ah, yes, just another wise ass."

"No, no", I threw my arms up in the air as a sign of surrender "just kidding, I hope you don't take offense."

"I might not, but I can't say my bull of a boyfriend might overlook the obvious... I'm just kidding too. But I am really interested, what's with the ponytail?"

Julie turns her back and starts cleaning up the bar. Five minutes later, she returns to continue the conversation.

"Ponytail, so what's with it?"

"Well my wife Gerti has a burr under her saddle about my ponytail, but at my stage of life, I felt a compulsion to grow one. Maybe its that my thick lion mane crop of hair is no longer that which I was so proud. It now has a life of its own, like the rest of my body, giving way to that of a man who can't possibly be the age I am."

"Wow, talk about being personal, let it flow Jackson. Jackson, right?"

"Just call me Jack."

"We'll you're on my clock now, best finish the story soon cause it's nearing 11:00 p.m closing time and I have a lot to do. Don't want me to be fired on my first day do ya?"

"Hell no", Rhino butts in," that would be a tragedy."

"Well, continue Jack, like I said, you're on the clock."

"Ya, well, the ponytail thing, well when I was drafted, like every inductee, they shaved my hair to the scalp. I was damn proud of my head of hair and when it was gone I felt an important part of me was taken away. Those were the "hippie" days, the "Haight Ashbury" ones, when everybody had long hair in fact the longer the better. As I recall mine was reaching my shoulders and just like that it was gone and did you ever see that baby food commercial, where the little girl, says to her mother after viewing her baby brother for the first time, "too bad, you had to get a bald headed one."

"No, can't say I have", Julie replied.

"Well, that's how I felt and I'm sure we all felt kinda that way, we were the bald headed ones, stripped of all our identities, every one of us looking the same. I went immediately from Jackson Krause, to Private Jackson Krause and there was a part of me that died there in that chair and I guess it's my time to recapture it. I guess that's maybe why I'm growing a ponytail. I guess that's why. Honestly, all this is just pouring out of me. The truth is I never really thought about it until now."

"Shit Jack, you could have just given me the Cliff Notes version."

"Sorry, I guess the scotch caused me diarrhea of the mouth."

"Well its 10:45 and time I have to shut this party down , it certainly was a pleasure to meet you. And about the Pats, well, there's always next year."

"Oh sure, that's what we said about the Sox."

Rhino and I left a generous $20.00 tip. What the hell, both of us agreed Julie was part of the evening's entertainment.

Leaving the VFW, Rhino turned to me "Well, she'll sure remember us."

"Why's that?"

"Cause, we're really memorable, plus we left her "you're one bitch'n good bartender" tip. It probably should have been more."

"More than $20.00, on a $52.00 bar tab?"

"Shit, you could have paid her more for the three hours of therapy."

"What are you talking about?"

"I'm talking about ...I never heard you talk so much. It damn well was diarrhea of the mouth. It was like she was your psychiatrist or priest, it just rolled out of you like high tide in a storm."

"Ya, you're probably right. I guess I just needed to get it off my chest. A lot of stuff has been weighing on me lately. I seem to be looking over an abyss and see my life spiraling down into an endless pit. I guess I just needed tonight."

"Well I can't say she wasn't interested, obviously she was. She was the one asking all the questions egging you on."

"She certainly has an inquisitive mind."

"Not a bad looker too."

"She has some miles - definitely seasoned but spirited."

"Ya, I wouldn't throw her out of bed."

Suddenly I found myself lost for words. Just minutes before I was rolling them out like a steamroller, now I was lockjawed. Then it just burst from me like a blast of hot air.

"Damn it, I wonder why Gerti never asks me any questions like that? As interested as Julie seemed to be, Gerti seems to have a lack of interest. Why the hell do you think that is Rhino?"

"Shit man, like you think I would know? But Julie's conversation was bar talk. She was trolling for tips. She ain't going home with you, ain't sharing your bed and your life. She didn't knock out two kids with you. She has no skin in the game, just barroom bantering."

"Really, that's how you see it?"

"Ya, from my little pin prick in the universe."

"Damn it Rhino, I see it totally different."

'You see it anyway you want Jackson. It's getting really late" Rhino walks over to his car. 'I'm getting the hell out of here."

"Ya, I best move my butt too. Gerti's gonna be really upset with me staying out this late."

"Well if that's the case, I don't think you had better bring up Julie."

"Ha Rhino, I might have had a few drinks, maybe even a little woozy but not close to brain dead."

Four months later, I was seeing Julie a couple times a
month gradually growing into once a week. I would sneak
away to Nashua New Hampshire under the pretense of mall
walking with Dirt and Rhino or saying I needed the afternoon
for completing my chore list. This was a bit difficult to serve
up because, God only knows if there was a man who had no
"chore man ability" skill set, it was me, Jack Krause. I hated
that stuff and Gerti damn well knew it, but she allowed me
to bullshit her nonetheless. She would fill her time worrying
about Riley, Bellows, her granddaughter Miley and the kid
on the way and wondering where our son Hendrix was as he
traveled the world (and there was no doubt in my mind) up to
no good or now quite possibly dead with not a peep from him
over twenty years.

The reality is that Gerti and I lived in a make believe world.
She would always run stuff by me, things that occupied her
knowing damn well I wasn't really listening and had little or no
interest, but to her, it seemed like it was the normal "bullshit"
things married couples do to each other. I was bullshitting Gerti
and she was bullshitting me in return. We both knew it but it
seemed neither of us cared. It was just the way we related. It was
just how we lived our life. It verged on the pathetic but I guess
we were doing the best in the world we built together. There
was no way it was heaven (some people, a few if any, have those
blessed marriages). It wasn't quite hell, although I'd be lying if
I said we didn't have more than a few hellish moments. We
could probably fill another short lifetime with those, probably
ten of the forty two-years we've been together. In short, our
marriage was "purgatory" that not so subtle itch that can never
be scratched, that more than aching toothache that never can
be relieved, the gnawing distant migraine that faintly wakes us
in the morning but grows stronger throughout the day and
by night is almost intolerable. Yes, purgatory was the category
in which our marriage fell, that disturbing "Limbo" where
nothing is quite right, and there will never be any opportunity

to get beyond the nausea it creates, knowing the only elevation from here would be to the gates of hell, where the writing on the doors, depressingly tells it all, "ABANDON ALL HOPE, YE WHO ENTERS HERE".

Cheating on my wife wasn't an easy thing to do. Believe it or not I had a "Jack Krause" morality. The core was pretty strong although I must admit it was rather frail around the edges. I have always thought myself as a fair and good man but as I looked back at my life I started to realize it was not good enough. There were just too many holes. There had to be more to *All of IT* than what I thought was fundamental, that of being a good soldier, husband, father and breadwinner. The truth was as a soldier I was passable, as a husband and father, I was significantly less, as a breadwinner, I was more than adequate and no one could take exception. In spite of my many short falls, I many times bullshitted myself I was beyond good enough. It sometimes was for me but never nearly for my country and my family.

When I returned home from Nam nobody gave me the badge of "moral righteousness" I felt I deserved. They didn't see me as a bastion of Good founded on an uncompromising moral premise, predicated on the simple belief that there was "WRONG AND THERE WAS RIGHT" and that every judgment and decision I made during my two year tour was based on the later. I thought I would return as a hero, a really screwed up one but one but a hero nonetheless. I expected some kind of recognition. I received none and came to conclude I might be on the wrong side of history. I despised the idea there wasn't any "wrong" or "right" but just political one-upmanship that put me, and my brethren in harms way. I thought about all the guys who died in Nam or were coming home with a part of them left in the bush, a hand, an arm, a leg, scrabbled eggs instead of the brains they had in their heads, never able to forget, never to experience another happy day, let alone a normal one. All of it sucked. It sucked to a fare thee well and

I had to learn I could not carry my war experience around with me, because frankly nobody really gave a damn. My father asked me about it only once before he died.

"So how was it over there?" I answered him in two words. "IT SUCKED." He never asked me again. My mother tried to support me the best she could. I saw her constantly reviewing my actions and speech, as if at any moment I would lose it all and would unwind as a ball of string and become unfurled right before her eyes, probably lying on the ground seizing out. It was in her mannerisms, in her eyes, that she was preparing for that day. Other than giving me a big motherly hug upon my return she never asked me one thing about my service other than "Jack, how was the food over there, was it any good?, to which I replied in two words, "IT SUCKED."

My brother Bobby was too busy attending North Shore Community and organizing with the *Students Against The War* movement, to spend any time at all to reconnect with me. He was brainwashed to the nines. He saw me as one of those, a freaking killer of babies, a rapist, an indiscriminate murderer, doing the devil's work. He was right because that is who I grew to be, a veteran who lost his pride in being one. An outlier who through no plan of his own was drafted in 1970 to help clean up the mess that the USA unfortunately found itself, through every damn fault of its own.

My wife and kids never really understood me. I had a hole in my heart as big as Fenway Park, but they for the most part didn't know it was there. They saw me as rigid, standoffish, unforgiving and unaffectionate. They viewed me as everything I probably was and more. They saw me the opposite than how I perceived myself. It was really wrong what I did to them. I never opened up and not knowing there was any possibility I ever might, they closed me down like a clam. They never asked me any questions why I was like I was. If they had, I'm not sure I would have answered, or at least given them the answers they were looking for. As a husband and father, I must admit I fell fairly short. I now grew to be the man my father was, except I fought my war in the fields of Vietnam and he fought his in the four corners of our two bedroom bungalow.

After my initial introduction to Julie, I saw her two more times, once in the VFW in Lynn and the last in the one in Marblehead. They were coincidental, I didn't know she would be there and she was now rotating at the VFW's in a fifty mile radius when needed.

As I recall the two meetings, it was the same as our initial. We bantered throughout the night and again it seemed she was paying a bit more attention to me than she was to the other patrons. Maybe it was my imagination, or my desire, but I clearly thought she had an interest in me.

"Hey, are you following me around?", she questioned.

"No, can't say I am", I responded.

"Well, I can make it easy for you. If you want my number, just ask." She turned her back and walked away.

I took a sip of my scotch. I turned to Dirt and Rhino, "What did she just say to me?"

"She said she wants to give you her number", Dirt replied.

"Ya, she's hot for you", Rhino interjected.

"Ah, Shit."

"Yep, I'd bet a dollar that's what she's interested in."

"You don't have a buck Dirt. If it wasn't for us you'd be back in your crate."

I was bewildered. I hadn't had another woman have any interest in me for at least thirty years, let alone having the darn 'hutzpah" to say she was prepared to give me her number if asked. I was rather perplexed being I was now a sixty-nine year old man. I have tried to avoid looking into mirrors for the last several years because I had to face it, what's attractive about a guy in his late sixties, (other than those who were filthy rich) I would have to surmise, probably nothing? Why any woman at my stage of life would be interested in me I hadn't a clue.

I was no means anywhere near rich, I was married for over forty years (Julie knew this, I told her during our first meeting) and I damn well must be at least twenty five years her senior. I came to conclude that she was just screwing with me, just having some play time inciting an old geezer, maybe even trying to get a rise out of me, something I also hadn't experienced in several years. I concluded she was playing me like a fool and the foolish needy guy I was. I was falling hook, line and sinker. Gerti has said several times "there is no fool like an old fool". If she saw me now all blushed up and pink, she would laugh her head off. I could hear her now, *"my husband Jack thinking he could attract any woman, let alone a younger one was a joke, never gonna happen."*

Dirt, Rhino and I left the VFW at 9:30 pm. I was diligently watching the time because I had been away from Gerti a lot lately and I knew it was starting to grate her. I really hadn't seen her for the last week. I would rise early and be out of the house. I would come back mid-morning and she would be gone which was unusual since she almost always preferred staying home. It was the same throughout the day, fortunately or unfortunately missing each other. Obviously our marriage was challenged but it was like we had a silent code, if we kept out of each other's way and tried to be civil then we could live under the same roof and at least have a pretense of a marriage. The reality is now it was nothing more than one of convenience. Gerti wouldn't move out because there was really no place for her to go, I wouldn't because, frankly it was just too damn much work and I just didn't have it in me to go through all the gyrations. Also with my pension (thank God for the UPS) there was just enough money to support us both with a few dollars left over each month for a bit of frivolity. If we chose to divorce, I just didn't know whether we would ever have the means to make it. The truth is Gerti and I laid a big bandage over our marriage and neither of us had the initiative to remove it because we didn't want to see what was festering underneath.

It was just fifteen minutes into my ride home when my cell phone rang. I looked at the number and hadn't a clue who it was except it had a 603 exchange. Then it dawned on me - a New Hampshire exchange. No it couldn't be, no possible way … the only way to be sure was to answer.

"Jack Krause."

"You disappoint me!"

"Why would you say that?"

"Well it's obvious, I basically roll over for you saying you can have my number and all you have to do is ask and nothing, NOTHING, no reply at all …. Like NADA!"

"We'll, like Julie … I thought you were just making light, kinda teasing this here old man."

"Well Jack Krause, you damn well have a lot to learn. First of all I'm not a tease. Second of all, I don't have a lot of expendable time to beat around the bush. Unfortunately, I don't have the luxury to play games, so here it is Jack Krause, *you interested or aren't you?*"

14

A Sick Dirt

Rhino called me. Dirt was in the hospital.
"What's going on with him?"
"Everything."
"Everything?"
"Shit Jack, the guy has been a vagrant for the last several decades, he lives on nothing, eats what he can scavenge. In the spring, summer and fall, lives in a wooden crate in back of Marshall's or wherever he can and smokes like a chimney. It's not that you would ever think someday it wouldn't all catch up with him."
"Where is he?"
"At Salem Hospital Emergency. Someone found him lying unconscious in the gutter at 2:00 a.m. this morning and phoned it in. The ambulance came and took him ASAP."
"I'll meet you there, it's 8.47 a.m. I'll meet you in half an hour."
"I'll be there, I'll bring you a Dunkin."
"10-4".
I arrived a few minutes before Rhino and scoped out the situation. Dirt was in the emergency ward. Visiting hours weren't till 10:00 a.m. We had a bit more than an hour to wait. We drank our Dunkin's and bullshitted about where the three

of us were at the moment and the unwieldy path that lead us here."

"We'll it's all catching up with us."

"Like what, you mean we're getting old?"

"Ya, something like that", I replied.

"Well it comes with the territory."

"Sure as hell does, but believe it or not, I thought there might be an outside chance we could grow old with a little dignity."

"You're fooling yourself - not a snowball's chance in hell, just isn't in the cards."

The nurse announced visiting hours were open. We got our badges and found our way to Room 114 on the first floor next to Radiology. We walked in. Dirt was all wired up. He had a tube in his arm and a breathing hose in his nose. He looked liked a pale version of a snowman caulk white. He turned his head to the right to welcome us and he waved his hand for us to come closer. We now hovered over him and under the florescent lights his skin looked tired, wrinkled and old. He gave the appearance he was already dead but his arm movement and his weak voice told us otherwise.

"What the hell happened to you dog soldier?"

"Hell if I know."

"We'll if you don't then nobody does," Rhino chimed in.

"Shit, I was just walking down the street and the next thing I knew I was here in this hospital bed."

"And what the hell were you doing at two in the morning walking the streets?"

"Couldn't sleep, ran out of Camels, was walking to the 7 Eleven to get some and just like that…vaboom, here I am."

A doctor entered the room and introduced himself.

"Hello, I'm Dr. Silver, I take it you are family or friends of Mr. Kearney?"

"Yes, we are", I answered.

"Well, which is it, family or friends?"

"Well, Doc, our friend we call him Dirt doesn't have any family other than us so we consider ourselves both."

"Dirt", that's an interesting nickname.

"It's a long story Doc, believe me it's a long story."

"Well, regardless", the Doc answered, "If you're both family and friends then I need to have a brief conversation with you."

"That's why we're here Doc, to do anything we can to support Dirt, so if you need to speak to us, we're all ears."

"Excellent."

Rhino and I followed the Doc into the hallway.

"Do you know your friend here is really in bad shape?"

"Not really, but that doesn't surprise me, does it you Rhino?", I asked.

"Christ, not in the least, I mean for the better part of the year he lives in a crate and as far as having enough money to feed, shelter and cloth himself he has a little but honestly…"

"Yes, honesty helps. It's a good place to start," said the Doc.

"We'll honestly then the little money he has, other than what Rhino and I give him, is usually spent on alcohol and cigarettes."

"Well I dare say that doesn't seem like a healthy diet, at least not one I would recommend."

"You see Doc, Dirt, here hasn't been right since returning from Nam."

"That's really not true Doc", Rhino chimed in, "He really wasn't in too good of a shape going in."

"So let me get this straight gentlemen, you're friend Dirt here, has been living this unhealthy kind of life since returning from Vietnam, that was quite a long time ago."

"Ya, like 1973", I said. "Like not to get personal Doc, but how old are you?"

"Well, that's privileged information but I don't mind telling you, I'm thirty-six."

"And this is 2017 let me see (Rhino was now doing figuring in his head) that means you were born in 1981, nearly eight years after Dirt and the two of us returned from Nam."

"So what's your point?"

"My point is that's a long freaking time living in a box and shelters, scrounging to stay alive on the streets of Salem."

"Well it certainly does seem like it's an interesting story but unfortunately, I have some doctoring to do and don't have the luxury to spend any more time with you."

This pissed Rhino off.

"See Doc, that's the whole problem, it seems that all us Nam vets have been lost in the cracks. Like nobody ever had the time or desire to help us, and a guy like Dirt needs all the help he can get."

The Doc brushed Rhino off.

"Like I said gentlemen, your friend here is very sick. I would try to get him into the VA hospital as quickly as I can. My quick appraisal is that there are a lot of things wrong with him. Definitely undernourished, lung capacity diminished significantly, possibly COPD if not something worse as if that isn't bad enough. I could go on and on but it's irrelevant because he should be admitted to the VA where he will get the best medical care the United States of America can provide it's veterans."

"Essentially, you're giving him a death sentence."

"I don't know what you mean?"

"Forget it Doc, I know you're busy - you got things to do."

"Well, it was nice to meet you and good luck with your friend."

"We wish you a good life", Rhino sneered back. "Well that's it Dirt is a goner."

"A "goner", what the hell are you talking about Rhino?"

"Dirt's as good as dead at the V.A., they don't have time and energy to waste on him with all these Iraq and Afghan vets returning, blown to hell, armless, legless, scrambled eggs for brains, do you honestly think a guy like Dirt is going to get any attention at all? Number one, he's an old shit, number two, he basically did all the crap to himself. I don't see a lot of time, energy or empathy wasted on him. It's just the freaking way it is Jackson, he's gonna fall through the bureaucratic cracks once again and I get the eerie feeling this time it might be the end of him."

"Shit, Rhino, you talk like you're giving up on him?"

"Honestly, and this is from the gut Jack, I was never the big Dirt fan like you, I think I gave up on him a long time ago, he's just a lot of work. He takes a lot of time and energy and the thing I really resent is that he did it all to himself."

"No Rhino, damn it man, I think you're wrong. Nam did the majority of it to him."

"Bullshit, it didn't make him give up on himself. It didn't make him smoke a pack of Camels a day for the last forty years. It didn't make him choose to spend all his vet and social service benefits on drugs, alcohol and cigarettes instead of food and a decent place to live."

"Ya, but Rhino, that was the effect, the cause was the war and how he was treated upon his return."

"I don't get you Jack, you see Dirt as some kind of hero, right up there with the Medal of Honor winners. He never had the courage to break through to the other side, he mailed it in when he returned and you parade him around as a symbol of how the good old USA has let him down, not really accepting he had choices and a damn critical role to play. I'm not saying he had the ability to rise above it because maybe he didn't have it in him. He didn't have whatever God gave you and me, the ability to piss in the wind and get on with our lives."

"Is that what we're doing?"

"Well, damn it, isn't it?"

A few minutes later Rhino and I were back in front of Dirt. He looked worse than he did minutes before when we left him to speak to Dr. Silver.

In a barely audible voice he asked, "I'm not doing well am I?"

"You've been in better shape", I answered.

"Ya, I suppose…but I can't seem to remember."

"Well, I will still bet that you have a hell of a lot of days ahead of you."

"Sure as hell", Rhino jumped it.

"Well I wish I was as sure as you guys, I would like to think I do but my body is telling me different."

"And what's it telling you Dirt?"

"It's telling me I'M GOING TO FUCK'N DIE."

"Whoa, big boy, you're far from Heaven's Gate. God has to torture you a bit more for you to qualify."

"You mean, I haven't suffered enough?"

"Ya you bet, you have a universe of suffering to go and you know God, he won't let you cross the bridge until you pay the tariff."

"We'll God and I have been estranged for a bit."

"Shit you're the ultimate prodigal son, he'd love to welcome a piece of shit like you back to the fold." Rhino added.

"Aye, aye, you can bet on that", I confirmed."

Dirt's voice was getting weaker like it was recoiling to a broken screech. He beckoned me closer. I looked at Rhino, he signaled me to go forward. I walked the five feet and then bent over to hear what Dirt wanted to say to me.

"Jackson, there is no doubt about it, I'M GOING TO DIE. A man knows when his time is up. I've been feeling it for a long while but it is nothing like I feel now and I knew it would eventually come down to this." Dirt paused, took a deep breath and then started again. "Well, like I was saying, I have a lifetime of regrets…I certainly understand I have pissed my life away." Dirt paused again, he took another really deep breath and I can hear his lungs grasping to take a hold of it.

He continued, "We'll there's no doubt I've been a real screw up but I want to thank you and Rhino from the bottom of my heart for all you've done for me. If it weren't for you two… I would have had no friends at all."

I really didn't know what to say. I never saw Dirt like this. It was like he was in a confessional and I was the priest. I didn't know what the hell good it would do, Dirt laying it on me like he did, I didn't have any direct line with God, in fact I cut him off years ago, but after seeing Dirt and hearing what he was saying, I might revisit that. God abandons those who abandon him.

I looked back at Rhino standing at the foot of Dirt's hospital bed.

He was just shaking his head.

Dirt struggled for another breath and continued, "Jackson I just have one more thing to ask of you. It's something I feel needs to be done to set my spirit free, to be one with the earth, this world, the whole damn universe. I hate to lay it on you but this might be my last request…you might say of a dying man."

"Yes, Dirt, I hear you. Tell me what you want, I'm sure Rhino and I will do whatever you're asking …I mean we were dog soldiers together. I can't think of a tighter bond."

Dirt in the faintest voice, "Well that's great Jackson. I want you to take my ashes back to Vietnam and throw them in the Song Sai Gon, the Saigon River. This will be the only way my spirit will find peace. I never truly came to grips with my service there, the shit I did, the killing and carnage so that's my last request …" Dirt rose off his bed and grabbed me by my shirt, "This is the last thing I will ever ask of you."

I straightened up and turned to Rhino. He mouthed the words "OH SHIT!"

Moments later outside Dirt's room…Rhino looked at me.

"What's he freaking nuts?"

"It's just freaking crazy', I mean him wanting to have his ashes scattered back in Nam."

"No Jack, that's not the crazy part. The really ridiculous crazy part is he wants you and me to cart his remains all the way back there and throw them into some piss hole of a river. And also, I don't believe one, that he wants his ashes scattered there and two, that he would drop that ultraheavy burden on our shoulders."

"Well I hate thinking this way Rhino, but he ain't dead yet, maybe he'll get better and we'll be done with this"

"What are you kidding me Jack, if he doesn't die now, do you honestly think he is going to outlive us?"

"No, he looks like shit, death warmed over. What is it the Doc said he has wrong with him?"

"Everything, just everything, Jackson ... Dirt has everything wrong with him."

"What's this COPD thing?"

"He can't breath, he smoked his lungs out, a pack of Camels a day for forty years will do it to you."

"Well, I can't believe the shit doesn't have lung cancer."

"Mark my words, I bet my last dollar he has or will."

"Well Rhino, I can't see him living much longer which brings us back to if we are or if we aren't going to drop his ashes in the Song Sai Gon."

"Well let me make my decision as clear as it can be. I ain't taking anyone's ashes back to Nam. In fact, let me tell you this, when I left that rice paddy I vowed never ever to return, my soldiering there was something I wanted to leave behind and for the last thirty plus years I've been struggling with. It already cost me two failed marriages because of the anxiety and horror I hold within. The truth is all three of us are suffering from PTSD, except I recognize it, and as far as Dirt is concerned, he's the absolute worse."

"Ya, Rhino, I understand, we all have a little PTSD."

"A little, you flirting with yourself , we have a lot of it - it's written all over you, me and Dirt, his is immeasurable."

"I know, well, I hear you loud and clear. I just have to think this through. I mean it is Dirt's last request. We owe it to him."

"See Jack, that's where you're wrong, we don't owe Dirt anything. In fact he owes us big time, especially you. You've treated him like your own personal charity. Whether you know it or not, your whole life centers around him."

"No it doesn't."

"Yes it does, and see, you can't even see it. He has you wrapped around his little finger. Whatever he wants he gets, it's like you're his Guardian Angel or something."

"Hey, I feel sorry for the guy."

"Christ, Jack, feel sorry for yourself would you?"

"Alright, okay Rhino, I had enough, like I said, Dirt isn't dead yet, he might recover."

"Not a snowball's chance in hell, he's already got his death sentence. He's going to the VA."

"What time is it?

"It's 11:15."

"I'm going to the mall to walk this off , you want to come?"

"No, screw the mall today."

Rhino, was really pissed at what Dirt asked of us. He never wanted to return to Vietnam again and I knew in my heart of hearts there would be no way he would.

I was in a quandary. Dirt dying was bad enough but him putting us in this position was unsettling. It sure as hell would cost me my marriage. There just was no way Gerti would ever let me do this. We didn't have a great or even a good marriage but we did have an "understanding" that there were certain things that would not be tolerated, that would end it all, and I sure enough knew taking Dirt's ashes back to Nam would not pass muster. That would be the end of it. Maybe that would be the best thing that ever happened to us, but even with that being so, the reasons I could never return to Nam were becoming crystal clear. Nam was one deep dark hole that led to another allowing no chance of escape. Going back to Nam for any reason...no fucking way. ***Fuck Nam***.

15

Family Guy

I arrived at the Mall at 11:45 am. I hate to get a late start. It knocks my whole world off kilter. I have always been an early riser. I like getting up before the rest of humanity turns the world into a turd. There was just something unencumbered by all the activity that brought a few hours of contentment I found in a day.

11:45 at the mall was way too late for me. There would be just too many shoppers who would get in my way. Won't they ever understand the mall is for walking, not shopping? Well it is for me. I'm sure the rest of the world doesn't see it that way, but being a non-conformist is my natural trait.

I just sat in my Merc feeling the heat generated by it nearing noon, ripping through my clothes. It's going to be one hell of a hot day. It's forecasted to be 101 with 80% humidity. It's going to be the ultimate "dog day" afternoon. It will be one of the hottest of the year and I'll always remember it as the one Dirt told Rhino and me he was going TO DIE and he wanted us to take his ashes back to Nam.

I just wasn't motivated. It will be difficult for me to continue my walking without Rhino and Dirt to support me. Dirt hasn't walked the mall in a while. He lost interest. He had more important things to do, like smoking his life away. He wasn't a good walking partner anyway, the Camels got to him.

One day, I calculated he averaged one pack a day for 40 plus years, meaning he smoked a total of 14,600 packs or 292,000 individual cigarettes. How anybody thought they could survive that must be delusional? Dirt did, but he was delusional on steroids.

It was just one of these days where the monkey wrench gets thrown into the soup and there was not a star in the sky let alone any lined up signifying at least there was a semblance of order in the world. I hated ones like this falling on me without a plan or purpose. I think in my retirement I was becoming lazy. If the day didn't roll as planned, I didn't have the creativity or the wherewithal to restructure. I just let it lay on me like molten lead, smothering whatever I had designed under it's weight, making me significantly more depressed than if I had structure to follow.

I just sat in my car in the mall parking lot, watching the frenzied people entering and leaving like ants scattering about as if desperation was in the air. Then I saw him. I wasn't sure, but a minute later he was more visible making his way between several people in front of him through two rows of vehicles, then finding his own, he stopped. It was my newly found friend Peter Strong. He unlocked the car with his remote and opened several windows, allowing the very hot, stale August air to escape.

He didn't enter the car's driver seat but just stood there scanning the parking lot as if looking for someone.

It was but a few minutes later his hand went up in the air as he started furiously shaking his wrist signaling. As I contorted to see who he was summoning, I saw a young woman and child making their way toward him. As she, child in her one hand and a bunch of packages in the other made her way through the crowd, it was obvious there was a connection. Grabbing the little girl in his arm and bringing her up to rest on his hip, he took the several packages the woman held and then reached forward and kissed her on her mouth. This was a part of Peter

Strong I didn't know, not that I knew much about him other than what he volunteered during our two previous encounters.

The young woman was absolutely beautiful and the child a perfect younger version. *That son of a B, Peter Strong"*, I thought, *the shit gets his ass blown up in Iraq and here he is like it just doesn't bother him and he's getting on with his life with hardly a misstep. What the hell's with this guy, doesn't he have any hurt or angst, any of the scars or shrapnel that inevitably finds those returning from war their host? This guy's got me all messed up. What does he see that I don't? He should be all screwed up like the rest of us and not coming home to a storybook woman and child. It's just too much of a stretch that I see his life falling into order … why him?* I couldn't believe what I was thinking but I honestly felt this way. I didn't want to but these emotions unwrapped within me, conjuring thoughts I wasn't much proud of. I asked myself, *"Why did I resent this kid?"* He was like us, a combat veteran but from a different war. His loss was physical but I damn well knew it had to very much affect him. How could it not? He lost his damn leg. Dirt, Rhino and me, we were mainly splintered emotionally, unless we checked off Dirt's COPD as a direct consequence of Nam, which I knew it was not.

No, I felt that meeting Peter Strong was just too much for me. I felt my life unfurling and hated myself for it. I wanted his life to as well and knew it had to be with all the stuff he saw and losing a limb but It seemed he never flinched, he manned-up, took it on the cheek and plowed ahead, right into (seemingly), the adoring arms of who I assumed to be his wife and those of the beautiful little girl, I imagined was his daughter. Peter Strong it seemed had broken through which I could not, that terrible residue I've carried for the last forty plus years, and whatever it is, I was still carrying part and parcel weighing me down more than it ever had.

I began to feel very alone. *Where were Dirt and Rhino? Where were Gerti and my kids Hendrix and Riley? Where the hell was the man I was forty some years ago who could take it on the chin?* All of them were nowhere, not to be found, but there was only me, now looking into my rear view mirror at someone I didn't even recognize, a significantly older version of who I was yesterday and dramatically aging by the minute. ***Dirt and his stupid cigarettes.***

16

Car Crazy

I told Gerti I was going to look for another car and even invited her along. I knew she wouldn't want to come. She had absolutely no interest in cars and the thought of following me around visiting dealerships on Boston's North Shore, in this stifling August heat, I knew she'd think was insanity. She sat in an old wooden rocker strategically positioned between our antique Sylvania air conditioner and several fans pushing the air around the room achieving what I felt was nothing.

"When you coming back?"

"Probably early afternoon."

"What's so important about looking for a new car now, in this stifling heat? You're sure this isn't crazy?"

"My Merc's making some really strange sounds. It seems it might be on it's last leg. I better start doing my homework, before it's too late. And what the hell, there's probably no better time to start, than now."

"Well Jack, do what you want to do, you're gonna do it anyway."

"Well Gerti, why the hell not, it's as good as you sitting around the house waiting for Riley's' and Bellow's four or five phone calls a day."

"They need to talk to someone, obviously, they can't to Humphrey and in your case, you never speak with them."

"There's just nothing to talk about, you know how I feel about Riley's pathetic life and Bellows and Humphrey living with her, and them knocking out babies they can't afford. Bellows is becoming nothing but a baby machine and he can't find a job and I know he's damn well not looking, cause it's easier to put his hand in someone else's pocket than his own."

"Christ Jackson, you have such a lack of charity."

"And they have such a lack of common sense ... I'm outta here."

I have now become a perpetual liar. I had no intention to go car shopping but had scheduled meeting Julie at her apartment in Nashua at 11:00. With medium traffic it would take me about forty-five minutes to get there. I really wanted to see her. It had been several weeks since we rendezvoused. It wasn't just for the sex, which after years of going dry was incredible, but rather more about her respecting me in a way my wife never has. The problem now was my having an affair with Julie, my first, and the little respect she was giving me, was diminished by the loss I had for myself. I knew I was now a cheat and a perpetual liar but I found it really hard to live like one.

When I knocked on Julie's door, she was already prepared to greet me. She put her arms around my shoulders and kissed me on the cheek, it was about five minutes later we found ourselves in bed.

"How long do I have you?"

"Well, I told Gerti I would be home mid-afternoon."

"Why did you have to tell her anything?"

"Like meaning what Julie?"

"Like meaning, if you said nothing to her than you wouldn't have set up any

expectations and also not put limitations on the time we spend together. I don't get it Jack."

"I don't get what you don't get!"

"I don't get that you always tell Gerti you'll do this or do that, and for some reason, the only one making any compromises around here is me. I mean, I feel like I'm being boxed in."

"Well, Julie, you damn well knew I was married from the time we met, I mean, like I never kept it any secret. It's not like I was trying to fool you."

The sheets were starting to get cold.

"Yeah, like I know Jack. Now how long has it been?"

"Since January, we met during the playoffs, remember?"

"Ya, how can I forget, so we're looking at what, I mean seven months now?"

"Ya, seven months."

"We'll Jack, have you ever heard of the seven year itch."

"Of course, I've experienced it six plus times over my forty-six year marriage."

"We'll then you'll understand. I am getting that seven month inch."

"What are you saying, that you are leaving me?"

Julie moved closer and started to cuddle.

"Leaving you, no, no, Jackson, it's just the opposite. I want to stay but I want you to leave Gerti."

"Leave Gerti?"

"Didn't you think it would ever come down to this? I mean, eventually a choice between her and me."

"Well, honestly, I never thought that far ahead."

"Well the reality is there is no free lunch and you have been nibbling at my table for way too long. Now it's time to make some decisions."

I was taken way off guard.

"Julie, I just don't get it."

"Get what?"

"I just thought you wanted a fling. I mean, look at us two we're from different generations, different worlds. I mean I'm a sixty-nine year old and you're twenty some years younger. I mean, really what do you even see in me?"

"Christ, Jack, you're dumber than I ever thought you'd be, with women it ain't a age thing, nor is it a hair thing, I mean here you are running around with a ponytail under your brigade baseball cap and it doesn't say Jerry Garcia "wannabe", but what it says is insecure to the bone. Yes, you Jackson Krause, sixty-nine years old, there is indeed a whole shit load of things in your life you haven't come to grips with and the reason is you never really tried putting your hands in your pant front pocket and jiggling around what you got there. Christ Jack, you got to grow yourself a pair of balls and start facing down the shit in your life."

I couldn't believe I was hearing this tirade.

"Jackson, you got to face your demons down, like this Dirt stuff, him wanting you and Rhino to take his ashes back to Vietnam. You play with this shit in your head all you want but the reality is you're not going to Nam with his ashes. Fantasize all you want but this will never happen."

"Julie, you are getting way out of line here. I mean if I wanted to deal with this kind of crap, I would have stayed home. I mean I never thought I would hear this stuff from you."

"We'll you're hearing it Jack, now the question begs, what are you going to do about it? But yes, to help you with your decision I do need to serve some things up for you. What do I see in an old married vet the likes of you - damn if I know all of it - but some I do. I see you as a really nice guy who somewhere, somehow lost your way. I see you as a guy who is vulnerable to the bone and did a lot of things for the right reasons but seemingly became very much disappointed with their outcome. I see a man quagmired in rage and no idea how to dispel it. In summary, I see a man, older than all the men I have ever been with but with a sensitivity and heart as large as all of them combined and a barrel of fun when he wants to be. In short I guess I have found a man WORTH FIGHTING

FOR, possibly one who just doesn't want to nibble at what I can offer but rather who wants to consume the whole banquet."

"Jesus, Julie, you're freaking me out."

"Jack, I don't want to freak you out, I just want you to start thinking about the stuff in your life keeping you up at night like number 1: when are you going to leave your wife and spend more time and make a commitment to me and number 2: when are you going to get enough balls to tell Dirt you're not taking his ashes back to Vietnam and throw them in no polluted damn river?"

I got out of bed, showered and left Julia pretty pissed off. I didn't now have one woman reaming me over the coals but two, and no more clarity of mind than a rowboat in heavy fog at sea. My life, it seemed, was getting progressively worse. I knew what I had at home with Gerti. It wasn't all roses. It wasn't like we had "Champagne" problems, the kind rich folk have, no we had the everyday kind, the type of the average couple, well, truthfully, probably way past those but at least with Gerti, we had an "Understanding" and although it wasn't like Romeo and Juliet, it was for the most part workable.

It was a day from hell. I lied and cheated on my wife and the girl I was cheating with thought I was cheating on her as well. In my heart of hearts, I felt I was cheating on everyone, especially myself. But I have to say in a very strange way I wasn't feeling really sorry for myself. I was on the verge of a mild melt down and after brief consideration, I felt I would throw my "pity party" at the VFW, because what the hell are VFW's for other than a lot of worn vets, playing back the horrors of their life, surrounded by those who had a box car load of empathy, but were not judgmental. Just a bunch of screwed up vets replaying the tapioca in their minds, trying to get a little peace, a little quiet respite from what's messing with them outside of the VFW's walls.

I was being over-served. I had five boilermakers (a shot of Jameson's and a beer chaser). It was unusual for Ted the regular bartender at the Lynn VFW to serve one patron so much. He was always responsible and watchful, but tonight there was a large crowd gathered and he seemed to have missed count. I kept ordering and he kept serving and I kept sucking them down as if there was no tomorrow. Unfortunately there was.

Before I knew it, it was 9:31 on the Miller Lite clock centered at the back of the bar. *Shit, I thought, my sorry ass is in big trouble, I left Gerti around 9:00 this morning and now its nearing 10:00 p.m., eleven long hours… there is just no way the shit isn't going to hit the proverbial fan.* I paid my tab and removed myself from my seat at the bar.

Ted turned and walked over to me, "Hey Jack, you be really careful driving home you hear, that is if you can safely drive. Jack, are you able to drive? If not, I'll get you a ride."

I guess Ted was counting after all. I waved him off.

"No, no Ted, I'm perfectly fine. Really, I'm good to go. Don't worry about me but thanks for the concern."

"Just be really, really careful", Ted replied.

I threw him a wave and out the door I went. I was drunk. There was no doubt. I hadn't felt this way since my niece's wedding and as I recall there was hell to pay in the Krause home that night and I damn well paid it. If there was anything that Gerti hated was a drunk, especially her husband being one. She was intolerant.

I hadn't a clue how I was going to explain my absence all day and then returning home three sheets to the wind. There were two things I clearly knew. The first I was drunk and the sanity in me was trying to convince me I should go back into the VFW and ask Ted to summon me a cab and the second, that there wasn't a chance in hell I can get pass Gerti without her knowing I was plastered and there would be hell to pay this night.

Against my better judgment, I started my Merc and with a wounded wing and a prayer, began my twenty-minute journey home. There wasn't a chance in the world if a cop stopped me

I wouldn't be arrested for DWI. I passed a cruiser with it's light flashing, the cops pulled someone over at the Dunkin' Donuts parking lot. *Better him than me*, I thought, *Better him, than me!* I finally arrived home and felt I had at least survived that, now for the rest of the story as it was about to unfold. I knew what lay before me was going to be twenty miles of bad road. *What the hell*, I thought, *whatever it was going to be is what it is going to be. There was no way I could avoid it now. Man-up, take it on the damn chin.* I tried to convince myself - really how bad could it possibly be?

It was worse than I could have imagined. I have never seen Gerti so mad. She was beside herself and attacked me immediately as I walked through the front door.

"Where the hell have you been all this blasted day?" Gerti screeched at me.

"Shit Gerti, like I said, I mean… I was looking at used cars."

"Looking at used cars from 9:00 a.m. in the morning till now after 10:00 p.m. at night. Who the hell are you trying to BS here? You weren't looking at used cars, you damn well have been up to no good (she now caught a hint of the liquor on my breath) and what is it that I now smell? Jack Krause, have you been drinking? Damn it Jack, is that all you've been doing all day … at some bar … at some damn VFW hall drinking the whole day away? Is that what it has come down to now, you spending no time with me but all of yours with your drunken vet buddies down at the VFW?"

Gerri, wouldn't let up for air, I figured I would let her vent, to ramble on hoping she would run out of gas, that her sanity would take over, but no freaking way, she was far from finished.

"Look at you Jack Krause, you look like a foolish old man. Always wearing that stupid Army baseball cap, every place you go, like it's screwed to your head. And that stupid ass ponytail, frankly, you look ridiculous. I don't know what's gotten into you Jackson but doesn't it bother you that you keep failing me and your family? Doesn't it bother you when you look in the mirror each morning the person looking back has been a failure all his life and has done almost nothing right?"

Unfair … UNFAIR… **TOTALLY UNFAIR!** I knew I was far from the perfect husband and father, there was no denying but I HAVE NOT BEEN A FAILURE ALL MY LIFE . Bullshit…BULLSHIT…**BULLSHIT**, the truth was anything but. I served me country with honor. I supported my family and put food on the table and a roof over their heads. I worked thirty plus years at the UPS and garnered a decent retirement and now Gerti doesn't have to do anything all day but just hang around. I never even cheated on my wife (other than the last several months) and isn't that worth something? Don't I get any break here at all. Don't I get at least one pass, one good "atta" boy? Not with Gerti. NOT A DAMN ONE.

I hadn't moved but five feet in the house and she was on me again.

"I don't know why I hadn't divorced you years ago. You have been the biggest disappointment in my life."

Then the train derailed. Gerti picked up the closest thing next to her, that happened to be my late mothers fake tiffany lamp and hurdled it at me, nearly missing as it shattered against the wall. Then she hurled several hardbound books at me, screaming at the top of her lungs.

"Get the hell out of here. Get the hell out of my house, YOU'RE A GODDAMN LOSER!"

Enough was a enough. I was damn well ashamed of my behavior today and cheating on my wife over the last several months, I was none too proud but again, ENOUGH WAS ENOUGH.

I went ballistic. Usually somewhat reserved, something exploded in me, breaking through all the restraint I had. I found myself approaching Gerti as a predator. Her my prey. I grabbed at her, barely missing, as she sprung out of my way. I lunged at her again and this time found myself on the floor, tumbling over the edge of the sofa with a thump. My shoulder took the impact of the fall and it felt I might have dislocated it but immediately rising to my feet, told me I had not. Gerti was but ten feet from me, holding in her hand the poker from the fireplace. She had a terrified look on her face, one I was unfamiliar with. It seemed both her and I were going to places we never visited, a dark demented part of ourselves we never knew existed or held in strict abeyance.

Seeing her standing there, now fully armed, set me off again. I leaped toward her and found my head meeting the poker dead on. Gerti hit me right across the temple, knocking my cap off landing me face first on the ground. I now felt nauseous and sick to my stomach. I felt like vomiting and before I could make my way to the bathroom, I upchucked all over the living room carpet. I could hear Gerti, beyond pissed, screaming out "CHRIST THAT'S THE END OF IT – YOU DEAL WITH THIS SHIT YOU ASSHOLE!" She threw the poker onto the floor, turned and walked toward our bedroom, I heard her slam the door, locking herself in.

I lay in my vomit, now feeling a welt on my head the size of a golf ball. I was feeling as low and ashamed as I ever had. In forty-six years of marriage, I never lifted a finger towards my wife and here I now lay, a man lowest of the low. Attacking Gerti was beyond me, or at least I thought, making me feel everything she said tonight was true. Maybe I was an asshole, a bum, a failure in everything I did, and I wasn't even man enough to face that. Maybe my family deserting me was really I deserting them. Maybe my whole life was nothing but a sack of crap and I deserved every last turd, because, that's exactly what I gave out.

It took me two hours to get me and the house back in order. I cleaned myself up and moved the furniture to lift the rug from the floor. Once freeing it, I rolled it up and dragged it to the back porch. I unrolled it and using a putty scrapper started to scrape away as much vomit as possible. Once completed, I blotted the area with some old rags and paper towels. Removing as much of the moisture as possible, I covered the wet area with baking soda and waited for about fifteen minutes before vacuuming it off, hoping not to disturb the neighbors being that it was already past midnight. I then left the rug, vacuum and baking soda on the porch before going to look for an enzyme cleaner in the kitchen to hopefully remove the smell. Upon finding one, I applied it on the rug and then retired to the living room to sleep on the couch. Even after showering, I could smell the vomit caked in my hair. It was a sign. Enough was truly enough. Something had to change. I walked into the bathroom, and taking a scissor and a razor from the medicine cabinet cut all my hair away and finally shaved my head clean. I stared in the mirror. *"NOW WHO THE HELL IS THIS STUPID IDIOT?"* I asked myself.

"YOU'RE A DISGRACE and I'm going to get a lawyer and file for divorce. Jackson, can't you see you're losing it? The hat and ponytail, now look at you, you look like an Aryan racist with your bald shiny head."

What could I say? I truly was out of control last night. I deserved the crap she was shoveling out in spades. I was wrong as wrong could be and couldn't justify raising my hand to a woman under any circumstance, especially my wife. I figured I would let this situation blow over and hopefully there would be no lawyer, no divorce. For whatever reason, although I had contemplated it a few times myself, I felt it was not the right thing to do. I hoped that Gerti, after a few days would feel the same. Nevertheless, I would have to make a lot of things right and to be painfully and brutally honest, I hadn't a clue where to begin.

The next day I went to the mall. I didn't bother calling Rhino. There would be no more mall walking for Dirt. He was moved to the VA, that didn't bode well for him. I did five times around the interior in record time. Maybe it was my baldhead cutting through the air, jettisoning me forward. Maybe it was my trying to distant myself from what had happened yesterday, trying to get as far as I possibly could from the other Jack Krause, who reared his ugly head.

The problem with completing my exercise in record time was now I was confronted with what to do with the rest of my day. I didn't have to wait for Rhino or Dirt, as I usually did, being Rhino was in passable shape but Dirt never was being totally neglectful about his overall heath. Over the last several months he had given up walking, like he had with every other aspect of his demented life. The only regiment he had left was his smoking and it was clear it had turned against him.

There would also not be any idle bantering with the boys today, consuming upwards of hours supported by at least two or three freshly brewed Starbucks. One thing I could say about Rhino, he indeed was one damn good conversationalist. He rose really early to read the morning papers after staying up really late at night to capture the late news. Rhino felt it was his duty to be informed.

"We've seen the best of days," he would constantly say, *"Yes, unfortunately the best of what America stood for is now behind us. We are fortunate in one way and then unfortunate in another. Fortunate, we had seen the Promise of America as it was visualized by our forefathers, unfortunate we will now watch it crumble before us, leaving just the residue of the exceptional country it once was."*

Rhino always had an agenda. There was always the topic of the day, which he delved into, pulling back the layers of skin to expose what it always came down to for him.

Damn it, I miss those conversations. It seems there has been too few lately. Rhino hasn't been as accessible as he once was. He seemed to be weighed down by his two ex-wives and a couple of kids, who were draining his already too few meager resources. He never spoke much about them, only that they were some of the wreckage of his life after several years returning from Vietnam. *"I made a shit load of mistakes, number one was going to Nam and thinking I could possibly change the world but I guess I could just chalk that up to being a eighteen year old and filtering through the little I knew. Ya, that was mistake number one, number two and three, were the two dames I married, thinking a good women could make a difference in me. There was no one, on this side, that could ever make me into the man other than I am. That's what really sucks about war, how it surgically cuts away at those who served, even years after experiencing it's horror. I still envision the same South Vietnam soldier cutting the ears and nose off some of the enemy captives. It is embossed in my memory and each day, every day, I ask myself, "What the hell was that all about?" The tragedy is there will never be answers and nobody really gives a damn no more. So there I was a Vietnam Vet laying this shit on my first wife and then a second, thinking one if not both would wade through the shit swamp of my psyche, and knocking out two kids in the process. What the hell must I have been thinking? WHAT THE HELL MUST I HAVE BEEN THINKING?"*

Rhino was indeed the verbal one. Dirt on the other hand held his feelings close to his vest. He didn't say much after returning from Vietnam. As Rhino said, *"The guy never spoke much before Nam and said little after."* When he returned home, it was as if he had just given up on his life. He was just there, hanging about, engaging in no way, other than bumming cigarettes from everyone who crossed his path. He was a lost soul and after living with his parents for the first two years after his return, headed for the streets as if he gave up on his family and they in turn on him. I never asked him why he left and he never volunteered any insight. It seemed for him it was the thing to do after totally giving up on himself, which was my quick and concise evaluation.

The street was where I found Dirt. We came into contact three years after both of our return. I just walked by him as he sat on the corner of Derby Street in Salem. I was making my way to the train en route to Boston and as I walked by him, I realized that somewhere we had crossed paths. Without reservation I circled back to get a better look. Without a doubt, I recognized him to be Danny Kearney, nickname Dirt, who was in the same high school class as me and who was drafted and then sent to Nam at the same time.

"That you Dirt?"

"Who's asking?", he questioned, as he sat in his dirty, grungy clothing, wearing a worn and tattered Boston Red Sox hat. My immediate reaction was he should be wearing a New England Patriots one because the Sox again were having a less than stellar season. They suck.

"Me", I answered, "Jack Krause, remember me, we went to school together and were drafted at the same time?"

"Can't remember."

"Well I damn well can you. You were the quietest kid in class, as I recall, never said a damn thing, in fact, this conversation is the longest I believe we ever had."

"Can't recall."

That's where it all started with me and Dirt. I looked at him as if he were a reflection of me. For the love of God, I could not understand how I was surviving my Vietnam experience (not that in no way did I find it easy) and a vet like Dirt was not. I felt blessed in a way. I felt God had given me whatever it was to break through (or thinking I had broken through) some of the walls I had built around me. I felt sorry for Dirt and strongly needed to redeem myself from some of the really bad shit I did over there by helping him get his life in order. As I look back, I must have been delusional thinking I would ever have any influence or power over him. Dirt was who he was, a man waiting patiently to self-destruct, and there would be nothing or no one who would ever stand in his way.

"Can't you see that Dirt's one of those flatheads, who took the war and his part in it way too serious?"

I could never understand how Rhino positioned it. War was a serious thing, participating in it, could easily and most often did, change a man's life, and in most cases not for the better.

"Let the sick bastard kill himself, if that's what he wants to do. You got to understand, "Sick-Os" like Dirt, create a lot of collateral damage along their way. People who involve themselves with him will wind up as the ultimate losers, because Dirt will never do anything to help himself. This is his ultimate "modus operandi". Mark my word Dirt will weight on you and sap you dry without you ever knowing. Damn if he won't."

The mall was quiet today. Too quiet. It was giving me too much time to think. I was looking for a distraction, any, that could take my mind off where I found my life.

I looked around and unpacked my knapsack holding my sweats, sneakers and socks (changed in the Men's Room) and started walking the inside perimeter. In a strange way, I was even hoping to run into Peter Strong the Iraqi amputee, my quasi acquaintance. I thought it would be an opportunity to finish, or at least expand on the previous conversation we were so emotionally engaged. He was nowhere to be found.

I settled myself down half way through the Mall, right in front of the

Apple store. Apple attracted consumers like flies. One thing is certain, that of all the stores in the mall it got the most traffic. It's secret is that its' technology provides the opportunity for its customers to embrace their self-importance. All their electronic gadgets play to people's insecurities, thinking others really cared about what went on in their lives. The insanity of it all, TWEET, #imeatingasaladatpanera, TWEET, TWEET,

#I just ran into Josephine, TWEET, #iamgoingtothebathroom, TWEET, #whothehellcares. Laptops, tablets, cell phones, Facebook, Tweeter, Instagram, stupid intrusions in our lives, stealing from us that which at one time was sacred - a little uninterrupted downtime where we could be one with our thoughts, or that could be shared with a person of important, a special time, once guarded not to be defrocked by a bunch of voyeuristic clones.

Dirt, Rhino and I were now the old guys. As the years passed we will be cast aside, rolled over, disregarded like yesterday's old news. Guys like us, who gave every bit of ourselves to our country, provided the foundation for the insanity now taking place.

I bet eighty percent of the people entering the Apple Store hadn't a clue when the Vietnam War was or why it was fought. It was as if yesterday never existed and the sacrifices were made irrelevant in the lives of the now significantly technologically efficient. I wondered if they ever "googled" anything about it or anything today induced a reason to do so? I just doubted it. I doubted it, *and felt a sorrowful deep regret*.

17

Not Worthy

I had to call Julie. I didn't want to but I hadn't spoken to her for ten days. Coincidentally, my wife hadn't spoken to me for the same. It was proverbially a week and a half from hell. Nothing gets to men like the quiet treatment. Women are so verbose we know they have to be really pissed off not to verbalize.

I hadn't a clue how Julie would react to my call but I dialed her number anyway. I also didn't know what I was going to say to her. My home life was in shambles and the little respite I had found in Julie's presence was receding with the fading tide.

The phone rang several times. There was a part of me that hoped she didn't answer. She did.

"I gave it fifty-fifty that you were going to call me."

"Well those are better than Vegas odds."

"Never been there ... have no desire to go."

"Never been there either. I, like you, have no desire."

"So what's this about Jack?"

"What, what's about?"

"The call. I can't say I wasn't weighed toward the fifty percent that said I would never hear from you again."

"Well, Julie, the last time I saw you was a tough night."

"Meaning for who, you, me or both of us?"

"Damn it Julie, you damn well know I mean the both of us."

"Well, to tell you the truth, the way it ended has indeed given me a reason to think hard about our relationship, not that I have taken it lightly - having a relationship with a married man."

"I understand."

"No how could you? I'm the one having the relationship with the "MARRIED" man, you're not."

"I understand Julie, I mean, I have never, for the last forty six years had another woman other than Gerti in my life.... although you're not married...you have to understand that this is all foreign to me as well?"

"Ya, sure Jack, I'd be a fool if I didn't think there wasn't any angst in you... and a fool is something I'm not. And I am damn well determined I won't let you make me into one."

I was hearing Julie loud and clear.

"And it was or is not my intention to make you."

"We'll Jack you certainly did that night. You left so damn hurried, you made me feel like I was a ten dollar whore.

If there was anything that was resounding to me, it was this. I remember in Nam whoring it up with some of the local street-walkers. You know as the saying goes, *"To the victor goes the spoils."* These young girls were everywhere, since there was almost no economy in the war zone, other than the underground, every civilian was scrambling to survive, doing whatever they needed to do to get by.

The average age of an American soldier in Vietnam was twenty-two. We were all kids. If we weren't fighting in the war, we would have been in college or if not, having another interest, but either way partying like there was no tomorrow. That's what kids do, party like the world is their playground, leaving as much of the seriousness behind and if circumstance becomes even more daunting, **party even more to get beyond it.**

I often wondered where I would have been and what I would be doing if I wasn't drafted into the service. Would I have been involved in the young aloof drinking crowd or evolved into the Cambridge, Haight-Asbury, "hippie" type brotherhood, smoking reefer and ingesting heroin and speedballs, thinking it was my generation's turn to save the world from itself and my patriotic American mission to stop the imperialistic country in which I lived, the "Good Old USA" from implementing its distorted view of world dominance. I really didn't have a clue where I would have been, but here I was now, again feeling caught up in the crossfire, not having any inclination to which way I should turn. My wife Gerti of forty-six years ready to drop divorce papers on my sorry butt, my girlfriend of several months thinking I have taken her to the level of a ten-dollar whore.

"You're no ten dollar whore."

"Wow, gee wiz, thank you for clarifying that … then why the hell do you make me feel like one?"

"Julie, this whole thing has just gotten away from me."

"Meaning?"

"Meaning, I never had any intention of having an affair with you, not that you're not a handsome woman, that you damn well are, but I would have never ever believed that one like you would involve herself with a sixty-nine year old worn vet like me. I just was not prepared to have such a beautiful intrusion in my life. I guess I wasn't prepared to meet this head on."

"Jack, I made the play for you. It wasn't the other way around. Remember it was me who reached out to you."

"Ya, Julie, that's just it. I haven't a clue what you see in me."

"You see, that's your problem Jack. You have a terrible low grade opinion of yourself. You just don't think you're worthy."

"Worthy?"

" Ya, Jack, WORTHY."

"Don't get it."

"I'll try to make it clear for you. You see Jack, I like myself. In fact I love myself, not that loving myself wasn't easy to get to, especially after one failed marriage. Mark my word, don't think I was exempt from the lowest of lows, but I broke through it and on the other side there was just me. I had to make the decision, whether to live in pity and be a victim all my life or discard the "Pity Party", find my own self-worth and be the best Julie I could ever be. I made the latter choice and never looked back…but you Jack…"

"Me?"

"Yes, you."

"Are we going to burn up the phones here?"

"Jack, I'm venting, it's the womanly thing to do. I'm on a roll here, please indulge me."

"Okay Julie, then go on …"

"Well like I said Jack, the Julie you know, the Julie, I love, YES, I LOVE, took a lot of years and effort to create and you know what the reason is, Jack?"

"No, Julie, I guess I don't."

"Well, because I'M WORTH IT and the crux of the matter and the explicit difference between you and me …"

"And that is?"

"Simply put, you don't love yourself. You think you are unhappy, unworthy. You don't believe in your heart of hearts you deserve to be happy and you will do everything in your life to sabotage that opportunity."

"Christ, that's not true."

"Of course it's true. See you have the inability to rise from the ashes of your past and create a person and a life that will bring you to where you desperately want to go."

I couldn't believe what I was hearing. Julie must have taken Psyche 101 and is relying on the little knowledge she had to pepper me with a bunch of crap. But right or wrong, I decided to let her continue in penance for how I treated her ten days earlier.

"Julie, I think we should see each other."

"No Jack, damn it, I ain't finished yet. Humor me."

My ears was turning numb, I was holding the phone so hard and close to my ear.

"The difference between me and you as I see it - is I have found myself, love, and you have none at all. So you live your life in desperate circumstance digging yourself deep into whatever you label your desperation and refuse to give anything else a try to break away from all that holds you back and steals your happiness from you. You just don't think you're worthy to be happy because you refuse to accept the journey that will take you there. Jack, it takes balls to walk away from that which is holding you back. Now tell me you still have a couple between your legs."

I had had it. I was looking for more than a scaling down, a total disregard for who and what I was. Julie knew just the little of me I offered up. There was a significant other that I didn't expose. Within each of us there is a vault which is hidden our true selves. It is kind of the root ball of our source and from which our branches grow. It is a sacred place, one not easily given up to anyone and sometimes not even to ourselves. It is the ticking clock, the heartbeat and pulse, the nuclear fusion that makes us ready at all times to close ourselves off to the world. It is the "red hot chili pepper alarm" that goes off without warning. Julie just triggered it.

"I can't listen to this anymore."

"I'm damn well not finished."

"I damn well think you are."

"Then I guess this is the end?"

"I'll call you."

Julie started to say something...*I hung up*.

18

The Phone Call

"Jack, the phone."

This was but three of the probably ten words Gerti spoke to me over the last four weeks. The silence was deafening. She was leaving signs all over the house she was indeed seeking a lawyer. I would have hoped things would have calmed down by now but honestly I didn't have a clue to what she was thinking or whether she was proceeding with the divorce. I knew the conversation had to be had but at the moment I was not about to approach it…call me a coward.

The phone rang several times more. Why she didn't pick it up I damn well didn't know. Why we still had a "land line" was another question I had to ask myself? Cell phones have made them obsolete like most things technology touches …G-O-N-E.

The phone rang again. I should have let it ring out, but I didn't.

I pulled my sorry ass out of my chair. I was reading the sports page of the Boston Globe. The Sox lost again. It's like they're playing in the minors, they still suck."

Who was it that said, *"A Man's Home Is His Castle."* Bullshit! Whoever it was I'd like to plant a hot poker up their butt. In my castle there was always a disturbance or a shroud of disaster about to happen. Indeed this was one.

"Jack Krause here."

The voice on the other end was barely recognizable.

"Jack…Jack…Jack Krause…is this Jack Krause?"

"Yes, it's Krause, who the hell is this?"

I started to recognize the voice now. It was my sister-in-law Ruth. She had the voice of a bird and over the phone, I could barely hear her every other word."

"It's you sister-in-law Ruth."

"Ruth, yes, I get it now, my sister in law Ruth, yes, I get it. Ruth can you speak a little louder. I can barely make out what you are saying?"

"Yes, Jack, understood, like what's happening and all, I've lost a lot of strength."

"Well Ruth, damn it, I haven't heard from you for like maybe three years. It's been some time. Is everything all right, is something wrong? As I recall Ruth you were never one to mince words - being from Maine and all. So what's going on up there? Robert and the kids okay?"

"No Jack… well, yes Jack, the kids are doing well, God is still blessing us there … but unfortunately, I can't say the same for your brother Bob."

I was now getting impatient with Ruth, it was unlike her to be ranting on for so long.

"Christ Ruth, cut to the chase, what's the nature of this call?"

"It's your brother, Robert."

"Yes, I damn well gathered that. Is he dead, sick, have a heart attack, stroke… come on, what gives here Ruth?"

"Jack, he got kicked by a mare. Bobby, turned his back on the horse and it inadvertently threw a kick, hitting him right in the back. He suffered fractures of the top two vertebrae. The Doctors said it is one of the worst if not the most serious of all spinal injuries…in fact…" Ruth started crying.

"Come one Ruth try to hold it together."

"I'm sorry."

"Nothing to be sorry about. Please continue."

"Well, like I said, the doctors said it's kind of the worst… much like the injury to Christopher Reeves.

"You mean he might be paralyzed?"

"No, I mean, he is."

I couldn't believe what I was hearing. My brother Robert paralyzed. I couldn't fathom. It was surreal. It changed the whole dimension of our relationship, at least from my point of view. It wasn't that we were very close. We weren't. Honestly I never really thought of him much and saw him even less, probably three times in the last ten years.

I looked at my brother, as strange as it seemed, like he was a kid from another family, living in the neighborhood. I looked at myself as the odd man out, especially after my being drafted to Nam. My parents looked at my poor high school grades and being drafted and all as my fault. I was the "failure to thrive" in the family, and couldn't compare and was immediately relegated to "also ran", once my brother was born. From

the youngest of age, Robert was the bright spot in my parent's life. I was just there, always getting in the way, becoming that immoveable presence adding to the stale air in the room.

When I left for Nam, I never looked back. If there was anything good coming out of me being drafted, it was that it broke the chain of command in my life. I no longer had to look over my shoulder and see what my parents were saying behind my back, no longer decipher all the innuendo and disparaging facial contortions finding their way in my presence as if my folks were sucking on a rotten lemon, leaving the worst aftertaste, a son who was a dire disappointment.

It was hard for me to love my brother. He distracted from my life, never really adding much good, being he was the baseline of comparison for everything I did. He always won out. I always lost. He went to college at Northeastern and got his Veterinarian degree from Tufts, (Cum Laude, 1st in his class) and I went to Nam. He would be educated and be a pillar

149

of society, I would do my tour and come back home more estranged than when I left. I refused to acknowledge I had a brother or that he was a part of me. We were both as different as two could be and I concluded living my life as an only child was for me the best way. I set my sights as orphaned and never looked back.

"Where is he Ruth?"

"Spine Institute of New England, the University of Vermont."

"Is that the best hospital?"

"Honestly, Jack, it's where his doctor suggested he be taken. He's paralyzed from the neck down. He unfortunately is the most extreme of cases."

"Like pardon my interference but don't you think getting him down here somewhere in Boston might be the best thing for him? I mean it's kinda common knowledge Boston has some of the best hospitals in the world."

"Honestly, I'm still in shock Jack, this all happened just yesterday, I haven't looked into anything. I'm just damn overwhelmed and haven't even put much thought into it other than getting him situated and reaching out to our two kids and you, his immediate family.

"What can I do?"

"Jack. You need to come up here, he wants to see you."

"Well…I, but."

"Jack, I know you two have never been close but you're still brothers and damn it, it's the brotherly, if not the Christian thing to do."

"Got it Ruth, I damn well got it. I'll be packing my bags shortly. Being it's probably a five plus hour drive, I'll be there in the morning. When do visiting hours begin?"

"They begin when you get yourself here Jack. It's damn well this kind of situation."

"I'll meet you there at nine."

"I'll be there Jack, just call me when you get in."

The phone went dead.

I was literally shaking after getting off the phone. I thought I had better inform Gerti what was happening. I found her in the kitchen slicing a pineapple. After telling her what was transpiring, she turned to me with her carving knife in hand and said,

"I'm sorry to hear what that call was about but driving with you to South Burlington - never going to happen."

"Got it".

She turned her back to me and continued slicing. I walked to our bedroom to pack my overnight things. I reached for my cell phone.

"Rhino, what you doing?"

'The usual, nothing of importance."

"Want to take a ride?"

"A ride to where?"

"To South Burlington, Vermont."

"What the hell you going to do up there?"

"Family emergency, my brother Bobby, the vet, got hurt."

"Didn't know you had a brother, didn't know he served."

"Yeah, my only brother, he didn't, he's a vet like a veterinarian."

"You mean like an animal doctor?"

"No, like a doctor who takes care of animals."

"Got it."

"Got kicked in the back by a horse, been told by his wife that he's in bad shape."

"Well, screw it, why not, I have nothing else to do. Haven't been that way for years. When you leaving?"

"In a few hours. I'm thinking maybe we can stop to see Dirt on our way. He's been at the VA now for a couple of days. Probably shouldn't have let this much time go by before we made a visit. So my plan is to visit Dirt then drive up to Burlington tonight, get a hotel room...don't worry, I'll pay... then meet with my sister-in-law Ruth, in the morning."

"Let's forget Dirt ... we'll see him later."

"No way. We haven't seen him, we'll see him today."

"Like I said Jack, this guilt with Dirt, just hovers over you, but what the hell, sure, we can stop on the way."

I said "goodbye" to Gerti. She grunted in response. She probably thought I was making the whole episode up and thinking I was running around with some other woman.

I picked up Rhino and not an hour later we were at the Salem Veteran Affairs Medical Center. It was a stark place, uninviting. We registered at the desk and walked up to the second floor and found Dirt, locked down in a bed, tethered to an oxygen tank. He was semi-conscious and looked patsy white. It seemed by the outline of the "johnny" he was wearing that he had lost several pounds off his already too thin frame. Dirt was wasting away. We looked to find a nurse but there seemed to be only one on the floor and she said visiting hours were over and we would have to leave. We said we just wanted an update on Dirt's condition. She said that would have to wait till tomorrow. We left.

"I told you Dirt is a goner. Once they put him in the VA hospital, he's got a "snowball's chance in hell.""

"Christ, think positive will you."

"Unfortunately, whether Dirt makes it or not, is no skin off my back."

"You're just one compassionate "son of a bitch" aren't you?"

"Just telling it like it is man..."

The ride to Burlington was a nice respite from Lynn. It was great to see all the trees in full blossom. It was a perfect summer's day.

The traffic on Rt. 93 and 89 was a bit annoying and something I was not used to. Unfortunately, it was Friday and a lot of folks from Boston and surrounding areas were getting a start to their weekend as they fast-tracked (or attempted) to distance themselves from the congestion of the cities."

"We're getting nowhere fast!"

"Quit bitchin Rhino this bottleneck will break soon. We're almost to Rutland, Killington's to the right here…you know the ski resort?"

"Sure, Jack, like you, I'm really familiar with ski resorts. What do you think I'm some kind of "blue blood" rich kid or something?"

"Sorry, I brought it up."

It took us six and a half hours to get to South Burlington. The next stop on the highway after our exit was Canada. Rhino was edgy as hell, he was being a pain in the ass (I wish I never invited him). I was getting a bit pent up myself and my butt cheeks were falling asleep.

After arriving in South Burlington, I called my sister-in-law and informed her of our arrival. She said she would meet us at the McDonalds at 1125 Shelburne Rd. in thirty minutes and we could follow her to the hospital to see Bobby.

I almost couldn't recognize Ruth as she walked through the door. It's been years since I had seen her and she looked now well past her prime. Although I hate to admit it, she was in her early sixties, an older woman now and didn't wear it well. She looked beyond matronly, as if she just let herself go. Her hair was white as snow. She had gained at least thirty pounds, which she tried to cover with an over blouse that made her look like she was wearing a tent. I probably didn't look much better to her but in a different way. The years had worn on me as well. *But Thank God I had the Northshore Mall to walk and exercise,* I thought, *or I might just look as big as her.*

I guess I didn't change that much (even with my new bald scalp) because she walked right up to me. She probably didn't want to ask if I shaved my head voluntarily or if something else going on. She was cordial as I introduced Rhino. We spoke not twenty words as she led us through the exit door on our way to the hospital. It was obvious Bobby's injury was getting the best of her. After thinking I would see him shortly, it was now getting the best of me.

Thirty-two minutes later we were at the hospital making our way to

Bobby's room. We were informed that his two sons (I wouldn't know them if

I tripped over them) had left just fifteen to twenty minutes before. I was glad, I just didn't want to be put in another situation where I had to explain my estrangement from my brother and his family.

We arrived at the third floor. The elevator opened and I felt more pensive other than the little control over my emotions I thought I had. I looked at Rhino. He shrugged his shoulders, like questioning what the hell he was doing here. I picked up on it.

"Rhino, you don't have to come in, why don't you amuse yourself for an hour or so."

This didn't fall on deaf ears.

"No big deal. I can always find something to do for a few hours."

"Well keep your cell phone handy. I'll call you when I get through."

I now found myself with Ruth in front of Bobby's room. She looked at me.

"Look, Jack, I spent the whole day with him yesterday. I think whatever we had to say to each other we said. I think this should be only brother's time. It was really important you came up to see him. He was very adamant he needed to talk to you, sooner …not later."

"Got it, I replied."

"Call me if you need me. I'll be down the hall."

Ruth turned and walked away.

I stood paralyzed in my tracks, seemingly as steadfast as Bobby in his chair - but damn it, I knew better. I really didn't want to see him, to stare into his eyes. The truth was I was a lousy brother which could be added to the laundry list of all the other pathetic things Jack Krause was.

I walked in. Bobby was in his chair, recognizable, but pained and older.

He immediately looked up at me. His eyes were clear but sad.

"Older brother, you've lost your hair."

"Yep Bobby, voluntarily, shaved it off."

"We'll hair or no hair, I'm glad you came to see me."

"You're my brother."

"A bit estranged but yes I am."

"It may be stupid to ask but how you doing?"

"I'm doing like shit, and the more I hear of my circumstances, I'm pained to say this might be the best I may ever feel. I'm getting a really bad omen I might have really messed myself up here… and I must ready myself for the worse possible options."

"Fucking horse."

"Shit Jack, it ain't about the horse. The horse had nothing to do with it other than being a tool or vehicle to send a message we are all fragile to the bone, living on borrowed time, all of us."

"But the horse kicked you in the back. How could he not be blamed?"

"The horse didn't make the decision to do so. He instinctively did what he does, he reared his hind right leg and it was me, the supposedly smarter animal that made the decision to step behind him, only not far enough, It's not the horse to blame, believe me it's not the horse that is the culprit. But this is a good segue …pardon me if my voice fades or breaks or if I take a lot to pause…I am as I and everyone around me must now accept - a paraplegic."

"I'm so sorry!"

"I know you are Jack. I know you are sorry and that's exactly the reason I so urgently wanted to see you."

"The reason?"

"Yes, the reason. I always envisioned me having this discussion with you but the time never seemed appropriate, not that we ever saw much of each other, but for whatever reason, this seems to be the desired format and the appropriate time to get what I need off my chest that has been weighing me down for years."

"And that is?"

"Something that needs to be said before I die, that for me might be any day now. An importance that needs to be said before we both face our mortality."

"I knew the shit was going to hit the proverbial fan. I knew all too well Bobby was going to lay twenty years of toxic dog waste on me and right now he had the license to do so. I was preparing myself. I heard it all before, like it was training wheels for what now was going to be expelled. What the hell, my brother was now paralyzed, I can take the brunt of what he's going to shell out …. me, the lousy brother, son, husband and father and I was now preparing myself for the hundred miles of gutted bloody road (toxic dog-crap included) I was about to travel through.

"Well here goes… I want to tell you that I LOVE YOU."

I couldn't believe what I was hearing. It didn't quit resonate what I thought he was saying …did he really say...**HE LOVED ME**? The paralysis must have made him of deranged mind. There was no possible way on earth that words or letters in the Anglo Saxon language could be put together or support the emotion of what came out of Bobby's mouth.

He spoke again. I walked closer and bent over him to make sure there was no way I would misinterpret what he was about to say.

"I want you to know what a great brother you've been to me."

These words wrapped around me like a noose around my neck. Paralyzed or not, why was Bobby was doing this to me? I hadn't a clue but whatever his reason, he was playing right into the mixed (mostly painful) emotions I held for him.

"I also wanted to tell you what a great son you were."

Enough was enough … I couldn't take no more. I was becoming "postal".

I wanted to pull all the hair out of my head, that is if I had any. I wanted to scream at the top of my lungs that what Bobby was throwing at me was JUST INSANITY. I tried to compose myself. I tried to bring myself down.

"Bobby, no, NO … what the hell are you saying? You meant to say the opposite, I know you did. Your words just got tangled up in your paralysis and wheelchair, that's all. What are you shitting me? I was a lousy brother, son, husband and father. THAT IS WHAT I WAS …AND AM!"

Bobby, in a calming voice. "Not to me. To me you were all the things I said you were. I can't speak to you being a lousy husband and father but to the others I can."

I was perplexed as hell. I just didn't understand.

"Explain, Bobby, please explain. I haven't a clue where you are coming from, I have to admit what I just heard from you is one of the greatest surprises of my life. You will need to explain it to me. Please."

"I'll explain. You were a great brother to me. When we were kids, you ran interference for me all the time whether it was with bullies at school or yes, even mom and dad, you did the brunt of the heavy lifting. Don't you remember the fight you had with Billy Giles after he bloodied my face. He was the upperclassman who always beat on the younger kids, you beat the crap out of him Jack. He never bothered me again and no one else ever did, and it was all because of you."

I barely remembered. It wasn't chiseled into my memory bank.

"I also want to tell you what a great son you were. Our parents were really messed up. In fact at times, very irrational and unjust. There is no doubt about it and the angst and the pain they were feeling was always taken out on you. It was really damn unfair".

Bobby paused to take a deep breath … he was struggling.

"It was really damn unfair, there was no doubt and it was all laid on you. Unfortunately, you were their whipping boy, not that they physically abused you but emotionally, I know damn well they did."

Christ, I couldn't believe what I was hearing … I certainly wasn't prepared for this.

"And because they keyed on you, they gave me a pass. I was indeed their fair-haired kid and had license to do whatever I wanted and you had none. As I looked from the outside in, I could readily see if they did not have you to direct their anger, not that I ever figured why they had as much as they did, they would have taken it out on each other and probably me. I can look back now and see how one thing could lead to another and there could have been "blood and guts" spilt. There wasn't because of you Jack, really Jack, there wasn't because of you."

Damn it, if this wasn't the craziest insane thing I've ever heard.

"So there you have it Jack. I just wanted after all these years, just to thank you and this just seemed like the right time, being I don't know where my journey will take me from here. I guess in summary, I'm sorry it took so long… so many years … but it just seems the right time to tell you that I LOVE YOU and that I THANK YOU."

I was dumbfounded. I stood there unable to move. It was but minutes later Bobby fell asleep. He had expelled all he had.

I walked over and kissed him on his forehead, turned and walked out of his room. I dialed Rhino on my cell phone. He picked up.

"I'm finished. We're out of here."

"What, not even going to spend the night?"

"No, we're just out of here … in fact … *as quickly as we can leave*."

19

Brotherly Love

As bad as Rhino was traveling up to South Burlington, he was worse coming home.

"Well that was a damn waste of a day."

"Well, Rhino, I'm sorry you see it that way."

"Not to say, I'm sure it had some kind of benefit for you."

"It damn well did."

"Then gone as planned?"

"Not quite."

"Then it was like a waste of your time ….. right?"

I felt like kicking Rhino out of the car. The problem was I was speeding at ninety miles an hour deadheading home and throwing him out would be way too large a task. Rhino was Rhino, a big lumbering kiss ass guy, who with his uncalculated edge certainly could kick my ass and probably everybody else's I know.

"Like I said, the whole trip didn't go down like I expected."

"What did you expect?"

"Christ, Rhino, it's a thing between my brother and me. Like it's kinda personal."

"Then why the hell did you invite me along?", Rhino questioned slightly pissed.

"Because, you're my friend and I thought you would be great company."

Rhino got into one of his "prissy" fits and pushed his back to me as he stared out the window.

"Okay, okay Rhino, my brother told me he loved me."

Rhino turned back at me.

"Well that seems like it was the brotherly thing to do."

"It blindsided me."

"Hey, at least he told you he cared."

"That's it, I don't get it. We were never close. We barely saw each other throughout the years. I scarcely knew his family and he mine, we saw the world through separate eyes. A day ago he wasn't paralyzed. Today he is. A day ago he wouldn't have said that shit to me. Today he did. I mean, I just don't get it. He didn't have to say anything to me. He should have been doing what any other recently paralyzed person would - shaking his fist at the sky and screaming in a fit of rage... WHY THE HELL GOD DID YOU DO THIS TO ME?

"Christ, Jack, God didn't do that to him...the stupid horse did."

Rhino laid his head back and quickly fell asleep. I covered the last fifty-three miles accompanied by his snoring. I wish I never invited him.

We had just turned off Route 89 connecting to 93, heading to Boston, when the phone rang. I didn't recognize the number but answered it anyway.

"Is this Mr. Jackson Krause?"

"Who's asking?"

"This is Nurse Beth Rosen at the VA."

"Then yes it is Jackson Krause."

"Well, Mr. Krause, it says on Mr. Danny Kearney's chart you are his closest next to kin."

"Not quite, I'm not related to him at all. I don't know any of his relatives and if there are any, I wouldn't have a clue how to get hold of them."

"So what's your relation to Mr. Kearney?"

"I'm his friend. Probably, his closest, if not only."

"Well then, I guess you're the person I need to speak to."

This conversation was going to a place I didn't want. I jabbed Rhino in the back with my elbow to wake him. He jumped in response.

"What the hell", he cried out.

I tried to silence him.

"It's the VA."

The nurse continued.

"Well Mr. Krause, then it's my duty to inform you that Mr. Kearney passed away at 5:45 this afternoon."

I looked at my watch. It was 7:10. Shit, I thought, I was just some twenty some miles away.

"Are you kidding me…Dirt's dead?"

"Dirt?" questioned Nurse Rosen.

"Yes Dirt, …it's Mr. Kearney's nickname."

"Then, well unfortunately, yes …. "

There was a long pregnant pause. Rhino was staring at me and I stared back. He had a glazed look on his face. He never really liked Dirt. He never understood him but was shocked at his passing as well … not that it was unexpected.

"Well then", Nurse Rosen continued, "Well, feel free to come and identify the body. We will be available until 10:00 this evening and from 7:00 to 10.00 tomorrow. I want to extend my and the VA's condolences and we are here to accommodate you in any way possible."

Nurse Rosen hung up her phone. I looked at Rhino, he returned my stare.

"We'll that's it."

"The shits killed him. I told you they would."

"No Rhino, he killed himself ."

"Well, I damn well know the VA contributed … like I said, once you go in there, there is the slimmest of chances you'll ever get out alive."

"Damn it, DAMN IT, **DAMN IT!** I didn't know what else to say.

There was a heavy silence in the car. It held for the half an hour it took us to get to the VA. I was pissed Dirt was dead. I was angry he lead the life he did and the only person who seemed to care about him now was me. I didn't give Rhino any license, although I knew he was somewhat affected by Dirt's death although he kept telling me he didn't give a damn whether he lived or died. He cared. I knew he did but like every other emotional attachment in his life he poised it as inconsequential.

"Well the bastard's dead."

"Shit, it's like it's surreal."

"Well he screwed us over in life and now he's gonna do it from the grave."

"Don't get it?"

"The Nam thing."

"Yeah…how could I forget?"

"I can forget really easy because, like I said to you before there isn't a snowball in hell chance I would ever go back to Nam. And in regards to taking his ashes and throwing them in that contaminated cesspool, the Saigon River - it'll never happen, see Jack, I'm okay with all this … my commitment is to myself, not to him. He's got no talons into me. Dirt is dead, Dirt is dead, praise the Lord … DIRT IS DEAD.""Christ, Rhino, you're disappointing me."

"No Jack, the disappointment is nothing more than homegrown. Listen to your brother, he loves you … START LOVING YOURSELF … MAKE YOURSELF YOUR OWN CAUSE and start getting rid of all the garbage in your life. You're doing too much heavy lifting. Believe it or not, IT AIN'T ALL ABOUT YOU … YOU'RE NOT THE CENTER OF THE DAMN UNIVERSE … you're not the cause of all the disorder. You're not the sole reason people's lives are in the toilet."

As much as I tried to dismiss it, Rhino's words did not fall on deaf ears. Maybe he was right. Maybe the big lug had it correct this time after all his missed starts.

"So what's it going to be?"

"What's what going to be?"

"The Nam thing, what are you going to do?"

"Well as much as I want to honor Dirt's last wish I know one thing is certain, it damn well will ruin my marriage. Gerti will never be able to put that one behind her. She hardly speaks to me now."

"Well, then maybe it is a reason to go over there."

"I ain't there yet ... I just haven't crossed that bridge."

"So I take it that you see it as I do, BULLSHIT, just another way for Dirt to influence us from the grave."

"No Rhino, I see it as it now relates to my life ... unfortunately, it's an intrusion and creates the kind of exposure I'm just not ready for."

"Look Jack, we pushed the damn envelope ... you know how lucky we are here sitting in your Merc. You know how many poor pathetic souls were lost in Nam, fifty some odd thousand, and we ain't talking here of the injured of limb and brain. We ain't talking about them. At this late date, they have either healed, been committed or vanished. Look, the way I see it is we are indeed the lucky ones and who knows, now maybe Dirt is the luckiest of us three because he never answered to anyone ... not a damn soul ... never ever had to worry what exposure or legacy he would leave behind because frankly nobody gave a shit. So he didn't have to give one either and wake each morning with the same question in his head... *"WHERE DID I GO WRONG?"* And not giving one iota of thought in regards to how he was living his deranged life because he had no one in it except you and me. Other than us there was really no one who gave a damn, in fact, the truth is you can take my name off that list because really I didn't have much use for him. I guess it was really only you who gave a shit… you stupid pathetic creature … it was only you who cared."

I looked at Rhino in the strangest of ways. I felt my face contorting as if I put a whole lemon in my mouth, but I finally spit it out.

"Does that necessarily make me a bad person?"

"No Jackson … just one stupid ass one."

Over the last forty some years, there were times I despised Rhino. ***This was one of them.***

20

From Dirt to Dust

I was on my best behavior. If there was anything I didn't need it was a blowup in the house. Gerti was speaking to me now, not a dictionary of words but a few suggesting there might be an opening for some civil communication. This was good by me. It was about all I could ask after my meltdown.

"Have you seen my Army dress?"

"Your Army stuff is in the attic."

Wouldn't you believe it, 103 in the August heat …must be 120 degrees in the damn attic.

I made my way up there. It was as I expected, stifling. Puddles of sweat dripped off me. I rummaged through my Army locker as quick as I could and at the bottom, I found my dress uniform, a little tattered and worn but nothing that forebode it's future use. It was coming out of retirement as I was going in.

Rhino and I picked up Dirt's ashes at the O'Donnell Funeral home in Salem. They were in a plan vanilla box, nothing fancy a lot of money could buy. Rhino and I both chipped in $25.00 a piece to purchase it. I was surprised Rhino volunteered , I guess he was a bit sorry about the things he said earlier about Dirt. He didn't say it but his actions indicated he was.

The next day at 7:00 a.m. I met Rhino at the Dunkin in Salem. He was wearing his Army dress as well. I was struck by how handsome he looked. We were a stark contrast to one soldier sitting at the counter attired in his battle fatigues, a kid in his twenties who probably was asking himself, *"Who the hell were these old farts dressed in these relic uniforms?"* I would bet my last dollar he didn't have a clue as to what war we were involved with, it was just we were then and he was now.

It took twenty minutes for Rhino and me to drive to Castle Rock on Marblehead Neck. We were to meet the color guard at 8:45am and as usual, they were on time. I never knew an honor guard to be late, it was a reflection of their pedigree. Rhino, the guard carrying a flag and a bugle and I, made our way to the sharply sculptured rock formation that hovered over the seascape. We chose this location with a westerly breeze hopefully to carry Dirt's ashes out to sea.

I took the urn from the knapsack I was carrying. Rhino stood at attention beside me as well as the two guard approximately six steps to my left. I held out the urn extended in my two hands. I began the ceremony. Just as I took a deep breath, I heard footsteps approaching from the rear. I hesitated and then turned around to see a Marblehead Policeman, not twenty steps away. He walked up to me.

"Are you doing what I suspect you are?"

"Yes, officer, we're scattering a soldiers ashes as he requested."

"It may not be appropriate. What campaign?"

"Vietnam."

"My father's war".

"Yes, ours as well."

"Well, at this time of day, I see no harm … is this the whole funeral party?"

"Yes, officer, it is," I replied.

"Then would it be all right if I participate? Indeed it would be a honor.

Marblehead has lost a lot of American heroes buried here. Your "fallen" would be proud to be among brethren."

166

"Yes, Army Pvt. Kearney would definitely be honored." I replied.

"I'm standing ready."

All five of us stood up and I proceeded as follows…

"We are here to honor Pvt. Danny Kearney, nick name Dirt. He was a warrior. He fought for his country with honor. When his country asked him to go to war, he went but in no way should we discount his fight ended with his return home. He was a warrior to the very end, fighting that which only soldiers know to be true … that once a soldier always a soldier … that honor and duty has a price only the brave and the strong are willing to pay. As we scatter Pvt. Kearney's ashes into the wind to find peace in the expansive waters of the deep blue sea, we pray for him to be at peace and thank him for his service. In God's name, he hence goes back from whence he came, a better man. A soldier elite."

With my final words, I motioned the guard to unfurl and then to refold the flag. They presented it to me. I would find it a home. Done with great command and authority, the bugler then began to play "Taps". I found a single tear breaking from my eye and a solemn apology extending from my heart.

Sorry Dirt it was the best I could do, with any luck, your ashes will find their way to Vietnam … with any luck at all …with any damn luck at all.

Rhino said I did okay. That was the best I could get from him and I took it as a compliment. I needed one, Dirt dying was one thing, not fulfilling his last wish was another. It bothered me tremendously but Rhino was right on, there would be no path I could have survived a trip to Nam. I was already on the thinnest of ice with Gerti, and that would have cracked and opened it up. I would have been a drowning man with no one to throw me a safety net. I had to admit it. ***Rhino was right… most of the time.***

21

Bombs Bursting in Air

Dirt had now been dead for three weeks. It seemed like light years and then only moments. Having someone I knew for forty plus years who I made my personal crusade, dead, quickly brought me to pause. I was now seriously re-evaluating my life. I was convincing myself the past held too tight a rein on me and since the future couldn't be forecasted, it was now pertinent that I live in the present, experiencing each day to the fullest, dusting the residue from the empty shelves of my emotional closet that I constantly found myself trying to fill.

I now found Rhino not to be the constant companion of the past. He more than frequently declined my invitation to walk the mall, or seemed always to have an excuse for not accompanying me on my less than exciting ventures that filled my day. I think Rhino was re-evaluating his life as well. I knew he was deeply troubled by the estrangement he had with his kids. I think he was spending more of his time and energy trying to break through to them. His off-spring, as with most parents, was his real legacy and as he told me several times over the last couple of weeks with Dirt's death, with just five people present to say goodbye, the thought of his children's absence from his funeral was unacceptable. He needed to make amends quickly. What unnerved me was that I felt the same way. I wanted to be a different person now. Maybe it stemmed from seeing my brother and him having the "balls" to say what he did.

The absurdity of it all, *My Brother Loved Me*. I didn't know whether to feel exalted or so angry the rage might break through the very little restraints I had built up over the years.

At sixty-nine years I felt like a school kid who had fallen through the cracks. One of those "throwaways" who I knew in school (me among them) who just took up space. The student who the teacher immediately relegated as "failure to thrive" and hoped would not be a drag on the year. The one who buried himself in his books, not reading one word or page, not learning one blessed thing until the frustration and anger built and finally broke out and then "the kid" becomes crazed, disrupting the class every chance he got. He now is relegated as a behavior problem and is pushed through the system like toothpaste through a tube. I felt like the student who years later the teacher meets and is surprised he can actually function and is astounded at his achievement and the fact that he had not destroyed himself or anyone in his path, had not been incarcerated or committed.

"Wow, I can't believe how well you are doing!" the teacher exclaims.

"Not due to anything you've ever done," the student volunteers. This is how I felt. Now paralyzed in a wheelchair, *my brother now loves me*. I really didn't need to know my parents, now dead and gone, loved me as well. It may be way too late for that. My scars have healed years ago or I have pretended they did. Frankly after denying myself of family for decades, I really now didn't give a shit.

Gerti and I have been civil with each other over the last several weeks. I paid strict attention not to cross her path, which was very hard to do in our small home. It was obvious she was trying to avoid me as well. We exchanged a few words. They were trivial and hung in the air like a helium balloon but at least it was a beginning. We weren't in total "lockdown".

I kept scanning the house to see if there was any trail of her communicating with her lawyer. I didn't know whether she was proceeding with the divorce or not. She kept me on edge by keeping this close to her vest. I felt it hovering over me, weighing on my every word and action. I walked around on eggshells. Being home was torturous at best. I looked for every reason to leave. The house was Gerti's refuge, in it she found solace and a little piece of mind especially when I wasn't there, which was becoming the new normal.

It was the 4th of July. The long weekend was arduous. Against my better judgment I invited Gerti to the Lynn VFW to celebrate the birth of our nation. At first, it was a big fat "NO" but for some reason, not a few minutes later, she acquiesced. I was shell shocked, but I didn't question her. I responded "Great" and after quickly dressing, we headed out to the car. The VFW was just fifteen minutes away. If there was any holiday that brought out its best, it was the 4th. There had to be five hundred people combined in the hall and parking lot. Almost everyone was wearing patriotic colors, red, white and blue. Young children were given miniature American flags. There were five grill masters strategically placed around the perimeter of the property. Staples were being served, hamburgers, hotdogs, chowder, beans, corn on the cob and my favorite "steamers" and of course, ice cold beer for the adults and soda for the kids. The meal was topped off with five large vanilla cakes glazed with frosting depicting the American Flag. The board had hired a seven-place band that performed every patriot song, the majority I knew but several I never heard before. The sun shown brightly and the crowd was enjoying a perfect New England summer's day. I glanced at Gerti as she garnished a hamburger and hotdog, she too seemed to be having a good time, which I was immensely pleased about.

THEN THERE WAS THE ROCKETS RED GLARE AND THE BOMBS BURSTING IN AIR … Shit …SHIT …OH… **S-H-I-T!** I couldn't believe my eyes. I took several steps back and strategically placed myself behind this six foot, two hundred pound biker. After a second and third glance ... it damn well … was …Julie… and my worst nightmare coming true.

I couldn't reconcile it. Julie lived in Nashua. I knew she no longer worked at the VFW. In the former of our last two conversations, she revealed she had taken another job. So the question begged, why was she at the Lynn VFW? The only logical answer was that she was looking for me.

I quickly accessed with such a large crowd there probably was an outside chance Gerti and Julie would not meet but it wasn't guaranteed. I quickly thought about tracking down my wife and leaving as soon as possible. I needed to keep my wits about me and finally concluded that they had never met and that in itself could provide space between them. They might pass in the crowd not ever knowing they had Jackson Krause as a common thread. It was now up to me to try to avoid Julie by all means possible. I walked over to a table where volunteers were selling hats, tee-shirts and sweatshirts to benefit the "Wounded Warriors Project". I laid down thirty bucks and purchased all three. I put on the hat covering my bald head already blushed by the sun and pulled the tee-shirt over my Vietnam campaign tee-shirt I knew Julie had seen several times before. I threw the sweatshirt over my shoulders and tied its arms at my chest. I felt secure she wouldn't recognize me now as the majority of my face was covered by my B&L Aviator goggle sunglasses, which I knew she had never seen me wear being I just purchased them ten days before on Amazon.

I now felt somewhat secure I might survive this encounter if I spend just another fifteen or twenty minutes and then gather Gerti up and be gone. It was the best solution to what I surmised might be a very troublesome encounter, uncomfortable at best. I was about to turn again to survey the room when I felt a tap on my shoulder. I turned. It was Julie. How she could have recognized me and tracked me down in this large crowd, disguised as I was, was beyond me."

"Jack?"

"Julie!"

"I guess I assumed right."

"Meaning?"

"I don't know…for some reason I thought I would find you here."

"It is the fourth of July."

"Yes, and my assumption was right …."

"And that is?"

"That any man routinely sporting his campaign cap, would indeed would want to participate in the 4th in a very big way."

"Well … it seems you were right …the 4th is a big deal …. well, at least to me and a lot of people who love this country … like me."

"Like me as well Jack. I love this country too."

"Well it's not the country it used to be but by all accounts, it's still the best."

I quickly scanned the area, hoping Julie wouldn't see my eyes moving behind my B&L's. I didn't see Gerti anywhere, she was not in the parking lot like us so must be in the hall. I hoped she would stay there so I could conclude my bantering with Julie and detach from her as soon as possible. Julie seemed to have other motives beyond the small talk.

"You know, this was not a coincidence."

"I somehow gathered that. Lynn Mass is a far cry from Nashua."

"It definitely is, but not a waste of time if the trip is worthwhile."

"Meaning?"

"Meaning, I need to know where I stand. I need to know whether we have a relationship or not, and if we do, how do we proceed from here?"

I was getting really nervous. Although I did not spot Gerti in the crowd, I damn well knew she would soon track me down. It was just a matter of time and I felt the quicker I dispose of Julie the better. Our relationship was what it was, a quick fling and over. Foolish as I was to engage, I did lead her on that something larger was going to evolve, but honestly, I didn't have the heart or mind to leave Gerti. I wasn't to that point yet, although someday it just might be, with me leaving her or more likely, she dumping me.

I must admit that I felt like a real fool. What Julie saw in me, I hadn't a clue. I couldn't bullshit myself. I was now old, worn and a lot of water had dried up in my pool and I doubt I now had the resources to fill it again.

In my heart of hearts, I hated what I had become, but resolved I had to face up starting immediately with setting Julie straight, that from my vantage point, the relationship was over and she should get on with her life.

"Julie, I'm glad to see you especially now. What I have to tell you, I need to tell you face to face."

Julie grabbed my arm.

"I don't think I'm going to hear what I want to hear."

"Julie, it's over. Indeed it was a special moment, but honestly I can't go on from here."

"You seem so cavilier about it. You screwed me Jack … physically, mentally and emotionally."

"We screwed each other Julie, obviously there was a need and a reason we hooked up and like I said …"

"What! **Like you said what!?**"

Julie was raising her voice. People were beginning to stare. I was getting nervous. I recognized some faces in the crowd. I continued.

"Like I said … it was a moment in time. Both our lives might benefit from it."

This pissed Julie off even more.

"What are you my freaking shrink or something?" You're much too homegrown to be talking so philosophically. You're a blue collar guy … so cut the bullshit and tell me you love me and are leaving your wife … in a blue collar way."

This caught the attention of the crowd and I started pulling away from Julie but she grabbed on tighter to my shirt and would not let go. To my chagrin, I looked over her right shoulder and saw Gerti making her way toward us. I was in really deep shit, the quicksand kind, the more a person struggled, the deeper they were sucked in. I decided to let whatever was going to happen, play out, because there was no possible way I could win. My only intention now, was simply to survive.

Within mere seconds, Gerti was standing behind Julie, looking over her shoulder at me.

"You want to introduce me to your friend, Jack?"

Julie let go of my arm and made a quick turn. Gerti and Julie were face to face.

"My name's Julie."

"A friend of my Jack's?"

"More than a friend."

I couldn't believe where the conversation was at this point. They were all in. No poking around to stoke the fire, no subtle conversation to size each other up, no attack from the flank, but an all out woman assault on both sides.

"You mean trying to steal my husband?"

"I'm not stealing anybody, it's obvious by the looks of you why the boy is grazing out of the corral."

"You little bitch. I don't know what you have in play here but let me straighten your pretty ass out. Jack is an old worn vet and even if you're interested, you would be a fool to be. He got you buffaloed."

I can't believe what I'm hearing. They're talking about me as if I'm not here …like I'm deceased or something. Honestly, I didn't know what to do to defuse the situation so I figured, as I concluded before, to let whatever it was play out. Then Gerti took several steps back and quickly scans Julie as if her eyes had x-ray.

"Not bad, you damn well don't need to get your claws into my husband. There's more than one guy out there you can brain fuck."

I couldn't believe my ears. I couldn't remember the last time Gerti referred to me as her husband, Jack, Jackson, Asshole, Son of a Bitch, but never that. They continued...

"Look lady …"

"It ain't 'lady', it's Gerti. "

"And what the hell is a name like that? But in reflection you look like a Gerti, an old rusted name for an old rusted hag like you."

I could see it in my wife's eyes. The intensity was such a crowd was gathering, just staring, hoping potentially something noteworthy was going down and they wanted front row seats. Again, I tried to defuse the situation. I put out my arms expanding my entire wingspan to separate the women but they weren't about to be deterred. Whatever was building inside them must have been for months and it probably wasn't all about me (although I damn well know I played an important part).

Gerti now came at Julie, I had to step between them again. I grabbed both by the arm and pulled them ten yards from where we were standing. It was like dragging raging bulls. I tugged as hard as I could but their resistance was steadfast. Now farther from the crowd they started again.

"You bitch, don't defile my name…it may be an old-fashioned one but I still perceive myself as an old-fashioned girl with a set of morals of which I'm proud. I make it a habit, unlike you, not to sleep around with other people's husbands. I take a lot of pride not being a whore."

"You calling me a whore, you ugly bitch?"

Julie took a swing at Gerti. To my amazement my wife ducked and swung back with a big lunging punch hitting Julie right on the side of her head. She fell to the ground with a thump. I was shocked. I had never seen Gerti act this way. It was a part of her I never knew existed. The crowd again was walking towards us and gathering around. Julie rose to her knees and pounced toward Gerti. I grabbed her around the waist. It was a distinct disadvantage for Julie because Gerti wailed her again, hitting her two more times. Suddenly I heard a lot of noise emoting from the crowd. Before I knew it I had my hands cuffed behind my back and two other Lynn Police officers holding both Gerti and Julie at the waist as each continued to attack each other. Neither of the women would listen to the cops as they tried to settle them down and eventually were cuffed as well. They kept yelling at each other.

"You can keep your cheating husband, overall he's nothing but a lying asshole."

"You're damn right ... *but he's my lying asshole.*"

I couldn't believe Gerti was defending me. She called me her "lying asshole". And I know as funny as it seems, they were the most affectionate words she had spoken of me the last several years, perhaps over the last several decades.

The three of us were put in a police cruiser and taken to the Lynn Municipal Jail. We were booked for disturbing the peace and disorderly conduct. In three hours Gerti and I both posted a fifty dollar bail and were back on the streets. I hadn't a clue what Julie did to capture her release and frankly at the moment didn't care.

Gerti didn't say a thing to me for the first forty minutes, then she spit out...

"You're a stupid shithead, Jackson Krauss."

I didn't answer but thought, **Yes, but I'm your stupid shithead, Gerti Krause.**

22

God Bless America

Three days later the incident was never mentioned. I knew there would be a day of reckoning but by some kind of silent agreement, it would be delayed somewhere in the future. It was okay by me. I wasn't quite over it and I knew Gerti would never be. I can't blame her for being angry, what person wouldn't, being put in such a compromising position? I really admired her fight and the way she stood up to Julie, and for me, if indeed calling me *Her Asshole* was really her standing up. After the last several months, I welcomed any small victories in my life and I considered Gerti not cutting me off at the knees, was one, knowing my indiscretions were considerably more than minor. Just why she didn't take me to the wall with them, I didn't know, perhaps, she didn't as well?

Still there was a calm in the house. As the saying goes "a calm before the storm." It was a droning stifling silence that drove my desperation to leave it behind. I felt I could capture better air outside and my lungs sought to suck as much in as possible. I found myself always wanting to leave the house and welcomed each opportunity to get into my Merc and set about, either to the mall to walk my miles or Lynn Shore Drive, the other of my preferred people watching places. I would park on the opposite side of the walkway and observe the people silhouetted by the flowing azure sea. On a stormy day, nature held my attention as it disrupted the walkway with waves so powerful and large they spilled over its railings and drove those curious onlookers who wandered too close, running for shelter.

I left the house around eight-thirty a.m. Gerti usually woke early but she was sleeping late this morning allowing me to get out of the house before she pigeonholed me with her daily chore list. I grabbed the morning paper, got into my Merc and immediately headed for Dunkin on the Lynnway. As usual it was slammed with the early morning construction workers, landscapers and Boston commuters getting the first of their caffeine fixes for the day.

I ordered a large hot black coffee and took several sips as I walked back to my car. I sat in my Merc and determined it was just too pretty a day to visit the mall. Humidity or no, I decided to drive to Lynn Shore Drive. It was a great "fly on the wall" day where I could sit in my car undetected hovering over the activity on the walkway and lawns. I had no pressing schedule, just the luxury of uninterrupted time. A lot of people were already out. I wondered who they were and how a lot of them could be here at 8:45 on a Tuesday morning. I understood the moms with the baby carriages and toddlers trying to entertain the kids as they participated in their daily exercise regiments. I personally understood the retired old farts aerobicizing, and walking back and forth on the walkway. What I didn't understand was all the people of working age sauntering about as if lost in a maze of confusion. I didn't understand the luxury of them doing this. Why weren't they working, doing what was age appropriate, like building a resume to participate in America's great (well, at least once great) economic machine? I just didn't get it, probably because these were just different times, and whatever was happening was just passing me by. I quickly determined this. Why should I care, even with all my life's challenges (even Nam) I think I've lived in the best of times. The best America had to offer was part of my life-scape and me not taking full advantage of it was nobody's fault but my own.

Yes, if there were any doors that did not open for me, it was me who kept them closed. I finally understood and was coming to terms with it and if I had to categorize myself, it would be I was just one "BIG SCREW-UP. Yes I was and there was no denying. I wasn't about to lie to myself anymore. This is what happens when the pages turn too quickly and a people find themselves in the last chapter of their book. They strive to be honest because it always comes down to this… the last person they try to bullshit is themselves. I'm sixty-nine years old and decided I wasn't going to lie to myself anymore. I hope the young people walking the Lynnway (when they sure as hell should be doing something else) weren't as well.

I picked up the Boston Globe and turned to the sports section. The Sox lost to the Mariners 11-2, humiliating. I threw the paper back on the passenger seat. The Sox losing again in another disgraceful defeat was now getting intolerable. WHO THE HELL CARED ANYMORE? I wasn't about to let it ruin my day. I scanned the walkway. It seemed to be getting more crowded. I guess people just had to get out since they were locked up the previous day because of a chilling Nor'easter. Living in New England is only for the brave at heart.

I closed my eyes for a second and before I knew it woke fifteen minutes later. I took off my B&L Ray-Bans and rubbed the crust from my lids. I focused on the walkway and I couldn't believe who I was seeing not fifty yards away. It was Peter Strong briskly walking down the concrete path heading toward me. I was amazed at how quickly he moved, having an artificial leg didn't seem to hamper him. He was in abeyance with the other brisk walkers. My eyes moved to the opposite side of the walkway. There seemed to be a group of guys walking down the path from the north. As they moved closer to me, I recognized them as the ones from the diner a few weeks earlier. It might have been the same guys who were pushing through the crowd a month before but I wasn't sure. They were maneuvering around the majority of the walkers and joggers who were in their path. Peter Strong and they were heading toward each other. As they saw the other, both picked up speed and with seconds banged into each other with Peter being absorbed into the mass of the five other men. Peter bounced from one body to another as if he were a ball ricocheting off a wall. He pushed away but as soon as he did he was engaged by another one of the five who pushed him back into the crowd. I wasn't sure what the hell was going on but one thing was obvious, Peter was in some kind of trouble with these punks and five against one (amputee leg not withstanding) he was outmatched. This was just not the way it was supposed to be. Peter Strong was an American veteran, a damn wounded warrior, the arrogant bastard as I knew him to be or not, he was a true American hero. I still didn't know what was going down but knew damn well Strong was about to take a beating. He was an American vet brethren and it wouldn't happen on my watch, no way.

I got out of my car and quickly ran to its trunk. I grabbed the first golf club from my barely used antique set that never moved the last several years. I slammed the truck shut and grabbing the club mid-shaft, ran across the street toward Peter Strong and the mayhem. Not ten yards away, I engaged the club tightening my grip and raising it over my head and screamed.

"Leave him alone."

All six guys including Peter Strong stopped in their tracks. I screamed out again.

"Let that fucking guy be."

I swung the club separating the group.

One of the six screamed out, "What the hell are you doing old man?"

"Kick your ass … that's what I'm doing."

The next thing I knew I was on the ground. As I rolled over and looked up I saw Peter Strong shaking his head.

"What the fuck are you doing? Jack, isn't it?

I didn't know what to make of this.

"Ya, Jack Krause, you remember me, from the mall."

"Remember you, how could I ever forget you? Now this?"

Another one of the six spoke.

"Damn it old man, you almost knocked my head off with that thing, what the hell is with you?"

"I thought you guys were beating up Peter Strong."

All six of the guys broke out laughing."

Another chimed in.

"Beat him up, Christ, he's one of us."

"What do you mean one of yours?"

"We're all Iraqi vets, every one of us, even (pointing to Peter) this knucklehead here."

"But you were beating him up."

"Beating him up? Shit we were only playing, screwing around as it were."

Peter spoke.

"Shit old man, I knew you were messed up in your head but this stunt was just over the top stupid."

Peter Strong extended his hand. I grabbed a hold of it and he lifted me from the ground.

"You okay?"

"Yeah, yeah, a damn bit embarrassed, like that hasn't happened before but yeah, I got all my parts. I'm damn happy one of you didn't hit me with my own club."

"Maybe if one of us did we could have knocked some freaking sense into you."

I shook myself off. One of the guys handed me my club.

"What's your last name again?"

"Krause."

"Okay Jack Krause, let me introduce you to my guys … Angel, Trace, Benny, Brick, and Guy and me, guess you and me don't need any introduction."

"No, I guess, we're getting to know each other really well now."

"Ya, Jack, but this is really funny or rather a bit delusional I'd say, that you thought my guys were going to do me some harm."

"Well, shit Peter, I didn't know who these guys were and the vantage point I had absolutely shown these guys were roughing you up."

"Well, it damn might have looked that way but it isn't the case. In fact these guys are all a part of my vets group. Each one of us is suffering from some amount of PTSD. We're all a bit screwed up in one way or another. Yeah, Benny and I are the only ones here that have lost limbs but the rest have lost something just as important. We have all lost a part of ourselves in the war and like all vets in any theatre, are trying to put the pieces of our lives together again. Believe me Jack Krause, we all are doing the best we can to make sense of it all. Hey, enough of this shit. We're gonna take a walk down to where the beach ends in Nahant. You want to join us?"

I was deeply embarrassed. I accepted Strong's invitation. I must have looked like a raging idiot, running across Lynn Shore Drive carrying a golf club like the grim reaper with his scythe. I'm lucky these guys didn't kill me or didn't want to press charges of assault and battery. After hearing I was a Vietnam vet and really still messed up as well, all five really opened up to me.

I learned that Angel did one tour of Iraq and another in Afghanistan and when he returned home, his wife served him divorce papers. He was enraged. She left with their two kids and filed a restraining order against him. Wrestling with this and unable to find a job, he found himself falling deeper and deeper into depression.

The big burly and older guy, nicknamed Brick (who reminded me very much of my friend Rhino) was involved in one of the earliest, largest and bloodiest battles of Desert Storm, which was a failed attempt to drive the Taliban from their mountain foothold. He told me he hadn't had a decent night's sleep in fourteen years, and now found himself more dysfunctional each day but is committed to fight through it.

Another vet, Benny, lost an arm when his HUMVEE took on a roadside bomb. He thought he was dead and says his brain has been scrambled eggs ever since. He's constantly nauseous and suffers from severe motion sickness and migraines. He broke off his engagement with his fiancée when he returned because he couldn't deal with himself and didn't have the heart to pull the girl into the "shit storm" of the life he saw coming his way.

Trace didn't volunteer anything to the conversation and didn't seem to be interested in asking anything of me. Peter volunteered that upon his return from Iraq, he tattooed his entire body from his neck down. It was like a roadmap of his assignments and "kills". Peter said there was nothing they could do to stop him. Every time he appeared to join the group or have a psych session, he would have another tat, eventually putting a four-inch spread eagle on his forehead. When Peter was speaking, Trace just cast a sinister smirk.

Guy had a lot to say, it flowed from him in uninterrupted expulsion. He felt the US had really let down its veterans. He said he was a fool for volunteering for service, that he was drawn into it like a lot of young men whose understanding was founded on Hollywood glamour and heroics and a slew of video games creating an adrenaline rush that couldn't be abated in civilian life. "How wrong was I?", he constantly repeated. "WRONG" to think that I would return unscathed, as the innocent, uninformed, idyllic eighteen year old I was. "WRONG", to think that death, destruction and mayhem would have no immediate and long term effect. "WRONG", I didn't realize everything I left before Iraq would not be the same when I returned, that I would look at those I loved with the same innocent eye and they the same at me. "WRONG", that the country I fought for wouldn't throw the best at us vets as we returned to its shores. "WRONG" to think there would be a job waiting for me upon my return and a grateful employer who would pave the way to help me get my financial house in order and not have to declare bankruptcy as I did." In summary he said, "Everything about this is "WRONG". My expectations were "WRONG". My deployment was "WRONG." My return was "WRONG" and the scariest thing about it is now I can't see how anything in my life could ever be "RIGHT" again. The most frightening thing that keeps me up at night and wakes me as if kissed by the demon seed itself as I open my crusted lids, usually soaked in sweat, is realizing that this is about as good as it will ever get. Even more depressing is that all this shit might circle back on me and bite me on my ass and I will never leave it behind. I damn well have a "RIGHT" to be pissed and this might be the only "RIGHT" left in my life because all I can see as I stare out into the landscape of my life is "WRONG"... "WRONG"... WRONG", a world of "WRONGS" and not a Goddamn "RIGHT" in my future. This is just no damn way to live."

Angel jumped into the conversation again, "Ya, it all sucks but you know what is the absolute worst thing about who I am and who the rest of you might be as well, other than America's Best and Brightest, the consummate warriors we are … do you know… do you know what the worse thing is?" In a consensus, three of the guys shock their heads to indicate "NO" and the others including Peter Strong mouthed the big "N-O-O-O-O". "Well I'll tell you what it is…I can't get it up anymore, haven't been able for years. My hard-on is dead on the vein. It has no life in it. It doesn't get excited any more. I can't get a rise. I sleep with women, my opportunities have been beyond description and all I do is sleep and some of them are so sexy and voluptuous that only a dead man couldn't get a rise and I keep thinking am I dead? … I pinch myself …. I pinch my pecker … I try to think of the most pornographic shit in my head … and then I say to myself, "What the fuck", I'm lying next to one of the most beautiful women I have ever seen with a body like a New England Patriots' cheerleader, ready to screw my brains out because maybe she never did a vet before or maybe it was her way of thanking me for my service…who knows. Maybe she was just horny as hell and luck bestowed her as a gift to me, and nothing, just a really disappointed woman and an even more disappointed me because the world is full of pricks and there is just no way in her life, looking like she does, that there won't be hundreds to choose from, but for me, mine is the only prick I have."

"Been there." Guy chimed in."

"Working through that", Brick replied.

I spent an hour and half with Peter Strong and his vet group on the Lynnway before they went to their support meeting at the VA. I couldn't believe how the time passed and how they engaged me and were so candid about what happened and is happening to them. I guess it was just part of the therapy and I was acting as a surrogate psychiatrist rather than being on the other side lying on the couch.

Upon our return, Peter walked me to my car.

"You get it now, Jack Krause?"

"Get what?"

'That all the shit's the same. It might be shoveled out differently at times, in fact all the time, it seemed that we all received different doses, but the end result is the same, the service left us all as damaged goods."

"So, that's how you see you and your guys?"

"Me and my guys and you, you Vietnam vets …Korea … any and all vets in any of the damn wars. We're all collateral damage and inconsequential in the scheme of things … that is if …", Peter paused.

"Is if what?"

"That is if, only we allow ourselves to be."

"Meaning?"

"Meaning, I don't know what you see in us or rather me, that you don't like but I get a feeling you really don't like me.

It was obvious from our first meeting. Your disdain stood out like a festering boil at the end of your nose. You disliked me and I don't even have an inkling or a clue why?"

Shit, I didn't want to go there. I didn't want to admit I was besieged by jealousy I just couldn't get over. I just recently was coming to grips with the feelings I had. Peter Strong was right, I didn't like him from the moment I met him and honestly I really don't like him any better now. *He just wore his service malady too damn well.* Now how the hell could I say to Peter Strong - *you look and act too good to be a vet amputee.* How can I tell Peter Strong that I'm uneasy being around him because he doesn't look like a victim or act like one? How can I tell Peter Strong that all the stuff I have in my head, all my Vietnam shit and the garbage dump full of crap that I could never seem to come to terms with, that he doesn't seem to carry its weight? How can I tell Peter Strong that I saw his family and seeing him and how they interacted showed me there was a love shared - an elusive one I would never experience because I was never open to it and never could nor would, express my feelings and emotions? How can I tell Peter Strong he was the mirror on the wall reflecting back to me the man I should have been but one I could no longer be because there was just too much water over my dam? I said to myself, *DAMN IT Jackson Krause, DAMN IT, SUCK IT UP!*

"You're right I have to admit, I didn't like you and honestly don't know whether I like you any better now."

"That's obvious, I guess it begs the question, why?"

"You just wear everything too well."

"You lost me here."

"Meaning, I don't see the pain, the hate, the resentment that all of us carry."

"All of us, who?"

"Us vets, all of us."

"I don't get it, we don't all come from the same cookie cutter mold. We experience and react to things differently.

That's what makes us who we are, civilians or vets. Again, believe it or not, we have a choice, we can choose to be victims all our lives or step out boldly and capture that incredible life we have left. That as we grow older asks us to purge the shit in our lives …and get honest and real … because Jack Krause, we aren't dead yet, there is still a lot of life to come. The question is, are we going to build from it, or sabotage the essence of who we are as we deal with all of it, which we now have little or no control over?"

Christ, I hated this guy.

"I understand, but you don't seem to be affected as the others, or as me, even with your loss of a leg. I can't say that I'm not envious."

"Envious of me? You must be delusional, I've struggled immensely with my loss. It is my leg and if you don't think there is a mourning process involved than respectfully, you're an idiot. I didn't wake one day with one of my limbs blown off and settle into it. I didn't wake without the mental torment that I had been violated, that a part of me had been stolen and it was far more than a leg. I am referring to the core of who and what I am and how I had to reinvent myself, and the struggle for me now is to continue to do it every day."

I knew what Peter was saying. He was damn right, who was I to argue with him. His journey is his journey and mine is mine.

"Honestly", Peter continued, "You're too damn self-absorbed. You got to get around the burden you carry. Get the hell over it, like I know it's not easy and I'll give that to you, but my problem Jack Krause is I don't think you're as screwed up as you think and honestly, that you use your damn service in Nam as a crutch … and I doubt very much you've really tried to do the best you can to get over it."

This is where the proverbial rubber met the road. Peter just sucked the air out of our relationship. I was listening and taking counsel and now he turned me off. Who the hell was he to tell me how I felt? Who was he to tell me my journey was not deliberate and honest in dealing with my issues? Yes, I probably caved into a mediocre life and lack luster happiness after Nam but expected nothing more, it was how I felt before I was drafted and how I felt after and honestly how I felt now. I didn't need no Peter Strong to to tell me this, screw it. This is something I already knew...something I had to deal with..it was *ALL ABOUT ME*.

"Thanks for your insight Peter ...you've really enlightened me."

I turned and walked away.

"Oh, one more thing Krause."

I stopped in my tracks and again turned facing Strong.

"And what is that?"

"It's all about America ya know."

"Meaning?"

"Meaning, we had the privilege and honor to fight for the greatest country in the civilized world. We were the chosen ones, now I know some of us went involuntarily, but we served and did it with honor and that is something never to be taken away from us. We fought for America, we were and are American Warriors. In that we should all not be prouder. GOD BLESS, AMERICA, Jack Krause."

"Yeah, GOD BLESS AMERICA, Peter Strong."

I turned from him again and walked the fifteen feet to my car. *I gave him the "middle finger" in my head.*

23

Hendrix

I barely could hold my phone. The purpose of the call was so surreal I hesitated and took a step back as I eyeballed my cell again. Calling Rhino, why? This has to be a dream, no a nightmare. His phone rang again. He answered it.

"Jack, how are you doing?"

How am I doing? I hadn't a clue. I felt out of myself, like a fragment of a puzzle that I grudgingly was trying to put together but could never now be completed.

"Hendrix is dead!"

"Your son?"

"YES MY BOY."

"My god, you haven't heard from him for over twenty years and now you learn he is dead…what happened?"

"I haven't received all the details yet but from what I did, it sounds like, as you know, he skipped bond to travel the world, to get out from under his life in the States and believe it or not, eventually found himself on the shores of Southeast Asia. You won't believe this Rhino but what I understand is he got himself all toked up with a couple of Vietnamese kids and rolled off a cliff on the Ho Chi Minh highway right before it connects with the Cao Bang Province."

"You're shitting me?"

"I wish to God I were, but this is as real as it gets. My son is dead. At least Gerti and I now know and not have to wonder anymore... and although, it may be the last thing I want to do in the world, I have to travel to Nam to identify the body and bring Hendrix's remains back home."

"You're shitting me?"

"No again, I'm beyond shitting anyone at this point and way beyond fooling myself. This is about as real as it gets... it's maybe the worst thing that could have happened to Gerti and me."

"And, yes, how is Gerti?"

"She's beside herself, it was her child, spit out of her womb. The loss of a child, no matter what the relationship, is absolutely the worst thing that can happen to a parent .... especially a mother."

"When are you going?"

"As soon as I can but before I buy my tickets, there's a hell of a lot of red type and paperwork I have to get and fill out. What makes this really complicated is that there is a criminal investigation involved because although they said the three in the car were suspected of being high, they also found more the a half pound of heroin. So you see Rhino, not only did Hendrix die all jacked up, he was also possibly trafficking the shit. I got really pissed off when I heard but with his history and all, I wouldn't put it pass him. Gerti and I lost this kid years ago and in my heart of hearts, he was always a heroin addict and there's no reason we have to deny it anymore."

"Whoa, this whole thing sucks."

"It more than sucks and it gets more complicated. I suggested to Gerti I fly over quickly, identify the body and have it cremated and bring the ashes back home with me. No damn way in hell, none, no way Gerti would permit it. She wants the body shipped back here and me to fly over there to accompany it so it doesn't get lost or damaged. Then she wants a wake, a Mass and a Christian burial. I tried to talk sense into her being he no way in hell led close to a Christian life, it's nothing but plain foolishness to me. But she's his mother and there's no convincing her."

"Jackson, I'm really sorry life is laying all this shit on you."

"It gets worse. Usually, the U.S. Consulate told me, it takes about seven days before a body can be shipped from Vietnam back to the States but that is under normal circumstances. Since this now is a criminal case, it may take up to ten, possibly twelve. And what sucks even more, not that it's anything other than what it is, but this is gonna take a bite out of me. It's gonna cost me about $6,000 for two tickets on the cheapest twenty-two hour flight and the cost of all the paperwork, fees, bullshit and flying the body back home with me will be in excess of $10,000, and that doesn't include the wake and ceremony when we get him back here."

"Damn it Jack, it's only money."

"Yeah, well, you're right and I'm probably sounding like a charlatan but over the last couple of years I've really been trying to get my life in order and "shore up" the loose ends, coming to terms in regards to who and what I am and now the worse possible thing in the world just knocked my world off kilter. Knocked me on my ass emotionally and financially. It just doesn't seem right. Life should be a hell of a lot easier than this."

"Hey, Jack, hey … hope I don't sound rude, but this ain't about you.

It's about your son Hendrix. He's dead, laying in some shit hole funeral home in Nam and you gotta get him back home."

Rhino was right. I had a rubber band wrapped too tight around my emotions. I had better calm myself down, take a long deep breath and get my priorities straight. There was a long pause in the conversation and I could hear Rhino pensively breathing heavy on the other end of the phone. I started to compose myself.

"Rhino, you still there … you still there?"

"Ya Jack, I haven't gone anywhere. I'm still here."

"Well like I said, or rather, was going to say, the authorities took the body to the Franco-Vietnamese Hospital in Ho Chi Minh City. I was told that Immigration was notified and it was demanding a diplomatic note detailing our request for the disposition of the remains ... in this case shipping the body. The authorities also wanted to do an autopsy because the death was of a suspicious nature and is required for all foreigners who die in Vietnam. I'm in the process of getting it waived which is the right of our family and also obtaining a Quarantine Permit for exportation of the corpse. Then I will need: a draft of the death permit produced by the Service of Health, a Customs permit produced by the Custom's office and a Laissez-Passer for Human Remains produced by the External Relations Office."

"Jesus, Jack, stop...STOP! This is way too much detail for me. What it sounds like is you're reading this off a piece of paper."

"I am Rhino, they're notes on a pad detailing the things I have done or are needed for me to do. And after they're all completed, I'll pick up our tickets."

"Our tickets", what do you mean ... OUR TICKETS?"

"Ya Rhino, our tickets ...you're going to Nam with me."

"Whoa Jack ... slow it down ... you're assuming I am traveling back to Vietnam with you?"

"Yes, I never thought you wouldn't."

"Damn it Jack, for one thing, you never asked and if you did, which I'm assuming by this conversation that you might now be - the answer is "NO", a big large chocolate with a cherry on top, NO! Once again ... NO DAMN WAY!"

"Rhino, you have to come with me."

"Jack, I don't have to do anything. I told you once, if not a thousand times, I would never return to Vietnam. The worst experiences of my life happened there and I have spent the last forty some years trying to forget what it did to me and what the hell I did to others. I told you, as plain as black and white. I thought you finally got it through you thick concrete block of a head that Vietnam is off my radar. It is and will be forever"

I couldn't believe what I was hearing. Rhino was my best friend after Dirt's death …. my only. I couldn't believe what he was laying on me.

"Rhino, I'll just pretend that I didn't hear what you just said to me."

"Jack, I couldn't make it any more clear. I'm not going, no way in hell. I refused to take Dirt's ashes back and throw them in the Saigon River and unfortunately for you I won't return to escort you and your kid back to the States."

"Rhino, but you're my friend and under crisis, this is what friends do."

"Jack, this may not be the conversation for it but what the hell, if this is going to be "A Come to Jesus" meeting, then let it be. You're not the only soul in the world that has felt the wrath of the world as it implodes on us. I mean I'm terribly sorry about you losing your boy. I have felt the anguish you have felt over the years dealing with your kid and have seen how it has eaten away at you, but I'm no stranger to my own kind as well and have to start cleaning my house and getting it in order. For as much as the hardships you are going through, I have a closet full of my own."

"Damn it, Rhino, I haven't a clue what the hell you're saying to me."

"Let me make it clearer, I'm no damn wordsmith, so I'll try to communicate this the best I can."

"I've been an asshole over the years. I've been more attentive to you and Dirt than to my own family. I have spent more time with you guys than I have with my own kids. I love you Jack but I never ever liked Dirt. I got to sift through my own shit. I got to find out who the hell I really am and what I'm hiding from. I've let down my two ex-wives and my kids think I'm a stupid asshole and they have every right. As dead

as your son now is to you …. I'm as much to my kids ….. even
though I'm lucky enough that I haven't drawn my last breath
yet. I need to be a father again. I need to reconcile with my
ex-wives, at least get to the point where we can communicate,
where they don't think of me as the piece of shit I've now
become. Christ, they must have seen something in me, they
married me for Christ's sake."

"Rhino, I don't mean to cut you off at the knees, but where
are you going with this?"

"It's plain and simple Jackson. I'm not going back to
Vietnam. I'm not going within a thousand miles of that place.
I'm staying right here where I belong…right here in the good
old U.S. of A. Because now, talking to you, it's a clear choice for
me. If it's Nam or the States, it's the States. If it's between you,
all the other Vietnam residue of my life and purging myself of
all this crap so I can have a meaningful relationship with my
kids, hands down… IT'S ME AND MY KIDS. If it's between
the little happiness I know can be gathered from the scrapings
of my life and for a couple nights of restful sleep…I'm damn
well all in.It's about time I grew out of my self-pity. As hard
as it is to do, I know it must be done. I feel like Prometheus
rolling my rock up the hill and in the streaming inner canal
where the angry waters of my blood line rage, I WANT TO
BE FREE …I WANT TO BE FREE … I WANT TO FREE
OF ALL THE CRAP IN MY LIFE and like it or not, you and
Dirt were and are part of it all. Don't take any of this personal
Jackson. It has nothing to do with you although I know you
feel you played a big part, but mark my words, it's all about me.
You and Dirt were just the life raft in the tumultuous break
waters of my life because I was and am a drowning man and
neither of you could see it because you were drowning too. It's
just time to swim to the safety of the shore."

Holy shit, I couldn't believe what I was hearing. Rhino was
expelling every little crap shit piece of his obviously demented
life on me. I really didn't know he felt this way … really never

knew he was as screwed up as he was but I will never forgive him for dumping this shit wagon on me at the worst time of my life. He didn't need to do this. He especially didn't need to do it now … not now… someday it might have been appropriate but not the fuck now.

"Are you kidding me Rhino? Is that how you really feel?"

"Yes, Jackson, that really is how I REALLY FEEL. But as far as your kid goes, I couldn't feel worse … no parent deserves that."

"Really Rhino…really?"

"Yes Jack, REALLY!"

I hung up the phone.

24

All Jack'd Up

I woke up at 4:30 a.m. I wasn't feeling well. I probably slept for about an hour, with all the turmoil in my head, I was lucky to get that. At least Gerti wasn't here. She was asleep downstairs in the little bedroom. I bet she got as much sleep as I did.

It was Tuesday, August 18th. It was forecasted to be 97 degrees in Boston and I was on my way to Vietnam to pick up my son's casket and escort it home. I was leaving on American Airline's flight 8475 with a direct to Toyko Narita. Then it would be a layover of nine hours and twenty minutes before picking up a Vietnam Airlines flight to Ho Chi Minh City. It would be a ten day journey since a lot of paperwork and procedures were to be done during the last couple of days, but I tried to cut off every day I could from that trip because I knew I would be in no mood for sightseeing.

Unfortunately, I waited too long to book the flight, hoping that Rhino might change his mind. He didn't. I didn't hear a word from him and probably the two of us were better off not ever seeing each other again, as we were both drowning men and going down together. Maybe if we didn't use each other as a life raft and unweighted each other allowing us, as he put it, "to swim to shore", I was ready, the weight of him was way too heavy, even though I was unaware of it for years.

As usual the airlines screwed me. My fourteen hundred dollar ticket now turned into $2565 fare, *GOT YA DUMB SHIT*, I could hear it now resonating through AA headquarters. They got me by the balls and someday, somehow they're gonna get theirs, and like a wise man once said, "Sooner or later we know it happens, everybody gets theirs." But wouldn't you like to be around to see it? I sure as hell would.

I walked to the john, I was getting used to my bald crown. I didn't look like a skin-head anymore, I looked more like a pumpkin. I was happy as hell about that. I did look like who I was, an overweight sixty-nine year old, soon to be seventy with a crusted, furrowed wrinkled face and now a cratered age-spotted bald head to go with it. I probably will never let my hair grow back. It was thinning out badly. God plays funny tricks. I now can't grow hair on the top of my head but Gerti is growing a mustache. Then again at our age, who the hell cares?

I had packed my stuff the night before and was preparing for my solo journey. It would be emotionally and physically draining. I hoped I was up to it. It would be ludicrous that two Krauses died in Vietnam, both of them young men, Vietnam stealing my youth as a boy and my son dying, who was just barely a man. I damn well wish I had someone to go with me. Rhino would have been the perfect choice. Gerti just wasn't up to it so I didn't ask her and then again, she didn't volunteer.

It took me almost an hour to get my things together. I thought I packed everything I needed last night, but I didn't do as complete a job as I thought, I couldn't even remember whether I packed my passport and where I placed it. The truth was, I was traumatized with the thought of flying across the world to pick up my dead son's body. There just wasn't an inkling of good about anything about this. IT WAS JUST ALL BAD ..... **IT WAS JUST ALL BAD!!!**

After several minutes with a sigh of relief I found it. I had put it in the most obvious of places, right on my nightstand but I constantly overlooked it as I was frenzied in my search. It's amazing how the obvious in my life was constantly overlooked. So much of my family's dysfunction was now so apparent to me. Unfortunately, to my great dismay, I had spent the majority of my life with blinders. I did not see what I did not want to see, and I chose not to see a lot.

My marriage to Gerti was a complex relationship at best because I made it that way. It could have been simple but the right words were never used. It seemed that I didn't have any of them in me. I don't ever remember saying to her that I loved her. For some reason these words always escaped me. As I look back over my forty-six year marriage, I now see so clearly the pain I caused. To live with a man and to never hear those words must be a terrible thing for a woman. Although painful as well for a man, it probably would not be considered excessive mental cruelty. In many cases it was the words, not said, that caused us the greatest harm in our marriage. The words said were THE WORDS SAID and no matter what they were, or how harmful they seemed at the moment, over time they usually would soften and may fade with a continual faint breeze, hopefully someday to be forgotten. Those never said are the ones that cause the greatest harm because Gerti just spent a lifetime wondering where the hell she stood in our relationship. It would have been kinder indeed if I dropped the cruelest four words in the English language on her, **"I DON'T LOVE YOU"**, but I didn't. I just let her hang out in Limbo, never really knowing, always constantly wondering, living in between the proverbial rock and a hard place. All these years must have been hell for her.

I remember when we first got married, I believe I said the words or at least carried the emotions in some verbiage or another. I faintly remember her accepting whatever I said as some kind of rendering that between the two of us there was indeed an attraction, a semblance of emotion that tethered us together as a boat to its mooring. Yes, there had to be, there could be no other way that we found ourselves walking down the aisle to vows both of us took seriously. There must have been something between us because no matter the challenges, interruption, stops and starts, quasi-tragedies and now the greatest tragedy a parent could imagine, we are still together or at least for the moment. The death of Hendrix will be the ultimate test. We may or may not survive it. I would give our marriage a 70-30% chance it may not and not because I, like the ass I am said that *I never loved her* but that I *never acted like I did* and now with Riley, Bellows and her kids moving in with us and Hendrix just a memory of everything that was wrong with us, or perhaps not with her but only me, it will just exacerbate to the point it will be intolerable.

I'm going to fly to Vietnam to pick up my kid. MY KID…I really didn't know who he was. I never really gave the father son relationship a chance to evolve. I guess I wanted no part of it. It was what I expected of myself after patterning my behavior after my father.

I remember watching Hendrix as a little boy running around the house, rearranging everything in his path. I remember saying to myself, *WHAT THE HELL AM I SUPPOSED TO DO HERE?* Gerti was away and I wished she was here but she wasn't and I was lost. I asked myself, *Should I discipline him or let him run free and do what he wants?* I reflected on how my father would react. He without a doubt, would have taken off his shoe and abraded Hendrix's backside as he did mine. None of that in his house. After reflecting on it, I decided I would do just the opposite. I would let my son do whatever he pleased. I was determined to be totally unlike my father. That would be my salvation, Gunther would definitely be in hell and I would gain my reprieve and worthiness by letting my kid run abandon like a "free-range chicken". That's just what I did all those parenting years, allowed him to get caught up in shit. Shit I had no idea he was involved in.

Hendrix's first encounter with the law was when he was just thirteen. He and a friend were caught stealing cigarettes from a local convenience store. I was called down to the Lynn Police Station and Sergeant Dileo said to me. "You know what you got here … YOU GOT YOURSELF A BAD KID HERE." I couldn't believe what he was saying …MY KID …A BAD KID? I wanted to knock the cops head off.

"What are you talking about? My kid, a bad kid? He stole a pack of cigarettes. No big deal."

"NO BIG DEAL?" When you get your kid, look into his eyes - he's high as a kite- your kid… Mr. Krause, is drugged to the nines …the kids how old?"

"Thirteen."

"Thirteen and already smoking pot and downing pills? It ain't a pretty start to a kid's life… doesn't denote a great future. Do you spend a lot of time with him?"

Shit, I didn't want to answer that cause the answer was NO. I spent a lot of time with Dirt and Rhino because they know me better. They have been through what I have, they understand who I am.

In retrospect the cop was damn smart. He saw what I didn't see. He hit it dead on and made every attempt, in the simplest terms, to get his message through. It was like I heard nothing, as though I wouldn't accept my kid and my relationship with him as anything but normal. Normal it was not. When we left the station, I sat Hendrix down on a granite bench and asked him, "You doing some shit I should know about?" He turned to me with the blankest of stares, his eyes dilated to twice their size, and answered "So what's it to you?" Before I could retort, he was off the bench, twenty steps from me heading cross-town on his way home. Our relationship changed that day, from bad to worse. In retrospect it was my one big chance to say something meaningful, to shed one emotion he could have understood and grabbed onto, and from which we could build a foundation. My words were far from thought out, they were flat, cut out of cardboard and I damn well knew he needed more, and at the time when needed most, there was just nothing. That I was unable to give it still haunts me today.

I lost my son that day. Before I knew it he was in high school and was very much removed from me. I hardly saw him. We were indeed "two ships passing in the night" and neither of us would reach out to the other but used Gerti as a buffer. She admittedly played this role well. She indeed was a great referee, a determined interloper, one who could keep relative sanity in an insane house.

Before I knew it Hendrix fell in with a bad crowd. He wasn't a gang member but rather supported their behavior by becoming one of its best customers. He went from pot, to speed, to heroin, to crack as if he were diligently working up the food chain to some euphoria he had not yet experienced. As his life spiraled out of control, Gerti and I saw less and less of him, and the majority of that was to post bail or drive him from one clinic to another. *SO THIS IS THE AMERICAN DREAM,* I thought, working like a dog at the UPS only to come home to constant dysfunction, waiting for the hammer to drop on my kid, knowing that all news would most probably be bad and the core of the problem was ME.

There was just no denying it anymore. My son was who he was because of me. There were no youth programs for him because I had no interest in motivating him to seek them out. There was no soccer, hockey, baseball, football, no camping or Scouts, none of that for Hendrix because the less interest the kid had, the more I applauded because it left me more time for myself, more time for me, Dirt and Rhino.

At thirty-one Hendrix never had a meaningful job. Although occasionally finding work, it was always part time and if there was an opportunity to entrench himself, he would find a way to screw it up.

One of the most embarrassing times in my life (one of many) was when I tried to get him into the UPS. It served me well over the years and I had hope it might support Hendrix as well. I told my son how important it was to remain drug-free so he would pass the mandatory drug test. He assured me he had beaten his addictions and he could pass the test easily. I must have been bullshitting myself because anyone looking at him would know he was a full-fledged addict and totally absorbed. In my heart of hearts I knew this as well but it was my only bastion of hope that I could do something for my kid and he could do something for himself that could divert him from the path he was traveling.

I accompanied Hendrix to his first interview. There were a couple of openings for package handlers at my HUB facility at 583 Chestnut Avenue in Lynn. I knew everybody at that HUB and hoped I might be able to catch a little break for my kid, like some of the Harvard applicants when their father or grandfather was an alumnus. I caught a bit of a break when I could accompany Hendrix and the supervisor Jim Erik on the initial interview that basically was a walkthrough of the facility and an overview of all the jobs but with much more detail in regards to the ones that had openings.

On the day of the interview I picked up Hendrix at his two-room flat that he shared with another recovering addict, which was subsidized by the state. Watching him walk down the several front stairs of his apartment, I knew we were in deep shit. Hendrix waddled side to side and after getting to the passenger door of my Merc, tried several times to pull the door open. After succeeding, he stepped in.

He didn't look at me, until I demanded he did.

"Hendrix … shit … look at me."

"What?"

"You heard me, fucking look at me."

Hendrix turned his head. His eyes were as large as saucers. I was pissed beyond reason. Here I was, trying to do the "fatherly thing", trying to save my kid from his demons within, trying to get him on a semi-righteous path to a semi-normal life, and he isn't doing squat to help me.

"Damn it, Hendrix … YOU PROMISED!"

"Promised what?"

I was livid. "The goddamn drugs, you promised me you would stay off the drugs and look at you…you're all juiced up."

"Shit, no Dad, no I'm not, I ain't on no drugs no more."

"You sure as hell are. Just sit there quiet and shut the hell up. I don't want to hear a sound from you until… I need to think this damn thing through."

I really didn't know what to do. I was lost. If I canceled the initial phase of the interview, Hendrix wouldn't have a chance at getting another. I used all the influence I had at the UPS. I would look like a fool if he didn't show up. And here was my "super" being nice enough to let me attend the interview with my kid.

I decided to take our chances. There was no way we could cancel out. It would have the smell of a rat and there wouldn't be a snowball chance in hell we would get another opportunity like this. I cashed in all my chips. It was do or die. I started the Merc.

"Where we going?" questioned Hendrix.

"Just shut your damn mouth now and try to get your shit together … we're on our way to the UPS."

"S- Shhiitt", I heard Hendrix say under his breath."

"Shit it is Hendrix … SHIT IT IS!"

When we arrived at the UPS, I convinced myself we might be able to pull this off. All my son had to do was act normal and show some interest. We met John Erik at the front desk. He greeted both of us, but with a suspicious eye. Hendrix was dressed like he was going to work in a garage rather than to attend a job interview. He wore dirty jeans, a soiled shirt and as skinny as he was (probably because he traded food stamps for drugs) he constantly tried to keep his pants up from falling to his knees. His complexion was pasty and his lips were parched. His hair needed washing and fell to his shoulders in oily strands.

Jim Erik was probably wondering *what the hell we were doing there.* He was nevertheless polite.

The interview took a total of forty-five minutes. Jim constantly reached out to my kid. Hendrix, however, was like a blank slate. No response, feedback or questions asked. He just stood there as if he were just a shell of who he was, occasionally, nodding his head, if he understood … HE UNDERSTOOD NOTHING.

After walking us back to the main entrance, Jim, polite as ever, thanked me and my son for taking the time to visit his facility and attend the initial interview. Hendrix nodded his head. I shook Jim's hand. Just after we turned to leave, Jim asked that I follow him into his office. My son was not invited and I told him to wait in the chair in the lobby.

Jim opened saying, "Jack, WHAT THE HELL?"

"What the hell?"

"Ya, you heard me, what are you crazy trying to get your kid in here?"

I wasn't shocked with what Jim was saying. He threw me a bone, he tried to help me and went out of his way. It was in UPS terms…I delivered a package to him and the package was crushed, ripped, broken. In essence, I delivered *"damaged goods".*

I didn't know what to say.

"Jim, I really apologize, I'm just trying to help my kid. The UPS has been really good to me and I was hoping it would be as good to him as well. I'm sorry I laid this on you. I really appreciate what you did in giving this interview, I owe you, I really do."

"Jack if the UPS has been that good to you then don't try ramming it up its' ass. You know that keeping a clean workforce is a really big deal here. In fact, it's PARAMOUNT!"

There was a long hesitation.

"Now, I don't want to see either of you again. Go back to your station and don't you ever bother me again."

Shit, I made an ass out of myself. I called in my chips and Hendrix didn't give a shit about the job. Why was I ever foolish enough to think he would. The one time I tried to do the "fatherly thing", it just blew up in my face. I was lucky not to have lost my job over this.

I connected with Hendrix in the lobby. He knew. He didn't say a thing. I would have smacked him on the side of his head if he did. I drove him back to his apartment where he got out of the car, turned and walked away. That was years ago but not too long not to remember. A year later he was picked up for trafficking drugs, selling amphetamines to a Lynn undercover. I once again did my "fatherly thing". Gerti told me she would leave and file for divorce if I didn't. I put up the two grand for bail. Hendrix was out of jail hours later, never to be heard again. *Until now*.

25

Daddy's Little Girl

Life has a way of coming at you really fast. And so did Riley. I remember her as a little girl carrying an innocence and purity that seemed to renew my hope after Nam. If there was anything for me to come back to after my service, it was a dream that I would get married and have a family just the opposite of the one I was brought up in. A normal one, a "Brady Bunch" or Father's Knows Best" kind. One that I would experience in the matinee part of my life. My little girl was essential to this. I couldn't see having a perfect family without a daughter but after the birth of my son and the estrangement in my marriage, I changed my mind, one kid was enough. But then Gerti did the unthinkable. Something I never saw coming and the result was Riley, a tortured soul at best.

Our daughter was born almost four years after Hendrix. By the time we had her, Gerti and I had grown out of our quasi-hippie part of our lives and weren't looking for any other kind of artist's legacy name. We named our baby girl "Riley" after a TV show, *The Life Of Riley* that we grew up with in the fifties. The title depicted (but seldom true) that after all the small challenges of life are met head-on, it would be nothing short of wonderful going forward. It seemed all too sitcom and after her birth, it was anything but.

The problem I had with my daughter was now I had two kids. I really didn't know how to father either. Unfortunately, I began where my father left off although not physically or mentally abusive I was rather detached and unresponsive to my children's needs. In retrospect, it's hard to forgive myself for this (I know my children and wife won't) and probably, I never will. A person like me, especially after Nam, dealing with the severest emotional problems, would have been better off not having kids. A real grownup would have sensed that and avoided that which was contradictory swimming around in his head. I was anything but and thought my life would play out just the way it did in a lot of the TV series. Father comes home from work, he's greeted by his loving wife and kids and dog and deals with the minor problem or challenge of the day and life goes on, weighing quite heavy on the *"HALLELUJAH, LIFE IS JUST GREAT"* scale of life, rather than, *"SHIT, I HAVEN'T A CLUE"* scale of what the hell I have gotten myself into. Each day I understand it less, especially the part I have to play.

I now had a daughter and a son. Riley was really the apple of my eye. It wasn't she did anything particular that gave her a head-up over Hendrix, other than the biggest surprise of my life that I never saw coming, it was, as truthful as I can be in retrospect, that Riley was a girl and I did not feel I would have much influence over her life growing up because it would all fall on Gerti's shoulders and that was damn well alright with me. I learned early, with the birth of Hendrix, I wasn't very good at parenting and felt extremely insecure in my futile attempts. There just wasn't a textbook on how to do it … and if there was, I probably wouldn't have read it. I would have just wanted the Cliff Notes version of "Parenting 101" and even that would not have simplified that which I found so complex.

It was early on that Hendrix was giving signs he was a problem child. He acted up constantly and was nearly impossible to discipline. At five, he was hell on wheels. He held us captive in our house because when we went out he acted so uncontrollably that it was an embarrassment. Gerti and I would rather be home than to be the focal point of all the pointing and staring. We knew what people were saying, *"Look at the little shit out of control… his parents can't contain him."*. I hated people who would point and stare. I wanted to rush right over to them and pound my fist against their skulls. What made me even madder was I knew they were right and if I was in their position, I would be saying the same things.

As each year progressed Hendrix was going from bad to worse. His young affectations were now pre-teen and teenage bad behaviors. There was just no stopping him. Nothing Gerti and I could do would detain his skipping school, his anti-social bad behavior in class, fighting, his constant stealing and drunkenness and evolving drug use. Yet, in spite all his demerits and bad scores, Hendrix was passed from grade to grade, eventually processed through the system as if the School Department was saying to me, "WE AIN'T PLAYING PARENT TO YOUR SCREWED UP KID … YOU FAILED HIM … YOU DEAL WITH IT."

Riley compared to Hendrix was a blessed child. From the time of her birth she had exceptional behavior and was quiet and introspective, so much she provided Hendrix a larger stage. Her presence paled compared to his theatrics. Gerti and I loved her for that. She was the salt to Hendrix's pepper, the "Ying" to his "Yang".

For as bad as we felt about our runaway son, we felt incredibly positive about Riley. It seemed to us (and wrongfully so) that each of them cancelled the other out. Were we to blame, Gerti and I? Was it really our fault Hendrix turned out the way he did? How could it be that as misbehaved as he was, Riley would be as comforting? Gerti and especially me, tried to escape from everything that was wrong with his upbringing. Basically ME, a father who couldn't relate because honestly, I didn't put in the time or effort. I chalked my son up as *Coming from the Demon Seed* and basically blamed him on the rogue sperm that had to find its way through me, but being jettisoned through my father's loins.

It was after Hendrix's third arrest, several months before he was incarcerated for dealing "ecstasy" now the date drug, that I almost wrote him off. Gerti held true to her motherly instincts that by hook or crook, by God's intervention and good graces, her son would reappear as the prodigal son totally transforming him into the one we wanted him to be. *Good freakin luck!!*

I just never saw it coming from Riley. She caught both Gerti and I by surprise. I knew something was amiss when she came down the stairs leading to our living room dressed like a hooker. Gerti and I were sitting watching the 7:00 news, the SOX were losing again , the world was out of control and here my daughter was parading herself as if auditioning for a cat house. The dress she was wearing was cut three inches shorter than mid-thigh, revealing just a hint of her red panties. She was platformed on stiletto heels that made her look six feet tall. She was wearing a pink blouse exposing her cleavage (for a fourteen year old girl she was amply endowed). She had bright red lips and rouge cheeks and sporting thick black eyeliner and shadow that made her look like a raccoon. She had brass rings up and down her arms, and gaudy earrings that fell to her shoulders.

Both Gerti and I were taken like a deer in headlights. I think both of us were thinking the same thing. *Who the hell is this? Is this our little girl?*

I shook my head as if trying to dislodge it from a cobweb and refocused again on Riley.

"Okay girl, what's going on here?"

My daughter didn't move a muscle. She just stood there on the lower platform of the steps as if modeling in a showroom window.

"What do you mean?"

Gerti looked at me and gave me a little nod, as if giving me permission to continue. I took the license.

"I mean why are you dressed like that?"

"It's Friday night and I have a date with Randy."

"Does your mother know about this?"

I turned to Gerti again and she shook here head indicating "NO".

"Well, I don't think I ever heard about this guy Randy" I turned to Gerti again and asked "Do you?"

"No", Gerti answered, "He's a new one, ain't ever heard his name in this house before."

"Well, you ain't going out with anyone until we meet him. Is that clear?"

"No, it's not clear at all."

"Well, then I'll make it as clear as I can. You're just fourteen and you will be dating no boys until either your mother or me meets them. And where are you going with this Randy?"

"He's taking me to the movies."

"He is, is he?"

"Yes, he is."

"And what is it you are going to see?"

"I don't know …. I guess we'll decide when we get there."

"Well you may get a pass tonight, just this once, but there is no way in hell you are leaving this house dressed like that. In fact, I never ever saw those clothes. Where did you get them?"

Gerti answered for Riley, "They were given to her by her cousin Jamie."

I thought to myself. *Now, I get it, given to her by her cousin Jamie … the slut.*

"Well you damn well get your butt upstairs and take them off …you're a fourteen year old …you damn well ain't no hooker."

"No. I'm not gonna do that!"

I couldn't believe what I was hearing from Riley. This was the first time she ever talked back to me. I didn't like it. In fact, it pissed me off.

I got out of my chair and approached her. I didn't mean to be threatening but I guess I was. Riley took two steps back.

"No… LEAVE ME ALONE," Riley spit out.

"I'm not doing anything to you, but mark my words young lady, you are not leaving this house looking like that, no way in a hell of Sundays."

"Yes, I am."

"No, you're not."

"YES, I AM."

Now I could not contain myself anymore, my voice became elevated.

"How dare you defy me Riley …this talking back stuff is not acceptable …"

"I don't give a shit." Riley blurted out.

I couldn't believe what I just heard, I'd be damned if I was going to take this crap from another of my kids. I already was up to my neck with Hendrix. I took two giant steps toward Riley, she turned and ran up the stairs. We heard her slamming shut the door to her room. I had had enough.

"THAT'S IT," I screamed, "THAT'S THE END OF IT … YOU'RE NOT LEAVING THIS DAMN HOUSE TONIGHT … IN FACT YOU'RE GROUNDED FOR THE WEEKEND…DO YOU GET IT? … HAVE I MADE MYSELF VERY CLEAR?"

"Screw you, I hate you!" I heard her scream from her room.

I had had it. I would never again accept this kind of behavior from my kid. I already lost Hendrix by my not paying attention. There was just no way I was about to lose Riley.

I started to run up the stairs after her. I felt a tug at my shirt. It was Gerti.

"Jack, let it be ….Christ, just let it be …"

"Let it be? What do you mean let it be? I can't let her talk back to me like that. This is just fucking unacceptable."

"Damn it Jackson, just let it be. YOU'RE MAKING EVERYTHING FUCKING WORSE."

In retrospect, this was the beginning of a tumultuous relationship between Riley, Gerti and I. What was going on with Riley caught both my wife and I off guard. Her home life was not the greatest. Gerti and I didn't hold back when we came to a head, we damn well didn't mince words. We were like two bulls banging skulls and it was obvious Riley felt the turmoil. How could she have possibly not? The truth was we were way too open when she was around. We created anxiety and uncertainty and for a fourteen-year old girl, it must have been quit unsettling. There was now no doubt she was pissed with what was happening in her home environment and now as a teenager she was acting out, pushing back.

Her older sibling Hendrix also set her no precedent on how to behave. Being constantly in trouble, seldom at home and creating a firestorm when he was, Riley found that whenever Hendrix was mentioned, the only safe haven was in her room, where she spent the majority of her time.

From fourteen years old and on Riley was on a "tear". It seemed in her defiance, she was trying to do everything wrong just to piss us off.

She constantly broke curfew and wore the clothes she chose (she would hide them in her locker at school and change into her fuck-me garb when motivated). She was now skipping classes and our usual B+ student now fell to C-. Gerti and I were constantly summoned by the teachers at Lynn Tech to discuss her anti-social behavior. She was now chewing tobacco and spitting on the school tile floors. She was involved in three catfights with several upper grade girls, something about disparaging remarks Riley made about one of them. There were also rumors, as one of the teachers advised us, she was getting a reputation as one of the "easiest " girls in the school.

"Easy meaning what?" asked Gerti.

"Meaning, she puts out for everybody."

"You mean…?" responded Gerti.

"I mean she's an easy lay."

"Goddamn it …"

"Shit, now our daughter's …A WHORE!"

"Stop it Jackson. NOW YOU STOP THAT RIGHT NOW. She's no whore."

"If she ain't, then pray tell, what the hell is she?"

Now with her high school years behind her, Gerti and I thought she would grow out of her bad behavior but it exacerbated. When choosing a college, we hoped (rather I did) that because of the proximity to home (and that there would be no need to pay board) that she would choose North Shore Community, right here in Lynn. No way in hell, Riley wanted to go to UMass Amherst. I knew damn well why she wanted to go, to get away from home, as far away as she could so she could do what she chose without scrutiny.

I can't say that both Gerti and I were not overly possessive and tried to control her behaviors. We damn well did. We already felt we were losing one kid, or rather that with each passing day, Hendrix (then age twenty-one) was getting farther away from us. He was now so distant that each time we saw him (which was very infrequent) he was more unrecognizable. We damn well wanted to save both our kids, but the odds were greatly against us and we decided we would now put the bulk of our efforts into saving one.

There was no doubt that as this played out, Gerti and I wondered where we went wrong. It was more on Gerti's side where the suspicion held. She had her faults but she was a damn good mother. She was there all the time when the kids were growing up, taking them here and there as her time warranted. She doted on them and as a home maker, she wasn't great, but the house was always clean and there was a hot meal prepared every evening and our kids went to bed with their bellies full and well nourished.

Providing the mothering she did, there was really no reason why our kids were estranged. Then THERE WAS ME and where the "rubber met the road". I guess if I have to be truthful with myself because at this time there doesn't seem to be much "wiggle room", I have to admit **I WAS A PISS POOR FATHER**. I allowed my kids to grow up without my constant presence and guidance. I provided little insight and direction hoping they would find their way without my intrusion and support. Admittedly, I didn't bring much positive energy to our home. I was just there, a disinterested mass of human flesh, lying on the coach, snoring away, or filling the over-stuffed lounger in our TV room. Unfortunately, my kids were an ancillary part of my life. They were the mandatory two back pockets on a pair of jeans, the rear two tires on my old Merc. I looked at them to be part and parcel of a struggling marriage, as the baggage our marriage carried and would always. I spent more time with Dirt and Rhino than my family, because honestly they were far less work and they understood that which my family could not, THAT I WAS REALLY FUCKED UP. They understood it all too well and I didn't have the constant pressure of being someone that I naturally could not be and they just didn't care and they never asked, *"Jack, where are you coming from?"* because THEY WERE FUCKED UP TOO!!!

Riley lasted just one and a half semesters at UMass, which was a Krause record as Hendrix's foray into college lasted less than three weeks. When she returned for the Thanksgiving holiday, she presented herself with her beautiful golden blonde hair streaked with purple, her ears weighed down with one inch brass rings, arms tatted from her wrist to her shoulder. It was obvious she damn well wanted us to know how far she was from the fold. We didn't need to see any of her decorative artwork, vipers spewing fire, crows eating worms, and the mandatory "Skull and Bones" but she made sure we did. The weather was an unseasonal thirty-four degrees when she burst into our house, carrying her coat on her shoulder, wearing a guinea T, arms naked and flushed. Gerti looked at her with a faint "hey" then turned and looked away. I just stood there, realizing that, which I did when Hendrix broke stride ... *My Damn Kid is Lost to Me!*

The "shit hit the fan" over the next year and three months. We heard little of our daughter until she showed up unannounced that she was leaving school and was pregnant. Gerti and I looked at each other and shared the same instinct, we wanted to wring her foolish neck.

"It's really great", she announced, "because unlike most of the UMASS coeds who get "knocked up" I decided not to get an abortion ... yep, gonna carry the child to term."

I checked myself because my first instinct was to throw her lock, stock and barrel out of the house.

"You know, like it's a moral thing...you know?"

"No, I don't know. This is all bullshit", I spewed out, "you are about to piss your whole life down the damn drain."

"Jack damn it, let Riley get it out, We're listening to you Riley, go on." Gerti interjected.

"Ya, like I said, I see this as a moral thing and everything's going to be alright because Justin, the kid's father is going to marry me."

Justin? Who the fuck is this Justin I asked myself. I figured I better cool myself down, there was way too much emotion in the room.

"This here Justin ...your boyfriend ...the so-called father of your kid. I take it he's a student at UMASS." *I said this hoping that at least the kid would have a father who would hopefully get a degree and job to support both Riley and the kid.*

"No ... no, he's no student at UMASS but rather is a friend of a student at UMASS who I met at a frat party."

"Well then where does he go to school?"

"He doesn't. He's a man of many skills. He does a lot of stuff."

"A LOT OF STUFF …LIKE WHAT KIND OF STUFF … LIKE WORK STUFF?"

I must be losing my freaking mind?

I looked at Gerti, she was turning white.

"You got to be shitting me. You're telling me you're leaving UMASS and just pissed away a couple of grand of tuition and boarding, you're knocked up and have decided to have the baby and that the so-called father is a guy who DOES STUFF ….STUPID STUFF THAT OBVIOUSLY YOU KNOW NOTHING ABOUT?"

"That's the brunt of it."

"Does this guy make any money?"

"Occasionally."

"Like what does occasionally mean?"

"Like, he DOES STUFF a couple times a month."

I had had enough. I just couldn't take anymore, I tried to hold it in. I tried to bring my heart rate down, to not let this circus bother me …to suck it up …to get from under the tent for a few minutes … to do what any sane father would. But the problem was that I WAS NOT SANE … not at this moment SANITY DOES NOT REIGN. I couldn't hold back anymore … it just rushed from me as a broken dam… the flood waters broke uncontrollably.

"Riley, get the hell out of here … GET THE HELL OUT OF HERE …FUCKING NOW!"

Without hesitation, she grabbed her jacket from the kitchen chair and headed straight out the door, slamming it behind. I could hear her faintly before the door jammed closed, "SCREW YOU ALL."

"Christ Jack, what the hell did you do that for ? You just threw your kid out of the house, out of our house. WHAT A STUPID THING TO DO. We have already lost Hendrix, now we are about to lose Riley as well. THIS FAMILY IS CURSED and I can't help feeling that it is all because of you."

Gerti started crying and headed toward our bedroom.

I damn well couldn't believe that I did it again.

Happy Fucking Thanksgiving, Jack Krause.

26

A Runaway Train

It was two years later that Riley, her dead-beat boyfriend Justin (they never married) and their kid Bellows wound up living in Lynn. Why she didn't stay in Amherst where he was from, I don't know. I surmised their "relationship" was going from bad to worse and in spite of being estranged from Gerti and I, she convinced Justin that being closer was the right thing to do probably as a failsafe for their daughter. I very seldom spoke to Riley, all the information I got was filtered through Gerti, who diligently kept contact. My daughter just pissed me off. She was my little girl. She held my hopes and ambitions. I looked at her as my last bastion of defense against an insane world, growing more so with each passing day. She unknowingly had a lot of weight to carry. She was (hopefully) my one good kid, destined to make up for my one bad one. It was foolish of me to think that even if she was the greatest and most successful kid in the world, that she could ever erase Hendrix from my life, perhaps MY BIGGEST FUCK-UP OF ALL.

Now Riley lived just twenty minutes away, a proximity most parents would love to have with their child. One where the relationship could be nourished on a different set of terms, whereby the parents could regularly see their influences as their offspring now accepted the responsibility of being an adult.

Unfortunately, the relationship between Gerti, me and our daughter became worse and eventually viral. We resented that she seemed to cave in to Justin's lack of ambition, that the daughter we hoped to achieve great things, helping us reclaim a little dignity as parents, like an anchor, pulled us down even further.

Both our kids seemed to have gone wrong, and the mirror reflected we had to blame no one other than ourselves. After all I have been through, I became callous at the thought our daughter, like our son was doomed to live a tired life with a dismal future. Both our kids were the casualties in the car crash of our marriage. The angst I carried was heavy but carrying it deep within, I tried to escape as much as I could. My avoidance of Gerti was common place, my drinking was now a rule instead of an exception. I tried to sweep my two kids from my memory, as a janitor would sweep dust from the floor. I now looked at Dirt and Rhino as the only lifeline I had. They were now more than friends and members of my band of brothers, but were the only justification of the life I was living. I was more prone commiserating with them than sharing any feelings with my wife. I let Gerti deal with the consequences of our marriage as her private war. I was a lousy partner. As I look back now, I can't believe I laid a private hell on the fine woman my wife really is. I may rot in hell for this and probably will.

Gerti was the only one of us who reached out to Riley. I had no motivation. My wife made excuses for me. I was sick, unavailable, caught up in the complexity of a life not well lead. In my cowardice I let her run interference for me. It wasn't that Gerti didn't have enough to manage, she damn well did. She had to manage Jackson Krause, because for the life of me, I couldn't myself.

Occasionally, I would inquire how Riley was doing. Gerti would embellish and always made things seem better than I knew they were. I let her play her imagination out knowing damn well she described things as she would like them to be rather than the way they really were.

"They're doing really well. Justin got a job and starts next week. He's managing a store at the mall."

Shit, I hope it's not one in my mall. I said to myself.

"Oh, that's great and the kid?"

"You mean Bellows?"

"Ya, you know who I mean, ya the kid, you know with the funny name."

"Yeah, I damn sure know who you mean, you're just one sorry shit Jackson Krause."

Gerti laid a whole lot of pressure on me because although most times she allowed me avoidance, the holidays were another matter. She had absolutely no tolerance that I would not be the paternal figure at the Thanksgiving or Christmas table. Holidays for me were a living hell. I grew to hate them and the role I played, being the father and grandfather I was not, being the person I pretended but damn well could not be. It was intolerable for me and only a bit better for the occupants at the table who knew the whole damn thing was a freaking lie.

Over the last holiday season, I blamed my lack of presence on the flu.

I was contagious or should I say, my terrible attitude could fill the room. I know I wasn't missed. It worked both ways.

The Krause family was like a runaway train. As the years passed, the more out of control our lives became. Gerti and I hardly spoke and when we did, it was nothing less than biting and cruel. It seemed our reason for being was to punish each other for what we were singularly and inexcusably together. Ours was the worst of marriages, why we stayed together I couldn't tell you, perhaps we were just too lazy to break from each other, or too masochistic and sadistic.

Like a flash of light before my eyes several years passed. My relationship with my daughter did not get better. It got progressively worse with her boyfriend Justin now non-existent.

We learned Justin finally did exactly what Gerti and I thought he would, he just got up one day and left under the pretense of going to get a pack of cigarettes at the local grocery store, abandoning Riley and his kid leaving them with nothing, not that he supported them in any way other than a menial job from time to time.

My daughter and Bellows were now existing on welfare and food stamps and this seemed to strip them of the little dignity they had. My daughter was now dysfunctional. She found herself totally disempowered in her ineptness to do just about anything. Eventually, unable to rise from her bed in the morning, she fell deeper and deeper into despair. The meager checks she received from the State were nearly enough to put food on the table and pay for her four room flat, a flat that should have been condemned. The little contact Gerti had was wavering. Although she reached out, Riley was unresponsive, creating within her tremendous foreboding.

"There's something really wrong here Jack."

"Damn it Gerti, there's been nothing right for years now. Did you honestly think things were going to get better?"

"We'll Jack, honestly, I need more from you than your pseudo psycho asshole comments."

Shit, Gerti was right again, I offered no solace. When will I ever learn to keep my asshole comments to myself? Probably never.

I agreed to drive Gerti for the umpteenth time over to Riley's apartment to see if she was there. I knew this was futile but I agreed nonetheless. I owed Gerti and no matter how I tried to frame it, all four of us were family and I damn well knew I had to fess up. Riley was gone from us and the hope of reconciling and lending the support Gerti and I thought she needed was nothing but empty air escaping on a crisp Northeast breeze.

As if things couldn't go from worse to tragic, when we arrived at Riley's apartment, there seemed to be no one there.

"Let's get the hell out of here, there's nobody here and I'm not waiting around."

"That's the problem with you, you just won't extend yourself, you just can't give anything of yourself for your family Jack. You just can't even wait for another ten minutes?"

We waited for another ten minutes and then waited a decade more. Now our daughter and granddaughter were gone and like Hendrix, the pain in our heart was deeper and more agonizing than we were able to deal with. Needless to say, Gerti and I were constantly at each other's throats, each blaming the other for the nightmare we were living. Our life was shit, why we didn't leave each other we hadn't a clue. I think we were just too damn depressed and tired.

Now both our kids were gone and Gerti and I were swept away in a world of despair and despondency.

It was a horrific thirteen years, we heard not a whimper from Riley. Gerti and I felt cursed. Now we had lost both our children and our grandchild, Bellows, we had no idea where her status lay, which just compounded the anxiety and despair that much more.

It was September of thirteenth year, when we were beyond wit's end, when the call came. Gerti picked up her cell phone and the blood drained from her face as she beckoned me to approach her. I did. As Gerti separated the phone from her ear, I could hear the weak and broken voice of Riley. I just stood not two feet from Gerti and heard the conversation as it unfolded.

"Mom, I'm sorry."

"Riley, that you?"

"Yes, Mom, it's me."

Gerti's voice cracked. "My God Riley, we thought you were dead."

"I know, I know. I know I must have caused you great heartbreak…I know I must have and I hope that someday, I can make it up to you…but…but Ma…"

"Yes Riley?"

"I'm really screwed up ... have been for years and it seems nothing gets any better ...if it wasn't for Bellows, I just wouldn't know what I would do?"

"Yes, Bellows...Bellows ...how is she doing?"

"She's okay Ma ... in fact that's one of the reason's why I'm calling you ... not the only one. Like I was saying before, I called to apologize too. I know with you losing Hendrix and my leaving, your world must be hell ... but I saw my departure as my only legitimate choice. I had to get away from the life I was living and leave everything behind. I saw it as my only option, the only anchor I had to save me from the storm around me. Ma, you have to believe me I had no other choice."

I stood listening to this bullshit and wanted to grab the phone right out of Gerti's hand and give my selfish daughter a piece of my mind. She sucked the little joy this household had in it, leaving nothing but the skeletal remains of a marriage cursed from its very start. I made a move toward Gerti and she back peddled away from me. Her knuckles were turning white from holding the phone so tight.

"When are you going to return home, Riley? We very much miss you and Bellows. It's been years now and your father and I have been overcome with worry and regret. You can't believe how painful it's been."

"Of course I can Ma, I'm involved in my own living hell as well. It's a constant saga of being lost and beyond the horizon, well that just spells out lost forever with very little hope to ever live a normal life, that is ... *if such a thing exists* ...which as I get older I very much question."

"No Riley, rest assured there's a life for you that you're running away from and believe it or not it's here with me and your father. Coming back home will be a wonderful start for you and Bellows and you know damn well it would be a great relief for your father and me."

"I'm not coming home, but in regards to Bellows, I'm separating from her and I'm going to put her on a bus to Lynn and am going to send her to you. To be honest, she's a great kid but at fifteen years now, she's just way too much for me to handle and I can't possibly support her anymore. I think also she might be the kid that you and Daddy always wanted you know, who might replace Hendrix and me, kids who have really caused you the greatest pain. Mom, Bellows is really special and in her there is redemption, I know there is. It's been a real disservice to not have allowed you to watch her grow up. She, I know as they say, will be the *apple of your eye*, as she has been to me , I know damn well she will be to you. And there's…well… there's other stuff."

"What do you mean ….*other stuff*?"

"You'll understand when you see her, but for me it's best that I go my separate way and try to make a life for me with the few good years I might have left."

"No Riley, you need to come back to us as well. Lynn is your home, you can move in with us again. Both your father and I would be extremely happy if you came back to us. It would be the best gift you could ever give us, if indeed both of you come home where you belong."

"Sorry, mother, it's just not going to happen.

I stood close to the phone, listening to this banter … WHAT THE FUCK!?"

Surprise, SURPRISE, **SURPRISE**. Two days later Gerti and I were headed to the Greyhound Bus Station to meet the bus from New York City. We both were incredibly anxious to reunite with our estranged daughter and our granddaughter. When Bellows got off the bus, we didn't recognize her being she was now fifteen and we haven't seen her for thirteen years. Thirteen years of excruciating pain … thirteen years of living hell.

We didn't recognize any one coming off the bus. There were several young girls and one carrying a baby and an overweight slovenly guy, with a patched beard following her carrying several small bags and then … THEN THE SURPRISE OF ALL SURPRISES …could it be Riley? … yes it damn well was, thinner and much older… I couldn't believe my eyes … it was our daughter by the grace of God …did we really get one of our kids back … DID WE REALLY …**DID WE REALLY?"**

AS GOOD AS IT WAS … IS AS BAD AS IT GETS.

Within hours we learned, that indeed, it was our daughter who walked off the bus. She had for the last thirteen years been working as a domestic in Houston. After passing several bad checks and the police following close behind, she decided to send her kid home to us and to move to California (hopefully beyond the reach of the law) but decided at the last minute she couldn't leave her daughter and decided to come back home with her. We also learned, again SURPRISE OF ALL SURPRISES, that the teenage girl carrying the baby was Bellows and the infant she was attending was her daughter Miley. Bellows who we never had a chance to know was now a teenage mother and the lard ass following her off the bus was the shithead who knocked her up. My first thought was he should be in jail. His name was Humphrey.

There couldn't be any more extreme emotions then what Gerti and I were feeling.

We wanted our daughter back but weren't expecting all the baggage. We knew deep in our hearts that Bellows was part of the package, although we knew very little of her as she was just two years old when Riley decided (like Hendrix) to run away. The infant Miley, we weren't prepared for and the thought our granddaughter giving birth at fifteen years of age was appalling. The only saving grace was all three were family. OUR, although fractured and dysfunctional, *FAMILY*.

Humphrey was another matter. I didn't like him from the moment I saw him. He and I were like oil and water. For one thing knocking up my granddaughter who was just fifteen years, he being six years older, was damn right sinful and criminal at best. He was a damn predator and what he was doing tagging along with my family was inexplicable.

I later learned from Riley, that having a pregnant teenager was just overwhelming for her and for the last several years, the strain of her lifestyle eroded her ability to make clear (if not good) decisions. Allowing Humphrey to move in with her was one of the worst. Once in her apartment, he refused to leave but rather bogarted the place, living off the meager income Riley worked so hard to bring in. He was a user and abuser but Riley justified his presence by his fathering Miley. He was Riley's boyfriend and hopefully in time, (Riley and Bellows hoped) her future husband. To me he was nothing but "twenty miles of bad road." I didn't want any part of him in my house or in my life. He already bore himself into my family and like a cancer was eroding it from the inside out.

What must we have been thinking, allowing the four of them to move in with us? Expecting only Riley and Bellows, we made no preparation to house an infant and a degenerate I considered a "criminal". Both Gerti and I didn't have the allowance, bedrooms or square footage to accommodate three more adults (if indeed you could call them that) and an infant. After several months realized that although Riley was our daughter, we lost the connection we had with her, after thirteen years, the three of us were indeed different people, and maybe it was best they stayed where they were (but that was now water under the bridge). Again, "BE CAREFUL WHAT YOU WISH FOR," that old adage loomed large in my life.

"THE OTHER" is what I now referred to our new family members. "OTHER" than them my life was almost tolerable. "OTHER" than them, my relationship with Gerti, although as imperfect as it was, was at least an "understanding" that we indeed breathed the same air. "OTHER" than them, our home was at least large enough for Gerti and I to hide from each other. Now there was no hiding at all. "OTHER" than them we occasionally now had a tolerable night's sleep. Now, it was weaning and crying of an infant throughout the night and day. "OTHER" than them, at least Gerti and I could relish the thought that somehow, someway, our daughter and kid were doing decent, although in our heart of hearts, WE DAMN WELL KNEW THERE WAS NO WAY IN HELL they were. Having the "OTHER" constantly underfoot was now getting intolerable. Riley, Bellows and Humphrey did nothing all day but hang around. My life was now beyond miserable and Gerti's less than tolerable. I left the house in the morning and tried to stay out all day. Thank God, I had Dirt and Rhino to run to. Gerti had no one. I really felt bad for her, but not enough to stay at home and share her burden and pain.

"They got to get the hell out of here."

"Jack, damn it. They have no job and money to get a place of their own."

" Well, I can't believe I'm saying this, but we'll find a place and support them as long as we can, until they get their feet on the ground."

"Christ, Jack that may be never."

"Well, Gerti, we damn well have no option, this arrangement is no longer tolerable."

It was a tough conversation any parent could have with their kid. I was literally throwing my daughter, her child and grandchild out of our house. As far as I was concerned, Humphrey could go to hell. It was a tough conversation but it had to take place. Riley said she understood but hadn't a clue how she would support themselves. I suggested the unmentionable, "Why don't you and Humphrey get a damn job?" My daughter looked at me like I had two heads.

It took several weeks before we could find them a place. I cringed as I signed the rental contract, knowing I was putting Gerti and me in harms way. I knew I had no other choice but to obligate myself to the monthly payment. I just couldn't believe the same "curse" was dropped on my family as it was fifteen years previous. First it was Riley impregnated by that loser Justin and now her daughter knocked up by another of society's "throwaways", this guy Humphrey, who barely spoke a couple of hundred words the several months he spent with us. He just moaned and grunted like a pig at the trough. I guess like mother, like daughter and so forth and so forth… the Krause family tragedy continued on.

Needless to say I stayed away from the "Others" as much as I could. Being around them was like hitting myself in the head with a hammer. I began to care less and less about their status, other than hopefully hearing Riley or Humphrey had found a job, hopefully both, but no such good news was forthcoming. I felt like the guy I learned about in school (one of the few things I retained) who was shackled to a rock, he kept pushing up the hill with no end in sight

Every month I mailed the rent check, I replayed the path I traveled leading to where I found myself. If I intentionally set out to screw up my life, I could not have done any better than what I had. *At least I'm good at something…* I said to myself… *At least I'm good at something.*

Gerti and I were always at each others throats about visiting Riley. She wanted to see her family. I had no desire. I wanted to void my life of any personal baggage, but the "Others" would not let me be. ***The Krause curse continued*** …

27

The Missing
Three Iron

It was a year later after moving to Lynn, Riley and Bellows came knocking at our door. I wasn't home. As always, when needed, I was never around. I was with Dirt and Rhino, doing some jerk-off stuff, basically nothing of importance, something fabricated, anything to get out of the house. My phone rang. It was Gerti. Her voice was cracking.

"Gerti?"

"You better come home Jack."

"Sounds serious, everything okay?"

"Just get home here Jack."

"Fifteen minutes later, I arrived. I hurried to the door. Gerti opened it. She held me at bay with one hand pressing against my chest.

"Now Jack, you have to promise me that you won't lose it … I mean, that is … let your temper get the best of you …"

I wasn't liking what I was hearing.

"What is it Gerti … cut the crap …what's going on?"

I now could hear Riley, Bellows and her kid crying in the background.

"What do I hear in the living room?"

"Ya, like I said Jack, don't make things worse than they are. Don't lose your temper now, you got to promise me!"

Shit, I would do anything to get past my wife, the gatekeeper.

"Yeah, sure Gerti, I promise."

I pushed Gerti aside and hurried through the small hallway leading to our living room. Riley and Bellows were sitting, the two year old was running roughshod jumping up and down on our newly upholstered couch. My attention immediately went to Bellows who was shaking and with baby and all, crying, tears running down her cheeks shadowed by her dark Alvira slut makeup. I could see her forehead was bruised and she had a split lip and a pink cheek. There were also welts on her arms and bloody cuts to her elbows. It didn't take a PhD from MIT to quickly gather the lay of the land. My first appraisal was that Bellows pathetic excuse for a boyfriend, kicked the crap out of her …seven months pregnant and all …THE LOUSY PUNK…

"Daddy …. !" Riley spoke.

"Don't Daddy me, I don't want to hear any shit from you."

Gerti jumped in. "Jack, Christ, you're damn well going to make this worse."

"You're right, I goddamn am."

I approached Riley, all of my six foot frame hovering over her like a palm tree over a sandy beach and as I looked into her eyes, I realized there was no real fight left in her. She was beaten, physically, and emotionally. There was nothing left in her eyes, they just focused nowhere …into infinity … into a very dark black hole.

"That asshole beat Bellows."

Riley just shook her head up and down.

"Pregnant and all, the bastard beat her."

Riley nodded her head up and down again.

"Piece of shit, son of a bitch. WHY?"

It took Riley a few seconds to gather herself but before she could speak, Bellows jumped it.

"Cause I told him that he has to stop doing whatever little stuff he was doing and get a real job."

"You mean, like W-O-R-K?"

"Like a real job", Gerti inserted.

Riley interjected again. "Like Bellows and I convinced him that he needed to come back here because Bellows needs a husband and Miley a father."

" Who gives a shit?"

"Jack please, you're making this worse!"

"See, I'm the one who made us move back here, he wanted to stay there because he has friends he does stuff with but they only do stuff a couple times a month and it's way not enough to support us so I convinced him that we needed to move back to Lynn because …because …well, I told Humphrey you would help with the kids and financially help support us if we moved".

I didn't hear a word Riley was saying. I was still focused on Gerti's last statement.

Making things worse? I'm not the guy who threw my pregnant wife down and punched her in the face."

"He didn't throw her down Daddy."

I was getting very upset.

"Quit this Daddy shit Riley you're pissing me off more. A few days ago you were the Iron Maiden and couldn't give a shit about your MOMMY and DADDY and now back to toddler speak."

Gerti's voice elevated, "Jesus Jack, enough …ENOUGH …she's your damn daughter for God sakes and these are you grand and great grandkids."

"My grandkids …I don't even know who they are?"

"And who the fuck's fault is that ?" Gerti snapped back.

"Enough of this shit, I want to know what happened here, that is before I go and knock this guy's fucking head off."

"You'll do no such thing", Gerti spewed, "This is for the police."

"Please no police", Bellows jumped in, " … please, please … No Police … NO POLICE."

"Bellows, I won't give that maggot you call your boyfriend the satisfaction of getting another arrest on his rap sheet. What he really needs now is a good ass kicking and damn it, if I'm not the one that's gonna give it to him."

"No grandpa … no, he didn't really mean it, what he did … it was nothing but an accident that's all. My coming here might have been an overreaction."

"Might have been an overreaction, bullshit, look at you. You're bloody and bruised and you're shaking like a leaf."

"It's really all my fault, if I didn't provoke him then I'm damn well sure he wouldn't have hit and pushed and kicked me"

Gerti angrily jumps, "KICKED YOU??"

"Ya, Gerti, what do you think, she got bloodied up and bruised all by herself?"

"Christ, Jack, SHE'S PREGNANT. He might have kicked her in her stomach and she'd lose the baby. Jack, you just got to go and do what you need to do …"

I couldn't believe Gerti was supporting me. A few minutes ago she wanted to call the Police, now, she wanted me to kick the shit out of Humphrey. I would have bet a million dollars she would have pushed back …but not this time. It seemed that Gerti was all in, she too had had enough of him. She now knew he was full of shit and a lousy lazy prick who didn't even try to support his family and worse yet, a cowardly woman beater, who preyed upon those who were unable to defend themselves.

Gerti's support made me even more determined to kick Humphrey's ass. He indeed threatened my family way too many times. Now his threats had turned into actions. There was just no way around this …Jack Krause had to deal with it.

I WAS OUT THE DOOR!

Honestly, I can't say that a few feet from the house, I didn't have reservations. I damn well was pissed and raging inside, but total insanity had yet to set in. Humphrey was a twenty two year old kid and at sixty-nine I had almost fifty years on him, years that had sucked from me my strength, my intestinal fortitude, my youthful impulsiveness. When I was young for the most part, I didn't know what I didn't know, and this alone empowered me. I fought for the sake of fighting, never realizing for what purpose. If someone or something provoked me I was all in, in a flash. I was involved in fights I had no stake in, brawls that I should have not been engaged. In my naivete I looked at fighting as a fun way to enhance my reputation at school, to brand myself as a "bad ass guy" not to be fucked with.

Obviously, less than a stellar student, I wasn't known for my brains (not that I didn't have any, only that I never really tried to use them), so at five eleven inches tall and a sturdy one hundred eighty five pounds, I was one of the bigger guys in school and possibly could have been one damn good athlete. I just didn't have the discipline or inclination. The ten or so fights I had during my high school years gave me the latitude I desired. The guys kept their distance and some of the girls found my rebellious behavior appealing as they unzipped my trousers on a bench in the playground or in the backseat of somebody's car.

In a few short seconds, my fears were gone. Humphrey indeed needed a damn good ass whipping and there was no way for me to back off now. I jumped in my Merc and made my way to Riley's apartment. It was a short ten minute ride away. I stopped in front of the house, and looking through the units window, I saw him.

He was a lot bigger than I remembered. He had to be nearly six feet, supporting well over two hundred fifty pounds. He was naked wearing only a pair of boxers.

He turned to look out the window. His "man-boobs" stared at me like they were another pair of eyes. He focused in on me, shit he was gone. So much for the element of surprise. I jumped out of my car and ran to the trunk, unlocked it and grabbed a 3 iron from my bag of rusty clubs. I looked at the club and reconsidered. This is ugly already so why make it uglier? Anyway, I wanted to beat this punk with my fists. I closed the trunk and walked quickly to the door. I knocked on it. The door was open and unlatched. I walked in.

Humphrey was standing, almost naked, but still sporting Calvin Klein boxers and a pair of tennis sneakers. I remember saying to myself, *Doesn't this shithead have any clothes ... and with a shit ass body like his...why doesn't he wear them?* We stood not ten feet apart looking at each other.

"Well, old man, I take it you have business with me?"

"Yeah, you're damn right I do. You beat up my granddaughter ... you beat on a pregnant girl ...you're a real piece of shit."

"So Granddad what are you gonna do about it? If you're smart you'll get the hell out of here?"

Humphrey reached behind the living room lounger and grabbed an Alex Rodriquez autographed bat. I couldn't help thinking this guy stinks in every way. *Not only is he a woman beater but a fucking New York Yankee fan as well?* I also remembered saying to myself, *You fool, you should have brought your 3 iron, dumb ass that you are!!*

I was now all in up to my sixty-nine year old ass. How I got myself into these situations I really don't know. It was like as a kid, I couldn't wait for the summers. In late July in Lynn, the carnival would arrive. I liked to play some of the games but the thing that really excited me were some of the rides. There was the Rotor, that was a cylinder and the rider attaches themselves to the sides. I remember myself pressing as hard as I could against the interior wall, hoping not to fall through. Within seconds the ride started up, I could feel my heart start to race. As the cylinder picked up speed I found myself in another world. It was as if I was on another planet. When the ride ended I was always disappointed. I could never get enough. It seemed that I never had enough money to spend the day and experience all the amusements, but there was one I looked forward to riding the entire year and I always made sure I had money for that. It was the Hurricane.

I loved the Hurricane. I could ride it all day. I remembered the first time I experienced it at the age of twelve. I peed in my pants. It just broke from me as the sweeping arm dropped with such great force. I couldn't hold back. No one initially noticed because, like me, all the riders were praying for their lives. I was literally scared shit and I knew that my fear was shared.

When the ride stopped, I looked down to my khaki shorts and there was a big pee stain. It covered my whole front. I remember seeing a couple of girls pointing and staring at me, unfortunately they were girls I knew from grade school. I knew that on Monday, every student at Sisson Elementary School would know that *Jack Krause was a pussy and peed in his pants because he was scared shit riding the Hurricane.*

I was mortified. I remember not wanting to go to school that following Monday knowing that I would be the laughing stock of every student there. It was humiliating. It took every ounce of courage I had to rise from my bed. If there was a dark deep hole I would have crawled in. I would have, but with my father screaming at me from the kitchen "Get your ass down here you're going to be late for damn school" I hadn't a chance. My life from here on, as bad as it sometimes seemed, was going to be inevitably worse than before.

My family wasn't very religious. We went to service infrequently. I was told we were Lutheran and at this very threatening time in my life, I prayed (my first time) to our Lutheran God. I didn't know if he existed, or what he looked like, or if he had ever heard or entertained any requests from any twelve year olds. The only thing I did was that I felt as depressed as I ever had and ran out of ideas how to survive the school day, week, month or years. Situations like this very seldom, if ever, blow over at school. Humiliations have a way of hanging like a black shroud over those who unfortunately experience them. UNFORTUNATELY, I WAS NOW ONE.

Life's a bitch when there is no place to hide. I wished I could just send my body to school, my perennial "earth suit" and leave the rest of me behind. A shell without a brain, a heart, emotions and soul. I would gladly give it up because it could act as a moat, protecting me from all the inevitable shit that was coming my way. No such luck, the package was Jackson Krause, the whole package with all his baggage, the twelve year old Jackson Krause who peed in his pants ... the twelve year old Jackson Krause, the cowardly bastard and pussy who got the living shit sacred out of him and pissed on the Hurricane to let the whole world see.

I knew damn well I could never live it down. I could see it now, Jackson Krause in the Sisson Elementary School "Hall of Shame". My picture, unattractive as it is, wearing my Khakis with a piss stain the size of a volley ball. I would be branded for life ... I fucking knew it ... there would never be any place for me. I damn well knew that too. Everywhere I went and every person I met, I would be exposed. I can see people staring at my groin even if it seemed they weren't ...I DAMN WELL KNEW THEY WERE ....and whispering at the very same time ... *it's Jackson Krause the pisspot inducted into the Sisson Elementary School Hall of Shame.* There was just nowhere to run from this. There just was no damn place to hide.

It took me twenty-five minutes to walk to school. I wished it took a lifetime. I didn't want to go within a mile of the place but I was running out of time and excuses. I mustered as much courage as I could and made my way, occasionally passing a fellow student along the path. I watched carefully how they reacted to me ... nothing, NADA. I was somewhat relieved. They didn't get any news over the weekend, that in itself was a good sign. Maybe my Lutheran God listened to me ... maybe

I should attend services more frequently, maybe, MAYBE, ah maybe not.

I knew it was just too damn good to be true. As I got closer to school I could see some students turn and then stare and then turn and laugh. I damn well knew now that the word had already gotten out and I hadn't even entered the school grounds yet. My ass was proverbial grass.

I wasn't fifteen feet into the schoolyard when I was approached by Bo Murray, a fat bully bastard of a guy and a couple of his bully friends. My worse nightmare was about to be realized.

"Yeah… pissed in your pants Krause." His two buddies laughed.

I didn't know what to say or do. I decided to say and do nothing.

"You're just the pussy I thought you were". His two buddies stared and chanted, "PUSSY…PUSSY."

Sensing there was going to be a fight a small group of students gathered.

I no longer had the liberty to say or do nothing, but what could I say or do?

Bo Murray was a mean kid. I saw not a few times him beating a kid badly.

I sensed he loved the power he held over others. He liked the effect of those screaming in his clutches as he hit them again and again, bringing them to tears if not a trip to the hospital.

When the prey looks the predator in the eye he knows he's TOAST. It was all too clear to me. I had to do something quickly. It was within seconds I made a decision that changed my life forever. I dropped my books and leaped toward Bo who stood not a few feet away. Unwinding my right hand in the process, I hit him right in the nose. I heard it snap. I broke it. Bo caved like a tent of cards. He fell to his knees and I kicked him in the head. He contorted in the fetal position. His two buddies looked with eyes as large as saucers, they couldn't believe what they just witnessed. well. The most surprised of all was me. I was astonished at what I did. I really had no intentions of doing anything but hoping to weather the storm, hoping Bo Murray would get bored and leave me alone. There was really no hope. I did what I had to do. I felt within me a greater power. It had to be the Lutheran God. I could think of nothing else possessing me to lunge forward… perhaps it was that *LEAP OF FAITH* that was the subject of a sermon at one of the few Lutheran services I attended. It must have been, because before this incident, I always thought of myself as submissive. I never had the courage to confront my enemies (which many times I felt my father was one) because there I felt there was no need to, as I envisioned myself all battered and bloody being ground into the pavement by one of the many people I disliked and by whom I was disliked in return.

I WAS NOW EMPOWERED! Me standing over the beaten, bloody body of Bo Murray was wonderful, it is what dreams are made of, it is the demarcation where trust meets reality. It was the best Christmas present of my life, not that I ever received anything memorable. It was me Jackson Krause breaking out of my fragile shell that was painted yellow for cowardice but now feeling exhalted that I just don't have to deal with any of this school playground bullshit anymore. **It's when Jackson "The Cowardly Kid" Krause became Mr. Jackson "The Courageous Kid" Krause.** I now had respect and the heavens were rejoicing!!!

My world now began to spin on a different axis. I no longer took shit from anyone (my father included). It was just my time. I watched with amazement as I grew from a scrawny one hundred twenty pound kid to a muscled packed steroid enhanced one hundred eighty pounder, with a forty six inch chest and a thirty inch waist, and arms as large as a midget's thigh. I was now more than most of the student body could handle. I had a new body, a new mind and a piss poor attitude.

I lived my life attacking, no longer submissive. I now walked the halls of Lynn Technical with an air of authority. Just about everybody was scared of me, the teachers too. They just didn't have any handle and looked at me as "twenty miles of bad road". Those who didn't were the baseball, soccer, wrestling and football coaches who tried to interest me in joining their teams. I had no interest, I was now Mr. Jackson Krause. I wanted them to beg me so that I could say "NO … Fucking NO." And as for the girls in my class, I wanted them to beg me so that I could say "YES… FUCKING YES."

So here I was fifty-seven years later posturing in my daughter's shit-ass rental in the same old city Lynn, ready to square off with her stupid, lazy, almost naked, shit-for –brains woman abusing boyfriend doing BAD STUFF GUY, going to war again.

What the hell am I doing here?, I thought, *I should be home bouncing my grand kid on my knee or taking her to the park or doing other things grandfathers do (whatever the hell they are) but I'm not, I'm about to do battle with Humphrey. LIFE IS GREAT!*

"I'm going to kick your ass, Grandpa."

"Not a chance in hell you piece of crap."

"You're an old senile man. You should be in a nursing home."

"You'll be in the hospital before I do that asshole."

I started to circle the room and Humphrey, with Alex Rodriquez in hand, moved counter-clockwise.

I was an idiot not to bring my golf club. I would take any of the irons now, in fact, I wished I had my Callaway Driver (my retirement present from the UPS, which has seen nothing but the dark interior of my car's trunk). I needed every advantage I could but I had none and the only person again I had to blame was myself.

There was a brief silence in the room and like a bull charging the matador, Humphrey ran toward me swinging the bat. Being pretty agile for an old guy, I just escaped its path as it missed my head. *This is serious shit.* I remembered thinking. *Really, like someone could really get killed here, that kind of serious shit.*

I stepped several steps back and tried to reposition myself. Humphrey bounced off the wall like a blubber ball and came at me swinging again. He looked like a sumo wrestler and I hoped I wouldn't be flattened. I got behind the couch and pushed it toward him. It did not deter him as he bounced from the seat cushion and leaped over it, I was amazed at his athleticism. For a large man he controlled his body well.

As I moved to the right corner of the room and Humphrey positioned himself once again, I picked up a brass lamp that was on an end table anchoring the couch. With Humphrey attacking again, my Lutheran God must have heard my faint prayer, because I swung the lamp and hit Humphrey square in the back of his head as his momentum took him past me. He dropped the baseball bat and hit the living room wall headfirst. His head smashed through it and I could see pieces of plaster falling to the floor.

I got him now. I thought. *Damn well got this shit piece of lard where the hell I want him.*

Humphrey, now on his knees, pulled his head from the wall, revealing a large hole in the plaster going right through to one of the two bedrooms. He managed to turn around and face me. Humphrey was panting like an old dog. With the lamp still in my hand, I was about to hit him again when I felt something startling. It affected my lower body and I looked down toward my groin, I found I had again (fifty some years later) pissed on myself. I was mortified and couldn't determine what had taken place.

I knew I wasn't a young man anymore but I wasn't as infirmed as many my age. I was a damn youthful sixty-nine. My plumbing was working well (or so I thought). I had no problems with incontinence or over active bladder. I never wore and hopefully never will, any adult Depends. I just didn't get it and then to file this away as quickly as I could to purge it from my mind, I decided that it is what it is. I was in a fight, perhaps, one for my life and in the turmoil and unpredictability of it all, I pissed on myself once again. What the fuck, twice in fifty-seven years, I guess I could live with that.

As quickly as I tried to think through "wetting" my pants, it just wasn't quick enough. The little time it took, that critical blind spot of confusion, that moment of fatal hesitation was just enough to allow Humphrey to regain his senses and composure. I thought I saw him leap to his feet and grab his "Alex Rodriquez" that was not but a few feet from him, balancing on the right corner of the couch, just enough to allow Humphrey to grab the handle. Seeing this I moved as quickly as I could, with lamp still in hand and stepped to my right hopefully to attack him before he did me.

I was not quick enough. Again, I have to give Humphrey credit for his fleet of foot and agility, being as big as he was, he moved twice as fast as I thought he could.

Seeing an opportunity, I unleashed another swing with the lamp, hoping to dislodge the bat from Humphrey's grip. As I reached back, with lamp in hand, I felt a sharp pain, on the side of my right temple. The next thing I knew, the lamp slipped out of my grip and flew across the room and I was down, staring at the filthy tattered shit ass rug on the floor. I could hear Humphrey scream, "Stay down you fuck, don't you make a move or I'll smack you again."

I laid there in a semi-conscious state, fading in and out of consciousness. I felt like my head ran into a wall; it did but in a different form, an Alex Rodriquez 34 inch, 31 ounce baseball bat.

I wasn't about to try to get up. The little brains that were not now scrambled told me don't move a muscle or Humphrey would smack me again and drive my head through the floor. Just then I heard him go into a rage, jumping around the room like a lunatic. I could hear the floor bouncing under his weight. He started to scream at me.

"You stupid shit ...I might have killed you over your stupid fucking granddaughter Bellows ... you asshole ... she's nothing but a whore ...a fucking whore. Miley? I don't even think is mine ... and the one she's carrying ...I doubt that kid is mine either ...your granddaughter's a whore ... that's why I smacked the bitch cause I found this shit out. You want to attack people with lamps, then you best smash your granddaughter across the side of her head and drive the "whorishness" from her. The bitch is a slut and I'm leaving her and the kids behind ... for all that I know ...neither of them are mine."

I couldn't believe what I was hearing but despite my trying to deny it, I knew it might be true. Her mother Riley had been putting out since she was a teen. Gerti and I were informed of that when she was just thirteen. We knew, we just didn't want to acknowledge it because she was our kid and what parents want to think that their kid is a fucking machine.

I felt nauseous and sick to my stomach, my head was spinning uncontrollably and I felt blood tricking down my face. I knew I couldn't lay here forever. I had to move. I was hoping Humphrey would move away from me, (go to his damn closet and get dressed and hopefully leave me here) but he didn't. He just hovered over me, then I heard him ask me, "Hey, you dead?"

I figured my best strategy was not to say a word, just to lie there as motionless as I could, hoping he thought he had killed me or at least injured me seriously. I did just that and it riled Humphrey.

"Fuck...you dead?" he questioned.

I held my breath.

"Fuck ...you dead?" he questioned again.

He started to panic.

I could hear him now talking to himself.

"Fuck ... FUCK ....**FUCK** ...I killed him... shit I have to get out of here."

I could hear Humphrey run the few short feet to the bedroom and a couple of minutes later return and I surmised that he was now fully dressed. Again, I didn't move a muscle hoping he would just leave without checking me again. He did just what I hoped and out the door he went.

After regaining the little sense I had left and making certain that Humphrey had left the premises, I tried to gather my wits. I attempted to get to my feet but I was very unsteady and felt, after getting completely erect I was unable to balance myself. I steadied my footing by holding onto the furniture that was scattered around the room. There were just a few pieces but enough so I could negotiate to the front door. A few feet into my journey, I picked up Humphrey's "Alex Rodriquez", which in haste he had left behind. I now had him by the balls. I had the wound to my head along with the weapon he used to inflict it. HUMPHREY'S ASS WAS GRASS AND I WAS THE FUCKING LAWNMOWER. Just a call to the cops would land the bastard in jail. Assaulting an unarmed senior citizen, nearly fifty five years his elder, with a baseball bat would surely send his sorry ass to jail for a good five years, especially since I would bet the farm (if I indeed owned one) he had a significant amount of arrests prior to this incident. Indeed Humphrey was in deep shit but the thought faded quickly as I became nauseous and felt I was about to faint. I started toward the door deciding whether I was going to call the cops or ambulance or try to make it to NSMC Union Hospital under my own volition. I decided to try it myself. My life lately had been a shit load of complication. I had no desire to make it any more than it already was. I made my way to the front door and eyed my Merc. Union Hospital was just minutes away. I knew my Merc would get me there. As usual, it was me and my Merc ... my Merc and me.

I sat in the emergency room for two and a half hours. As always, it was jammed packed with everyone from a child with a cold to a young man who broke his leg in a motorcycle accident, two inches above his knee. He was wearing leathers with some crest on the back. It was in Italian, or I thought it was. As ill as I felt I got a chuckle out of the thought he might be a member of a "Spaghetti" motorcycle gang. As tough as he looked and he looked very, he didn't now as he winced in pain. Even the tattoo of the skull and bones and dragonhead on his arms, looked a little dismayed.

It was starting to get late in the day. By nightfall and into the early morning hours, this place will be packed. There would be more of the same and in every other infirmary as well, knife and gun wounds included.

Gerti had been calling every fifteen minutes for the last two hours. I started to Riley's house at 3:45 p.m. My mano-to-mano with Humphrey lasted but a short fifteen or twenty minutes. I knew Gerti (and hopefully Riley and Bellows) were worried about me and curious as hell about what had happened. I should call them but I just didn't feel the desire. For some unexplained reason I wanted them to wait - to wonder - to worry about whether their husband, father, grandfather had indeed found Humphrey and what resulted from the encounter. I wanted them to worry whether we banged heads, and if we did, what was the result. Was Humphrey the victor or victim or their good old husband, father, grandfather - asshole extraordinaire - their's truly Jackson Krause. I guess in the most selfish arrogant sense I just wanted them to worry damn hard and long.

It was now over three hours and finally my name was called to see the doctor. To say I was pissed would be an understatement. I was beyond words and with my bloody forehead wrapped and my clothes covered with blood I followed the nurse to an examining room.

The doctor walked in. He couldn't have been over thirty-five. He already looked like he was burned out. In a quivering but angry voice I immediately attacked him.

"Shit, I could have died in that waiting room, it took so damn long."

"You wouldn't have been the first", the doctor replied, unsympathetically.

"Well, I don't give a shit about the others this is the only body I have."

"Well, that's very Christian of you."

"There's been nothing Christian about this day."

"Obviously, with the welt on your head and the one inch split in your skull, I surely can see why. How do you feel?"

"Like shit. My head is spinning three sixty."

"How did it happen?"

I didn't know what to say. If I told the Doc the truth, he might have to inform the authorities, then the soup would get even thicker, as if it wasn't thick enough. So I decided to do something I was good at. I lied.

"Slipped off a curb."

" It doesn't look like a "slipped off a curb" injury to me."

"Ya well… why is that Doc?"

"The placement is all wrong for that kind. The split is almost on the crown of your head. To experience it like you said, you would have to have dove into the pavement."

I was getting pissed again. Who was this young ass doctor to question me? I was old enough to be his father.

"Well, believe me or not. I really don't give a shit."

"Well, we doctors like to have a honest communication with our patients. It might not always be attainable but at least we're hopeful."

Hopeful, my ass …boy, does this young Doc have a lot to learn. An honest relationship with his patients … BULLSHIT … I haven't had an honest relationship with my wife and kids for over forty years …probably never had. I decided I had enough of Union Hospital and their kid doctor. If he wants to play "Hospital" then let him play it with someone else's mind and body.

"I'm outta here … gone … I want outta here."

"It's against my best advisement Mr. Krause, that you go anywhere. First of all, you damn well took a damn hard blow to your head. It's placement is very consistent with getting hit with a blunt instrument. Secondarily, this is no minor cut on your head. It's margins are better than an inch long and very deep. Your head is split down right to the skull. You will need at least fifty stitches. Last, but not least, I recommend strongly that you spend the night for evaluation. You might have a severe issue here not really knowing until the testing and evaluation is done, but I would say, the least of all, is that you might have one serious concussion which will cause you dizziness and nausea. Something I think you are already experiencing, at least the dizziness."

Smart, "wet behind the ears" young punk ass Doctor that he is, the shit might be right. I felt like crap. My vision was getting away from me. When I looked at the Doc, I could see no less than four of him and my head was swimming uncontrollably. Even worse, I felt sick to my stomach like I wanted to barf.

"Yes, well, I guess … well, you're the Doc … Doc … I guess I'll take your advice …cause I really don't feel that well."

With those last words I felt very weird … I felt very faint …I started to fall, I fell … I FELL… and before I hit the floor, I felt the Doc catching me. Then I remembered… *absolutely nothing…*

28

All Stitched Up

I woke up several hours later. I wasn't quite certain where I was, a hospital or an insane asylum. With the absurdity of the last few days it could have been either. My recollections were now coming back and I started remembering my conversation with the doctor. I was now happy that he was as strong minded as he'd been. He was damn right. I needed medical attention. My head was pounding uncontrollably and it seemed as though my insides were eating away at themselves. I hoped whatever issues I have would resolve shortly. I don't do doctors, nurses and hospitals well, they are anti-Jackson Krause. I hate to be dependent on anyone or anything. The doctor entered my room.

"I see you're doing better."

"Better than what?"

"Than you were before. You almost passed out in the exam room."

Wow, I couldn't even remember that, just a haze of recollection but the detail was lost to me.

"Well, what's the prognosis?"

"The prognosis Mr. Krause is that you have a very bad concussion and a cracked skull and you will need several days of bed rest before you will be able to go home."

Several days of bed rest, shit, I don't have time for this. I have important things to do like tracking down Humphrey and finishing what I began.

"No Doc … I can't stay in here that long."

"You're not going anywhere Mr. Krause. You may not think it but you are a damn lucky man. If you'd fallen a bit harder you might very well be dead now. Your demise was much closer than you think and it would be unwise for both of us to push the odds."

"Alright Doc …alright … I got it."

"Excellent, then I'll take my leave and see you when I make my rounds later today."

"Yeah, Doc. Sure as hell will see you around."

Well there was no way I was leaving the hospital. It was to my betterment that I stay and in spite of my surliness I was very much relieved. According to Doc I was all stitched up and it would take a few days for the affects of the concussion to be gone.It had been over seven hours that I have not spoken to Gerti. I'm sure she had put out repeated calls to me. I bet the number of attempts have been in the teens. She is going to be bullshit when she learns I'm all right and have been at the hospital for several hours now and haven't picked up the calls, text messages or responded.

It was unlike me not to respond. Whether in sync or at odds with Gerti, I always answered when she called. It was something I did well, she sure as hell was going to think I've been injured or most assuredly worse than that since she hasn't heard from me.

For what reason was I not responding or reaching out to her, I really didn't know but deep inside me there was a part that said, "SCREW HER", let Gerti and the kids worry the hell over my well-being, then all of a sudden like a bolt of lightning it hit me. I had to question why was Gerti so adamant initially, that I not chase down Humphrey? I had to question why she would have me rather call the police and not a few minutes later contradict herself by saying with firm conviction that I shouldn't contact them but rather track Humphrey down and hopefully, teach him a message he'd not soon forget, or even worse. It wasn't that Gerti was beyond reason, Humphrey had degraded her granddaughter, hit and kicked her and Bellows now well into her pregnancy was at risk of terminating. Sure, it might have been part of the reason but not all, there was more to it than that, as I recalled the conversation, it now came as apparent to me as falling snow on a hot scorching August afternoon that Gerti wanted me to track and confront Humphrey so that he WOULD KICK THE LIVING CRAP OUT OF ME OR PERHAPS, KILL ME DEADER THAN DEAD.

Yes, it was a revelation. I could now not deny it. My wife Gerti was blaming me for all the shit that had occurred in our marriage, the years of miscommunication and dysfunction, the years of our son Hendrix's alcohol and drug addiction, his bad behavior, police convictions and ultimately, his leaving. She blamed me for Riley's rebellion against her family, her lying and deceit, her slutty behavior, her tattoos, her now sixteen year old daughter with a kid and another on the way. She also blamed me for Bellow's degenerate boyfriend, a downright lazy, belligerent, woman beating piece of shit.

YES, IT WAS **ALL ME**. YES … YES … AND YES. I WAS TO BLAME FOR IT ALL…JACKSON KRAUSE ….THIS LEFT NO ROOM FOR SPECULATION … NO ROOM FOR DENIAL … NO "WIGGLE ROOM" AT ALL.

The more I thought about it, the more pissed I became. Here I was again, a pawn in another person's game, my wife's. It is as if nothing with me ever changes. It seemed I was always the scapegoat for what ails the world. It was like that with my Nazi-like father, Gunther Krause, who ruled the roost like he was a commander in a prison camp. It was the same as a draftee in the military, whatever went wrong in my unit, I or someone other with my shit-ass rank would be to blame, but it usually came back to me. It was the same with my relationship with Dirt and Rhino. I still have guilt for not traveling to Vietnam and throwing Dirt's ashes in the Saigon River. I feel a deep down sorrow that at the very end, where the rubber meets the road, that I did Dirt wrong. My relationship with Rhino ended the same. He told me he was a drowning man and it was I, who was dragging him down and now a relationship of fifty-plus years is marginalized, or possibly, non-existent. Now it is my family that is laying on me the biggest and most cutting guilt-trip of all, affecting my very seed and legacy. Yes, me Jackson Krause has failed once again, but in no small way, my wife and kids. There was no shadow of doubt this was the shit now being dropped on me and from the vantage of my hospital bed I felt totally disempowered. There was nothing I could do about it now or perhaps never. My wife and kids hated my guts and wanted me to die even at the hands of a shit bag, lazy scum of the earth bastard, pretend boyfriend and father - that douche-bag Humphrey Ravens.

I found myself shrinking into the bed's mattress. I looked down toward my toes and profiled my body. It was now that of an old man. At sixty-nine, I couldn't discount that the years had drifted away and the end result was that there were far more that past than those that lay ahead. If I could rescind any of the things I have done, it was now nearly impossible, because I was running out of time, energy, and those who would be willing to give me a chance. Who and what Jackson Krause is and was is now engrained with indelible ink. It had now dried and I lay here in the residue of my legacy, a failure on all fronts.

Gerti, Riley, and Bellows had found me. I couldn't believe it as they busted through the hospital door to my room with Miley in tow. By the looks on their faces, they were far from happy. They were more than upset, hours had past and they hadn't a single utterance from me. Even me being confined to a hospital bed and wired to an IV and a two-inch bandage around my head, didn't deter them as they dropped tonnage.

Gerti held rank, she was the first to attack. "You asshole, Jackson Krause. You shithead. Riley, Bellows and I have been worried sick over you."

Sick over me, bullshit. They wanted me dead and I fully knew it.

"Why didn't you fucking call? You have a cellphone?"

Why didn't I call? That was a really a good question. It cut to the crux of the matter. My answer would have been, *I didn't call because I wanted to punish or severely hurt you because I know all your darkest secrets... YOU ALL WANT ME DEAD!* I didn't say a word but just lay there looking at them with the deepest contempt.

"Damn it Daddy", now Riley jumped in.

I hated her when she called me Daddy. It was so childish coming from her. She has called me every name possible over the last five years and now for the last several months she has resorted back to Daddy. Daddy my ass.

"Daddy, really with everything happening in my life how could you ever do this to me?"

Now what the hell is this? With all the shit in her life? Like now she is going to lay all this crap on me, her slutting around, her dropping out of UMASS, her being knocked up before the age nineteen and her daughter Bellows with a kid and another one on the way (possibly by two different men if what I heard from Humphrey is true) and continue living with and possibly making the greatest mistake of her life - hoping her daughter would someday marry the asshole Humphrey Ravens.

"Well Daddy, are you hearing me? Mom and I were really scared that Humphrey killed you or something."

Killed me or something? The way I look at it now is that I have been dead for years. Yes. me Jackson Krause and the man I am or possibly could have been if I didn't get wrapped up in all the crap in my life is dead. Jackson Krause, the nice guy. Jackson Krause, the doting husband and father. Jackson Krause, the best friend a man could have. Jackson Krause,

the lover of life and the doer of things. Jackson Krause…
the almost … maybe … possibly …perhaps …complete …
fulfilled ….and happy man **… IS DEAD AND HAS BEEN
FOR DECADES.** Praise the Lord, May Jesus have Mercy.

Three days later I was out of Union. It confirmed my
suspicions, that hospitals are not the place anyone wants to
be. They are as it has been said, *where the sick people go*. I was no
longer sick, my concussion was well on the path to healing,
that is, if I heeded my doctor's advice and remained steadfast
and calm, limiting my activity and movement. I was committed
to doing what I was told (not the Jack Krause way) because the
dizziness and nausea rendered me almost helpless.

As far as Humphrey was concerned, just the thought of
him turned my stomach. I decided not to call the police and
hoped never to see him again. In regards to Riley, Bellows and
Miley, Gerti and I decided to allow them back in our home.
Having my daughter and her family underfoot was something
I dreaded but we had no other option.

Gerti and I hadn't a clue how we would make this
arrangement work. As before, our small bungalow strained
with four bodies under foot. What made things worse is that
Bellow's date of delivery was just six weeks away. We now
would have three adults, one teenager, a toddler and a baby
although it had been quite a while since both our kids left, now,
three adults and one (soon to be two) grand kids, there would
certainly be no privacy or quiet, and certainly no order. And
our one and a half bathrooms would now always be crowded
leaving no longer any sacred space or time, to do the little
reading I did, mostly fingering through the sports page of the
Boston Globe.

My life although "hellish" before, was now going beyond.
This I knew and I surmised Gerti did as well because hers
would be running parallel for the most part, well that is when
I was home which I decided would be as little time as possible
under the circumstance.

The problem now was multiplied because, unlike a few months before, I really had no friends now. Dirt was dead and as funny as it sounds, I missed him. Yes there was no doubt he was a pain in the ass, as irresponsible and homeless as he was, but there was something in him that for whatever reason, (I'm still trying to figure it out) held me, like glue. I was drawn to him in the strangest of ways. At times I thought his attraction, was he had made such a mess of his life. He didn't do it happenstance. It wasn't because he was caught off guard or because the fickle Gods of disorder threw a tonnage of crap in his life, not to say that his tour of Nam was anything but … it was rather that years before he decided whatever life served up in the pursuit of being a responsible adult, he wanted no part. For whatever reason it was overwhelming and he decided he was much better suited to live in various shelters and even an occasional box in the back of Marshall's in Vinnin Square than he was any place else.

Whether anyone else would ever think that "rolling over" in life had one inkling of courage, I was very much in doubt. Most would think like Rhino, that Dirt was nothing more than a lazy, user, alcohol, drug and tobacco addicted totally irresponsible street person. Maybe he was but I saw something else in him. He was a guy who knew his limitations and he had a shit load. He was a man who knew his ambitions, and here again, his cart was empty. He was a man who understood as uncomfortable as it had to be, to make this decision, he would just live his life on the dole, expecting nothing from it and him giving nothing in return.

There was no doubt Dirt would never be anyone or anything singled out as a pillar of inspiration. He surely would be walked over as anyone who gave just an inkling of respectability to his existence. Dirt would most assuredly be labeled a bum, a loser, a parasite, a despicable example of wasted human spirit and life. He was the dust that is swept under the carpet, the rat who lives in the sewer, the pure example of who not to become or be.

It might sound stupid but If indeed I had a hall of fame, most assuredly, Dirt's picture would be hanging there. Because no matter what he was, he was all in. There was no pretense about him. He didn't try to bullshit anyone at all. He was comfortable in his skin and no one had to peel layer after layer from him to see what was at his core. Unlike me and a whole lot of other people who play at our lives, we don't make the sacrifices that Dirt did and do not voluntarily accept the consequences of our decisions. I have skirted responsibilities in my life and just touched the surface, never going beyond the fringe where it could have made a dramatic difference.

There is an honest truth about Dirt in accepting the fact he wasn't cut out to be a valuable member of society and instinctively choosing not to be. There was little disappointment in his life because he expected nothing of it. The few people he knew, he never let down because he expected little or nothing from them, and they indeed expected the same. I was one of those people. I wondered sometimes to obsessiveness whether it was Dirt who really needed me or the other way around. I also pondered what kind of a man I am, needing a person like him to emotionally support me in my life. It puzzled me that I was drawn to such a presence to maintain a firm foothold. What a fool was I not to think that my relationship with him was nothing less than clinical, knowing that as bad as my life was or was going to be, that in no way could it equal Dirt's. Being the lowest of the low, there was no upside to his, just a constant spiraling down into the abyss. There was a lot in mine if I chose to see it and committed to work toward it.

I remember many times using Dirt as the baseline from which to compare my life. I might have a sucky day and I would hear myself say "Fuck it, it ain't as bad as Dirt's." In some metamorphic sense the air would go out of my balloon and I would again resonate, "Fucking Dirt, I know damn well he is having a shittier day than me." Gerti and I would get into it and I would say to myself, "Shit, at least I have her."

There's someone in my life and although it may not always be "Wine and Roses", the fact was that our relationship was more like Arsenic and Rag Weed, I would again be saying to myself, "Unlike Dirt, I am not lonely." Even though many times I longed for someone other to fill the hole in my heart. As funny as it seems, many times I looked at Dirt as the giver and myself as the beneficiary of our relationship. Our friendship was superficially based around a few hours a week, a cup of Dunkin's and a cinnamon donut, a trip to the diner, occasionally a short ride around Salem, Swampscott or Lynn, nothing more … most times less.

I spent a lot of hours lately trying to think through our relationship. I had it now down to the simplest terms. There was however that one perplexing matter, his request that Rhino and I take his ashes back to Saigon and throw them into the Po River. Where that came from I didn't quit know? Dirt hated Vietnam. His tour broke the back of an already weakened spirit. Why he wanted to go back in any form, cremated ashes not withstanding, I really didn't know and Rhino had less than a clue. Maybe it was just to test us both, but for what I asked. What the hell would he want to test us for? It wasn't his way. Maybe he thought Rhino and I needed to go back to make peace with our past and this was a sure fire way to get us there, that is, if indeed we did choose to go. Yes, this idea carried a certain weight. This summation was plausible and not totally without reason. Lastly, maybe it was that Dirt, as stoic and emotionally detached as he seemed, hated Vietnam beyond description and in his inner gut, although he put on a great pretense, hated himself as well. Maybe, yes, maybe it was just that, that Dirt hated himself as much as the country that finally took him down and that in death he concluded there would be no better place for him to rest for eternity than in the shit-ass, polluted river in Saigon. Maybe I was right, maybe I was wrong, maybe it doesn't matter at all.

It now came down that Rhino was my last bastion of Hope. I was down to one friend and he was it. I hadn't seen him for quite a while, in fact ever since Dirt's ceremony on Marblehead Neck. He was MIA. I wasn't comfortable not having Rhino around. What I was to Dirt, Rhino was to me. He was the calm in the storm, the salve on the wound. He was the voice of reason in an insane world. He was a pillar of strength that held the walls in the crumbling fortress of my mind.

Without Rhino involved in my life, there was no doubt I would have been a lesser man than I was (although at times, I found that would be impossible). For whatever reason, Rhino was my anchor. In the fiercest and most terrifying of storms, he held true. I could count on him.

I knew Rhino didn't like Dirt. Although differing in opinion, I couldn't take issue for him feeling this way. Dirt was the anti-Rhino. Rhino was responsible to a fault and didn't let up on himself. He believed that every man had a solemn duty to fend for himself and not be a drain on the rest of society. He believed people should educate themselves on everything that was important or pertained to their lives. Believing that the brain was a muscle and would atrophy when not used, his dogma was that all people should seek as much knowledge and understanding as possible. Rhino didn't read books, he consumed them, he digested newspapers like popcorn and sought out every and all media seeking that which he did not know, that which he felt was a missing but critical component of his life source. He believed those who would not educate themselves were lazy, foolish and dumb. He hated people like this, he believed Dirt was part of this club and Rhino had no use for either.

Rhino believed that every person should have a moral plane. He believed they should have that at the center of their lives. He often spoke of "selective morality" and "selective inattention", his verbiage for constantly making excuses for not leading a purposeful life, one of moral fiber and conviction.

When God made Rhino, he did not only make him of sound body but of sound mind. As fucked up as I could be (and as he perceived Dirt to be all the time) he was sane and stable while occasionally being crude, jarring and ragingly un-moveable. When Rhino voiced his opinion, it was not just a fleet of thought. It was well researched and thought out and once it was said, Dirt and I knew it would be etched into his mind and stored in his mental war chest, ready to be loaded into his voice box when needed as a bullet in his gun. Rhino didn't say much but when he spoke people listened. He commanded a room and everyone's attention when he stated his opinions, but sometimes in such a bombastic manner the perception was that there was no doubt of error. As large a man as Rhino was, his opinions and their presentation spoke louder. I missed that about him. He was studied, he was learned, he was "in your face", he was Rhino.

The big contradiction in Rhino's life was the failure of his two marriages. He constantly pained over them as he did his relationship with his two kids, who were their result. As far as I could tell, he tried as hard as any man to hold onto both. What separated him was his insatiable need to overperform. Rhino smothered both wives with love and affection to the point he was overbearing. He did the same with his daughters. Wherever they were and whatever they were involved, he wanted to know every little detail. Working or not, over the years, (Rhino fashioned himself as a highly skilled mechanic, which he truly was) he would call them incessantly throughout the day. There was no escape from him and as the years unfolded, six years of marriage to his first wife and nine to his second, there was a breaking point in both. Literally "one" because both his wives had to break through his compulsive, addictive behavior having to be one with them all the time. Fortunately his kids were too young to realize how controlling their Dad was.

Rhino's obsessiveness drove him and his wives to counseling throughout the years. Neither of the sessions had any positive result. Knowing now obviously there were big problems in his marriages Rhino became more of who he was. Afraid that his wives (and children) would leave him, he patterned both the same, he quit his jobs, and now constantly underfoot with no income to support his family, he watched as it crumbled under him.

Rhino became a perceived threat to his wives. They both eventually put a restraining order against him. He was now out of their home and not able to get within a thousand yards of them and the kids. Rhino was miserable and angst-ridden as his life was falling apart.

It was ironic and a bit comical that Rhino saw just the opposite happening in his life. He felt he was a great husband but didn't spend enough time with his wives and kids. It was incongruous that he felt this way because there was hardly any degree of separation between them, and that was indeed the crux of the issue. It was strange as hell that he saw it as he did and he made a strong case for how all of us live in a strange, sometimes unrealistic world that has absolutely no relevance to the real one.

For Dirt and me, Rhino was always there for us over the years. The little time he spent away from his family, he spent with us, usually at the mall walking or occasionally having breakfast or tooling around in my Merc for a few hours. Other than that, he was either engaged or tracking down his family's whereabouts. In the years he was working, which were the majority, Dirt and I didn't see as much of him. He would end work and immediately return to his family – not that he didn't communicate with them throughout the day with a barrage of phone calls and questions.

I remember Rhino saying to me in one of his pensive moods…

"You know Jackson, I don't really know what the fuck went wrong in my life. I mean I damn well know I'm a good man and damn well I'm a motivated one by doing only the right things, but although my intentions are noble, or at least I think they are…there's always a fly in the ointment. I never wanted to scare my wives. I only wanted to protect them and as for my daughters, they are indeed the center of my universe. I have to ask you, can a father show too much love, can he show too much affection, can he ever be too close to his wife and kids? Now I'm asking you this Jackson, because God knows, I need to know. Can he? CAN HE? For Christ's sake answer me."

I didn't really know what to say. I was damn well at a loss for words. I wasn't a shrink, social worker, counselor … no, I was none of the aforementioned. I was just a retired UPS driver and the only license I had was to get behind the wheel of a car or maybe a truck, but I answered anyway, certainly with little aptitude and strength of conviction but just enough "flim-flam" that I no longer had to pay his inquiry any attention.

"No," I answered, "Fucking no. No father can ever show his family too much love nor too much affection. No father could ever be too close to his family. And I answered one more unasked question of my own. And no father could ever want enough for them ….their welfare and happiness is paramount … YES PARAMOUNT … it is above all things."

My answer crucified me. It hung me on the cross. It punctured my fractured life like the point of a thousand spears. It was the mirror that I for years avoided … one reflecting back the sickness I carried to the detriment of my family. I was the anti-Rhino. I was motivated by no moral premise other than my innate laziness to break through that of which I am. In reflection, I never gave my marriage a chance. From the very first day, it was designed to fail, not that it had in the traditional sense because Gerti and I were still married for forty-two years but the path was laborious and it was me who made it that way. I never gave Gerti a chance…never…from the day I met her forty-four years ago.

Rhino turned and looked me straight in the eye

"Jackson, do you think it was Nam that fucked us up?"
There was just no other way for me to answer it.
"Yes, Rhino ... *it was Nam all the fucking way*."

29

Magical Mystery Tour

Rhino and I were just back from Nam, I for six weeks and he for four. Upon our return, we both had the same estranged feelings. We were in the jungles of Nam one day and the next back in Lynn Massachusetts. It was so surreal. I kept wiping my eyes to see if I had just fallen into a rem sleep and was living in a world of hyper imagination but I was not. It was indeed real that I returned with all my arms and legs intact. My brain was another thing, it was scrambled to the nines. It fried over there like a poached egg on just laid tar. There was now just a big disconnect.

Rhino and I would just keep asking ourselves, will we forever be tethered to the war? Will we ever be free from it to the point that the consequence of our being there will be minimal at best?"

"Jack, can I tell you a secret?"

"If you can't tell me than who can you tell, Rhino?"

"Well, then hear me out. I had my reservations about returning home."

"I understand believe me, I've had mine as well … and yours?"

Rhino picks up his Coke as we both wait for our sandwiches to be served.

"Well Jack, I have two."

"And they are?"

"Well for one, leaving my guys behind. It really is a strange feeling I'm here and they are not. I mean here we are having a Coke and BLT at Heck Allen's Sandwich Shop and our guys are probably prepping for another mission, possibly another insane "fire fight" and unfortunately some of them will be injured and possibly killed and here we are a few blocks from a friendly ocean that separates two extremely different worlds …. and I can't say that I'm not consumed by guilt."

"Shit Rhino, you know what my CO said? The easiest part of our returning home is our getting there. He said don't be surprised by the emotions that reveal themselves once stateside. They will be a war all by themselves. I really didn't know what he meant by that, but in retrospect, there were probably no truer words ever spoken …. "

"Yeah, well, at least you received some advice. I received nothing more than a pat on my ass and "you're outta here soldier." That and a dime won't buy me a cup of coffee."

"Well, one good thing is that we have each other. We won't have to go through this shit alone."

"Well I'm not totally sure of that as well. We are different people, we live in our own heads."

"And the second thing?", I asked

"I can't relate to anyone but you. I can't talk to or even want to see my mother. It just pains me to be with her. Ever since my father died last year, I had no desire to return home. I think part of it is I didn't feel prepared to see her. My father doted on her, he did everything for her, every blessed thing from unlocking the door, writing the monthly checks, cooking and doing the laundry. His entire reason for being was she was the center of his universe, his absolute core of existence and he in return, hers. I damn well know I will never do this to my wife. I will imbibe her with an independence that her life is her own and if indeed I was plucked from the face of the earth she would remain whole … well at least functioning through life's mundane responsibilities. No way I will I ever be like my dad. There's just no fucking way."

"That feeling too will past", I tried to cajole Rhino.

"Yeah, well you tell me when?"

"I haven't a clue, but like everything else there is a timeline."

"Well it had better be quick. I don't want to return home. I try to do as much as I can. I can't face a fifty–eight year old elderly woman who finds herself lost every day and spends the better part of it crying and lonely, reminiscing about all the old times that have past and will never again be replayed. I go home and my head is still in the war and hers is the lost love in her life, the hole in her heart as large as the Grand Canyon and we are just at the polar end of the earth."

As fucked up and feeling as bad as Rhino, I for some similar and other reasons found myself in the awkward position of giving out advice. If there was anyone in the entire world who I would not solicit it from … IT WOULD BE ME.

It was just then the girl walked in. I didn't know who she was. Rhino seemed to move his head several times in her direction. It seemed he knew her or at least she looked familiar.

"Gertude Boguslawski."

"You're shitting me?"

"No that's her name."

"Really?"

"Really, you asked me her name and I told you, what's the big deal?"

"Gertrude, that's all."

"What's with Gertrude?"

"What do you mean?"

"I mean the strange look on your face when you asked."

"Well, Rhino, Gertrude seems like such an old name."

"Old, meaning what?"

"Meaning you don't hear of many girls named Gertrude anymore."

"No and you don't hear of any Myrtles, Ada's, Beatrices or for that matter, Alfred's or Bartholomews, so what the fuck?"

"I get it Rhino."

Rhino and I sat at our table for another twenty minutes ravagingly consuming our BLT's and coke. When we were finished and ready to leave, Rhino turned to me and asked, "Gertrude … do you want to meet her?"

I was not inclined at first to say "yes" but I quickly decided "Why the hell not?"

We took the fifteen steps toward her and once a foot behind, Rhino declared,

"Gerti, is that you?"

Gertrude turned around and questioned, "Whose asking?"

"It's me, Danny Rowkakowski and my friend Jackson Krause."

"Wow", Gerti replied, seemingly surprised, "Wow, like I honestly wouldn't have recognized you."

Rhino for some reason, was a bit embarrassed. *Danny Rowkakowski?* "Well yes, like Jack and I have just recently returned from Vietnam."

This was my first, but obviously not my last, meeting with Gertrude Baguslowski. Honestly, I don't know what attracted me to her. Gerti wasn't what anyone would call an attractive girl. She stood about five feet, four inches or so and weighed approximately one hundred and twenty five pounds, not to say that I had any reason to believe I was anywhere near accurate.

She was medium busted but a little heavy around the hips and her legs were a bit thick at the calves giving the perception she was anchored to the floor when standing and steady on her feet while ambling about.

Facially, Gerti had strong Polish features. She had a prominent nose, a tad too long and a bit too wide for her face. Separated by two round button eyes, which were light iridescent blue and unquestionably her best feature. Her lips were marginally too thin but when smiling revealed a row of perfectly balanced teeth, white as new fallen snow.

Gerti had an effervescent personality that waned over the years. When she was young, it took over the room. It seemed she always had the most interesting and entertaining stories to tell and told them in such a way it firmly held her audience captive.

The thing I really liked about Gerti, after dating her several times, was that she was incredibly easy to be with. Unlike other girls I met, a few months after returning from Nam, she was almost no work. I returned "all fucked up' and it seemed the others kept prying deeper and deeper into areas I felt very uncomfortable. They kept asking me about my war experiences and what my views on it now that I returned. Their barrage of questions just kept on coming at me and I was of no frame of mind to answer them. I locked up these feelings in my upper vault and it would damn well take a shit load of time before I figured the combination to unlock them. Vietnam was my private hell and I did not expect my return to be more of the same but it was and in several ways worse. The most hellish of these were when several asked me to justify my involvement in killing innocent men, women and children in an unjust American Imperialistic war. I remember recoiling from these. Right or wrong, I was drafted into the army. I served my country well. We soldiers might have different opinions about the war, but we did what was paramount. We had a job to do and we did it. I can't say that these girls didn't really piss me off when they asked me these things or voiced their opinions on shit they just didn't know about, the crap they read about in all the liberal anti-war newspapers, magazines and other rags.

The way Rhino and I were treated by some men of our generation was even worse. They would say the same things and ask the same questions as the girls but it was even more intolerable. When we heard them, Rhino and I thought the very same thing, these guys were assholes. At least they could have shown us a little tolerance and respect. We were the ones fighting the "damn war" that somehow escaped them. Right or wrong, we were the guys (and thousands of others like us) who have or were putting our asses on the line.

It wasn't a few times things got out of hand. I was a lot more tolerant than Rhino and he was just about bigger than anybody. On three separate occasions he busted up a few assholes who didn't understand their "poking fun" was taking them to a place no sane man would want to be, which was at the focused end of Rhino's wrath.

Gerti Boguslawski was just easy to be around. She didn't ask questions or try to pry back the layers of my subconscious. She knew there were rules and although they were never discussed, she stayed within their boundaries. The great part of our relationship was that she made me laugh more than I had ever before. I laughed more during the first six months of our dating than I had in my entire life. Whether she knew it or not, this is what drew me to her. I wanted to laugh as loudly and frequently as I could. I just wanted to laugh, to laugh my life away because when I stopped laughing I was just *in so much pain.*

Gerti and I dated for two years. It seemed incongruous that at the height of the sexual revolution in the late 1960s, that it took us over a year to become intimate. It should have been a telling consequence that there was indeed a lack of passion or inquisitiveness in our relationship (not that it was on my part but hers) that as the relationship evolved from boyfriend to girlfriend, fiance to fiancée and eventually man and wife we had the fortunate luck to find a new best friend, *POT- Marijuana – Hash.* and as strange as it seems not only did I embrace it, but for whatever reason, Gerti did as well.

Weed became my friend in Nam. It was there as if a divine deliverance was bestowed on us dog shoulders as God's way to make an intolerable situation almost barely. When I returned stateside I tried to leave my addiction behind. It was far from easy but I felt it was the smart thing to do. I wanted to start a new life and carrying the ghosts of my past would only prevent me from reinventing myself. It was a very difficult decision at best because in Nam when the "shit-storm" happened, a few tokes turned a firefight into a fireworks display. How my brothers and I survived was a miracle. It was an absurd calculation that a bunch of stoned G.I.'s had enough wits about them to fight off a determined crazed enemy. War is an indiscriminate thing, my platoon, stoned to the nines not a few times, survived a firefight without a single casualty, while others as sober as a judge, were completely wiped out. In Nam it just didn't matter, there was no right or wrong, there was only luck and the lack of it. We must have had a "Guardian Angel" because as foolish as war was, my platoon was beyond, doing things that most often lead to certain death, but I guess it wasn't our time. Ours was somewhere down the line, but as I now sat stateside, I wondered what form it would take.

Rhino introduced me to "weed" again. He never gave it up, but knowing that I was trying to kick it, he honored my decision by never smoking around me. It lasted almost two years and I felt there was something missing in my life, something other than sex in my relationship between Gerti and me. I began to long for that eerie, detached feeling that served me so well in Vietnam. I started to think through the plus and minuses of starting again. I was clean for almost one and a half years, that alone told me that I was not an addict. It reassured me that I could smoke and quit at will.

It was one Tuesday afternoon, there was absolutely no doubt in my mind that Rhino was high. His eyes were glazed, holding firm as though he was guarding a secret that was beyond us both. He was constantly snorting as a bull in heat. His words fell intermittently, without structure or reason. Rhino was laughing insanely out loud. I decided I didn't know what was in Rhino's head but whatever it was I wanted some.

"Rhino, you got some dope?"

"Shit, am I hearing you right?"

"Yeah you're hearing me right. I proved to myself I could live without it so I look at it not as an addiction or crutch but rather just a little indulgence that doesn't mean shit in my life."

"Ya, sure, so what the fuck you trying to tell me Jackson ... like I'm some kind of addict or something and you're not?"

"I'm not trying to tell you anything other than I need to elevate my mood. My personality's so stable I'm boring myself to death."

"Well, at least it's your choice."

"Ya, would you say, even my relationship with Gerti is the same old, same old."

"Well my advice to you is that you better rethink that relationship then. It's not been a year since you've married and there seems to be no jump in your jeans. It ain't a good sign Jackson, take it from a man who knows ... as a sign, it sure ass ain't a good one."

"Well, like I said, maybe some weed will give me some juice."

"Yeah maybe, but what I'm damn well hearing is that Gerti needs a little spur under her saddle as well."

Rhino and I drove behind Home Depot. He pulled out his nickel bag and rolled me a heffer of a joint. If there was anything Rhino was good at, it was rolling a joint that looked just like a store bought cigarette. He handed it to me. I took two long drags, fucking "Hurrah", WELCOME TO DREAMLAND. Then surprise, surprise, Rhino took the joint from me and handed me this little pill.

"What the hell's that?"

"None of your damn business. Just take the fucking thing."

"What do you think I am a complete asshole, taking a pill and I don't even know what it is?"

"Christ Jackson, am I your fucking brother or what? Like I'm going to do you wrong. Have I ever done you wrong?"

"I can't believe I took the fucking pill. I stuck it on my tongue and swirled it around in my mouth."

"Don't give up on the thing Jackson, just trust me, swallow the tab."

"I did what Rhino told me and swallowed."

Rhino turned and looked at me with this big old wide mouth teeth-sucking grin.

I stared back. He smiled again and broke out laughing.

"Wait."

It had been about five minutes, that seemed like a century - Then BAZAAM…

DREAMLAND ON STEROIDS. I didn't know where I was but I damn well knew I wasn't on Mother Earth, maybe in the black hole of the universe as I was being swept away and all I could hear was Gracie Slick's "White Rabbit" playing in my head but the words were mine, not hers.

Another year past I can't remember the last
A minute ago it was another year
I was another soul

I can't remember from where I came
I lost my perspective and you are to blame
But then it seemed like another Nam day
Now it seems to be like any other... to be fading away

I think I can see the flame from the light

The years they pass like a distant plight
They've been taken from me ... whether wrong or right
As I welcome a new day
Just another twenty four hours that will be stolen away

So the hell with the days weeks months and years
I won't celebrate with the passing of tears

It's with my new dopey friends that I will again look past
Knowing how the new year will begin but won't last

A dog soldier I shall forever be
Until my death ... that will ... eventually ... let me be free

Everything started spinning around me, faster... *faster*, I remember asking myself , *Where am I? What am I doing here?"* I have never been out of myself before. I have never had the feeling of strange detachment. I had never had that out of body experience like I was a fly on the wall observing my every thought, action and feeling my every emotion. I squinted a few times and saw Rhino through the thick haze, I could tell he was trying to say something to me, I finally heard him.

"LSD"

"That's what it was?" I asked Rhino.

"Yeah, LSD, great shit huh?"

LSD, I've heard a shit loud about it but this was my first experience taking it. It was four hours later and I was just getting my wits about me. Now I knew what the commotion was about this hallucinogenic. It was *amazing*, it was *scary*, it was something that I would love to drop on Gerti as my mind entertained me with the thought of what she would be like under its' influence. My sexuality burst through my skin after taking it. My body lusted for her (but I must admit any female would do) I was in rabid rabbit heat. With a new perspective now, I wondered who she would be like under its' spell and I strategized a plan to see if I could entice her to participate knowing damn well that there wasn't a snow ball chance in hell she would.

"Jack, what do you say happened to you?"

"Like I said Gerti. This LSD shit is simply amazing. It takes you to places you never ever would believe, like in the Beatles song "The Magical Mystery Tour", it really is a gift from God."

Gerti looked at me in the strangest of ways. We had just been married for over a year and I couldn't help thinking what she was thinking. *WHO THE HELL WAS THIS GUY I MARRIED?* Honestly, many times over the short span of our marriage I was thinking the same. I didn't really know how to say to Gerti, *I want you to drop acid with me, so that I can get into your head, but most importantly get into your body and have ravenous unlicensed sex with you. I want to turn you inside out, upside down... I want it all ... everything I felt denied over the last couple of years ... sucked from me like air from a balloon.* This was in my head but not in my word well.

"Got any?"

Was I really hearing what I thought I was hearing? Did Gerti really ask me if I had some?

"Yeah, I got a couple of tabs."

Should I ask her? Should I...ask her? Why the hell not?

"Yeah, want to take some with me?"

The world is indeed a strange place and interaction between people even stranger.

The relationship between husband and wife is the most absurd of all, uncalculating at best. Gerti's answer to my question supported the reality I hadn't a clue who the hell my wife was. If I were to bet my life, I would have wagered she would dismiss my enticement as a sick proposition from a very sick man. I would have bet life and fortune and her answer would have rendered me dead and broke.

"Sure, what the hell, sure I'll try it."

Render me stupid, render me dumb, render me the worst judge of human character, render me delighted, render me enthralled, render me speechless, render me horny as hell.

Without hesitation I reached into my pocket and pulled out one little tab that within it held enough power to open up the world, the universe, the hemispheres to the person who dared use it. Gerti was now at that threshold and her decision (as surprising as it was) would roll back the carpet on the dance floor of her life. She would fall into a new rhythm as she heard and perceived things as never before. If her experience mirrored mine she would be thrown into a state of euphoria, unsettling at first but she would quickly become one with it as she surfed through her unconscious seeking that perfect wave of understanding where mind, body and soul became one as she morphed from one state to another on her incredible, customized "MAGICAL MYSTERY TOUR.

It was still bewildering to me as she reached and took the tab from my hand that this was not a dream and the residue of my acid run not a few hours before now seemed like a lifetime in the rearview mirror of my life.

Now as if Gerti was a lifetime user, without hesitation or lingering thought, the pill was gone. It disappeared from her index and forefinger as if it were but a particle of dusk, blown into the air, dispatched to a place beyond mortal vision, never to have existed, leaving not a trace.

Gerti swallowed…I had second thoughts. Fuck, what if her initial use turned bad? What if she reacted in a way that I heard some users sometimes did, that instead of getting a euphoric ride they were thrown into a subconscious that wanted to fight back. What if it demonized her with the deepest, darkest, incredible nightmarish thoughts. If this were the case, there would indeed be hell to pay. Then another thought broke in knocking at the anterior lob of my brain. Damn it, what if it fries her like a broken egg on the Las Vegas strip. What if it marches her toward insanity by frying up her wiring leaving nothing in her place but a vegetable, with no reason for being other than occupying a chair in a padded room.

I was second guessing myself now. I might have made a huge mistake, a disastrous miscalculation. I now found myself honed in on her every moment, every blink of her eyes, every breath as it ebbed and flowed. I watched the heaviness of her chest, the placement of her arms as they fell lifeless at her sides. I grew restless. I needed to know what was happening as the effects of the LSD worked their way through the miles of neural highway composing body and mind.

"Holy shit!"

Did I hear what I heard?

"WOW ….. holy shit!"

Yes I did!

"WOW …HOLY SHIT …WOW."

Gerti to the bell tower.

As amazed as I was during and after my experience with my LSD trip, I was even more with Gerti's. I was like a fly on the wall cheering her on, hoping what she would experience was the best of things, that I was presenting her with a gift that would allow her to break through that which prevented her living openly and fulfilled. I wanted Gerti to rise from the ashes of her former self and elevate me as well bringing us together in a cauldron of pleasure and delight. We now had a common bond beyond marriage, we were acid users and I hoped for so much more.

It was July but Christmas came early. Gerti was high as a kite. I pulled a joint from my trouser pocket and lit it up. I now was there as well. I extended my hand to her. Another surprise, not only did she reach for it but lifted herself from her chair and walked over to me and sat not two feet away on a small stool and beckoned me to join her. Without hesitation I found myself in her space, my arms wrapped around her and again if Christmas and my birthday were all wrapped up in one, this was it. We found ourselves on the floor, popping buttons and zippers and ripping our cloths from each other, flesh on flesh excited us more, we were raging with desire, which I had never experienced and knowingly she hadn't as well. I thrust myself into her causing her to roll her head back emitting sounds so guttural and inhuman I felt I was hurting her but she beckoned for more. I was all consumed. I wanted nothing more than to please my wife. My desire was to re-engage, to build from this moment our relationship from the ground up, starting from where the sex would end and an insatiable appetite for more would begin.

Gerti's and my relationship was reborn. When we wanted sex, we got high and had it. When were wanted to stimulate the mood, we took acid or smoked pot and there we were, once again held captive by the seduction of the moment. *HAPPY DAYS WERE HERE AGAIN.*

It was still incredibly interesting to me that Gerti was still Gerti when she wasn't stoned. She was the same old girl wrapped in the same old introspective space as she always was but still again, always with the power to make me laugh. When we were high, we laughed all the time, when we weren't we laughed almost as much, probably more than most married couples. This was the *fantastimo* part of my marriage, three years of exceptional sex, acid, pot, mushroom caps and what they now called Ecstasy drugs. We were consumed. We were held captive and watched our nights dance away in our dreams as the reflection from the telephone pole street light not twenty yards away from our bedroom window bounced from our blinds to our ceiling every night. Every night… ***until everything changed***…

30

And Baby Makes Three

Gerti had an ectopic pregnancy. Normally an egg is released from the ovary into the fallopian tube with the hope that it meets with the sperm and resides nine months in the lining of the uterus. However, in one out of every fifty pregnancies, the fertilized egg does not move from the fallopian tube. Referred to as an ectopic pregnancy, it attaches to one of the ovaries, another surrounding organ or possibly the cervix. It now becomes life and death for both mother and child.

Gerti was diagnosed in the eighth week of her pregnancy. If she brought the child to term, it would be extremely difficult and a dangerous to both mother and child. I was ready to abort. Gerti would do no such thing. There was a spiritual side of her that very seldom was brought out but there was no clearer decision for her to make than to bring her baby to term. It was a terrible pregnancy, severe bleeding, unbearable cramping, long periods of nausea and dizziness and several bouts of fainting.

Gerti's surgery was in the twelfth week where the fertilized egg was clipped from the fallopian tube and inserted into the lining of her uterus.

"There is a slim chance that this child will come to term. You know this?" questioned Dr. Raylor.

"I know that if my child has a one in a million chance to live, I'll not stand in the way of that slim chance that it can have a life."

"Understood Mrs. Krause, I'm not here to deter you, only to inform you."

"Understood, Dr. Raylor. Perfectly understood."

It was a painful experience at best. Every waking hour we were burdened with the fact that Gerti's body could naturally abort the baby that had gone rogue in the womb. There were many nights I lay awake, Gerti by my side, with both our eyes wide open, not experiencing a single moment of rest. These were hellish times. I knew Gerti was thinking the same thoughts as me but even more serious personal ones. I was obsessed with the two options that clearly confronted me. The first was whether Gerti and the child would survive and the consequences of that? Second, if either one or both did, what would life be on the other side? Although I tried very hard, I just couldn't get over the feeling that a hellish pregnancy could produce nothing less than a hellish kid and that life for the three of us would be challenged at best. I rolled many thoughts around in my head trying to think through every possible outcome. I thought I had exhausted them all but there always seemed to be another that would create additional angst and concern. I finally resolved my uneasiness by relegating it to the fact that I thought probably every father experiences the same during the pregnancy and eventual birth of their child.

The child was taken from Gerti three weeks premature. I now had a son pried from the womb, a purple-veined "primie" having no resemblance to either Gerti or

I, but perhaps alien life somewhere in a distant universe. I honestly can't say that I was elated with the birth of my son, the journey was long and treacherous, a lot like Nam, but I had this hollow feeling inside that maybe, I wasn't quite cut out for fatherhood. I had barely come to terms with my marriage (although I must admit that for the last several years the drugs had really helped and the sex was as good as could be imagined).

Gerti responded to the birth of our son like he was the second coming of Christ. I saw it in her eyes that it was beyond anything she could have prepared for. It was like as a woman, she had been tested and unflinchingly rose to the occasion and beyond. Gerti was all in. She journeyed through the pregnancy like a trooper, hardly complaining, but suffering nonetheless. I knew as she took the baby to her breast that perhaps I had gotten myself into the firestorm of my life and like Nam, it would haunt me till my death or until I caved into being who I was not, the man, the husband, the father that I could not be.

Gerti, baby and I weren't home from the hospital but for a few hours when I had the dire need to see Dirt and Rhino. I felt like I was smothering under the weight of my new responsibilities. My son Hendrix, the name we decided on if a boy and Henrietta if a girl, both in tribute to Jimmy Hendrix, arguably the greatest "Rock and Roll" guitarist of all time but baby Hendrix was sucking all the air from the room. I understood that this would happen in any family but honestly I was not prepared. A crying child, constantly feeding, dirty diapers and the lack of restful sleep was a recipe for disaster if I didn't get my emotions under control. Abruptly, I left the house, leaving Gerti to fend for herself, one of the stupidest things I had done in my life, but it seemed like the natural thing for me, like a drowning man reaching for a life preserver in the midst of a turbulent sea, I had to touch, feel and hear Dirt and Rhino to help me make sense of what I felt I was unable to do.

I met with Rhino and Dirt at the Dunkin. I looked at both of them in a strange way, they were who they were, Dirt and Rhino, two disassociated, disenfranchised Vietnam vets just like me. I wondered what I was seeking from them. Dirt couldn't take care of himself and my looking to him for answers bordered on the absurd.

Rhino on the other had been in the first of his several marriages. He got married a year before me and already had a one year old daughter. Looking at him, I realized he owed me …he owed me *BIG TIME*. Rhino was the one who got me into drugs again. He was the one that opened up both me and Gerti to the MAGICAL MYSTERY TOUR. He was the one who gave me "Mother's Little Helper", the acid tab that I dropped on Gerti. It was Rhino who helped bring sex back into our marriage. It was he who helped bring Gerti and I together in a passionate assault of our senses, taking pot and instigators into my life, constantly challenging me to burst beyond who I thought I was.

"Cave into it?"

"Cave into it …what are you saying Rhino?"

"I'm saying there are things in life you have to flow with."

"Like the birth of my son?"

"Yes, exactly like that. If you think there wouldn't be any pushback for you, you were mistaken."

"It ain't like that Rhino."

"Ain't like what you think it is?

"What am I thinking it is? Huh Rhino, what do you…well to be honest…Gerti and I were having a hell of a time for the last several years. If you ever told me that she would ever get into drugs even as a one-time user, I would say you had your head up your ass, but as a recreational drug user, well that just went beyond my wildest dreams."

"Yeah, I know."

"Ya, you should. It's because of you that we both got into it."

"Ya, so what?"

"Well I was just thinking that the drugs might be the reason for Gerti's difficult pregnancy."

"Jackson, you're thinking way too far into it. Shit happens, it ain't about the drugs, it's about you having a kid very much like you."

I didn't like what I was hearing from Rhino.

"I don't get what you're saying ... *"a kid very much like me?"*

"Yeah, sure as hell as Dirt and I are sitting in front of you."

"Still don't get it."

"You've been a outlier all your life. You've been against it all. *"It all"* meaning everything that an ordinary normal guy your age would have caved into over time."

Dirt shook his head in agreement. *What the fuck does Dirt know? He knows fucking squat.* For all intent and purpose I tuned Dirt out of the conversation going forward.

"Rhino, I still don't understand what you're telling me."

"It's like this Jackson. You've never had EASY in your life and the payback for you is that in the lives you've touched you never brought EASY in. What I'm saying in a very convoluted way is that this difficult pregnancy and now the birth of your son is just another link in the heavy chain that makes you Jackson Krause. You're life isn't about EASY. It's about just another difficult thing you will have to wrestle with."

"Rhino, whatever you're saying to me and mark my words, I'm not sure I have a fucking clue, is nothing but bullshit, typical Rhino bullshit. Here I am asking you whether you think that any of the drugs Gerti and I have been taking in the past could have possibly lead up to us having a screwed up pregnancy and maybe a screwed up kid."

"And my answer is Jackson? Who the hell knows. Do you think I am God or something and drop on you a "cookie cutter" answer that will make everything right for you? You damn well know that there are none of those and if there were, you're boy here, Rhino, would be first in line to receive."

Rhino wasn't serving up what I wanted to hear. He was delivering what he was good at, lip service. I could ask him anything about the majority of things and he would give me a well versed truthful answer but now was just rapping his mouth, jawboning for whatever reason. I just wanted to make sense what was happening to Gerti and me and our new son

Hendrix. I wanted to try to put the shit in order, knowing that for me to come to terms with it, I very much wanted to know it's source or at least to get focused in to eliminate some of the variables.

"I don't get any of this Rhino, as far as the answer man, you're falling way short."

"Then let me make it distinctively clear for you. MAN UP, IT IS WHAT IT IS!"

"Meaning?"

"Meaning, whether the pregnancy was caused by the rogue personality that you are and your kid is a chip off the old block and started his pregnancy outside the uterus instead of in, or whether your and Gerti's drug use was the cause it doesn't matter. You need to live with the damn consequence either way."

Damn it, Rhino nailed it. He was right. It really didn't matter. My wanting to know was just for me to take a highway to nowhere, a place where I could drop the blame on something or someone other than myself, my wife, and what we did together to really sabotage our kid.

No matter how I tried to hide or displace it, there was the fear of God in me. Having a child was scary enough but for me to have one who started from the very worst of foundation, was dauntingly overpowering. I was scared shit. It was a greater fear than I ever felt in Nam, it was a scared shittiness rendering me paralyzed, knowing in the best of circumstances, I would be only a mediocre father and in the worst, probably marginal at best.

"So that's what it comes down to Rhino, "IT IS WHAT IT IS?"

"Jackson, that's the key to it all. Didn't you ever hear of Werner Erhardt?"

"Haven't a clue who he is."

"Well, regardless of you knowing, he was the guy, who in the 1970's created the philosophy of EST. It was a sixty-hour two weekend course that after you pulled back the peel of the onion and get to it's core, that just in the living of your life and accepting the consequences of it lies control and true happiness. Basically, giving up on controlling everything about you renders you the ability to enjoy life as it unfolds before you."

"Christ, Rhino, it sounds like a lot of bullshit to me and I'm really disappointed in you, here you are my friend and I'm asking you a civilized question because I'm really "fucked-up" about the birth of my kid and you lay some pseudo-intellectual bullshit dogma crap on me that doesn't mean "squat".

"It is what it is Jack."

"It is what it is AND IT'S NOTHING BUT BULLSHIT."

To say I was disappointed with Rhino's lack of concern and direction was an understatement. Unlike Dirt, from who I expected nothing, I expected at least a little serious attention and understanding from Rhino, a learned response that somehow, someway would provide just an inkling of resolve to the unbelievable insecurity that I felt at that moment. I guess "it is what it is" and "it is" a bucket of crap.

When I returned home, Gerti wasn't speaking to me. She was pissed that I left her as I had many times before. If it was a choice between Gerti or Dirt and Rhino, it seems that I always chose the latter. I was really a screwed-up husband. It was clearly apparent to everyone other than myself but I was seeing it now, with great clarity and although I didn't like it, my greatest fear was that I knew I could do nothing about it. My greatest sin was that I never tried. And now, it's Gerti and me…and baby Hendrix makes three.

What our marriage was before Hendrix, was quickly cancelled out with the birth of our son. There was no more alcohol and drugs. Sex was a thing of the past. "Mommydom" consumed all of Gerti's life. She strived to be the greatest mother of all, forever doting on our kid, addressing his every whim and need with the greatest urgency. Other than proving a meager living at the time (I was just beginning as a journeyman at the UPS) I had as much importance in my family's life as the old torn leather chair in our rented apartment's living room. When I was home which wasn't that often, I was there to be walked around, as just another intrusion in Gerti's way to being "SUPER MOM".

My wife's inattentiveness and her new found role, continued giving me license to leave the house at whim and spend as much time (other than working) with Dirt and Rhino. I should have been married to them … and in many ways I was.

"How things going?" Dirt asked me one rainy autumn morning as I watched the colored leaves clogging up the sewer in front of Dunkin.

"Like shit, that's how they're going. You know Dirt … well, that was stupid …. course you don't know … well maybe, yes, one part of you does …nobody can really prepare you for what you experience in war, marriage and fatherhood."

Dirt shook his head.

"But at least the military takes the time to train and get you in shape so you may have just an inkling of a chance to survive. Marriage, it just ain't like that. There's no preparation. It's not like living together is a stepping-stone or training wheels for the married state. Once the vows are said, and the "I Do's" are recorded with the state, and the rings are slipped on the fingers the whole relationship changes. It ain't boyfriend and girlfriend no more. It ain't roommates no more, it damn well now is "man and wife" and from that one great screw on your wedding night and the several on your honeymoon if you are indeed lucky enough to engage, everything from the moment you take the vow changes."

Dirt looked me with the blankest of stares. He hadn't a clue what I was talking about, not a damn one and I stared at him and noticed he had just pissed in his pants. I felt like an asshole running my mouth and expecting some kind of intelligent feedback from a street person who just voided himself and who like a dog lives in a crate. *I must reign in my insanity.*

It was well into two years Gerti and I although living under the same roof, sometimes felt tortured by each other's presence. We somehow made it work through the smallest but critical efforts on both our parts.

I was now getting used to the intrusion my son played in my life. Unfortunately, I looked at Hendrix that way. His needs so outweighed mine or so I thought that at the end of the day, Gerti was spent. She had nothing left and habitually fell into a coma-like sleep, leaving me usually sitting by the bedroom window gazing out into a large black hole that I knew was another universe which had a far different purpose than the one I lived. I many times wondered if there were indeed other worlds why I wound up in this one? I finally concluded there had to be one "great power" holding the key to the universe and everything and everyone in it and watching with great dismay how his or her great design was falling apart at the seams.

I now knew in the twenty-seventh year of my life that this POWER was pissed. HE or SHE was pissed to a fare-thee-well and why wouldn't HE or SHE be? Humankind had "thumped" HIM or HER on the side of the head - dissed the great POWER by paying little or no attention anymore. In the GREAT POWER's design, there were everyday subtleties that constantly played out, if indeed anyone paid any attention and cared enough to look for them. There were signs everywhere that there was indeed a GOD who reigns above all the chaos. Sometimes it's just a crack in the sidewalk that brings us to a path that we need to follow, sometimes just a feather spiraling to earth from a bird that takes our imagination to wing. Then there were the not too subtle signs that was something much greater in play here, something beyond that of us mortal beings, *life itself.* My child being born should have been one of these. Yes, I look upon it now, Hendrix coming into this world was indeed the greatest sign that the POWER bestowed to me and Gerti. A child being born is a renewal, a reprieve from all things wrong spiraling to a bottomless abyss. It is *hope* that can be garnished that indeed with the birth of this child there would be a new awakening, a dismissal of all the wrongs, a celebration of all the good things to come. Hendrix was indeed a gift from the POWER to Gerti and me and the rest of our lives should be in celebration.

Why couldn't I have seen it that way then? The very thing I felt weighing me down was that which should have renewed me, recreating the man I forever wanted to be.

I was lost with the birth of my son. I didn't at all see what piece I played in the puzzle. I was a fly on the wall, an outsider looking in, an outlier who had far less than what a father must feel and be. It was a terrifying realization that what should have been coming naturally was not coming at all. When I stared down the tunnel where the natural fast track of fatherhood was coming toward me, I felt that meeting it head on would not be a renewal, it would not be a new refreshing page comfortably fitting into my book of life. It would be nothing less than a collision between me, a man, who after Nam was barely getting a handle on where the war experience and civilian life met up. My returning to the States was a woeful experience at best, and the farther I tried to distance myself from it, the harder it seemed to get.

I wanted so hard to forget what several years before was survival at its worst. That if I found the right person I could right my sinking ship and sail into the calming waters of civilian life. It was not so, not so at all, but rather my personal seas became more troublesome, treacherous and turbulent when I had a woman in my life. I could have looked upon Gerti as a captain would a first mate. I could have looked upon her as the compassionate soul who could share the comforts of the boat as we sailed through life. I did not. These were my troubled waters and I refused to allow anyone to paddle around in them. I held everything that I feared within, every little trial and turbulence I tried to iron out as one would the wrinkles in a shirt. I found myself a lousy launderer, and a sailor navigating the fickle waters of my life less than adequate.

I wanted to be a good father, but I wasn't even a good husband. This was the brunt of it. I wanted to be it all but concluded in the shortest span of time that I was neither. I just couldn't get over Nam. I couldn't really cut to the chase of the matter that I saw things I couldn't quite digest and come to terms with. The death, the blight, the carnage, my friends dismembered, many of them dying and lastly but more significant than anything else, the several if not dozens of civilians and enemy I killed.

My marriage was what it was. It wasn't like I didn't make an effort to include myself in my family. I did. I was very much aware of the circle of importance where no matter what transpired in my life there would be no excuse for me not to participate, to be present even though I was a shell of the husband and father I should have been. I never missed a birthday or our anniversary and usually man-upped to it, pretending beyond an Academy Award performance that I was dutiful as well as doleful.

I finally came to realize Nam scared me worse than I thought. I came to conclude that the Jack Krause Way, was the hardest damn way a person could ever come to terms with anything. That my feelings for my son Hendrix stemmed from three major germs. Firstly, that Gerti and my influence under drugs gave me a respite from all the "noise" in my head that continually played back to me. I honestly looked forward to and enjoyed those moments when drifting into a hallucinary state. Gerti and I became one as we screwed into the night not giving a shit about anything or no one. Those days were gone, I really miss those days. Second, the birth of my son pronounced me unworthy as a father because for what I knew, I was damn well unworthy as a husband and I had never gotten to first base so I could not fathom running to second. This deep-rooted feeling of failure and insecurity stemmed from feelings of unworthiness and how it would translate from father to son. I was just scared that Hendrix would grow up just like me and would be the mirror upon what my reflection shown. And third, kids fight wars. I didn't want my son to fight in any war and by the looks of what was happening in the world, I damn well believed Vietnam would not be the last. I didn't want my kid to see what I had seen, to do the things that I felt compelled to do and finally, but most important of all, to come back with a missing limb and a tapioca brain, never again to be free of heart, mind and of the constant unrelenting residue of the most hellish of times. I wanted all these worries, all this troubling shit I loaded on my wagon of crap that was burdened with way too much weight to just go away. *And then came Hendrix*.

31

Magical Mystery Tour – The Sequel

I couldn't believe what I was hearing. I thought there was wax in my ears and immediately ran to the bathroom to flush them out. I heard Gerti again through the bathroom door.

"Jack, you and me gotta talk."

Shit, this was not a good sign. We barely had social banter. We were more prone to serious conversation, that is, when we weren't fighting. I looked around the bathroom as a prisoner would his jail cell. There really was nowhere to go, nowhere to escape. I felt foolish as hell. *What the hell was I escaping from? My wife, my son?*

Gerti reached out again but in a much calmer seductive voice.

"Jack, you and me, we need to talk. It's something that has been on my mind for quite a time."

What the hell? I said to myself. *Maybe it's time to break through what it is that has been dividing us, a chance to get the strangeness out of the house.*

I walked from the bathroom. Gerti stood there, not twenty feet away looking the best she had for some time. Maybe she did something to herself that made her look different. Then again, maybe I hadn't really focused on her for some time now.

We were for several months, two strangers living under the same roof.

"Yeah, Gerti? You seem intent on having this conversation."

"Yes Jack, it's something I wanted to discuss with you for some time. I just put Hendrix down for his afternoon nap, we got a few hours here. It just seems that the time is appropriate."

"*Appropriate for what?*" I queried. I was about to get nervous again, that "caged in" felling was rearing its ugly head.

Gerti turned and walked to our living room couch. She sat and motioned for me to come join her. I really didn't know what was happening but decided to let it play out. I didn't see a gun or knife, a bat or a garret, so I figured the worst I would take would be a verbal beating. If it came to that I was okay, this wouldn't be my first spin on the dance floor.

I was really surprised at Gerti's demeanor and the tone of her voice. The angry, standoff woman seemed to have faded as she snuggled closer to me on the living room coach. Surprisingly, she reached out and touched my hand. I was bewildered. We hadn't had physical contact in a long time, in fact too long for me to remember. Then she spoke words that still resonate, as unbelievable as they were.

"J-A-C-K-KKKK." She said in the slowest and most seductive tone I had ever heard from her. "J-A-C-K-KKK", damn it she mouthed it again.

"What?" I suddenly volunteered.

"Jack, I've been wanting to have this discussion for some time now, like I said, I believe this is the right moment to discuss something that honestly", she hesitated and took a deep breath and then continued, "it's been festering in my mind for so long that if I don't let it out, I damn well am going to explode."

I was getting just too antsy to sit and listen to this anymore. *If she had something that she wanted to say to me then damn it, say it!*

"I want to have sex with you."

My heart fluttered and then skipped a beat. This was the strangest dream I ever had. I snapped my fingers and didn't wake. I pinched myself and it didn't snap me out of the deep semi-conscious state that I was in. *"SEX",* the word even sounded strange to me since I have for years been estranged to it. It seemed to have a "dirty" connotation, that somehow said to me this is the deepest and most threatening of waters. When a woman mentions SEX, it damn well has an underlying reason, a subliminal message that somehow she was putting forth that men don't understand it, or understand in its simplest form. Woman want to make love, men just want to get laid, in the simplest form that is the crux of it, but after several years of abstinence there just has to be more to it than that. I was surmising, way more, way the hell more...

"SEX", Gerti regurgitated.

"Shit Gerti, I can't remember what the hell that is."

I pushed back on the coach. I don't get it (I swallowed my words) they seemed acidic as they retreated back into my throat.

"Jack, now don't be a hard-ass here. We've been married for almost three years and honestly since the birth of Hendrix, well I must admit, a lot of the romance and chemistry has gone out of our marriage.

Duh... do you think? I wanted to add.

Gerti continued, "And I remember back before Hendrix's birth, remember those days?"

Remember them? How could I ever forget our Magical Mystery Tour!? Toking up, dropping acid, the ecstasy drugs, making love throughout the night into the early mornings until we were raw and rawness or not, repeating again and again. These were the most memorable and beautiful of times as we or perhaps only me, thought they would continue forever because we were just like every young couple who came before us and who will come later ...blinded by our youth, renegade passion and the delusion that only it can provide thinking that the good times will go on forever. Forever. The MAGICAL

MYSTERY TOUR by the Beatles, I couldn't remember all the words so I made up my own.

Ah, Ah, Magical Morning Renewed

Ah, ah, every day is a magical morning
Ah, ah, when your head swims in the sky
And you find yourself far from shore
And not a reason why

Ah, ah, it's you and me lost at sea
Ah, ah, drifting aimlessly at bay
Far from who we were on land
Not caring that we stray

Ah, ah, a little this, a little that
Ah, ah, makes one feel glee
And the two, that are but one
Are now enabled and are free

I reached for you, you disappeared
And immediately you're here
And a little this and a touch of that
And now no longer any fear

Ah, ah, every day is a magical morning
When your life is spiked and loose
A little this, a little that
A touch of crazy juice

I wanted so much to relive those days. They were perhaps the best I ever experienced. Zoning out not worrying about a blessed thing, just Gerti and my body coming together as one. WHY? Because God made the parts fit this way and that was just a good enough reason for me, the only one I needed to know. There was just no more thinking beyond that. Gerti and I came together because our plumbing was different and it was what it was…and damn it…*it was fucking great*.

I must have been in dreamland. Gerti broke my trance.

"J-A-C-KKKK, you listening to me?"

"Yes Gerti …I'm sure as hell listening but I can't say I'm not surprised."

"Well J-A-C-KKKK. I honestly can't tell you that I'm not surprised as well. I mean speaking to you like this, my body now craving that which it hasn't for years."

I must be delusional, did she say "craving"?

"Ya, J-A-C-KKKK, there has been a lot missing between us over the last couple of years. I know I have doted on Hendrix and that it has been hard for you ."

Hard for me…was she kidding? I was damn well *persona non gratis*, the odd man out, the damn outlier in my own home. Hearing this from Gerti was like Christmas all over again, beyond Christmas and anything else I could imagine.

"Well, J-A-C-KKKKK, do you wanna?"

Wanna..do I wanna? Did she really have to ask? I was panting like a dog over a bone, rather actually like a dog in heat. Do I wanna , my ass, you bet the hell I wanna.

Five minutes later we were in the bedroom. Gerti stripped first. I stood in awe watching her unwrap herself. It had been so long. With each piece of clothing she discarded I felt more aroused. I focused on her breasts, a C cup that were firm round and full. My eyes then followed the curves of her body as they made their way to her flat belly. I was amazed it remained as firm and profiled as it was, a bit thick through the hips but nonetheless acceptable especially after the birth of our son. My eyes naturally fell to her light brown nape and then flowed uninterrupted as they made their way to her long thighs, then to her calves, then down to the floor where her clothes fell in a heap. Gerti was more vulnerable than she had been for years and I did crave her, not with romantic passion but rather with pure lust. I wanted sex with her and let my restricted waters break through the dam of unrequited desire that manifested itself in more anxiety and depression that I was ever aware of. It was damn well time to purge myself before my pipes became rusty, before they became so damn backed up that my member had no more life and fell like a damp rag, never having the ability to ever again be provoked.

Gerti stood before me in wait. She was in no way a beautiful woman but in her plainness had a pleasant look that I became comfortable with over time. Her body however was strong and hard. It was one of a younger woman. I was pleased and amazed she held up so well after childbirth.

I stripped in a frenzy. My desire was working faster than my ability to undress. What should have taken a minute, took several as I stumbled all over myself. I felt the clumsiest, since my days in boot camp where everything I did was wrong and had serious consequence.

I was in bed and on top of Gerti in minutes.

"Now J-A-C-KKKKK be gentle, it's been a long time, I mean don't treat me like a longshoreman. I mean it's been a really long time, play on the gentler side of being rough."

I heard Gerti loud and clear but as I inserted myself into her she shouted out with pain.

"AHHH ... damn it Jack, a little bit of foreplay is needed here, you just can't jam it in like WAM, BAM, THANK YOU MAM..get down on me."

I now found my head between Gerti's legs. She had the smell of a woman in heat .... it was the cross between a flower and toilet water, subtle but pleasing. I engaged, Gerti groaned with delight. I worked my way down her legs tickling her with my tongue, licked the bottom of her feet, sucking her toes. I then entered her again. She was now far more than ready to take me. There was now no resistance, just two bodies in ebb and flow, vertically dancing minds and bodies giving over to what was natural for men and women to do.

I tried to hold back but to no avail. It broke from me in rapid spasms that provoked from Gerti small bird like sounds that reminded me of those I occasionally heard in our small garden in spring, delicate pleasantries tweaked out by the several sparrows who visited it and eventually made it their home.

I lay motionless. Gerti lay the same. It was short and sweet. I wish it could have taken longer and I knew damn well certain Gerti wished that as well. It was not one of our marathon sessions but rather a new beginning from which we could hopefully build. I was pleased that at least there was more than some interest from Gerti to re-engage. I felt I was stuck in a dry unresponsive desert for years, with no hope of ever finding an oasis to drink, but we had now found a bit of that which has been missing, just a taste with hopefully more to come.

It was a marathon. I felt I was reborn and my relationship with Gerti like an inverted clock brought us back several years before the birth of our son. Hendrix was still a major presence but the attention she gave him was more guarded. He didn't demand all of it. The constant hovering over his every moment and attentiveness to his every whim was something of the past. Gerti was now making time for me, not a lot, but enough that made me feel like staying home, reinforcing her desire to have sex and my constantly seeking out Dirt and Rhino less of an alternative. The only thing that got in the way now was my job at the UPS. It took up my weekdays but at lunch I would call Gerti to see if she was available and had interest. The majority of time she was and I took great pleasure, walking past my fellow employees, knowing that within five to ten minutes I would be home in bed with her while they would be eating their BLT or chicken breast sandwich and them not having a clue what I was partaking in was only in their faintest dreams. I always returned with a smile on my face. They would stare at me wanting to know whatever was served up for me at lunch, they wanted to partake. They hadn't a damn clue. Not one.

When I returned home at night, the marathon would begin again. If it was a good night Gerti and I would have sex twice, if it was a great one, we would add one more time. Weekends were out of control, it was a screwing joust and was about as good as it got, other than our being a captive in our small bungalow.

My father used to say "Bu da gecer ya hu", it literally means "this too shall pass". He said that he picked the saying up from some Persian guy working alongside him at the Eastern. My old man said the Persian said nothing all day but every hour or so gutted this saying and then continued piling the skids. My father said each time he heard it, he wanted to take a hot poker and shove it up the Persian's butt.

"The damn guy says nothing but this stupid saying, I walked over to him one day right after he spit it out and grabbed him by the collar, and holding the jackal three inches off the floor, asked him what the hell are you saying? He said "Dis do shall piss", I asked him again, and he said the same stupid thing. Pissed off the Persian wouldn't tell me what he was saying, I hit him on the side of his damn head and sent him tumbling, asshole over tea kettle, over a half piled skid. He was knocked for a loop and scared shitless. I never heard the Persian say another thing over the next seven years I worked with him, not a one, NADA, NADA, NADA." This was how my father told my brother and me the story.

It was three and a half months of extreme screwing then there was nothing. Nothing, *nada, nada…nada*. This too shall pass and like everything else, all the sex was gone.

"Jack, I'm pregnant!"

"You gotta be shit'n me?"

"No Jack I'm pregnant, eight weeks."

I couldn't believe what I was hearing. Gerti and I never spoke about having another kid. After the difficult pregnancy she had, I never figured she would ever want one. As far as my feelings went, I knew I was messed up to a fare-the-well.

Having another child, just the thought of it brought me to my knees. I couldn't pass, not that I gave it a noble try, getting through Parenting 101. It wasn't in my makeup. I knew I would be an adjunct failure and my son Hendrix played to that truth. One child I could possibly deal with. I damn sure would kinda try to man-up, hoping that I could break through the barriers that made me "standoffish" around him. Two years into it I was no further along than my first hour of fatherhood.

THERE WAS NO MORE SEX. It was gone like a piece of grain in a truck load of sand. Gerti got what she wanted and I was made a fool. She sucked my seed from me in the most malicious way. Her intentions from the first afternoon were dishonest. She used me like the foolish man I was. The power she held over me was so obvious. She was as cunning as she could be and in my demented world I thought I had some kind of control over my life, but the reality is that I had none. I once heard some boilerplate business guy say "You have to control the controllables". "Bullshit", there aren't any controllables. I lost control of my life years before, most importantly in high school and the several years following, especially the first time I stood before Sgt. Randall Cliff, a big burly black man who had the presence and vocal authority of someone larger than life. When Sgt. Cliff spoke he put the fear of God in us dumb ass draftees who were in a half mile ear shot of him. I guess I never really had any control over my life but I constantly tried to fool myself I had. It was a game I entertained myself with. Jack Krause, kick ass son of a bitch who had (unlike most people) a pittance of control over his life. Yeah, good luck. *YES... GOOD LUCK.*

32

Ginger Lee

"I'M PREGNANT!" It was a flashback to 1967, my steady girlfriend, Ginger Lee Bacon laid it on me on the back steps of her parents small two bedroom cottage.

"You're what?"

"Pregnant, I think I'm pregnant."

Pregnant, what the hell was she talking about? We only had sex a half dozen times and used a rubber all but once. There wasn't a chance Ginger Lee was pregnant or was there? I didn't know a hell of a lot about sex only that I was like every other seventeen year old boy in the sixties, trying to learn as much as I could pretending I had a world of experience while having almost none. Ginger Lee was the first real girlfriend I had and the first sexual experience that was meaningful. The other few were just "first base" episodes, while the sex with Ginger was "all the way there", rounding all the bases again and again. She was amazing for being a Catholic High School girl, she was without inhibition. She manhandled me like a Greco wrestler. I found myself doing things and in positions I never dreamed. At times, honestly, I felt intimidated but Ginger forged ahead screwing me in ways I questioned were natural, not that I had any reason to believe they weren't.

"PREGNANT!" Shit, her saying that was like getting hit in the face with a baseball bat or kicked in the stomach with iron construction boots. It was like the worst kind of Asian flu, sucking from me every ounce of strength, every bit I thought I could muster for the future. THE FUTURE? THERE WAS NO FUTURE, if indeed I was the father, I was screwed, ironically being screwed by being screwed.

I looked at Ginger Lee, knowing fully well all the blood had drained from my face. She returned the look with a hard lined stare of someone who had been violated and would absolutely demand her due, would absolutely get her pound of flesh and more. I couldn't stop staring at her, not knowing quite what to do or say.

"DAMN IT Jackson Krause, didn't you hear what I said? I'M PREGNANT. There's a baby inside of me and it's all because of you. You said the time we didn't have a rubber that you would pull out."

The only thing that I could think of saying was "I DID … I DID PULL OUT."

"Not quick enough because inside of me is the result of your fucking up. Inside of me is the worse possible thing happening, a kid inside me, your kid to make it worse. Now we gotta do the right thing Jackson, we have to get married."

Get married, what the hell was she talking about? Get married, we're just seventeen years old. Getting married was out of the question, the reality of this was as far away as Mars is from Planet Earth. There just was no damn way.

"No Ginger, we can't get married. "

"Why the hell not Jackson?"

"Firstly, I won't live long enough to get married if my father finds out that I knocked up a girl."

"What do you mean knocked up a girl? We're not talking about any girl here Jackson. We're talking about me, Ginger Lee Bacon, a Catholic High School girl, this is my worst possible nightmare."

"I know. Yes, I know Ginger, but my father will kill me if he finds out. I mean he will literally ripe me apart so there's no damn way you're going to have the baby, you got to get it aborted.

"Aborted? No, never, I can't do that Jack. I have a life within me, a breathing and living entity with a pulse and a heartbeat and I'm a Catholic girl. Catholic girls don't get abortions. I might have to go away and have the baby, like to a place in New Hampshire or somewhere, but getting an abortion? Never, Never, NEVER!"

I wanted to jump down Ginger Lee's throat. Catholic girl or not there was no way I could let her bring this pregnancy to term. It was against everything I planned for in my future. What lay ahead I had no clue but I was damn sure being a father at the age of seventeen would damn well be a deterrent to anything that was.

I didn't sleep a wink the first night after hearing about the pregnancy. My heart was full of the unthinkable. What if Ginger indeed gave birth to a kid, my kid, her kid, our kid. What the hell would it be like? I don't even know who Ginger Lee was. We dated only eight or nine times us being in different schools, that is if you call meeting at twilight and trying to find a place to screw dating. In an essence that was what our relationship was about. Ginger Lee had one of the worse reputations in Lynn. She was known to be one of the "easy girls", one who would at a drop of a hat, put out like tomorrow would never come.. That's why I sought her out, because I needed to get laid more than the few times I had. I was seventeen and to only have had sex a few times was an embarrassment, especially when I heard a lot of other guys saying they were getting it two if not three times a week and not with one girl but several. I felt short changed. I felt inexperienced and almost like a virgin. I felt I had gone not anywhere near where an experienced male needs to go, close to the sexual edge where nothing would be foreign, like the clear, crisp sunshine on an autumn afternoon.

I couldn't believe where I found myself as I returned home, knowing I was one instant from a good kick-ass beating, if indeed my father, Gunther the Nazi found out. He would definitely take a belt to me. There was and never would be an opportunity to reason with him. With my father there was only the Gunther way and not that of the rest of the world.

There was no peace of mind the day Ginger Lee informed me she was pregnant. My mind was in a frenzy. I was caught up in a whirlwind of emotions. There was no way I wanted to be a father at seventeen and there was no reasoning (much like my father) that would not convince Ginger to have this child. I couldn't believe what a shit ass situation I had gotten myself into, screwing one of the biggest "put outs" in Lynn and now anchored to her and the unborn kid. I was determined there must be a way out of this. If indeed a man could be sent to the moon there had to be a path to relieve me, what up to this time in my life, was the biggest mistake I had ever made. I started to pray to God again, because if there was a bastion of hope, just one damn smidgen, it was not of this world so it had to be of another. I prayed. I hoped that God would listen.

"Okay, okay Jack, if you pay for me to have an abortion, I'll do it."

Thank you God, THANK YOU. I couldn't believe what I was hearing. Just a few days before, Ginger Lee was adamant she would bring the child to term but now everything it seem had changed. Why and what caused her to change her mind, I did not know, and although I was curious as hell, in fact, beyond that, I wasn't about to get into it any deeper than I was for fear she would change her mind.

"Ginger did I hear you correctly? You said if I pay…you'll have the abortion."

"Yes, although it's against everything I stand for, being a Catholic school girl and all, but I decided having an abortion under the circumstances, meaning that we are both just seventeen years old and hadn't graduated from high school and unemployable at best was the only right decision that could be made. But, it is based on your ability to pay for the abortion. If you can't pay, then the deal is off."

"No, no Ginger …I'll pay … mark my words … I'll get the money by hook or crook." I really spoke way too soon, with just way too much enthusiasm, as I hadn't a clue what an abortion would cost until Ginger laid it on me like a ton of cement flattening me to the ground. My enthusiasm and energy were now leveled as could be, having no dimension of my former self.

"Three hundred dollars."

"THREE HUNDRED DOLLARS, ARE YOU SHITTING ME?" Three hundred dollars then was the equivalent of approximately three thousand today. It was more money than I could have ever dreamed, more than I saw myself making in my entire life."There's no messing with this Jack. I checked around and three hundred dollars is the cost of getting it done. I mean I probably could get it cheaper by some butcher or somebody, but Jack, there's no way I'm gonna take that risk, no way I'm gonna let some asshole screw up my plumbing."

"I'm not asking you to screw up your plumbing but I am asking for you to shop around. I mean three hundred dollars is more money than I ever dreamed of."

"GET IT JACK. I MEAN GET IT OR I'll MAKE YOUR FUCKING LIFE MISERABLE!"

I hadn't a clue how I could ever get that much money. I'd been working part time at a grocery store, Pleasant Family Shopping, since I was fourteen, I lied about my age and the proprietor didn't give a damn. Over the years I had saved and occasionally skimmed approximately sixty-three dollars. I was damn proud of saving that money. It gave me a sense that I had a little control over my life and one little secret that emboldened me where I felt some day, I could break away from my family, especially my old man, the bastard he was.

Sixty-three dollars was what it was. If indeed through some great miracle or if it multiplied itself twice over (by God's divine intervention) it still would not be enough. I was in deep shit and envisioned myself pushing a stroller and my stomach turned on itself. I wasn't made for Fatherdom, in fact at the tender age of seventeen, I wasn't sure what I was put on the earth for but it wasn't to marry a girl who I knew almost nothing about and having a kid.

My imagination now was taking me for a wild ride. I envisioned all my problems going away ... if I robbed a bank like Whitey Bulger ... breaking through the doors, gun in hand, displaying it in the intimidating manner resulting in me getting away with a bounty of cash. Yes, without a doubt that would solve my problem, but it would create ones that made the one I was dealing with pale by comparison. Yes, my imagination was running rampant but it was getting me nowhere because there was just no real way out of my dilemma other than Ginger Lee having the baby or me paying for it to go away. There is nothing worse than a trapped man, nothing worse than having such great regret while living not even one quarter of my life.

"So Jack, you got the money?"

Every few days Ginger and I would meet. The meetings were useless because nothing had changed. They became monotonous, me making excuses for not having the three hundred dollars and Ginger describing her morning sickness and how now in her thirteenth week she was beginning to show.

"I feel like shit." She would constantly say. "Pregnancy is a bloody curse, it's a sin women have to go through it and men get off scottfree. You're just lucky bastards you men, you just don't know how lucky... you shits."

Our meetings were going nowhere. Ginger bitched, moaned and complained, reinforcing what a smart shit she was now hiding her pregnancy from her parents and everyone at school.

"I'm wrapped tighter than a rubber band, coiled tighter than a golf ball."

"A golf ball?"

"Yeah, a golf ball, haven't you ever seen one with the cover off? A bunch of rubber bands coiled, like I said, in a damn ball, and that's just the damn way I feel."

"Got it", I said, not seeing any relevance at all.

"We're up shit's creek Jackson we're going nowhere. Obviously, you don't have and or can't get the money. If I don't get it aborted now, you and I are going to get married and have the kid."

I was now grasping at straws.

"No way in hell, Ginger, I got some money, maybe you can put down a small amount and pay the rest later, maybe there is somebody that will do that?"

"Not likely Jackson, I'd say that has about enough chance as that stupid "snowball" surviving in hell, like probably, no damn chance at all."

"You never know unless you try?"

"Okay Jack, so what you got?"

"Sixty seven dollars and eighty cents."

"Sixty seven dollars? Are you shitting me?"

"Sixty seven dollars is a lot of money?"

"Not when you need three hundred it's not."

"Well that's all I have, until I can get some more."

"Well maybe we can do something with it, do you have it with you?"

"Hell, no. I don't carry that much money around with me."

"Well, the next time we meet you better have the money on you. If this is gonna work, you know damn well they will want to see the money."

"Yeah, like sure. I damn well guess that they'll want to see the money."

The following day I gave Ginger Lee the money. At least now, I had a little bit of hope. I might be able to survive this episode if I indeed remained working at Pleasant Family Shopping and scavenged and stole every penny I could. Nothing was guaranteed but there was within me a semblance of optimism as I went about my life, hoping my challenge would quickly be a thing of the past.

It was suspicious that our regular meeting that usually lasted an hour or more didn't happen. We decided we didn't want to meet at either school to stir up any suspicion for what was going on. We weren't known to be boyfriend and girlfriend. I waited for Ginger at the entrance of Lynn Woods our scheduled rendezvous but she never showed. The next day I tried to track her down at school but she was nowhere to be found. I was getting really concerned something really bad had happened. I asked around her campus and received a big "NO" from her circle of friends, if they had seen her. Finally, after asking everyone I knew, I caught up with her after class. I saw her walking down the front school steps in such a hurried fashion that it seemed she was trying to escape the school grounds. I ran after her and finally got close enough where I could grab her by the arm and stop her cold in her tracks.

"Shit Ginger, where the hell you running to and why didn't you meet me last night as planned?"

Ginger jerked her arm away from my hold.

"Because bad shit happened to me last night."

"What do you mean bad shit happened, WHAT KIND OF BAD SHIT?"

"Well let's just say that our worries are over now."

I was getting pissed, I didn't want to play any word games, I JUST WANTED THE DAMN TRUTH.

"Don't screw with me Ginger. I want to know what the hell happened to you last night and why you didn't meet me at the Woods as planned?"

Ginger was getting emotionally riled.

"Okay, okay, screw it, I'll tell you, you asshole…I had a miscarriage."

A miscarriage? I heard of them but honestly didn't really know what one was.

"A miscarriage?"

"Yes, a MISCARRIAGE. You don't even know what a miscarriage is do you? You are such a dumb shit and to think I was stupid enough to have sex with you. I must have been a fucking fool."

I didn't now have an opportunity to mutter another word. Ginger stormed on.

"A MISCARRIAGE you asshole is I lost the damn baby."

I didn't know whether to be elated or sad. A day ago I was going to be a father and now I'm not. After a second and third thought, I found a semblance of a smile breaking from my lips. Ginger saw it as well.

"You asshole. I had a miscarriage, lost the baby and could have died and you stand there with a big shit ass grin on your face. You are truly a fucking asshole."

Maybe I was, but that was all right with me. I might be an asshole but I won't be a father and pushed into a stupid marriage with Ginger Lee Bacon. I no longer had to worry about getting any more money and now would get my sixty seven dollars back.

"Ginger, I'm sorry about the miscarriage, are you alright?'

Ginger seemed to soften a bit …

"Ya, I guess I'm alright."

"That's great, now when can I get my sixty seven dollars back?"

If there was a question that should have never been asked, one in the universe of all questions at the most inappropriate moment of all, it was the one I just did. Ginger's face turned "Chili Pepper Red. Her eyes rolled in. Her face contorted as if she had swallowed a lemon whole. She tried to say something, but whatever it was, was caught up in her throat. All I could hear was something resonating.

I wished I could have taken the question back but it was still out there, hanging over the two of us with the weight of insanity just a step beyond. I knew there would be hell to pay which were training wheels for every other relationship I had with a woman my entire life.

"YOU FUCKING ASSHOLE...me being on the verge of death and having to endure the physical and emotional agony of A MISCARRIAGE and you ask me for your money back. YOU ARE THE SCUM OF THE EARTH ... A DISPICABLE HUMAN BEING ...THE CRAP ON THE BOTTOM OF MY SHOE."

Yes, I probably was, but I could live with that, I still wanted my money back, it was mine, I worked hard for it, stole it, scavenged it, like a rat after a crumb.

Well, I knew I was in the RED ZONE, I was screwed so there was no stopping me now. I was all in and there would be no walking it back.

"Ginger, I'm sorry for the shit that has happened but it's not all me that was the cause, it was both of us together and you damn well know when you asked me to "belly up" with the money I did, well that is, with at least part of it."

Ginger in her most defiant tone said, "The money, THE MONEY IS GONE.."

The money, my damn sixty-seven dollars gone like shit through a goose. I damn well need to know where it went.

"THE MONEY, WHAT DID YOU DO WITH IT? YOU DID'T HAVE AN ABORTION!"

"No you asshole, but I was planning for one and I met the person who was going to do it. Like we discussed before he would probably want some upfront money since I told him that we would have to pay over time, pay over time with thirty percent interest. The point here "Shit for Brains" is that the sixty seven dollars is gone and you're no longer the father of my kid and best of all, I don't ever want to talk to you or see you again. After school I will avoid you like the plague. For all I care, YOU ARE DEAD AND CAN ROT IN HELL."

Ginger Lee turned and throwing me the finger ran out of the school yard. It was finally over, no more worry, no more anxiety or angst, no more fucking sixty-seven dollars.

I thought it was done. Episodes like these never go away in one's life. It needled and picked away at me every day. I had made a terrible mistake, the first of many, I should have known the ink where I dipped my pen. I should have known things just weren't as transparent as they seem. What was my perception was in error, what was in my head was misaligned, what was in my heart was misappropriated. I was many things but none rose above that of ASSHOLE, especially when I heard the conversation that drove a stake through my heart and tore away at the little well-being I thought I had.

The little twerps stood in a circle laughing and talking about me. It was a reckoning of the intolerable, unimaginable, unforgivable.

There were five of them, no one better or more gracious than the other. A flock of hens picking away at everything I thought I was or pretended to be.

"I can't believe that he fell for the whole thing?"

"Ya, Ginger played him like a fine tuned guitar, she said he didn't see anything coming, he believed everything she told him."

"What an asshole."

"Ya, surely not the smartest guy in his school."

"Yeah, at least he got laid."

"But he had to pay sixty-seven dollars to get it."

"It's a lot of money."

"I would have loved to have seen Krause's face", a third girl chimed in, "when she told him she was pregnant."

"Ginger said he was white as a ghost."

"Poor pathetic asshole."

"Boys are jerks."

"The majority… not all."

"I beg to differ", another of the five replied.

Just then one of them looked over the others and saw me standing just an earshot away.

"Shit!"

They all turned and looked at me and quickly dispensed like a bunch of coakroaches when a light switch is turned on."

Some wounds never heal. As the years go by they somehow manage to hold onto the core of my soul. I became a different man after I was made a fool. I had been the brunt of laughter before but never to this degree. I felt I could no longer trust anyone, especially a woman. I was now in no man's land, drifting aimlessly out to sea, looking for a port in my personal storm. There were none, just one towering wave after another driving me deeper into the ebb and flow of an uncontrollable deep blue. I had only a thin raft under me that was but one leak away from a certainty I didn't want to entertain, so I latched on to anything I could to hold my course true and they failed me again and again and I failed myself by hoping anyone could save me other than myself. I latched onto my parents if only for a moment, and then my brother if only temporarily, and then anyone who could shelter me from the storm, even those who could not swim like Dirt and those who now swam to a different destination like Rhino. Gerti was my last bastion of hope and I knew I had let her down in so many ways. How she stood as a pillar of strength for me to hold true in the relentless storms of my life I would never know or understand.

"JACK…I'M PREGNANT!"

I couldn't believe what I was hearing. My life flashed before me like it did eleven years earlier. They were the same words with the same intonation. They could have come from Ginger Lee Bacon but they came from my wife of almost four years, Gerti Krause.

The last few months replayed in my mind like a broken video recorder. There was a dry desert of sex and not an oasis to be seen. Then before my very eyes one appears in the form of my usually docile wife, whose hormones seem to be raging out of control. Then the marathon sex began and then without any indication ceased as quickly as it appeared. Now the desert looms before me again and the call to arms for Gerti was that she was again pregnant, hopefully this time with a girl, the one I so desperately wanted only a few years earlier and now with the son we already had. ***We would make the perfect American family.***

33

Psyched

"Jack, I don't care what you say, you are going to start seeing Dr. Andrews, and I don't want to hear another word of it."

That was twenty some odd years ago, Dr. Russell Andrews has been my psychiatrist. Gerti told me he would help me navigate through my emotional turbulence and help me find peace within. I answered Gerti that day in one word. "Bullshit." Guys like me, Rhino and Dirt were men, we could handle problems no matter how bad they were. We didn't need to sit on a guy's couch, a guy who was wearing a tweed jacket and a PhD hanging on the wall and cry our eyes out holding a box of Kleenex.

"Well Jack, BULLSHIT or not, if you want to stay in this house with me, you're going to see Dr. Andrews."

I acquiesced, once Gerti has put her foot down there is no prying it off the floor.

Doctor Andrews was everything I was not. He was centered. I lived my life at the fringes not totally aware of where true center lay. It was out there somewhere but I didn't have the skills, desire or determination to seek it out. Every time I felt I was getting close, I sabotaged my pursuit by going directly to that point I so desperately tried to avoid. He was also a scholar and received his medical degree from Washington

University and did his psychiatric residency at Harvard. I was anything but a good student, although I went through high school and finally graduated, I did barely nothing and like a hot potato or a live grenade, was passed from class to class without reservation. My college was Nam, it was the source of my true education. I like to think I went to THE WAR COLLEGE, that prestigious high bred military institute I heard was in Newport Rhode Island. Again, I was just bullshitting myself. There was no war college for me. I just swam the swamps and cesspools of Vietnam waist deep in the sewage of life learning what I could in between being paralyzed with fear and regret.

Truth be told I liked Doctor Andrews because he was respectful, compassionate and focused. He could hone in on an issue and squeeze the life from it. I damn well could bullshit the best of them but Dr. Andrews had this uncanny ability to separate the fly shit from the paper. That's not to say I was an easy case for him. Shit, I have been seeing him every other week for the last twenty some years and I'm still pretty messed up. I'll admit many things have changed, but then again, many have stayed the same.

Off THE RECORD

Although Dr. Andrews and I have a doctor-patient relationship I like to think of as friends. We didn't have the kind I experienced with Dirt and Rhino, with them my relationship went beyond friendship, they were my BAND OF BROTHERS, guys who saw the world through the same distorted lens. War makes those who participated unlike anyone who didn't. We were different from those who escaped it's touch and belonged to a special club, the club "FUVA"... the *Fucked Up Vets of America* club with a jaded and sinister view of the world.

Dr. Andrews got it or at least I like to think he did. He once told me he practiced martial arts for thirty something years. That's a long time. I was in Nam for only two, to me they were thirty plus a lifetime. He told me he had a BAND OF BROTHERS too, guys he trained with, who shared busted arms and noses. He too knew shared agony and how it could bond guys together with Gorilla glue in ways other people couldn't understand. Once he told me about his Sensei, a man who now in his mid-eighties had dedicated his life to the martial arts at the expense of everything else, family included. That takes a lot of balls, but having only one thing in life paramount above all others must be the most liberating experience. I think it was Bob Dylan who said, "If you ain't got nothing, you got nothing to lose." Maybe all that karate training built something from nothing, a center so deliberate and strong it was unwavering.

Me? I had no center. My life was a whirlwind. Within its cyclone was a number of relationships that went wrong and each day I wrestled with what role I had to play in them. My son and daughter held my sanity hostage. They have gone beyond the worst I imagined. My wife Gerti has at times pleasantly surprised me and at other times disappointed. As complex as she is I could never really get a handle on her. Whether she loved or hated me was still very much a mystery. I wrestle with that every day. Yesterday, I thought I would "belly up to the bar" and ask her but the truth was I didn't have the guts. I didn't really want to know the answer.

ON THE RECORD

I was about ready to quit my sessions with Dr. Andrews. I even told Gerti and she didn't put up a fight which actually troubled me, but since tomorrow I was leaving to go to Vietnam to pick up Hendrix, I figured what the hell, this would be an appropriate way to end my psyche sessions.

"It was indeed my shit that I can never quite free myself from, the subject in case today Doctor is Rhino. I miss him in the strangest of ways."

"Let me understand that better."

"What?"

"On missing your friend Rhino."

"I've spoken of him many times over the years."

"Yes, you have … and passionately I must say.

"He was my closest friend, I mean along with Dirt, the two of them, they were a pair, honestly Doc…"

"It's good to be honest Jack."

"Honestly, It doesn't seem right we're not together. I mean it's like they have been with me in my entire life…well, the thirty some years that is pretty much the better part of it."

"True friends are hard to find."

"Ya, Doc … I heard say in a person's entire life they might count their real ones on the fingers of one hand."

"Possibly, some people less, then again, some more."

"And what about you Doc, do you have a bunch of friends?"

"Me? Jack this session is not about me, it is as it should be, about you."

"Yeah, I know, I know it's about me. Well I miss Dirt and Rhino more than anyone in my life."

"More than your wife and your children?"

"My wife hasn't left…"

"No, not physically she hasn't, but many conversations over the years-"

"Yeah, I know Doc, I know...like emotionally maybe she has."

"And what do you think?"

"Well, yeah, okay…like Elvis has left the building."

"Interesting analogy!"

"Ya, Doc, I got it …emotionally like Elvis has left the building."

"Let's not make light of it Jack, you have said how emotionally detached she's been over the forty years of your marriage and that has caused you great concern."

"Well the greatest concern was on her side Doc, she's the one who always said I don't allow people in my head, to get into my emotional flow."

"And?"

"And she's right?"

"And your daughter Riley, you miss Rhino more than her as well?"

"Yeah, I do Doc. It sure as hell isn't an easy thing for me to say, but although I always wanted a daughter, she sprung into my life under the most malicious circumstance. I guess as we discussed many times before that although I thought she would be the light of my life, we never emotionally connected and possibly never will, although now she and her teenage daughter and her kids live under the same roof as Gerti and me. Like I told you a couple of weeks back, while the irresponsible men in their lives roam the world like my long lost son... doing stuff..."

"Yes, then of course there is your son Hendrix."

It took every ounce of strength I had to hold back tears because I was determined not to cry in front of Dr. Andrews.

"Let it go Jack."

"What?"

"Just let it go."

"Hendrix?"

"Yes, do you miss Rhino worse than Hendrix?"

"I never knew my son Doc, of course I have a hole in my heart, but it's like I never gave him a chance... but he never gave me a chance either. I think we were very much alike."

"In what way?"

"Christ Doc... you know ... the apple doesn't fall far from the tree. Meaning he was very much like me."

"Well Jack, the next time you see Hendrix, just remember it's not too late. It's not too late to get him back in your life. Just be honest with him."

As hard as I tried, I failed to hold back one crocodile tear. I'm sure Dr. Andrews noticed, but said nothing.

"Yes we have had many conversations about Hendrix, but this is the first time you have mentioned your dire need for Rhino."

"Ya, Doc, like I said, I damn well miss Rhino the most."

"And how do you feel about that?"

I feel strange as shit. I mean I should miss Gerti, Hendrix and Riley more, and possibly even Dirt, but it's clear to me ... it's Rhino I really miss."

"And why?"

"I guess I never had to mince words with him, not saying we always saw things eye to eye, but even in our differences we had the war and our marriages in common and the big thing was we didn't have to act like normal people around each other. There didn't have to be this big stupid façade, acting like we were really happy and the whole world was spinning on axis, when it damn well wasn't. Well at least not for Rhino and me. Do you see where I'm going with this Doc?"

"Yes, I see Rhino might be what you might perceive to be your last bastion of understanding, a man who sees most things through his eyes as you do."

"Not all things Doc."

"Jack - I said most."

"Well, I dare say he is the only bridge I feel I have left."

"Bridge ... interesting ... go on."

"Well, isn't that what Rhino is to me?"

"I don't know Jack, is he?"

"Well, I see him as a bridge between where I was and where I'm going."

"Let's start with where you were."

"Christ, you know Doc, I was in Nam and before that here in Lynn."

"Yes, but it's Nam that eats you away isn't it, as it always has. It's Nam that is the issue here as it has been for the two decades I've seen you."

"Yes, It's Nam, a war I can't get beyond."

"Jack, you'll never get beyond it if you fight your private war every day …it's been some forty plus years now."

"Shit Doc, you're right. I guess I've been at war with everything and everyone, with Gerti …my kids …and just about everyone else."

"It's your war Jack, only you can confront it, accept it or walk away.

"Well, the truth is, it's got the best of me. It took me and it took my son."

"What do you mean it took your son Jack?"

I looked at the clock on the wall. It was getting late. It was time for me to go. I had a lot of things to do to get ready for my trip to Vietnam and frankly, I had enough. The basic truth was I wasn't Peter Strong who could deal with THE SHIT. I was Jackson Krause, WHO JUST COULD NOT. I abruptly pushed myself off the chair.

"Sorry, I just got to go Doc."

"That's obvious Jack, so what are you going to do about missing Rhino?"

"I'm just going to call him Doc …*just call him*."

34

What Could Have Been

Ican't blame everything in my life on Nam, although now, I'm seeing I definitely tried. With my kids, I used my service as a crutch to escape from responsibilities I felt uncomfortable with. Unfortunately, my wife and kids picked up on my insecurities and the uneasiness that I felt with them underfoot. It must have been really hard for them to be around me and perhaps that is why they seldom were. From the earliest ages, both of them were always out of the house. I never really thought much of it, because I again, used every excuse I could to find reasons to leave as well. *Gerti, I have to work a double shift... Gerti, I have to take Dirt to the V.A. ...Gerti, Rhino needs me to help him with some stuff.*

Any excuse I could, I would use. It was all about me getting away from the house as often and as far as I could to shrug my responsibilities. And again, unfortunately, my kids picked up on this and grew up very much like me. I have only me to blame. Hendrix and Riley...oh, what could have been...***What Could Have Been***?

It was 5:15 a.m. It was time to leave my room. I closed and locked my suitcase and wheeled it to the door. Opening it, I stood in place, hoping the others in the house were still asleep.

I heard nothing. In fact it was weirdly quiet. Ours was a small house, noise resonated off the walls and ceilings and hardly anything or anyone could stir without being noticed. I heard not a sound.

I walked the several feet from the hallway to the stairs leading to the first floor. It was a quick fifteen steps, pulling my suitcase with a thump as it rolled down and over the stair threads. It was but seconds later I found myself on the first floor, staring at Gerti, who was fully dressed sitting in our captain's chair.

"Whoa, I didn't know you were up."

"It was a tough night to sleep. A lot of things were swirling around in my head."

I put my suitcase down on the floor and walked over and opened the blinds. It was going to be another stifling hot day in Boston. I could see the sun starting to make its way over the horizon. I turned to Gerti. She still sat in the chair, barely moving a muscle.

"Yes, I never ever thought I would be doing something like this."

"It's the worst possible thing to happen to any parent, we have certainly had our share of problems, but we have only ourselves to blame."

"We can't take all the blame Gerti. Hendrix was a grown man, he made a lot of decisions on his own, of which we were not part."

"Damn it Jack, you're still trying to figure out a way not to blame us for what we made of our son."

"I don't get it Gerti for what we made of our son?"

"Yes, you and me, see Jack, I'm taking my share of the blame as well."

"I don't know what you are talking about Gerti you were a damn good mother to both our kids, you did the best you could."

"Not good enough Jack, just not good enough. In parenting, it always comes down to the end result, the final grading is our kids wind up living a good and healthy life or they don't. The final grading is that ours did not and are not."

"You're being way too hard on yourself. "

"And Jack I would say you're not."

"I've been hard on me, let me dare say, I've been hard on myself."

"It's like building a house Jack, if the foundation isn't set correctly, the house crumbles from the ground up. We built a lousy foundation for our children to grow from."

"Shit Gerti, I know I wasn't the greatest father, there's no doubt about that."

"No that's where you're fooling yourself, you were a great father to your buddies, Dirt and Rhino. You spent more time with them and cared for them more than your family."

I couldn't believe what Gerti was saying, "Not true ... not true."

"Jack, there has never been a greater truth."

Gerti got up from her chair. She walked over and shut the blinds that I had just opened.

"What are you doing? I just opened it. And why are you dressed so early in the morning?"

I looked at my watch. "This isn't really the time for this. I have to get to the airport or I'll miss my flight. This security stuff sucks, for international, you have to be at least several hours early at best."

"Jack, I'm going with you."

"Going with me, to where?"

"To Vietnam."

"To Vietnam? It's too late...you don't even have a ticket and a passport."

"I do have a ticket Jack, I saw the flight you made scribbled on a piece of paper on the desk in the living room ... called and bought a seat. I was damn lucky there were a few left … and the passport, I just got one the last thirty days."

I was shocked, I just couldn't see Gerti doing this. She never took the initiative to do anything, her life was buffering the kids from me. If there was anything that really pissed me off, it was her interfering with my plans, her constantly second guessing me. Maybe this is why I felt overwhelmed in my life and constantly sought out Dirt and Rhino because I didn't have to explain myself to them like I felt I constantly had to… to my family and the rest of the world.

"But you're not even packed, we just don't have a enough time."

"I've been packed since yesterday. My suitcase is in the broom closet in the kitchen."

I was frenzied, I didn't need this shit. Gerti parading around with me in Nam … again, second guessing everything I do.

"Gerti, I just don't know about this. I'm not sure this is a good idea. I mean, this is really going to be tough …I mean … it's really going to be emotional."

Whatever I said, set Gerti off. Her voice raised three octaves.

"Really being tough, you are really an asshole Jackson Krause. Going to be tough … living with you has been a living hell for the past forty-six years …you don't know what tough is!"

I tried to reign her in, there was a flight to catch.

"Gerti!"

"Don't Gerti me, I'm not finished. You haven't a clue Jack, what it is to live with an emotional shell of a man…a man who must have left the better part of himself in Vietnam. You see Jack, you soldiers weren't the only victims of the damn war. The family you guys came home to were as well … we too experienced the pain, the horror, the emotional voids, the detachments. It wasn't no walk in the park for us either and the brunt of the damages might have been to the children involved Jack, our children."

"I know, I know, but this isn't really the time."

"Damn it Jack … this isn't the time …it's always been like that … it's never the time with you."

I was beginning to panic. I looked at my watch again."

"Damn it Jack, stop looking at that damn watch, I have a cab picking us up in twenty minutes."

"Us?"

"Like I said Jack, you're not leaving this house unless I'm going too - end of discussion - end of argument!"

"Gerti, like I said, I don't think you going with me is a good thing."

"Well Jack, I really don't care what you think. It's come to that."

I have never seen Gerti as adamant. She was determined to go. I don't know what came over me, but I looked at her and started to cry. I felt one single tear and then another and another and then a deluge flowed from my lower lid down my cheeks. It was unsettling. I couldn't remember the last time I cried. It was probably when I was very young. Never as a young man, never as an adult. Yes, there was an abundance of anger and rebellion, but never a tear …well, at least one that I could remember. I started to think about all the reasons that could make me cry, that could render me an emotion so strong it just took me over. There were so many, they seemed to "POP" in my head, like a popcorn in a maker. POP … I failed my wife of forty six years because of all my selfish behaviors … it was all about me … never about her … how so very sad… "POP". I failed both my children, spending more time with Dirt and Rhino than I ever did with them, trying to find that part of me that was lost in Nam… the part that I left behind upon my return … how so very shameful… POP… POP… I cried because I was now about to retrieve my son who found more comfort in a pill or at the end of a needle than he ever felt from me ...was there anymore I could have done? ...of course there was but I failed to do it, how foolish I was even to ask myself... POP .. POP .. POP... I cried for Dirt who no matter what he was, was a friend, one of the two I had in this world, and the lost life he lead ... and me not being able or rather not deciding to fulfill his last wish and scatter his ashes in the Saigon River... POP .. POP .. I cried for Rhino, who like me had a "call to Jesus" meeting with himself and realized his life was proportionately out of control ... and its wreckage was scattered about in the form of two ex-wives and two estranged kids... POP ...POP.. POP...I cried for Peter Strong and all the soldiers like him who gave the better part of themselves in all the crazy wars, and somehow had the strength and courage to try to rise above it, I cried... POP ....POP.. POP... for all those soldiers who for whatever reason were unable to recapture their lives or for that matter never, never were able to build a new one... I cried... POP ..... POP... for Julie who would resort to the likes of a broken down me to fill the loneliness and great big hole in her heart and for all the families that have experienced the same because their soldiers were never able to heal. I cried for myself, Jackson Krause, my brother Bobby, now not able to ever walk again, my father, mother .... in all their dysfunction ... I cried...POP ...POP.. POP... for my sixty-nine years and not another sixty-nine ahead ... but rather just a short few, to start to make right the many wrongs in my life ...

Yes, it all came upon me suddenly, like my whole warped world was unfolding before my eyes, like they say happens when a person is on their deathbed. Gerti just looked at me as ghostly white as I was, with a river of tears falling from my cheeks. She didn't say a thing but let the minutes unfold, uninterrupted as I melted down, right before her eyes. I could think she looked upon me with amazement, not one single tear in forty-six years and now a virtual waterfall where I was unable to find the spigot to turn off.

She walked up to me and looked straight into my eyes. I tried to avoid her gaze. I have never felt as vulnerable as I did now. For years I had built this moat around me, deep and inaccessible, backed up by walls so high, no one could scale them, or bust through. They were impenetrable, as I to the outside world. Now it seemed they were crumbling and I was feeling emotions I hadn't for years. I was somehow, surrendering to all the turmoil and rage within.

Gerti, put her arms around me. We hadn't been this close for years. It felt good to have her so near, after avoiding her in the most carnal sense for over the last several decades. Her presence was comforting. She had a scent of her own, that now seemed to play to my senses, quieting my heartbeat, my rambling thoughts, calming my troubled waters.

"It must have been hard, harder that we would have ever known Jackson Krause. I know me and the kids couldn't in our wildest imagination understand what you experienced in Vietnam. It damn well must have been hell. I've seen you deal with it for the last forty some years and the kids for the last thirty. In all honesty, it has somewhat destroyed your, our life, but this now is the end of it. This is where it bottoms out, it just can't get worse than this Jackson Krause.

Gerti lifted my head so I could look into her eyes.

"You and me Jackson, whatever it is, we are going to try to work this out together."

I couldn't believe what I was hearing from Gerti. All these years, I never confided in her. I never spoke, perhaps only a dozen or so times, about my Vietnam experience and glazed over it at best. It was on a "need to know" basis and as far as I was concerned, there wasn't any "need for her to know".

"Gerti, I'm sorry for all the pain and suffering I have caused you. It was never my intent to treat you and the kids like I did. I was and still am in a *no man's land*, a place where I've struggled with to break through for years and here I am still carrying the burden of it all. And you carrying it as well …

honestly, I don't know why you have stayed with me all these years. I know it must have been a living hell."

"Jack, it was…it is. But Jack, we have an *understanding*."

"An understanding?"

"Yes, Jack. We've always had an understanding."

I looked at Gerti and then at my watch. Seconds later, we heard the taxi cab driver blowing his horn.

"Gerti, it's time for us to go."

"Yes Jack …***Let's go get our boy***.

THE END

Made in United States
Orlando, FL
13 November 2022

24494813R00195